Sadie's Freedom

Connie L. Heron

Sadie's Freedom

Connie Leonard Geron

To order additional copies of this book, contact:
Xlibris Corporation
1-888-795-4274
www.Xlibris.com
Orders@Xlibris.com
48754

Contents

Give me your lantern and compass,
Give me a map,
So I can find my way to the sacred mountain,
To the place of your presence.

Psalms 43:3 (The Message)

Chapter 1

The Reality

It is such a strange feeling, sitting here in this small café having coffee and a sweet roll. The sounds of early morning traffic announce that the day is well on its way; a honk here, a bus braking there: whoosh, whoosh. The fragrant, warm smell of fresh brewed coffee is like a healthy elixir to the senses. Sadie wishes she could just sit back and enjoy all this without having something so pressing to occupy her mind. On the countertop beside her, is a newspaper turned to the classified section. Red pen in hand, Sadie scans the rows upon rows of small print. *This is like a movie scene,* she ponders. *This can't be happening to me, not really. But it is! I need a place to live, and I must have a job. I'm 53 years old and this is not how I pictured my life at this age.*

Sadie bows her head and silently pleads with the Lord to guide her steps and help her out of the mess she's created. *I am your child, Lord. I'm in trouble. Right now I need your help or I will be lost. Forgive me for the mess I've made of my life. I'm sorry . . . . so sorry. Please take this 'cast away' and make something new and useful out of me. I know you can, because you are the miracle worker. Work a miracle in me. I'd like to be useful again. I want to make a difference in people's lives. Help me dear Lord, I pray.*

As soon as her prayer is finished the old doubts start rushing in again. *You are a loser. You messed up. You are too old now to start over. What skills do you have? You might as well tattoo a big 'L' on your forehead.* She takes a deep breath and looks up. An overhead fan is spinning the air; moving out the old stale air and sucking in the new, cool air from the open doorway.

"More coffee, ma'am?" asks the perky, young waitress. She stands in front of Sadie, chewing her gum, pencil behind her ear.

"Yes please!"

Sadie determines that it is time to get serious and 'jump in and start swimming for all she's worth.' That's an old adage—a piece of advice she remembers from her youth. Down by the river near her childhood home, where the current got rough and the frothy, white water tumbled over boulders. Sadie's daddy would stand next to her on the edge of the precipice and look down into the churning white water.

"When you jump in, start swimming for all you're worth or the water will suck you down and not let you up," her daddy warned, and away they'd leapt into the froth. Their bodies would be tumbled about like clothes in a washing machine—the power of the water controlling and pressing down. Sadie would start pin wheeling her arms and kicking her feet to resurface and gulp in air. Then she had to continue to swim for all she was worth to reach the safety of the side. What an exhilarating ride in the rapids; it was dangerous, but fun. She and her dad would do it over and over till their strength would ebb, and then and only then would they retreat to join the family lying on the towels in the sand.

Now it was time to jump in again and start swimming for all she was worth. Could she do it? Could she survive on her own? She was ready to give it a shot. Sadie glanced outside to see people coming and going on the sidewalk. All of them had established places to go and obligations to fulfill. It seemed that everyone out there had a place in the world, a set pattern and routine that naturally gave each of them a feeling of security and purpose.

Across the street, his back against the wall of the pharmacy, squatted a man in dingy clothes. His face was gaunt and weathered by too much sun and wind. His eyes were a bit vacant. He sat with a sign that read, "Will Work for Food!" He held a paper cup stained with old coffee so that people passing by could slip in a little change now and again. *Oh Lord,* she thought, *How close am I to that?* She turned back determinedly to the classified ads and began to read.

There was mostly secretarial work (administrative assistants) and openings for computer analysts and programmers. Let's see: janitorial jobs (custodial engineers), wait staff positions and hostesses for new restaurants, nanny jobs, construction workers wanted. Was there anything here for an "over the hill," frumpy woman who had given most of her life to take care of her family (kids and husband) and who had failed to hone any useable skills in the real world? *Take heart, Sadie, take stock of your skills.* Well, she did know how to cook; there was that. She could plant a nice garden and keep flowers blooming. She could sing a moving solo. She could write a good letter. Did that count? She was a good listener. Lord knows she got plenty of practice in that skill.

How much money did she have to work with? How much was left after the long bus ride out to this bustling little town in the North Carolina mountains? Whatever possessed her to take this step and actually dare to live out the dream she had harbored for years? Did she actually think that there was magic that would settle in around her and work everything out to the standards of her dream?

> A dream is a wish your heart makes,
>> when you're fast asleep.
> In dreams you can lose your heartache,
>> whatever you wish for you keep.
> Have faith in your dreams and some day,
>> your rainbow will come shining through.
> No matter how your heart is grieving,
>> if you'll keep on believing,
> The dream that you wish will come true.

That used to be her favorite song from an old Disney movie, 'Pinnochio'. When she was just a little girl she would sing that song over and over and dream that her life would evolve into this wonderful dream come true. But life just doesn't work that way. Life is what it is—life.

Many years before, she had vacationed in a lovely little town up in the Appalachian Mountains. She had dreamed then that life there would be ideal. She had wished for it and pondered on being part of that close-knit community. So now, years later, here she was, so physically close to that special dream place and yet logistically and financially so far. What now? Just because a bus ticket had dumped her off in this quaint city didn't guarantee there was a place here for her. Could she find a purpose and a means of earning a living among these people, along these streets amist the hustle and bustle of this mountain town? She loved the smell of the high mountain air. There was a hint of fall in the air. Oh, how she loved that fragrance. It was a promise of colder days and nights, and of leaves turning gold and crimson, of smoke from chimneys and crisp apples being plucked from trees. It was Sadie's favorite time of year.

"Excuse me, ma'am! Is there something else I can get for you?" The waitress was clearly eager to get her to move on and leave a space for a new customer.

"No thanks! I enjoyed it so much . . . just sitting here taking it all in. Thanks for putting up with me. Appreciate it!" She wrapped up the remains of her roll in a paper napkin and left money to cover her bill along with a generous tip. She knew the plight of waitresses who made so little salary and had to depend on the tips to make ends meet.

The young girl's eyes widened in surprise and her pouting mouth lent a genuine smile to Sadie. "No problem. Didn't mean to rush you off. Come back again!" But Sadie was already out the door. She crossed the street and dropped a dollar in the stained cup of the homeless man. He barely glanced up. The warm sun peeking over the storefronts was caressing his face and it must have felt mighty good to him.

Sadie walked slowly setting down her feet, step by step, feeling the solid earth beneath her feet. She breathed deeply of the morning air. She had time to relax and think. She wasn't destitute yet. *You've been a long time getting here girl*, she said to herself. *So don't waste it by rushing and worrying.* She kept walking and watching the people. Some of them were set in their single-minded purpose and looked straight ahead and made no eye contact. Others glanced at faces and smiled tentatively, nodding their heads here and there, acknowledging a fellow soul in this world. It felt good to be a stranger in a brand new place. It was like a clean slate ready to be written upon.

Chapter 2

The Proposal

There was a quaint, emerald park with tall shady trees. Near a gurgling fountain, Sadie found a bench and sat upon it. She stretched out her legs and lifted her face to the tops of the trees. Pigeons, sometimes referred to as rats with wings, gathered around her hoping for some offering. She always thought pigeons were so lovely and fat. Their feathered coats were glistening in myriad phosphorescent colors. She unwrapped her roll and broke it into pieces and fed them. A pair of doves came strolling in to partake of the meager feast. She loved doves too. They were said to mate for life. When one died, the other was lost and alone for the rest of its life. It was a sad thing to see a single dove.

The peal of church bells suddenly filled the air, ringing in the morning. It was so uplifting. "How Firm A Foundation Is Jesus My Lord"—the bells sang the song and the reverberations laid a blessing on the little town. Sadie closed her eyes and hummed the tune along with the ringing bells.

"You sound like you know how to sing."

Sadie opened her eyes and sat up straight. Sitting beside her was an elderly man, dressed in a fine wool, gray overcoat and scarf. He had a smart silver-tipped black cane leaning on his knees, and he too was feeding the birds. Even through the gloves, she could tell that his hands looked a little twisted with arthritis. His wispy hair was white and windblown. He had a neatly trimmed mustache of pure white. His cheeks were sunken but rosy. "Didn't mean to disturb your reverie, young lady, but I was enjoying your humming."

Sadie glanced beside her to see if he might be speaking to someone else. But no, she was the only one there. He had called her a young lady! *Well it all depended on your perspective,* she reasoned. At any rate, she liked the old gent immediately.

"I was just soaking in the glories of this city. Everything seems to be perfect!"

"I would hardly call Rose Creek a city; more like a nice sized town. And believe me, it is not perfect by any means. I've lived here all my life. Are you new here?"

"Just rode the bus in last night. So I guess you could say I'm pretty new here."

"Where are you staying—with relatives?" He lifted his bushy eyebrows in an inquisitive manner. "My, but I'm being nosy, aren't I? Forgive the intrusion."

She had been a bit taken aback by his forthright questions, but his recalcitrant manner caused her to soften and she answered him truthfully, "I am here by myself, hoping to find a place to settle in. I've always loved North Carolina. I vacationed up in the mountains south of here in Highlands years ago, and I always wanted to live there one day. Now I have the chance, and I'm hoping I can find a way to do it."

"Well everyone wants to live up in Highlands. It's pretty ideal up there. It's a hard seventeen mile trek up there on steep winding roads, but once you are there, pure heaven, heh? Ever been there in the winter? The town nearly shuts down. Just the diehards stick it out. The Old Highland Inn closes up and the shops too; but it is lovely there even in winter."

Sadie was delighted to find a fellow admirer of her favorite little town. "I don't really expect to get the chance to live there. I think it is out of my reach. But even living this close would be nice."

"Don't give up on your dream so easily. Where are you living here? Oh, there I go again," he hit his knee with his balled up fist, "always prodding in like I deserve to know everything. Sorry!"

"Don't be silly! It's so nice to have someone asking after me." She replied. "I stayed last night at the Motel 6 right near the bus station. It's cheap there and I have to conserve my resources till I find work and a place to live." She was instantly repentant that she had divulged that much of her plight to this stranger. It felt like she was thrusting out a coffee-stained paper cup for sympathy and charity. She held up the classified ads and her red pen. "See, here is my feeble attempt to find work. I'm new at this as you may easily recognize."

He turned his face forward cupping his hand over his mouth and supporting that elbow with his other hand. He was grimly pondering the scene before him. She had the notion that he was disturbed at her for some reason and maybe he was even sorry he'd started this conversation.

She decided to slip away gracefully and not cause him any further consternation. "So, I guess I'd better get going. I'm 'burning daylight' as my daddy used to say." She started to rise, but he stopped her with a look.

"Hold your horses little lady! I've just been thinking on this. Give me a minute!"

She sat back down and tried not to giggle at how closely he had sounded like John Wayne. What a sweet old man he was to be so concerned about a virtual stranger. Then she remembered her prayer at the coffee shop. *Work a miracle. Help me dear Lord.* She knew how real the Lord was and how He had come to her rescue before. Maybe this was yet another answer to desperate prayer. She folded the newspaper carefully and set it beside her on the bench; then she folded her hands together in her lap and waited.

How sweet it was to wait and let time roll over her. Her senses were open to all kinds of things that normally were shut out due to being too busy. The twitter of birdsong, the rustling of the breeze through pine boughs and limbs, the faint smell of wood smoke in the air, the delicious warmth of sun filtering down through the trees to touch her face like a soft kiss.

"What can you do?" His question was abrupt and to the point. "What skills do you have? What are you good at, and what do you enjoy?"

She smiled at him and replied, "Funny you should ask that. I was just pondering on that very thing this morning as I read these classifieds. Let's see—I love to cook and I enjoy so much seeing people relish what I prepare. I love to read, but that wouldn't count for much in the workforce. I can write a good letter and keep good financial records. Hmmmm . . . let's see. I can grow a great garden and nurture lovely plants and flowers. I like people generally and enjoy listening to them and learning about them. Does that count for anything?"

"Well, indeed it does! There's a shortage of good listeners in this world. Most people have to pay at least $125 an hour to hire someone to listen to their woes."

"Now if I could just have a little shop with a sign out front that said, 'Good Listener. Inquire Within. Fees Reasonable.' Do you think I'd have any customers?" she laughed.

"You might be surprised at how many you would eventually get!" he mused. "But let me cogitate on this a minute. Just give me a second here!" Once again his craggy face screwed up into a fitful and contemplative pose.

Sadie took a deep breath and realized that she was having a very pleasant morning with this old gentleman. *Thanks Lord! For these few moments of friendliness. Thanks! I'll take all the little blessings you can throw my way.*

"Okay, here's the deal. How hearty are you? I can't guess your age, but you look rather able and healthy. Can you do some manual labor like cleaning and fixing a place up?" His wild, white eyebrows were furrowed into a gruff question mark. It was like a test, and she knew her answer would determine how much more of his plan he would reveal.

"I'm 53 years old, and yes indeed, I am still able to sustain a hard day's work. I like a good challenge, and I've had my stab at fixing up places and making nice places to live out of slovenly sites. Is that what you are asking?" she inquired with arched eyebrows to match his.

"I don't mean to delve into your past, or reasons for your being here or any of your circumstances that brought you here. I admit freely that I am honestly curious, but the main reason for the questions is that I need to know if this is just a passing thing for you. Will you need to run back to wherever you came from, back to your old way of life? Is this just a passing phase that will soon grow stale for you? Are you ready to really get into a new kind of life for a good long time? Whatever your answer is," he paused, "make it a true one. I need to know these things so I can determine if my proposal to you would be beneficial to us both." He held up his head like a monarch and looked down on her, waiting for her response.

Sadie looked at him eye-to-eye and held that pose for several seconds. Finally she admitted, "I have no place to go back to. I've severed my obligations and ties to the past. I must move on and truth be told, I want desperately to move on. In fact, I relish the prospect of settling into a new life. Does that answer your question?"

He sighed deeply and closed his eyes for a second or two. Then he nodded his head a few times and began. "I didn't expect to come today to this little refuge of a park and find the answer to my dilemma. But here you are and, Lord help me, it feels so right, that I'm going to go ahead with it." He turned to her and pulled off the black leather glove on his right hand and stuck it out for a handshake.

"My name is Colonel Everett Shaw." His handshake was firm and warm. "I include the Colonel in my title, not as a braggart, proud of my stint in the military, but because that is how I am known around these parts. Everyone calls me 'Colonel'. My ancestors from three generations past have lived in this area. My family home is pretty near the center of this town. The town has grown up around it and at times it seems to be pressing in on all sides. We have a walled garden surrounding the house. The place is way too big for my wife and me, but we stay anyway because it is familiar and expected of us. My kids are all grown and two of them live away from here and one lives in this town. My wife is not really well and can no longer prepare meals or clean the house. We have a cleaning woman who comes in twice a week to keep things somewhat tidy. We try to live on the ground floor of our big house and keep the upstairs pretty well shut off for utility bill purposes. What I'm proposing is for you is to come and live in the little gatehouse, out back of the big house. You would have to fix it up, since it has not been lived in or used for so long. I'm not even sure what is stored out there." He took a deep breath and quietly sat looking at her.

Sadie's eyes were wide and full of anxiety. What was he getting at? What is it that he wanted from her? Did he want her to be a nurse? A housecleaner? A cook? Did he want a companion for his wife? She sat waiting for him to continue. A sudden peace came over her and she felt confident and sure of herself—unafraid. She felt the Lord's hand in this—plain and simple.

"My proposal to you, if you are willing, is to fix up the gatehouse to live in so that you could have your complete privacy away from us. In return for the use of that house and the utilities, I would expect you to cook good meals for my wife and me. Three times a day: breakfast, lunch and dinner. You would be responsible for cleaning up the kitchen and doing the shopping for groceries. I would give you the use of my old pickup truck for going here and there. It is reliable for short hops, but a long trip might be asking too much of it. You would have 2 days a week off with the hope that you would prepare dinners for my wife and me to warm up on those off days. We will have to manage for ourselves the other two meals on your free days. You would get all your meals from our kitchen to be eaten with us or away from us, your choice. You would get a stipend of wages. We'll work that out to our mutual agreement. I'll work out a deal with our insurance company to cover your medical care when needed. I would not expect you to clean up anything but the kitchen. How does that sound to you?" He threw out the last question like a Colonel would do, with authority and yet with masked anxiety.

Now it was Sadie's turn to cogitate and sit quietly and think about things. She had to hand it to the old gentleman; he did wait patiently for her to respond. Finally she spoke quietly. "Colonel Shaw, my name is Sadie. Sadie Jamison." She used her maiden name and it felt like stepping way back in time. "I think your proposal sounds ever so intriguing and worthy of consideration at this point in my life. I would like to meet your wife first and see the place and the garden house out back. Before I agree to anything, I'd like to see what I'm getting myself into."

He slapped both knees with both hands and stood up. "Well that sounds just about right to me, Sadie Jamison. How about we walk, right now, to the old homestead and meet the little woman and check things out?" She stood up and they began to walk out of the park together. The pigeons scattered and waddled away.

Chapter 3

The Mansion and Cottage

They walked down past the little Rose Vine Café where she had taken her morning coffee. The young waitress glanced up from wiping a table and waved at Sadie as they passed. The old man said, "I see you've already met Cherie? She's the young single mother who is determined to stick it out here against all odds."

"I always wonder about how young mothers like Cherie manage. Who watches the baby? Where do they live? How are people treating them? So many questions go racing through my mind."

Sadie glanced across the street to see the grizzled, homeless man napping in the sun. His stained cup was still held loosely in his relaxed hand. Colonel Shaw saw her point of interest and offered, "That's our resident bad luck story. His name's Peter Combs. He used to be a big time stockbroker up in Chicago. At one time he might have been on top of the world with lots of portfolios to manage and the knowledge of inside information. People depended on his expertise and advice for their wealth. Then the bottom dropped out of his life and he ended up beaten and he just gave up. It's a long story; too long for you to contemplate right now. Suffice it to say, old Pete there has struck bottom and just doesn't care anymore. I'm not too sure he is not still wanted by the law."

Sadie glanced once more back at the man in question. She just couldn't help it. Her heart went out to him. She'd have to get a hold of herself. She needed to consider her own plight right now and not worry about those around her. She'd always been a sucker for lost animals and hurt things. *Focus, Sadie!* She chided herself.

She and the Colonel walked past the downtown area and across the street into a more wooded residential part of the town. Nicely restored old Victorian mansions lined the streets. She marveled at each one and thought about the history of lives that had passed through these old homes for nearly 150 years. Then she saw it;

the high stone wall with a growth of vines creeping over the top. Huge treetops showed above the top of the wall. They followed the massive wall to a corner, turned and continued along the wall until they came to an arched, wrought iron gate. "Here we are. Our property covers three blocks," announced the Colonel.

She peered into the shady green refuge inside those high walls. A bricked path bordered with slightly overgrown shrubs led up to the front of a white columned two leveled front porch. The house needed new paint; the steps needed repair, but the mansion still stood proudly in the midst of the towering trees that surrounded it. She just stopped and stared. Her gaze went up, up, up taking in all the massive oaks, sugar maples and pine trees.

"This is a park all by itself," she marveled. Squirrels scampered up and down the trees chasing each other in utter delight. Birds flitted here and there in the upper reaches of the trees. She saw the noisy, pesky blue jays and red-winged blackbirds and the flash of the red cardinal. She wished she'd had her bird book in hand. She took into her lungs the misty, fresh, cool air. She breathed in deeply again and again. The smile on her face must have expressed her utter delight, for Colonel Shaw stopped and nodded his head.

"Yes it is a special place here. It's way too much for me—but I can't give it up—not yet!" he sighed. "Come on, let's go meet my love. You'll have time to ponder this overgrown acreage later!"

He walked her around to the side of the massive house and they entered into a mudroom area just off the spacious kitchen. The ceilings were very high—at least 14 feet. High wooden shelves were stacked with varying sizes of old pottery bowls and pitchers. A big six-burner gas stove stood with an old marble countertop skirting both sides. A deep old porcelain sink stood below a bank of windows that looked out to a big screened-in back porch. The sink was full of crusty bowls and plates and silverware. Some pots and pans with leftovers inside were on the sideboard waiting to be scrubbed. The cupboards were glass-fronted with haphazardly stacked dishes inside. One shelf near the stove held dusty glass jars of canned fruit and veggies. She spied a jar of pickled peaches with the whole cloves dotting the sweet, syrupy juice inside. Her mouth started to water up. Remembrances of her own grandmother's golden pickled peaches raced through her mind. In the middle of the kitchen was an old wooden table with four wooden chairs around it. The white paint on the table was peeling away and there were gouges in the wood. The table itself was piled high with junk mail, letters, and unopened newspapers. It didn't look like anyone ate at that table.

The old man led her through a swinging door into a huge dining room. She nearly bumped into a heavy dark table with ten matching chairs. More chairs stood around the edges of the room, promising that there was the choice of adding a nice-sized extension that would make the huge table even larger. The massive dining table sat on a thick, old Oriental rug with tattered edges. An electric crystal chandelier hung above the table with actual places to put candles. A tall, heavy, dark mahogany cupboard held fine china and crystal. There was a buffet for linen and silverware under heavily draped windows. The long ornate piece was made of the same dark wood as the china cabinet and was topped with a fine old white porcelain pitcher and bowl set. She was pretty sure the wood was teak, for the signature fragrance of that wonderful wood permeated the stale air.

A sterling silver serving set rested on one end of the cabinet. On the other end stood a collection of amber candleholders. The early morning light barely slipped in to shine through one or two of the golden pieces showing the preciousness of them.

Sadie looked up to see the Colonel waving her onward down the entranceway past the side of the sweeping stairway. She wanted to linger and study each room, but he seemed anxious to get on with the introductions. She glanced into the room further down the hall opposite the dining room and caught a glimpse of a spacious living room or parlor. The room was unused and looked like a museum. The couches were upholstered in worn, shiny, heavy, silk brocade with chenille spreads draped here and there. Tasseled pillows in paisley prints with gold-threaded cording were stacked on each end. Huge ottomans with the stuffing a little lopsided from so much use were shoved up against overstuffed chairs. A monstrous fireplace stood at one end of the room. It was so big that Sadie could have stepped into it by just hunching over of her shoulders. Someone had set the makings of a real wood fire. Carefully arranged on bunched up paper were kindling, bigger pieces of wood, and then logs. It was ready to be set a-fire. The mantle was high, and placed haphazardly on it were family pictures in frames. Above the mantelpiece was an ominous looking gilt-framed mirror. Flecks of dark mold were creeping along the edges to claim it. The drapes were heavy, just like in the dinning room, and were drawn shut to keep out the light. So far, Sadie did not see much life in this house. Maybe in times past it had been bustling with it, but that time was long past.

They passed through the foyer where the stairway split halfway up and gracefully curved upwards to the second story. Two, sort of shriveled up ferns sat at either side of the staircase. Bits of dried up fern fronds lay on the floor. They passed on to the room straight across from the dining room, which had at one time been another parlor or maybe a library. Now it was the living quarters of Colonel Shaw and his wife.

She took one last glance up the stairs, longing to go explore up there too. This all reminded her of a haunting dream she kept having periodically. It was of a big old mansion where room after room held all kinds of discoveries and each room was piled up with old furniture—too much furniture—sort of like a warehouse. She could never get enough of exploring the rooms in her dream and always longed to go back and find more rooms through which to search. Those dreams were not satisfying and never lasted long enough. They always left her feeling unfulfilled and hungry for more: like searching for unanswered questions.

Chapter 4

Victoria

"Sweetheart, are you decent? I've brought someone to meet you," the Colonel called out to the seemingly empty room. A big messy bed sat at an angle across one corner of the cavernous room. A bedside table held used tissues and at least seven bottles of medicine. The room was stuffy and the air stale from a night of sleeping. A vase of dried and drooping roses sat on the dresser. A few of the dried pink petals lay on the stained crocheted dresser cover. A silver-filigreed brush and mirror lay atop the dresser; long gray hairs were caught in the bristles of the brush. The other end of the room held a cozy little area where the old couple could sit and watch TV, read or just talk. There was a chintz-covered couch and a couple of easy chairs well worn and inviting. In the middle of this little living area was a nice coffee table strewn with magazines, newspapers, and novels. On a side table was a tray holding the remnants of last night's supper. On one wall were shelves of books, floor to ceiling. *So maybe this had been a library at one time after all,* she thought. A small fireplace, shut up and unused now, was set in the wall adjacent to the book cabinets.

Sadie could not help thinking how nice this room would be with a cozy fire going to scent the air with fragrant, wood smoke and adding warmth and light to the otherwise depressing room.

Through a little door a tentative voice could be heard—a sort of mewling, frightened sound. The Colonel walked to the door and knocked gently, speaking softly. "Now Vickie, there's no need to be frightened. I would never bring someone in here who would scare you. I want you to meet the nice lady I found in the park today. I'm not entirely sure, but I think she just might be the answer to our prayers."

Slowly he opened the bathroom door and reached in. It seemed to take forever for his hand to come forth bearing with it a slender wrist and then finally the whole person of his tiny wife. She was clad in a pale violet dressing gown. Her hair was in disarray with wisps of white hair curling around her wide-eyed face. She was shriveled and small and sort of hunched over at the shoulders. She peeked around the doorframe and took in the presence of this unwelcome stranger. She reminded Sadie of a frightened, wild animal that was cornered and was looking in all intensity for a way to escape.

"Honey, this is Sadie . . . . ," he looked to her for the last name again.

"Sadie Jamison. Thank you for letting me come in unannounced to meet you, Mrs. Shaw. Your husband has made a proposition to me to come and cook for you and maybe live nearby. I'm just taking him up on his suggestion to come and have a look to see if things might work out. Forgive my sudden intrusion."

"Let me properly introduce you to my wife, Victoria Louise Shaw, the love of my life now for 57 years." The Colonel still held fast to his wife's hand and proudly nudged her forward. The fear seemed to subside from her countenance, and she shyly reached forth her waxy-boned hand to greet Sadie as a gentile lady would.

"I apologize for my appearance. I was not expecting guests this morning. My husband is always surprising me," she uttered with a playful slap on the Colonel's arm. "Won't you come and sit and tell me what scheme he has cooked up for you?"

And so it began. They reiterated to her their morning meeting on the park bench. The Colonel told her how he had been inspired from their initial talk to ask Sadie to consider living in gatehouse and cooking for them. He suggested she accept the position on a trial basis for a couple of weeks to see if they all agreed it would be a good match. If not, Sadie could go on her way and they would be no worse for the try.

"Oh Everett, she very well may run when she sees the condition of that little house out back," his wife warned.

"I know, I know. I've already warned her what is out there. Why don't we go have a look right now, Sadie, and leave my wife to get dressed and presentable?"

"I have a suggestion of my own," Sadie offered. "Why don't I cook you both some breakfast first? That way you can see if I'm just bragging when I say I can cook. Then I'll take a look at that nightmare residence and see if it is feasible." All of a sudden Sadie wanted to cook something and get that big old kitchen smelling good.

They all agreed that it sounded like a grand notion. Sadie rose, picked up the tray from last night's supper and found her way back through the rooms to the kitchen.

Chapter 5

First Breakfast

Sadie pulled off her coat and hung it on a peg near the kitchen door. Her first move was to stack up the dirty dishes, pots and pans and run a big sink full of soapy, hot water. She soaked the dishes and dirty cooking pots.

Then she began exploring the cupboards, refrigerator and pantry, and quickly formulated her plan for a quick and easy breakfast. On the pantry shelf were a couple of Granny Smith apples almost past their prime. She found some walnuts in a sealed jar and some golden raisins in a box. Eggs were in the refrigerator along with a few slices of bacon. She uncovered a little wooden potato box and found a few potatoes that were still edible. She pulled off the sprouts growing from them, and peeled and grated them, washing off the starch and patting the moisture out with a hand towel. She mixed up an apple/walnut muffin mixture using the flour, baking powder, soda and Crisco she found. She popped those into the oven and started the bacon cooking. Already the smells began filtering through the room casting out the old stale smells. She found some coffee in the freezer and perked a pot in one of those old-time percolators that can only be found in antique stores now. Adding a little vanilla to the grounds gave an even more succulent scent to the air.

She stacked up all the newspapers and found two paper grocery sacks to sort the catalogues and junk mail into one and the business letters and important-looking stuff into the other. Then she found a cheery red-checkered tablecloth, worn but clean, and covered the table. She discovered a candle on the windowsill and dusted it off and lit it.

As the muffins were baking, she quickly did all the dishes and stacked them on the sink's edge on old, clean dishtowels she discovered in a drawer. It really did not take much effort to shine up a kitchen. She glanced at the floor and shuddered a little. It would take a great deal of time to get that shining.

When the old couple came into the kitchen, the room was steamy with warm scents of walnut-apple muffins, coffee, bacon, eggs, plus hash browns all crispy golden brown. The lady quickly gasped and her hand flew to her chest in a fluttery sort of way. The old gentleman ushered her gently to her seat and audibly breathed in the fragrance of everything.

Mrs. Shaw expounded, "My doctor says I can't eat like this anymore. But, by George, I'm going to do it just this one more time. This brings back such good memories of my younger days." She helped herself to a muffin and a small portion of fluffy scrambled eggs, (not beaten, but the whites just gently stirred and the yolks busted and mixed in at the last minute and tossed till barely done). She poured cream and sugar into her steaming hot coffee and even took a small corner from the plate of potatoes. "Oh this is so delicious", she announced.

The Colonel took generous portions of everything and helped himself to a second muffin. "There's some honey up in the cupboard above the stove. I wonder if you'd be so kind as to reach up there and get it for me?"

Sadie was happy to comply. The golden honey melded with the melted butter on the muffin and soaked in for a tasty treat to the tongue. Sadie turned to the sink and began washing up the skillets and spatulas. The warm, sudsy water felt so comforting to her hands. She had always loved washing dishes after a good meal was accomplished. It was just peaceful to immerse her hands in warmth and scrub away the grime and remember all her blessings. Even here she counted them. Never a day went by without having something for which to be grateful.

"Why don't you postpone that for a minute and come join us?" the Colonel requested. Sadie dried her hands, poured herself a cup of coffee, and settled down at the cheery table. The look of pure joy on Victoria's face was worth every effort she'd put forth. "As soon as we are finished with this marvelous repast, I will settle my wife down to watch her morning programs and then you and I will go out back to the little caretaker's house and see if you think there is any hope for this arrangement."

Sadie was thinking that maybe she should just pinch herself and get it over with. There was really no way this could be anything but in a dream. Would the Lord choose to arrange things so clearly and openly for her future here after what she'd done? She felt so very unworthy. She felt as though she deserved to be chastised a great deal more severely than this. Here was this old, relic of a house, so similar to the one in her dreams with so many rooms yet to see, plus nooks and crannies to explore. She already felt nearly at home in this tall-ceiling kitchen. Surely, something would happen soon to dash all her hopes and teach her a lesson with discipline and poverty.

Chapter 6

The Cottage

Sadie's mind went back in time a few weeks ago to see the group of deacons ushering her out the door of the church and shutting the doors with a solid thud behind her. She had just been in a meeting where her husband had pretended an attempt to spare them all the shame of having to deal with such a wife. He convinced them that he had tried so hard to dissuade her from her adulterous ways. Yes, he admitted that part of the problem was that he was way too busy with so much work to do as the church's pastor. He had tried to schedule time just for her, but evidently, it was just not enough. He protested that he was heartbroken and feared they would no longer want him to be their pastor. They had called her in to face their governing body. She had sat in front of them with no more tears to shed. She knew she appeared hard and calculating. She didn't care. The object of her cheating heart sat in the back of that room with his head in his hands, moving his bedraggled head back and forth in an anguished manner of guilt.

Oh Jacob, she had thought, *I should have seen that you would crumble to the will of this place. Your loyalty to me is truly touching,* she thought sarcastically. *You appear to be the harmed and used person here. Don't worry. They will forgive you and welcome you back into the fold for your repentance. Soon, you will once again stand up on that stage and you will lead the choir and congregation, turning the heads of all the women.* What a fool she'd been to turn to him for comfort and expressions of love.

"Miss Jamison, Sadie, are you okay? You seem to have gone somewhere else for a minute." The Colonel looked worried and held his wife's hand in reassurance.

"Yes, I'm just fine. I did sort of space out there for a minute. There's so much on my mind and so many changes in my life right now. I'm just sort of pondering on things I guess. Sorry to have worried you."

"What say you let these dishes sit a spell and come out with me to that infamous abode I've been warning you about?" He smiled wanly as if hoping that she would not get discouraged when she saw that little unused house near the back gate.

"Just let me get my wife settled in her room. She likes to watch her morning programs. I'll be right back." He turned adoringly to his sweet wife and beckoned her to come with him. Victoria smiled warmly at Sadie. There was a flush of peach on her cheeks. She appeared to be satiated and content. "Thank you so much for this lovely repast. I feel like I've stepped back in time. I do hope for the best for you no matter what you decide about staying here."

What a sweet thing to say, thought Sadie. *No pressure, just good wishes for my future, no matter which way I choose to go.* While Colonel Shaw was off getting his wife comfortable, Sadie whisked off the dishes into the sink and gathered up the tablecloth, shaking it out the back door and then resettling it on the table. By the time the Colonel had returned to the kitchen, Sadie was nearly finished with the cleanup. "My but you are certainly fast," he commented approvingly.

Sadie put on her coat and followed the Colonel out the back door. Clouds had gathered in the sky like sheep running together. Still, there were patches of blue. The temps had dropped some and Sadie suspected that rain was coming soon. They tramped back of the house along a trail that was overgrown and deep in pine needles. It was still a path, or what was left of one. She could see the outline of the little house through the foliage. It was small, for sure. The walls were stone and the windows set deep giving room for something to sit on the ledges. The screen door was hanging on one hinge, but the front door itself looked sturdy enough, although the paint was peeling and the wood crinkled with age. Colonel Shaw reached into his pocket and pulled out a set of keys. He searched painstakingly through the bunch and finally settled on a long bronze one. As if he were placing lots of hope in this proposal, he removed the key from the set and put the rest back into his pocket.

The door creaked open as the Colonel slowly pushed it open. A dim darkness stared back at Sadie. The air was a bit repugnant with whiffs of mildew, mold, old papers and maybe even mouse droppings. It had been a very long time since anyone lived here. Sadie sort of wanted to turn and run. *Oh dear, what am I getting myself into here?* she thought. Colonel Shaw flipped on the light switch and a dusty low wattage bulb lit up to cast a sickly pall over the scene. Sadie nearly gasped, but checked her response with a quick cough.

"Yes, it is dusty in here to be sure. If the windows are open to the fresh air, and all these cobwebs and dried leaves and debris are swept out, maybe this could become a home again," he remarked hopefully. "I can't even remember the last time I stepped foot over this threshold. When I was a boy, I spent many a fun day here with the caretaker and his wife. It used to be one of my favorite escape spots. One of my sons used it as an art studio for a while. My daughter used to have tea parties out here for her friends and even a few slumber parties." He rushed forward tripping over an old rake. He wanted to open the other doors to let her have a look.

What a challenge this place would be! The living room and kitchen were all one room. Flaps of old mildewed wallpaper were hanging from the walls. Cobwebs were filling almost every corner. There was a little fireplace all sooty and chipped. Sadie closed her eyes and prayed. *Lord, what is this? Is this where you want me to settle in?*

Am I up to this? In my younger days, I did make homes out of run-down houses and one that even had been a chicken coop in a former time; but I am older now. Can I do this? Do you want me to do this? She waited there a second for some epiphany or assurance to seep into her being, but there was nothing. So, she followed Colonel Shaw farther into the room. The kitchen part of the room had an old wood cook stove there. A tiny wooden table had two chairs stacked up on top. No refrigerator was in sight. She spied a chipped enamel sink with mouse droppings and dried leaves and dirt in it. The linoleum on the floor was curling up and was some indistinct gray color. A window above the sink looked out over the acreage. Sadie noticed a blue jay sitting on a pine bough right outside the window. It seemed to be looking at her with a sort of curiosity. A loud squawk came from that bird and nearly made Sadie jump. *Thanks for the nice welcome,* Sadie thought with humor.

"Over here is the bedroom. There's only just one of them; the place is small."

Sadie stepped in with trepidation and it was nearly pitch black. It took a while for her eyes to adjust to the darkness. Then she recognized that stacks of boxes lined the walls and covered up the windows. The light switch did not work in this room at all. "Must have burned out," the Colonel apologized. Sadie quickly retreated back to the kitchen. "The bathroom is just a toilet, sink and shower. There is a little screened-in back porch where the refrigerator is kept, and a sink for washing clothes and stuff. That screen will have to be replaced for sure"

Then the Colonel said the very thing that almost made up Sadie's mind to leap happily off the cliff and swim for her life. "Our big old house is so full of unused furniture. Six bedrooms upstairs are full of everything you could ever need here. There's even a nice-sized bedroom downstairs. We use it as an office right now, but there is still a bed in there. All you have to do is go looking for what you need and haul it down here and set up housekeeping." Her heart leaped with joy. It was her dream, come true. To be free to explore that wonderful old mansion, going from room to room searching through the troves of treasured furniture. What an adventure this was going to be. Her whole being was suddenly fused with energy and hope and right then and there she began seeing that little hovel with new eyes and with plans for its revival.

"I'll tell you what I'll do, Colonel Shaw. I'll go back to my Motel 6 tonight and think this over, and I'll come back tomorrow morning with an answer for you. Right now I'm tending to think it just might work; but I need to consult with my boss to see if this is what I should be doing."

"I didn't know you had another job. Why would your boss let you do this?"

"I try not to do anything major like this unless I've prayed about it and run it by the Master for approval," she clarified.

He smiled at her with new respect. "That's good enough for me. If you decide to come onboard here, I will get some workers to help you clean out this mess and slap a fresh coat of paint all around. I'll even replace this old kitchen floor and put in a regular electric stove," he promised.

"Sounds like a plan," she quipped. "But I really do like this old wood stove and would like to keep it along side the electric one for use once in a while and to warm up this house. My grandmother used to tell me that food cooked on a wood stove could beat out anything cooked on one of those modern conveniences. I'd just like to try it out and see for myself."

The Colonel locked up the old door and they walked back along the path to the big house. Sadie finished up her work in the kitchen and set two of trays for their dinner. She looked inside the refrigerator and found some leftover beef roast. She quickly put together a little stew with cubed roast beef, potatoes, carrots and onions browned first in the skillet. She found a bit of port wine, all dusty, pushed back in the cupboard and flavored the stew with that. The house was full of the moist, hearty fragrance. She made some sweetened iced tea and set up a little skillet of biscuits for the Colonel to bake in the oven when it was time for their dinner. After all this was ready, she felt free to leave them.

Chapter 7

The Past Revisited

The air was heavy with moisture as she hurried along, back through town. The little café was still lit up with a few customers there having a late lunch. She wondered if she would be hungry tonight. Nah! She had too much to think about and decide. It surely wouldn't hurt her to skip a meal now and again, anyway. She looked around for Mr. Combs, the homeless man. She couldn't help but wonder where he went to find shelter from a night such as this.

She rushed down to the bus station and then to her motel room. The rain let loose and doused everything in a sudden downpour. She stepped into the lobby of the motel and breathed a sigh of relief to have avoided that deluge. It felt so alien to be in that barren, cold room with its stiff bed and worn coverlet. It always made her wonder who had been in this bed and what person had sat on this bedspread before her. Motels were not friendly places and certainly not her favorite thing. Sadie's thoughts were focused on this most life-changing decision. Inexplicable tears welled up in her eyes as she realized how close to destitution she really was, and yet she felt such hope and such incredible love and care surrounding her. Her tears were expressions of grief and shame; and yet she felt great joy at being forgiven and presented with this chance of making a new life.

For 33 years she had tried to endure that loveless marriage with a man, so adored and respected by his flock. He gave himself to the church wholeheartedly. When he walked out their door, he was completely focused on charming people and being clever with words. He would be so kind to anyone in need of his counsel and commiserations. His sermons were powerful, moving and eloquent. He was one of the leaders of the community; his advice widely sought out and adhered to. Pastor Anthony Golden worked his way up from small country parishes to small town churches. Then he did a stint as the youth director of a big city church, and finally he was called to be a pastor of one of these huge congregations. He had his own ministerial assistants to handle choir, youth, senior citizens, bus, education and children's ministries. He earned an extravagant salary. Even the members of the church, who were not in the governing counsel, were not allowed to know about the amount, but it was a good six figures.

Why then, could she not just bask in the residual glory of this handsome man, her husband, and not worry that behind the closed doors of their home there were no tangible expressions of love for her. Sure, he told her that he loved her and patted her on the back like she was a well-behaved dog. She found that words were weak and unsatisfying. Why couldn't she just do what was expected of her? Through the years, she'd fallen into the pattern of keeping the house and preparing meals punctually. The home was open to Bible studies for men during the week. She would quietly retreat to the other rooms of the house to see that the children were put to bed. After serving the coffee and snacks, she would escape to her bedroom to read or just go to sleep.

She was expected to play the piano for church and sing solos, be friendly and cheerful, never complaining or demanding anything for herself. How many years did she sacrifice herself to this, all the time telling herself she was doing this for the glory of God?

Her three children came right after the marriage was consummated. Eighteen months between each child: a son, a daughter and then another son. Andrew, Rebecca and Matthew; all biblical names of course. Andy, Becky and Matt. How she had loved those precious little people! When they had been small, she was so absorbed in their nurture and care that she had hardly noticed the lack of physical love between her husband and herself. She received her joy and self-esteem by creating experiences for her children to enjoy: tents in the living room, puppies to raise, picnics and exploratory hikes. As they got older, she had school plays to attend, sports practices and games to sit through, not to mention the school lessons that needed her input. She had tried not to think too much about the fact that their daddy was too busy to even be home at night, or that he had no time even for Halloween trick or treating. She made excuses for him, assuring the children that their dad was a servant of God and that he really did love them so much, but could not be like other daddies. His job, as a preacher and pastor, just took up too much time.

It wasn't very long until her children began to notice their mother's sadness and isolation. When they got to be teens they confronted her with it, telling her to stand up for her rights as a person. "It's not even a real marriage, Mom," her son, Andy, would admonish. Becky would plead with her saying, "Mama, he treats you like a servant. You are a really attractive lady, and I don't think he even notices it. Tell him what you feel, please!"

The thing was, she **had** told Tony for years how frustrated and unfulfilled she felt. This could not be how God intended a marriage to be. She cried tears of rage and threatened to take the children and leave. Sometimes she pleaded and then felt so humiliated afterwards. He would charmingly agree with her, shaking his handsome head as if he had failed her for sure. He would promise to do better and try to reason with her to be patient and be willing to sacrifice. One time, 'Pastor Tony' penciled the family in for Thursday nights of each week and really seemed determined to set that time aside for them. Remembering back on that time, Sadie was saddened to think of a father scheduling time on his calendar for his very own family. As it turned out, something almost always came up on those Thursday nights: emergencies or special meetings, or someone sick to visit, or a young woman needing counseling for her own, struggling marriage. Pretty soon, he just gave up on saving Thursdays for them, and he didn't even pretend that he was sorry.

He even brought home books for her to read; books that told her how to be a better wife, a submissive wife. There were tapes on how to understand the pressures of a pastor. She would reason with herself and set aside her personal grievances. She tried again and again. Inside she was becoming sadder and sadder with no real self-esteem. She felt unattractive and invisible, just someone that he needed around to cook and clean, and smile in church, and raise his model children. "A pastor needs a wife and good family, or it doesn't look right," he would remind her. "Just stick with me. Retirement is on the horizon and we will travel and be together all the time then, and you'll be sick of having me around." He had no idea that she was already to that point.

Whenever Anthony could sense that she was getting to the breaking point, he would come home with flowers, or candy, and sometimes perfume. She remembered one time in the early stages of the descent of their marriage when she was expecting their third child, she was so tired of being home and being huge. He promised her he would take her out to eat and to a movie that weekend. She was surprisingly giddy with joy. The night arrived and they drove into a residential area instead of heading downtown. "Where are we going?" she inquired worriedly.

"Oh, I forgot to tell you. I have to stop by the Martins' house just for a minute to drop something off. It won't take a minute. You can come in with me and just say hello and then we'll be on our way. I promise."

Well, she was so disappointed, but once again reasoned that in this business, she had to comply and realize that the church and God had to come first. So they walked up the walkway to the front door. She noticed lots of cars parked all around and wondered what kind of meeting was being held here. When the door opened to balloons and crepe paper streamers, she wanted to bolt and run down the street screaming. It was another baby shower. All these well-intentioned women were cheering and clapping. She began crying and the tears would just not stop. She looked at her husband, who was beaming down at her until he recognized how betrayed she was feeling. Then he took his leave very quickly and promised to pick her up in a couple of hours.

As the door shut behind her, she was at the mercy of that situation. The tears would not stop and all the ladies thought that she was just the most, tender woman showing her appreciation with profuse tears. They surrounded their pastor's wife with hugs and adoration. She did not know how she got through that evening, sitting in the center of all that attention, enduring the frivolous games and comments. She opened each gift and smiled until she thought her jaw would break. She expressed words of thanks and sighs of surprise. She felt like the worst phony that ever walked the Earth. Finally when it was all over, she waited at the door while all the guests departed one by one. Her energy was so low she thought she just might drop. Finally after she began helping the sweet hostess clear up the napkins and dishes and stuff the wrapping paper in garbage bags, Anthony came to pick her up. He was late. He couldn't help it—another emergency. She rode home in the car in total silence. He kept asking her if she had a great time, and wasn't it just so good of all those ladies to give her a third shower? She stared out the side window, not even wanting to see his face in her peripheral vision. Silence reigned. She didn't even care if he thought she was ungrateful and acting crazy.

It took a long time to get over that disappointment. It was like the last straw, and yet she stuck in there and stayed with it year after year, until now. How had she been so determined to make it work? Unbelievable.

Chapter 8

Forgiveness

Now she was alone and free and had to make choices on her own. It felt so exhilarating and yet frightening at the same time. She dropped to her knees and threw her arms over the frayed bedcover. She cried out to the Lord to give her the assurance that this was the right option. She prayed for strength to take it all on. She knew that if she would just acknowledge God when she was making life choices, then the Lord would direct her paths and bring her the delights of her heart. She bowed there quietly with sighs and sobs breaking the silence. The Spirit would have to pray for her, for she could not articulate anything in words, just feelings.

Suddenly she felt as though she were being covered up with a big, fluffy, warm, downy blanket. It surrounded her with comfort and peace. The feeling was so tangible that she gasped at how real it felt. She was being hugged and loved and nurtured right in that Motel 6 room. It felt absolutely wonderful. Forgiveness surged through her and washed her soul clean. She felt like laughing through her tears. She wanted to stay that way forever and never have to be outside His presence ever again. Finally she eased herself up and crawled into bed with all her clothes on and fell into a deep, healing sleep.

The morning sunshine peeked through the drapes of the motel room that would just not come completely together. Sadie woke slowly. She felt so at peace and well. She lazily roused herself. It was a new day—a brand new, empty page upon which to write. She showered and put on fresh clothes and headed out to the Rose Vine Café for breakfast. She was famished. Cherie, the waitress recognized her and welcomed her.

"How you doing today?" she asked. "Isn't it so nice to see the sunshine? That was quite a rain we had last night. My baby was so frightened by the lightning and thunder."

Just small talk but it was there to show Sadie that she was glad to see her and hopeful for a good response. Sadie smiled back at her. "Oh yes, children are indeed prone to be afraid of wild weather. They have to be taught to enjoy storms and not be afraid of them. Maybe some day soon your baby will grow to love storms and wind and rain and feel so safe in her home."

"Well, that's how I feel for sure. I guess I'll have to work on showing her by my 'no fear' attitude that storms are interesting and that we just can look forward to them. Say, what can I do you for?"

It had been a while since Sadie had heard that endearing term. It reminded her how people are connected by certain traditions and sayings from past history where families touched families from long ago. "I'll have some pancakes and link sausages. Oh, and coffee too," she added.

"It'll be right up," Cherie replied pouring Sadie a nice steaming hot cup of reviving coffee.

Sadie glanced around and noticed that the homeless man was not out there this morning. *I wonder where he slept last night during that downpour,* she pondered. Then her thoughts went to the Shaw's, waiting in their old plantation-like home for her to bring them her answer about the proposal. What else could she decide? The Lord had seemed to be the one who led her to this opportunity, and who was she to say to the Lord, "Nah, thanks anyway, but I think I'll just find my own way." That wasn't going to happen. What lay ahead of her was hard work and lonely nights and adjustments to new people and their needs. She would plant herself here and make a life and just take it one day at a time and see what happened.

"You look so deep in thought. Everything all right?" Cherie tentatively asked. She had the steaming, fragrant hotcakes with pats of butter melting on top and sausages and a pitcher of hot maple syrup. Sadie's tummy started to rumble just at the sight and smell of everything.

"Oh, I am deep in contemplation for sure. You see I've been offered the position of cook for the Shaw's who live near here. It will be a big leap for me to take this on. So I am just trying to figure it all out."

"I just love that old man. He comes in here for coffee and an éclair at least once a week, and he is so very nice. I heard his wife is not doing so well. You will love working for them." Cherie assured her. "He was very good to me when I had my little girl. He gave me an envelope once with a hundred bucks in it. You cannot imagine how much that helped me."

"Yes, I can imagine it. He offered me a chance to survive here, and I'm taking it. It is always amazing to me how a day unfolds and presents such surprises to us if we are just open to seeing them."

"Some days I don't see many blessings—just problems. I don't have a husband and yet I have a little baby girl to raise. I know lots of people look at me like I am such a messed up girl. But Colonel Shaw was one of the good ones who gave me hope to carry on and do the best I could." Cherie confided.

"Who takes care of your baby while you work and where do you live?" Sadie inquired. "Oh, I'm sorry to get into your business; I am always so curious about how people live and get by. It is none of my business and I'm sorry to be so bold to ask that."

"Not at all. There's just something about you that I trust. So I will tell you that my baby and I live above the bakery across the street, there. It is just one room with a tiny bathroom stuck on one end, but it does for us. There is an old woman who watches Joy for me while I work. She lives above one of the other stores on this street. It is convenient for me. I wish I could spend more time with Joy, but I have to earn money to live."

Sadie looked at this brave, young girl making do with what she had and with her circumstances. "Well life just has a way of working out and weaving itself into a pattern that suits us. I just know that you and your little Joy will be fine. You have so much love to give her. She will be your best friend for a long time to come."

Tears began to well up in Cherie's eyes and she blinked them away and grabbed a napkin to blow her nose. "It is so good to hear encouraging words. Thank you for that."

Cherie got busy with the other customers and Sadie savored every bite of her breakfast. It was time to get going and act on this decision about her life ahead. Of course she would do it; she had to. You don't just ask the Lord for answers; and then, when they come, cast them aside. She got up and left a sizeable tip for Cherie and paid her bill with the cashier. She headed across the street to the bakery deciding at that moment to take some fresh baked goods to the Shaw's so that she could just get started right away on her new abode. Maybe if she worked really hard and fast she could move into the gatehouse in a few days' time. It all depended on how quickly Colonel Shaw could hire the workers to redo her kitchen floor and paint. She would have to get help carrying down the furniture she would need from the upstairs rooms of the mansion; but that was an easy problem and did not worry her. She closed her eyes and sighed at the thought of the work that lay ahead of her.

Chapter 9

Peter and the First Day

The fragrances from the bakery were so succulent—the fresh baked breads, donuts, rolls, cookies and cakes. A bakery had to be one of the best places in which to stick in your head and breathe. *Ahhh . . . . wonderful.* She chose some bear claws and some maple Danishes and a big loaf of fresh crusty French bread.

As she worked her way down the streets toward the walled-in mansion, she noticed the homeless man wrapped up in two coats walking along in the sunshine carrying a cup of steaming coffee. His eyes looked only to the ground, his mind on private thoughts. He had a sad presence, so heavy with grief and regret. She spoke to him, "Good morning. This sun sure feels wonderful, doesn't it?"

She was almost sorry she had ventured to speak to him, for his eyes came up to hers and she read all the pain and loss there, and something else as well. Was that anger and resentment? He said not a word but just walked on toward town. *So much for trying to be nice.* Who did she think she was anyway—God's angel to the needy? She was needy herself.

The stone wall around the Colonel's home looked so dark and heavy. Today she had another view of this acreage. The woods inside were way too crowded and did not allow much sunshine to get through to the ground beneath. She slightly shuddered at the oppressive dark shadows underneath the heavy foliage. She hurried up to the Shaw's front door and rang the bell. Peels of sound came pouring out of the house as the Colonel opened the door to her. "I've been watching for your arrival. So glad you came back. I was wondering if you had decided against my job offer. I was surely hoping you would come. What have you decided?"

"Good morning to you, too! You are a man who gets right down to business that is for sure!" Sadie replied. "Yes, I've prayed about it, slept on it, and I've decided to do this thing. And furthermore, we won't have to wait two weeks for me to make up my mind, either. I will be happy to be your cook and to live in that little house out back. I'm ready to get started on fixing it up."

The Colonel's face lit up and a big sigh of relief welled out of him. "Oh, thank the Lord! I'm so relieved. I haven't seen my wife light up like she did yesterday in a very long time. I could tell she liked you and trusted you. This will be a great thing for us and I will try to make sure it is a great thing for you as well."

She showed the Colonel the bakery goods she had brought, holding up the bag for him to sniff. "You are a woman after my own heart," he exclaimed. "How I love that bakery downtown. I frequent it quite often, maybe too much," he quipped, patting his flat tummy. Sadie could tell he was very proud of his slim physique.

"Let me get some fresh coffee perked, and I'll carry in this simple breakfast for you and Mrs. Shaw, so that you won't have to bother coming in this morning to eat. Then I can just get to it. I'll need a broom, a mop, a pail and dust cloths. Can you point me to where they might be?" The Colonel led her to the back porch and pointed out a little end closet where everything she needed was waiting.

Sadie ventured into the dining room and searched through the big china cabinet. As soon as the coffee was brewed, she carefully filled some fine-boned china cups with the hot coffee. She discovered some lovely matching salad plates with gilt edges and tiny rosebuds. She used these to serve the bakery goodies and included two soft-boiled eggs and a cut-up orange. Oh, it was delicately enticing. She stepped outside to search for something growing that she could include on the serving tray. She found a few tiny pine cones and some pine tree greenery that had fallen during the storm. There were some new orange berries growing down the overgrown path and she clipped some of that too. She found a tiny pottery vase and put these pieces of nature in the vase and added it to the tray. Oh, that looked so nice.

Victoria Shaw was waiting expectantly in her comfy wing-backed chair. Her hair was combed, and she wore a nice organza dress with pearls and earrings to match. She smelled of clean soap and talcum powder. It was a delightful scene. Sadie greeted her with exuberance and respect, telling her how nice she looked. Mrs. Shaw was visibly moved by the compliments and faintly blushed. She was so happy to see her fine china in use again and clapped her hands lightly. "Well, Mrs. Shaw, Colonel, I'd better get to it. I'll work this morning in my new home outside, and I'll be sure to stop long enough to get your lunch ready. Enjoy your morning together. Don't worry with the dishes; I'll pick them up later."

She was about to retreat when she heard the quiet voice of Mrs. Shaw. "Please dear, this may seem too soon to you, but I'd appreciate it if you would call me Victoria. Already I feel close enough to you, through your kindnesses, to request this familiarity."

Sadie was nearly moved to tears at the gentle ways of this beautiful old woman. "I . . . . I'll be happy to comply . . . . Victoria."

Finally she was free to dive in and get started on that house. She found some high wattage light bulbs and grabbed up the broom, mop, bucket and cleaning supplies. The sunshine seemed to smile on her as she set her life on this new path. It felt so warm and Sadie was determined that by the end of this day that same sunshine would be streaming into her little abode.

As she headed out the back door, Colonel Shaw called to her. She turned around to find his hand extended holding the big brass key. "I think you will be needing this, young lady." There it was again—his reference to her as young. God bless him! "Thanks so much. I am feeling like I'm home already!"

The key creaked in the keyhole and the door swung open. She was once again assaulted by the scents of mustiness, dirt and rotting vegetation. She wrinkled her nose in disgust, but then she remembered a favorite scene in a great movie. She pictured Whoopi Goldberg as Celia in "The Color Purple", tackling that disgustingly ruined kitchen, scrubbing and sweeping the place to a livable state once again. She took a deep breath, coughed, and stepped in boldly to face this task. First, she opened all the windows and replaced the old light bulbs with nice bright ones. She began to sweep out the kitchen and had to run back to the main house to get big black garbage bags. She soon filled two of them with debris old papers, and garbage. The fresh breezes began to blow in and gave her courage to carry on. She carried hot water from the house and added dishwashing soap until there were suds and steam coming from the bucket. She began to scrub the sink, walls, cabinets, and floor. After several buckets had been dumped in the woods, the place began to smell and look a bit better. She suddenly realized that she had just wasted a lot of effort cleaning that damaged floor since the Colonel was going to replace it soon. Then she reasoned that it was worth it to keep from tracking dirt to the other rooms.

Sadie took a break and walked to the market a few blocks away, purchasing honey-baked ham slices, chips, pickles, olives and a roasted chicken from the deli plus 2 sides and dessert. That would do for today's meals: sandwiches for lunch and roasted chicken for dinner. As soon as lunch was served to the Shaw's, this time on rough-looking pottery plates, with big mugs of root beer, she ate her own sandwich on the run as she continued her work.

The Colonel came out to check on her progress. He smiled at how different the place already looked. "My, my, but you've really done a lot of work out here already! I'm going to call right now to the home decorating store and have them bring you some samples of new flooring. They can install it in a day or two, whenever you are ready. As for those boxes in the bedroom, just push them out the door onto the path and I will have them removed by the junk man. I don't know what is in them, but I'm sure it is not worth going through. If anything is priceless in there, my good buddy, Ralph, the junk man will return it to us or at least ask permission to sell it and use the proceeds for himself."

"Sounds like a great plan to me. I was wondering what I would do with all that stuff. I think I shall try to get someone to move the boxes out for me. My back needs to be protected for all the work I have ahead of me. Maybe I can use that same person to help me haul down the furniture I choose for my little house. What do you say?"

"Now that's the ticket!" He said as he reached into his back pocket and pulled out a leather wallet. "Here's some money to pay you back for the groceries you just bought and to hire someone to help you do these chores." She took the money and nearly swooned to see four $50 bills there.

"This will be more than enough, I imagine. And I will keep a record of all the things I purchase for the kitchen and for meals and for this renovation. Thanks so much."

"Don't be silly. No thanks needed. I am paying you to be here and I appreciate so much your willingness to do all this. No amount I paid you could be enough to compensate for what you've already done for my sweet Vicky. How about I pay you the end of every week? We'll agree on an amount soon."

Sadie smiled at him and genuinely just wanted to hug him. She was a hugger and loved to show people her feelings by touching them or hugging them or kissing them on the cheek. But something told her that it was too soon to advance on the Colonel with expressions of gratitude.

Really it was that boldness to express her deep heartfelt love for people that got her in trouble at the church. After a fine program in which she and the music director had labored over for weeks, the congregation had clapped and given the choir and drama team a standing ovation. Afterwards, in the hallway, she hugged him to her and kissed him on the cheek in delight at what they'd accomplished. He had looked shocked and stood back from her. "Sorry," she apologized, "I just get carried away and wanted you to know how much I appreciated all your effort in this."

Then he said the one thing that started her heart rolling. "Oh, don't apologize. I've been wanting you to do that for a long time now."

She had hidden her surprise at this admission and excused herself with smiles and pats on his back, but the jolt of someone admitting that they actually desired to hug her was salve for her wounded spirit and low self-esteem. After that, every time they worked together they hugged in parting. They found lots of excuses to work together; sorting music in the choir library, or consulting with each other on the musical selections. Just being near him and smelling his woodsy cologne gave her sensations she had scrunched for a long, long time. She began to smile more and have more energy. She was happier at home and nicer to Tony. He was delighted at the change in her countenance and attitude.

Sadie was sure that he congratulated himself on solving another counseling dilemma by all the books and tapes he'd offered her. The fact was she had thrown each self-help manual into a rarely used closet. The pile of them was getting big there in the corner of that dark place.

As time went by, she confided this little infatuation to her daughter, Becky. "I don't know what's come over me; I should be running the other way. What's gotten into me?"

Becky lived nearby with her one son, Treat and husband Stan. It was having her near that saved Sadie's life. They had lunch once a week and confided in each other truthfully. Becky knew of the sad state of her mother's marriage and had little respect for her father and his self-promoting ways. She recognized that he loved being adored by the congregation and had apoplectic attacks if anyone barely indicated that they were upset with him in any way. Becky had seen her mother get old before her time, with a deep sadness that permeated her features and left her somewhat lifeless and unenthusiastic. Becky had been pushing her mother to step out and do something about it for years. She had finally given up, thinking there was no hope for her wimp of a mother.

Now she responded with this, "Oh Mom, it was bound to happen sooner or later. You are a beautiful woman and one of the most talented, super people I know. Of course your being my mom makes me prejudiced a little, but there is so much untapped potential in you. You have stagnated so long and settled for so much less than you deserve. This nice man has discovered something wonderful about you, and of course he loves to be with you. Don't worry about it; you are not doing anything wrong."

"He's only 48 and so handsome it makes me dizzy. I just have to be sure to keep it completely friendly. When he just touches my hand, I nearly jump. I sound like a little high school girl. I can't believe I'm telling you all this."

"That's the great thing about you and me. We trust each other with our deepest secrets. I've told you all about my marriage and how disappointed I use to be. You've shown me to be patient and loving, and to wait for Stan to grow up some more. And he has. I might have jumped out of this marriage a long time ago and wasted a good match that just needed time to settle in together. My little Treat loves his daddy so much. I'm glad I didn't choose to quit and run. With all that said, Mom, you have stuck it out in your loveless marriage for 32 years now, and enough is enough. Mom, please stand up and be counted."

Sadie pondered on the fact that her two sons, grown and living far away, were probably disappointed in her as well. They called once in a while and seldom even sent photographs of their lives. She treasured each short visit they made to come see her at Christmastime and maybe Fourth of July. They could not stand to be around for long, because they both resented their absentee dad, and they both abhorred hypocrisy so much. Neither one attended church now. Andrew would kid and say he was a member of the Bedside Baptist Church and that he was the preacher. Matt didn't even pretend to be interested in any of it. Neither of them had found a sweet girl to marry, and Sadie was sure it was because they'd seen how unhappy their own parents' marriage had been. Oh she wished for healing for them and their ability to forgive their dad and her. Bitterness like they harbored was only poisoning them

She snapped her mind back to the present and watched the old Colonel walk slowly back to the big house. Now there was little she could do before those big mildewed boxes were removed from the bedroom. She decided to walk back to town and see if she could talk to someone about who would be willing to help her with the chore. She stopped at the dime store for a little notebook and a couple of good pens. She wrote down her expenditures so far for food. Then she saw the homeless man whose name was Peter Combs, as she recalled. He was sitting on an old chair outside the café enjoying the sunshine. His eyes were closed. An inspiration struck her. His little shabby sign sitting beside him said, "Will Work for Food." So why not let him work a little? She approached him carefully and cleared her throat to rouse his attention. He snapped open his eyes and glared at her intrusion.

"Do you really mean what that sign there says?" she inquired.

"What?" he barked.

"Your sign says, 'Will Work for Food.' Do you really mean that?"

"Lady, what do you want? Can't you see I'm trying to get some rays here?"

"Well, your cup is empty and I have some work that needs doing. It's just some old boxes that need to be dragged out of a house and put on the side of the street. Do you think you are up to it?" she queried. Sadie had just had about enough of this loser's attitude.

"Where's the house?" he asked gruffly.

"It's near the big old plantation house. You know, the one with the giant wall all around it?" she offered.

Peter Combs let out a big sigh of resignation, slapped both knees with his hands and stood up. "Well, I could use a little cash to get me by for the next few days. Let's see what you have for me to do."

"Your sign says that you will work for food. That was how I was planning to pay you," Sadie responded. When she saw the glaring look on his face, she amended, "but I'm sure I can add a bit of cash in the bargain as well. Come with me and see if you think you can handle the task."

This seemed to set him off and he snorted and shook his head as though she should easily see how able he was to move a few boxes. He would not walk beside her, but followed along a few steps behind. People in the stores along Main Street gawked at the spectacle of Sadie leading the town's homeless eccentric down the street. She held her head up high and marched resolutely on.

Not a word was spoken between them. When he got a little too close and the breeze was just right, or wrong as the situation might fit, she could smell his unwashed clothes and body. It made her nose crinkle up in disgust.

"The house in question is that little place back there in the woods," she pointed down the path at the sad, little cottage. "I'm planning on making myself a home out of that."

That snort again. She turned to glare at him. "That may seem silly to you, but it is rude to show such disdain to someone you don't even know."

He chuckled and she was surprised to see that he even could laugh anymore. "Don't get me wrong, lady. I have no room to judge where someone lives. My favorite spot right now is under the bridge at the end of town. There's a cozy spot up under the concrete where I make a little fire and curl up out of the wind. Compared to that, this little shack looks like a mansion to me. It's just that you don't look like the type of lady to choose it as a home."

"Well it is my choice and I'm going to make a go of it. Come right through here and I'll show you the boxes I need moved."

He was stronger than he looked and was easily hauling the boxes to the street's edge where the Colonel's friend could come to pick them up. He was nearly done in about an hour. Then one of the last boxes toppled sideways and split open to reveal a bunch of old clothes neatly folded inside. There was a heavy wool coat and some work Pants, shirts and heavy woolen socks that had a few moth holes in them. Long underwear were scattered in there too.

"I don't mean to be forward, Mr. Combs, but you look in need of some clothes. Maybe you could air these out and find some good use for them," she offered.

"How in blazes did you know my name? I never told it to you. And what makes you think I need someone's old cast off clothes, anyway?"

"Colonel Shaw told me who you were because I asked him. And it looks to me like you could use some clothes that have less wear and tear than the ones you are wearing at this moment. Pardon me if I've offended your tender sensibilities."

Peter just snorted again and carried the busted up box of clothes to the street along with the rest of the boxes. When he was finishe, she asked if he would like to work a little longer. He shrugged and said he figured he had a little more work in him for that day. So she set him to washing the windows inside and out. He went through so many rags, that she had to go search for more in the house. Those rags were blackened with the soot and grime from those windows. Sadie warmed to the sunshine now streaming into the house through the shiny glass. She opened the windows again after Peter cleaned them and washed out the dead bugs, dirt and pollen accumulated over the years in the windowsills. These open windows brought in more fresh air, and soon the place had a smell of pine trees and pine cleaner. She had Pete clean all the windows twice. Some of them were antique-looking, with wavy glass where the years had caused the glass to slowly settle toward the bottom leaving the top of the panes thinner than the bottoms.

"How about some lunch now?" she offered. "Sandwiches, chips, a coke and a Danish?"

His eyes had a glimmer of light and she could tell he was hungry. That was a lot of hard work he had just accomplished. She reckoned he would be sleeping pretty soundly under his bridge tonight. She quickly went to the big house and fixed sandwiches for the Shaw's and for herself and Peter Combs. He ate outside on the front stoop. She sat at the little wooden table covered with a nice red-checkered cloth she'd found in the big house's kitchen. She contemplated just how much more work there was to be done. She wondered if Pete was up to helping anymore. Maybe she'd better not push it too much right now.

Colonel Shaw walked down the path to the house and greeted Pete warmly. "Looks like she put you to work out here. I really appreciate your help here Peter."

Pete just shrugged and kept his eyes to the ground as he ate. Colonel slipped in behind him to the house and sat at the table with Sadie. "My, my, but it looks like you've accomplished so much in just this one day. The man with the linoleum samples will be here soon, and you can also pick out the paint for the rooms from samples he will bring."

Sadie was delighted. "Is it okay for me to choose without conferring with you?" She asked. He assured her that he would not mind anything she did to the place.

"It already looks tons better than it has in years. Go for it! Pick out whatever you think will look nice. Go right upstairs and pick whatever furniture you need to fill this place to your liking. I never even go up there anymore and the place is never used up there. I wonder if Pete will be able to help you with that. It will be too heavy for you to cart all that furniture down those stairs. You might want to find at least two people to help you."

When Colonel Shaw left, she approached Peter. "Well, you've done a fine day's work here. I'm going to give you a bit of dinner to take for later, and here's $25 for today's labor." She handed him the bills and rushed to the big kitchen to fix him a plate of chicken, mashed potatoes, green beans, and a couple of soft yeast rolls. She covered up the plate with tinfoil and took it out to Peter. He looked sort of subdued as he eyed the plate of food.

"Well that's really great of you to fix me a supper plate. I usually don't even bother with late eating. My stomach is going to wonder what is happening. If you have any more work for me to do tomorrow, I'll come by and I'll bring back this plate to you."

She brightened at that. "Why that would just be fine, Peter. I'll see you tomorrow bright and early, say about 8:00? Tomorrow, we will tackle the paths around here and clean out the old refrigerator and back porch. I was wondering if you'd like to help move some furniture down from the big house to this one. I'll have to find you another set of hands to help you. Colonel Shaw seems to think a lot of that old furniture is too heavy for one man and a woman to handle."

"It's been a while since I used my muscles for this kind of work. I'm sure I will suffer for it right at first, but truth be told, it sort of feels good to stretch out the kinks. Maybe I could borrow a furniture dolly from the moving company. I'm sure that if we offer to rent it, they will let us have it for $10.00 a day," he offered.

"What a great idea! Tomorrow, I will go upstairs and pick out what I need for this little cottage and we'll be good to go as soon as the new floor gets put in the kitchen and the walls painted. Now I am getting excited and anxious to get moved in here," she admitted. "I'll have your breakfast ready for you in the morning too. After all this is a work-for-food agreement," she laughed.

Pete moved off down the path and Sadie watched him go. What a sad sight he was. There walked a life that had once been full of promise. Now, it was just wasting away. She stood at the door of the cottage and saw him stop at the pile of castaway boxes on the street. He glanced back her way and she quickly stepped back out of sight. Then she saw him pick up the box of clothes she had offered him. He hoisted it up to his shoulder and walked off. She smiled at this concession he was making against his pride.

Chapter 10

Calling Becky

Sadie was wiping out the windowsills for a third time when she heard a knock on the door. It was the man from the home decorating store in town. He sat with her at the little table and Sadie picked out a textured linoleum that appeared to be big squares of tile. She picked out a pale, creamy yellow paint for the kitchen. For the bedroom and living room, she chose a soft pale green that was almost creamy white. He promised that his men would be there early in the morning to install the flooring and then paint the walls. The place would be ready to move into by 1:00 that afternoon.

Sadie was dizzy with the swift resolve of all that needed to be done. Before she left for the day, she went into the big kitchen and fixed the dinner trays for the Shaw's. Then she started walking toward the motel. On the way she spied a pay phone and stopped to get her thoughts together. She knew her daughter's phone number by heart, of course, but had to calm herself down and take several deep breaths to actually dial the operator to get that number on the line. She had piled up all the change she had and was ready to shoot it down the coin slot as needed.

"Becky? Hello dear. I'm just checking in to see how you are doing and let you know what is up with me."

Rebecca's voice was a wail of emotion with an urgency that nearly caused Sadie to drop the phone. "Mother, thank goodness you called. I've been frantic. Are you okay? Where are you? Are you hurt? What in the world have you done? The town is buzzing with suppositions about you. It seems that you are infamous! Dad keeps calling over here to see if you are with me. I had to admit that I had no clue what you were doing. He acts like he has no idea what happened to you. From the sound of it, he thinks you have gone off your rocker and that you need to be hospitalized."

"Dear, take a deep breath and let me talk for a minute, okay?" Sadie responded. She could hear Becky on the other end of the phone gasping for air and sort of snuffling. "Becky, I'm fine as rain. I'm not crazy and I'm not sad. As a matter of fact, I feel quite pleased with myself and oh so very free indeed. I haven't felt this free and unencumbered in ages. It's wonderful. The Lord is with me. Oh, you have no idea how really true that is. I won't tell you where I am right now, because I don't want you to have to lie to your dad. Just know that I am safe and fine and warm and fed and have found work and a place to live."

"But Mother, where did you go, and how did you get there? I am frantic worrying about you. I don't know if I'll ever forgive you for not including me in these plans of yours."

"Well, sweetheart, there were no plans. It was sort of forced on me all of a sudden. I had no other choice but to get out and away from it all. I took a bus on a long, long ride. Let your dad explain the why of it to you. He is well able to tell you all about the reasons I left. I'm sure he will color the facts with his own special brand of the truth. Never mind that! I will tell you all about it after I organize my thoughts and get truly settled here. Don't worry about me. The truth is I am rather happy. I do miss you and my boy, Treat, and Stan too. But seeing you will just have to wait a while. Be patient with me and quit worrying. I'll call you again soon. Please know that I love you so very much. You are my girl and my friend too."

"Oh, Mama, I miss you too. I'm so relieved that you called me to let me know you are all right. I'll just have to trust that what you say is true, and that you are finding a way to live wherever you are. I'll call Andy and Matt because they are frantic and mad at Dad about the whole thing. Of course they blame Dad for everything even though he's not said a word about the 'why' of anything. I know you left alone, because I saw the music director still roaming around town."

"Oh, my wonderful, loyal daughter; just be rest assured he is the least of this and out of the picture completely. I will call you soon and let you know how my life here unfolds."

"Mama, one more thing! Do you need any money? Stan and I could send you some. Would you actually tell us if you needed anything?"

"Of course I would, dear. I need nothing. I'm doing fine. What I did need I just got—your reassurance that you love me and care about me. That is like pouring vitamins into my soul. Take care there and hug little Treat for me. Tell him his grandma misses him. Oh, there is one thing you can do for me; I'm glad I just thought of it."

"Just name it, Mama!"

"I need you to go get Wheezer and bring him home with you. Your dad always hated animals in the house and I doubt he'll take care of that old cat, and he might even give him away. I plan to get my big old tiger cat back someday. Can you do that for me? I know it is a lot to ask, but that cat means so much to me. That furball kept me sane for years."

"No problem, Mama. I'll go right now. Wheezer knows Treat and me. That boy will love having a kitty around. Stan will just have to understand. I'll tell him it is just a temporary condition."

"There is not a dearer daughter in the whole world, Becky. My change has run out now, so I will say a swift goodbye."

After Sadie hung up, she cried some, with relief and joy and wonderment of such a daughter—such loyalty. She was full of happiness for the encouragement she felt coming from Becky.

She stopped along the way to pick up a juicy hamburger and chocolate malt. When she got to her room, she wolfed down the welcome food, enjoying every greasy, fatty swallow of it. Then she showered and fell into bed exhausted. Her heart was filled with joy. She was making a home for herself and it felt darned good.

As she was slipping off to sleep, her mind raced through old memories. They were the steppingstones that brought her to where she was now. She had left the church that fateful day having given not one answer to their belligerent and demanding questions. She just sat there stone-faced and unmoving. The object of her misguided affection refused to quell his sobs long enough to answer questions either. She knew she appeared to be so cold and unfeeling, but she was past caring. Finally she just stood up, turned and walked out leaving them all stunned and open-mouthed. She drove to the bank and pulled out the monies she had saved over the years in her special account. It was the funds she saved up to do special things, like trips to go see her sons, and to have some fun with her daughter and Treat, her beloved grandson. Someday she planned to drive the car across the country on a long trip to Highlands and stay a day or two at the famous Highland Inn, refreshing her sore soul there on the big expansive front porch of the Inn. She just knew in her heart that being there would restore her. Little by little she had deposited a few dollars into that vacation account, never really realizing it would become her escape money. $2400 was not that much, but it was good to know she had it.

After leaving the bank, she had driven home and began to pack. She looked around at the accumulated evidence of 32 years of marriage: the big old beds and quilts she so loved, the tiffany lamps in every room, the fine pictures she had chosen and framed to go with her cozy home. She took down from the attic, the biggest suitcase she could find, and began packing her clothes. She only took what she knew she would need and nothing frivolous or extra: a good coat, boots, tennis shoes, loafers, one pair of heels. jeans, sweaters, a couple of skirts, two dresses, some tops and a jacket. She gathered up pictures of the kids in frames from the mantle, dresser and the top of the piano. She emptied her wallet of all credit cards and placed them on the dresser, adding the checking account book to the pile. She didn't know if it was silly pride that made her throw this all away. It was as if she didn't want one thing to remind her of her attachment to this farce of a husband. She wanted nothing of his. She wanted to be free indeed. She gathered up her makeup, toothbrush, shampoo, and her necessary medications. What-ever would she do without them when they ran out—she didn't know and didn't care at the moment. She grabbed her well-worn and marked-up Bible and then added a pen, envelopes, typing paper and stamps, should she need to write someone. She included her address book and one of her favorite novels, *The Prodigal Summer.* Reading was one of her passions, but surely there would be a library wherever she landed. She left all the wonderful books she had collected over the years. She looked on bookshelf after bookshelf, and regretted the loss. As she was heading out of the bedroom, she stopped stock still and pondered a moment. Then she pulled off the two carat diamond ring from her finger and placed it on top of the credit cards. Anthony had insisted she get this huge stone to show the people in the church his prosperity and to make a show of his devotion to his wife. What a phony he was! She didn't even look back at the ring.

Then she took a deep breath and called a cab. She called her kitty to her for one last hug. The tears began to well up in her eyes, but she willed them to stop. There was no way she could take that cat with her now. She never even looked back at the fine brick house that she had once called home. She marched to the cab dragging the full suitcase behind her. The cab driver helped her in and stowed the suitcase in the trunk. It felt so wonderful to be finally heading away from that prison of a house.

The bus for North Carolina was leaving in half an hour and she sat calmly in the bus station waiting, ticket in hand, trying to let her mind rest. During the next 2 days, she did not remember much of the traveling in that smelly bus from stop to stop. She recalled babies fussing. There were people with breaths redolent with alcohol, and perfumed old ladies clutching their purses like a lifeline. She slept fitfully once in a while. Food tasted like cardboard and she found herself relieving her hunger with fresh apples or bananas instead of heavy meals. Although her ticket was for Asheville, it stopped first in the wee hours of the morning at the little town of Rose Creek. She stumbled off the bus. She knew she could not take another minute of that confinement.

Now here she was, just a couple of days after arriving here, and her immediate future was seemingly being plotted out for her. She shivered with anticipation at the wonder of picking out the furniture for her own little house. The dreams came and she rushed into them.

Chapter 11

Progress and Mrs. Fortenbrau

The new day dawned bright and shiny. Blue skies like cobalt served as a backdrop for the beginning hints of gold, red and orange leaves of fall. There was a crisp sting in the cold air and the promise of warming sunshine close ahead. Oh, it was good to be alive and good to have a plan. It was good to be free, yes free. That's just how Sadie felt. Being away from Preacher Anthony Golden was like being let out of a long hard stay in prison. She wished she could do a cartwheel, but she had never learned how and now she was too old.

Sadie vocalized a prayer. "Thank you, dear Lord, for this day. The beauty of your creation just overwhelms me. I love having this day stretched out ahead of me. Please give me strength to see it through, and let me be a blessing to those I meet."

Sadie dressed quickly and left her luggage at the motel room. She wasn't sure if her little cottage would be ready or not today. There was so much yet to do. At the front desk, she grabbed some coffee and a donut and a bagel, and then headed out to meet the challenges of the day. She stopped at the local bakery, winsomely called Winnie's Sweet Shoppe, to sniff the fragrant air. She purchased a little bamboo basket in which to carry her purchases. For good measure she bought some almond croissants, so soft and flakey that they were nearly bending. It was obvious that they had just come out of the oven.

Next, she stopped at Clyde's Grocer, the small, local grocery store, and bought some fresh Braeburn apples, tiny Clementines, a sack of lemons, a sweet onion and two sweet potatoes. This basket was going to come in handy. She found a couple of thick pork chops in the butcher section. She added two nice big candy bars to her basket. Her money was quickly dwindling away. She would have to keep tabs on which items belonged to the upkeep of the Shaw's and which were just for her own pleasure.

Sadie was very surprised to see Peter Combs sitting on her door stoop waiting when she arrived. She greeted him warmly to which he made a mumbled response. She noticed he had on some of the cast-off clothes from that box in her house, and he looked rather clean and warm in that old coat. She never mentioned it at all. He seemed to be daring her to notice the clothes.

"Give me a second and I'll get some fresh coffee made for you. I just had a cup of java at the motel and ate a donut along the way here. If you want to get started right away, I'll get you the rakes and show you where the wheelbarrow and heavy lawn bags are located."

When she had gathered all these items for him, she turned quickly for the kitchen door and let herself in. Colonel Shaw had shown her where he hid the keys. They were tucked away in a heavy pot of geraniums, right down in the middle of the thick stems.

The kitchen needed airing out and she started by opening all the windows and lighting some candles. She found a sprig of dried rosemary in the windowsill and laid it on a plate and struck a match to set it afire. Just for an instant, the herb flared up and then settled down to make the most fragrant white smoke. She carried it all through the kitchen as the incense rose filling every corner. She rushed into the dining room and let the last fragrant spurts of smoke trail in there. Oh, that just smelled so heavenly, like a nice cedar fire roaring in a fireplace. She remembered that the Indians used to cleanse their prayer huts with burning rosemary. They believed that the smoke scared away any evil spirits looming in the place.

'I wonder if there are any evil spirits here,' she thought with a smile on her face. She didn't actually believe in ghosts, but she did believe that if unhappiness had taken place here, then the rooms were permeated by that sadness and anger, and she knew that it needed to be expelled.

Sadie got the coffee perking and added a pinch of salt to it. That would take out some of the bitterness. She fried some eggs and bacon and made some oatmeal and toast. Soon, she had a tray of that hearty breakfast in hand and delivered it to the Shaw's. They were watching the morning news and seemed delighted to see her again. "Oh that looks wonderful Sadie. We are starving this morning, aren't we, Vicky?"

"As a matter of fact, I am," she conceded with a twinkle in her eye. "It is good to look forward to eating again."

Sadie picked up the tray from dinner last night. "I'll be busy out in the little house again today. There's plenty more to do. Hopefully the flooring man will come to install the kitchen floor, and the painter may come to paint too. The sooner the better is what I say, I'm anxious to get out of that motel room."

"Why don't you just stay upstairs in one of the unused bedrooms until it is completed?" queried Col. Shaw.

Sadie thought a minute and replied, "No, I'd rather just move right into that little house. I'll wait. It will make the moving in that much more special." She added, "Peter Combs is back and already clearing away the overgrown paths and raking up pine straw."

"You know, pine straw makes a very nice carpet on a path, as long as he clears out all the leaves and pinecones in it," ventured Colonel Shaw. "There's nothing sweeter than the smell of pine straw; it cushions the path and keeps the mud from forming."

"Great idea! I'll tell him to do just that. I'll see you two a bit later, when it is time for lunch." Sadie started for the door, but stopped abruptly and turned to ask, "I was wondering if it would be alright for me to explore the upper rooms and pick out the furniture I will need for my little cottage. I don't mean to be aggressive and forward, but I thought if I have time, I should just get started on it."

"My dear, that will be perfect. The sooner the better. Search away. And remember there is nothing sacred up there. Just pick and choose. We will be thrilled that some of that stuff up there will be used by someone."

As Sadie was headed for the kitchen she heard some rattling going on in the dining room, and she ventured in to take a look. A sour-faced old lady was snorting around and talking to herself as she perfunctorily dusted some of the furniture in there. She made half-hearted swipes at the thing and looked not one bit happy to be there.

"Good morning there. You must be the cleaning lady," Sadie said.

The old lady jumped and whirled around toward Sadie. "Great Jiminy Crickets! You scared me half to death. Who in tarnation are you anyway? Does the Colonel know you are skulking around here?"

Sadie bristled at this remark, but took a deep breath and answered calmly, "My name is Sadie Jamison, and I am the new cook and bottle washer here." She tried to make light of it by chuckling a bit, but Sadie's attempt at hilarity was met by the stony-faced, sullen woman. Her appearance was slovenly: dirty apron, torn pants and a mismatched shirt. Her hair was in disarray like she owned not a comb or brush. Her skin was close to the color of mahogany and was lined with heavy wrinkles. It was obvious she had had too much sun in her youth. Sadie looked at her and wondered at her upbringing. *I wonder if she had any sort of an enjoyable childhood.*

"Well, it don't make me no never mind who you are. Just don't sneak up on a person like that agin. Ya heah me?"

Sadie was taken aback at her confrontational attitude. She decided to take a stance and show some authority here. "What is your name, if I may be so bold as to ask?"

"Not that it is any of your beeswax, but my name is Gladys. Gladys Fortenbrau. I've been the housekeeper here for nigh on to 15 years now. I only work 3 days a week, and half days at that. When it is raining, I don't show up. When it is too hot, I don't show up. I sort of make my own hours."

"Well, Mrs. Fortenbrau," (Sadie refused to use her first name) "I think after you finish with the dining room, you should clean the entryway and take those ferns out for a good soaking and shaking and picking over. There are plenty of dead, dry fronds and they are cluttering up the floor by the stairs; and speaking of stairs, they could use a good polishing too."

Gladys' mouth dropped open and she began breathing very hard. She put her hands on her hips and said, "Now wait just a cotton-pickin' minute, missy. You are **not** my boss. I answer only to the Colonel. There's no way I'm doin' what you tell me to do. I've been doin' this job for a long time, and I certainly don't need your help figuring out what to do!"

"Well hello there, Gladys," said the Colonel entering the room. "I thought I heard your voice in here. Decided it was fair enough weather to come to work today, heh? I want you to meet Miss Sadie. She is the new cook and overseer of the house. From now on she will determine which jobs you need to accomplish for the days that you show up. It's going to be nice having her manage things, because Lord knows, I have been letting up on my responsibilities in that area for a long time. Carry on then!"

He walked slowly away glancing over his shoulder at Sadie with a wink. She felt so grateful to him for that act of confidence in her. Sadie gathered herself to exit the room. "And Mrs. Fortenbrau, be sure you sweep off the whole front porch before you go today. I'll be baking some cookies soon and you can have some with a cup of hot tea at your break time . . . say at 10:30?"

A sort of snort came from Gladys' direction and she turned around and started dusting again. Sadie feared in her heart that this arrangement would not work out for long. The woman was too resentful and had such a bad attitude that the heaviness and darkness of her mood permeated the rooms. Sadie turned back one more time and said, "Take the ladder in the back porch and take down those heavy drapes. Let's get some sunlight into these rooms. Open the windows and if you have time, clean them as well. I'll take the drapes to the local cleaners and have them freshened up." With that Sadie turned to head for the kitchen, but not before she saw Gladys' mouth screw up and her eyes squint shut. *Mrs. Fortenbrau is formidable looking,* she thought.

Sadie had not even intended to be the overseer of the house, and boss the maid. She saw that if she were expected to work in this big house and be content in the atmosphere of it, a pecking order would have to be established. Right now she felt pretty much like the head hen. It felt mighty good to be in charge.

She quickly fixed a big plate of eggs and sausages and toasted bagels slathered with cream cheese and raspberry jam for Peter. He was busy raking and piling up pine straw. He pulled up branches and made a pile of them as well. She called to him. "Take a break, Peter, and come eat your breakfast."

He eagerly set aside his rake and came to her. "Do you like juice? I will get you a big glass of orange juice."

"Oh, thank you, but coffee will be fine for now. My, but this does look mighty good. All this working has revved up my dormant appetite."

He sat on the door stoop and began to eat voraciously. Working tended to bring that out in a man. Soon, his tray was sitting neatly inside the house on the floor, napkin folded up like he'd been brought up right. His plate from dinner last night was added to the pile.

Sadie got busy herself, cleaning out the refrigerator in the cottage. Oh it was a musty mess with black mold clinging to the sides. She mixed up hot soapy water and added a little Clorox for good measure. Lo and behold, that little old frig cleaned up right nicely; gleaming in fact. She plugged it in and found some old ice trays in the big house's kitchen. She filled them with water and set them inside. She planned to get some treats and things she liked to eat as snacks. Now her refrigerator was ready to go.

"Hello there. Is anybody home?" It was the flooring man and his helper. They carried between them a roll of linoleum and they wore tool belts. She was delighted to see them. She moved the table into the bedroom, and left them to their job.

Sadie went on into the main kitchen to make some cookies. She mixed up a bowl of butter shortbread cookies made with real butter and vanilla. The scent of those cookies baking was like sweet, sugary, cotton candy to the nose. She peeked in to see what Gladys was doing and found her on the shaky ladder pulling down the heavy drapes. Gladys seemed petrified up there.

"Let me help you with those," she offered. "You can pack them up in these garbage bags and I'll carry them out to the pickup truck for hauling to the cleaners."

"Don't put yerself out!" came the curt reply. The room was filled with dust from the disturbance of long ignored, dusty drapes, and it meant that Gladys would have to redo that dusting job too.

Sadie ignored her remarks and insisted that she be the one to climb the ladder and loosen the drapes. Gladys then gathered up the musty, grimy, drapes, and stuffed them, panel by panel, into black garbage bags. Sadie hauled them to the back porch, and then washed her hands and blew her nose. She plated some cookies for Gladys and made her a cup of hot tea with lemon and sugar.

"Mrs. Fortenbrau, your snack is on the kitchen table when you are ready for it. The tea is hot right now, so you might not want to wait too long." Sadie heard another audible grunt. It made her shake her head to think of that miserable woman begrudging even a kind act.

Sadie stacked another plate with hot cookies and took them across the foyer to the Shaw's residence. Victoria informed her that the Colonel was out for his morning walk.

"Won't you come and sit with me a moment please? I have so few visitors and it would be nice to talk for a bit," said Mrs. Shaw.

"I have a better idea, if you are up to it Victoria. Why don't we put on our heavy sweaters and go sit on the front porch in those sturdy white rockers there? We can talk there and enjoy the freshness of this beautiful morning."

Mrs. Shaw visibly shuddered just a little and answered in a tiny voice, "I would rather stay in here if you don't mind. Maybe some other day we could venture out there."

So Sadie, realizing that the old woman was petrified of going out of the house, settled on the settee to have a chat with her.

"How is it going out there? Big job, I imagine. That little house has been unused for more than 20 years. My kids used it for playhouses, and workshops and such. Once I even planned to go make it into a little getaway place for myself. You know, a place where I could go write and read in silence, but it never seemed really appropriate since I had this huge home with so many rooms in which to do just that."

"Oh, I think it would have been a most delightful retreat. I'm sure you were so busy with the raising of your children and guests and people running here and there, that quietly going off to that little refuge would have been good for you."

Victoria brightened and said, "Well, whenever you get it all fixed up, I just may come and give you a visit now and again. Then I can remember my dreams for it and be happy to see that it mostly came true."

"It's a deal! When I have it all prepared to my liking, you and I will have a high tea party there, fine china and all. We'll have dainty cakes, and fresh strawberries and fine Darjeeling tea with honey. I'll make tiny cucumber sandwiches and maybe even a fresh scone or two with coddled cream and raspberry jam. How does that sound?"

"It sounds wonderful to me. It will remind me of the time I traveled to England with Everett. What a grand time we had. We were so young then. I shall look forward to having high tea in your sweet cottage, and I hope that day comes soon. You spoke of my children. Did you know that I have three?"

"Yes, your husband told me that two live away from here and one lives nearby."

Victoria nodded and said, "Stephen is the oldest and he is the one who lives nearby. He is a good boy, and so smart and successful. But now that he is grown and 55, he thinks that he knows what is best for us too. He's gotten to where he treats us like we are already in the 'Old Folks' Home'. I love him so much and am proud of him, but I wish he would not be so eager to settle our affairs and take over for us."

"I'm sorry about that. Perhaps he doesn't see how able you and Colonel Shaw still are. Perhaps he worries about you in this fine old place. He probably thinks it is too big for just two people."

"Well, now you sound just like him. I know his reasoning is justified. But my husband is very capable. That is for certain. I'm not so sure about myself anymore. I had a small stroke a couple of years back, and it has taken me a while to regain the use of my limbs and mouth. I have slowly retreated into these few rooms, and it is here that I feel safe and comfy. Just the thought of venturing outside is nearly as frightening to me as if you asked me to travel to another planet and step out there. I hate being so afraid, but what can I do?"

"Well, maybe you can venture just one small step at a time until you get your confidence back. And you wouldn't have to venture out alone. I will be here for you when you feel a sudden surge of bravery. We'll do it together. I, for one, know how good it feels to step out on faith, against your fears, and move forward to a new adventure."

"Is that what you did? Did you become brave and set out to lands unknown and take on a new adventure?"

"Indeed I did. No one could have said it better than that. I waited too long to show my courage. I waited years and years. Now I just hope I have years left to enjoy my new freedom."

"Oh, my dear, you are so young yet. A mere whippersnapper!"

Sadie smiled and rose. "Well, I'd better get crackin', as Gladys would say. I still have plenty to do before my head hits the pillow tonight." Victoria struggled to rise. Her thin arms seemed not strong enough for such an effort, but she slowly rose to her feet to bid Sadie farewell.

Sadie was overcome with gratitude and affection for the old woman. She stepped forward and gently hugged her. She kissed her on top of the head. Victoria gasped a little and did not raise her arms to return the hug. Sadie quickly left the room with a slight wave.

Now, what did I go and do that for? I am so forward with my affections. When am I going to learn that not everyone welcomes a hug? she pondered on her forwardness.

Pete was outside picking through the piles of straw and bagging the clean fresh straw. He had carried out a huge mound of sticks and fallen limbs to the street, stacking them next to the curb with the pile of discarded boxes. Sadie wondered when the Colonel's friend would be by to pick those things up. The paths were down to bare earth now. The dirt was so dark and damp and musty smelling.

"I'm going to let that pathway dry out a bit before I spread this pine straw."

"Sounds like a good idea," Sadie remarked. "Things are looking so much nicer out here, Pete, as if someone cares. I like it!" She watched Pete turn away from her quickly, but not before she noticed a satisfied grin begin to spread across his face.

She found the old pickup with the key still inside. She got inside and tried to turn over the engine. Nothing but silence. She tried again. Just dead! She put her head on the steering wheel. When she looked up, there was Peter right by the window.

"Let me give this a look see," he suggested. "I used to be handy with this sort of thing when I was in high school. Let's see if I can remember anything useful."

She thankfully surrendered the seat to him and went to sweep the back porch and mop it. Some of the screen out there was poked through and ripped and was rolling up in the corners. She remembered that the Colonel had said that new screens were part of the bargain. That should make the place look oh so nice. She peeked to see what progress was being made in the kitchen and was happily surprised to see that the flooring workers were done with the job.

"How in the world did you accomplish this so quickly? It looks wonderful. It is so light and airy and clean. I love it!"

The two installers were happy to hear her praise. They looked at one another like this kind of response was not very often forthcoming. Sadie said, "I'm going to bring out a plate of cookies and some iced tea. You two look like you could use a break." This made their faces register real wonderment. She quickly brought out a colorful plate of cookies and two big icy glasses of sweetened tea. The two workers took the tea and cookies outside to relax just a minute or two and breathe in the fresh fall air.

Back inside the big kitchen, Sadie heard Mrs. Fortenbrau mumbling. Sadie found her kneeling on the stairway polishing the steps. The smell of lemon oil was very tangy and clean.

Oh, Mrs. Fortenbrau, those stairs are indeed coming back alive. And the scent of that oil . . . . ah lovely!" A half smile started on Gladys' face and suddenly Sadie realized that Mrs. Fortenbrau was not really old at all—just worn out. Sadie guessed that Gladys was probably no older than 46. The weathered face and bent-over body made her look old. She had indeed had a hard life.

All of a sudden she heard the startling roar of an engine and rushed out of the kitchen to see Pete bent over the old pickup's engine with the hood up. Blue smoke was puffing out from under the hood and Peter was waving it away with his hand. Sadie guessed that his unused knowledge of cars had not let him down. She did not want to make a big deal out of it, so she stayed in the kitchen and left him alone to tinker with the old truck. It needed a good wash and most of all a new paint job, but it would be a blessing to have some conveyance and not depend solely on her 53 year old legs.

Sadie got out a Pyrex dish in which to bake the huge thick pork chops. She sprinkled over them some olive oil, soy sauce, salt and pepper. Then she covered them with plastic wrap, and let them sit for a while in the windowsill to marinate. The air was nippy enough that she did not fear them being out of the refrigerator. Then she cut up a big sweet onion into thick slices, and she thinly sliced a lemon. She searched around and found the catsup and Worcestershire sauce. Later she would put all of those ingredients on top of the pork chops and sprinkle it all over generously with brown sugar. Those chops would slow bake in the oven, covered with tinfoil until they were steamy tender. She would serve them with fluffy white rice. She wrapped the washed sweet potatoes in tinfoil and set them aside too. She would bake them at the same time she baked the chops. Everything was now ready to put that dinner together.

She fixed sandwiches and soup for lunch and delivered a tray to the Shaw's. Mrs. Shaw was sleepy and ready for her nap. Pete was hungry and glad to get his lunch too. He seemed sort of proud that he'd accomplished so much that morning, especially getting that old Ford pickup to run again. Mrs. Fortenbrau was putting on her coat and hat when Sadie came back into the kitchen. "Oh, Mrs. Fortenbrau, I was just coming to give you your lunch."

"I don't get lunch here. I leave about this time every day and I just stop at McDonald's in town to grab a hamburger."

"Well that sounds mighty good too, but I already made you a big sandwich and chips. Just let me bag them up for you to take. Just in case, you don't have time to go to the McDonalds." Sadie handed Gladys a paper sack of lunch.

Gladys took in a quick breath and her eyes widened. "Well, since you already made it I guess I'll have to take it. But there was no need. I ain't use to no special treatment, 'round heah' ya know!"

"Anyone who works as hard as you did today, Mrs. Fortenbrau, deserves special treatment in my books," Sadie replied honestly. "When will I see you here again?"

"Well, not tomorrow. I have to work over at the school buildings tomorrow. I guess I'll be back on Friday, day after tomorrow. That is unless it is raining. Then don't expect me."

"See you later then," Sadie said. She turned to go inspect the work in the dining room, stairs and front porch. She had expected Gladys to leave straightaway, but she walked behind her, curious to know what Sadie thought about her day's work. Sadie saw that the big dining room table and the cabinet and bureau were all beautifully polished. She noticed the clean windowsills behind where the heavy drapes had hung. She nodded approval at the well-vacuumed Oriental rug. The fern fronds were all swept up and the ferns picked over and refreshed. The stairway was glowing with polish. The scent of lemon wax was pungent in the air. Sadie breathed in deeply with a satisfied "hmmmm!" Then she progressed through the front door to the front porch. The tiled porch was swept clean as a whistle and the old white rockers were angled to encourage cozy conversation. Cobwebs were swept down from the corners. Huge pots of geraniums were manicured and watered and set on either side of the steps going up to the porch. It wouldn't be long now until there would be no more red blossoms in those big pots.

"Mrs. Fortenbrau, bravo! This looks fantastic. What a great job you did here. I appreciate all your hard work."

Gladys just huffed and walked away. "See you Friday. Just leave me a list of what needs doing and I'll get right to it."

Sadie went back into the house and shook her head in amazement and confusion. The woman clearly loved approval, but didn't want anyone to think that she needed it. Sadie wondered what kind of life awaited Gladys at the end of her day. She wondered for the second time what had happened in Gladys' life to make her seem so bitter and joyless. Sometimes life had a way of beating a person down.

Chapter 12

Exploring

Sadie started back to the kitchen to get dinner ready for the oven. She happened to look up the stairs to the mysterious realms up there. All of a sudden she knew it was time. to venture up there and look around. It was as though she'd been saving up this special treat as a reward for her own hard work. She took a deep breath and headed on up. The stairs divided halfway up at a landing. They lead to two halls going in opposite directions, like the proverbial East and West wings. At the top of the stairs dividing the two hallways, a door led into a room straight back from the stairs. She chose to start with this room. *My, but this house really is huge.* The door opened into a spacious, cavernous room with a baby grand piano set by a vast bank of windows. The light streaming in would make reading music so easy. The ceiling in this room rose to a diamond point in the middle with stained-glass skylight letting the sunshine stream in all colorful and brilliant. She quit breathing. Her mouth opened in amazement. Her eyes scanned the beauty of this magnificent room. At last her breath took hold again, and she let it out in a big exhale. This was better than any of her dreams.

The floor was so spacious and made of some sort of rare hardwood. It was polished to a golden hue. A huge colorful, rich oriental rug stretched out to cover at least half the room. The colors in that lusciously woven carpet were bright reds, blues, greens and violets. Golden threads complimented the pattern as outline hues. She reached down to touch it. The pile was so deep her fingers sunk down at least three inches. She could sleep comfortably on this masterpiece. Most of the floor space was open with little areas of furniture gathered into sections of the room. A party of 25 would find plenty of cozy niches in which to sit and chat. The high square-sectioned windows were in a bay shape, and looked out on the expanse of the property. She wondered if there had once been a time when a well manicured garden graced that view. Dances could be held here. She could picture rows of folding chairs arranged to face the piano. In her mind's eye she could envision small recitals and a private string quartet giving concerts here.

Sadie was drawn to the piano. It was covered with a dust cover and she dared to remove it carefully, so as not to disturb much dust. She didn't want it to fall upon the ebony wood of that splendid instrument. She sat down on the bench and began to play. "One Day at a Time." She played the tender, melodic chords and the sounds reverberated throughout the room, bouncing back to her as from a distant wall of a cave. She sang the words of the song: this wonderful song that had been given to her by a good friend at college. There was no written music for it; just the song itself, living in her memory and in her hands.

One day at a time, I'm serving the Lord.
One day at a time, I am trusting His Word.
The future may hold much sorrow here for me,
But one day the face of my Savior I'll see.

All that I need is strength for today,
But for this strength to the Lord I must pray,
Tomorrows are His, but today is mine,
I know I can serve Him one day, one day at a time.

Sadie felt the inevitable tears burn her eyes as they formed. She choked on the last of her words. Her hands came to her face and her body was wracked with gasping sobs. Once again, she felt the Lord's presence so near and that realization made her feel so unworthy. The tears flowed and flowed. Finally she gathered herself together. She felt marvelously washed clean once more with tears. *When will these episodes of crying be over?* She thought. She didn't really care. She knew these moments of release were good for her, and they helped her rid herself of the resentment and pressure that she harbored. She desperately needed to let go of all of it and move on. Sadie covered the piano and walked out of the door closing it quietly behind her.

At the foot of the stairs stood Colonel Shaw looking up. "That grand piano hasn't been played in ages. I'm so glad you woke her up. Someday you must play and sing that song for me again, when I am right there to hear every word. It sounded so beautiful."

The tears threatened to come forth again. The kind words of the old gentleman were like a balm to a weary soul. "It is just an old, old song that comforts me. I hope I didn't wake Victoria from her nap."

"Are you searching for the furniture that you need?" the Colonel asked.

"Well, I am about to do just that," she replied.

"Good. And remember, there is nothing sacred up there, so choose whatever you like. By the way, the porch and these stairs look so clean. Thank you for taking Gladys under your wing. She just needs some gentle prodding and instruction."

"I think Mrs. Fortenbrau and I will get along better and better as the weeks roll by."

Colonel Shaw walked on into his living quarters and left Sadie to her adventure and search. She wandered down the east hallway and opened the first door on the right. Here she found a small sitting room with a sewing machine and a good-sized alcove full of linens and blankets.

Sadie moved on to the next room down the hall. She looked into a huge bedroom with a high-canopied bed. White lace draped down on all four corners and formed a little cozy cave at the head of the bed. The bedspread d was silken white, with crocheted patches on it in squares. Huge fluffy pillows were thrown at the head of the bed all in various shades of white, cream and champagne. There were three enormous white sheepskin rugs on the floor. Two comfy, soft cushioned armchairs sat cozily up near the small fireplace. The inviting chairs were upholstered in pale peach and cream with a nondescript pattern of tiny flowers in the fabric. Little footstools sat in front of the chairs. Each footstool was covered with the same fabric as the chairs. The lampshade was made of stretched, pale rose silk and had an alabaster base. Sadie switched on the light and the room took on a rosy glow.

There was a nice-sized bathroom with a claw foot tub tucked in one corner. It was made of white shining enamel. The faucets and pipes were a rich, shiny brass. An enameled pedestal sink stood under a gilded oval mirror. Vanity cupboards were on either side of the mirror. Sconce wall lamps flanked the cabinets. The fluted light fixtures pointed to the ceiling. She turned on the lights and the reflection off the ceiling lent a sort of scalloped shadow. It was very feminine and flattering.

Back in the bedroom Sadie noticed an oak chest, usually referred to as a cedar chest or hope chest. It sat under a bank of tall windows. She opened it to find a stack of quilts strewn with cedar chips to ward off the hungry moths. She would definitely come back to these. The long drapes streaming down from the windows were of the same material as the huge bed cover. They hung long and draping onto the floor in a puddle of fabric. This room was fit for a princess.

She wandered across the hallway to another spacious bedroom. Sadie caught her breath when she saw that room. She felt like she'd just come home. This room was done up in subdued smoky primary colors with the feel of calico. What a drastic difference from the royalty bedroom across the hall. There was a cannonball bed, very high and made of dark pine. A king-sized, colorful quilt was used as a bedspread, with an extra quilt folded neatly at the foot of the bed. The pillow shams matched the quilt. The bed looked so inviting she nearly succumbed to the temptation to climb aboard. But she opted to just place her hands on it and test its softness.

The windows were framed in long, simple calico curtains, drawn back on the sides and held with thick plaid ribbons. There were two big wing-backed chairs facing the windows with a table and a tiffany lamp between them. This was the perfect place to read and contemplate life. Against the east wall was a huge chifforobe, or standing closet. It was made of dark teak, and she inhaled the wonderful fragrance of that wood as she drew near. She opened it to discover coats of all styles and sizes stored in there. The faint smell of mothballs wafted out. She wondered how such a magnificent piece could sit so securely against the wall. It was so tall and heavy. Since she had no closet in her bedroom at the cottage, she could definitely use this piece. But oh, how in the world could it be carried down the stairs? "Well, they got it up here somehow, so there must be a way to get it back down," she spoke aloud. She tried to pull on it a bit and see how heavy a piece it was, It would not budge an inch.

A nice teak dresser and vanity graced the rest of the room. More tiffany lamps were placed on these two pieces. The walls were a creamy pale yellow. All the dark wood and fabric in the room was a welcome contrast to the light walls. To whom did this room belong? Sadie could feel the camaraderie with that person as she walked that warm, cozy room.

One corner held a rugged oak bookshelf filled with the good old classics. There were Newberry Award books like "Wrinkle In Time" and "Miracles On Maple Hill", "Island of the Blue Dolphins." There were some of the favorite Dickens adventures. Her eyes scanned the titles as a warm flood of longing just to sit down and curl up to read came over her.

A six-foot rag rug lay beside the bed. The colors woven in it were proof that this was made by a loving and artistic hand. Oh, this room tugged at her heart strings more than any room thus far.

She quickly searched the last room on the east side. It spread across the end of the upstairs and was partially divided by a bathroom that went only 10 feet back. The two sides of the long back room held two full beds. It was plain and serviceable. Certainly had to be a guest room. There was little personality here. The bathroom opening to the main hallway was tucked between the two sections of the room with an open space joining the two sides of the room behind the bathroom area.

Chapter 13

Stephen

Sadie did not want to leave her exploration of the upstairs, but she knew she would have to postpone for another day her journey to view the rest of the rooms on the west side of the stairway. She needed to get dinner in the oven and check on the progress of the work at the cottage. She was suddenly invigorated. This new life might just turn out to be mighty fine after all. She could not believe that she had no regrets about leaving her husband. Instead, she felt so full of joy and happy anticipation, and most of all, freedom.

Rushing down the stairs to the kitchen she caught sight of a big man in a business suit coming onto the veranda and heading for the door. She hurried to the door and opened it to a surprised, gray-haired man holding forth a key in his hand. He had been ready to unlock the door.

"Yes sir, may I help you?" Sadie was standing in the doorway barring the way in.

"Who the blazes are you? Where's my father?" The man rudely exclaimed.

"Oh, you must be their son. They told me you lived in town nearby. Please come in. I'll tell them you are here. I am Sadie Jamison, and I have been hired to be the cook here. Glad to meet you." She was offering her hand in greeting when he just snorted indignantly from his nose and pushed past her, nearly brushing her aside with his shoulders.

"I won't be needing any introduction. This is my house and I know where they are!" With that he barged into the Shaw's suite with a bellowing voice. "What the heck is going on around here? What have you done now?" He slammed the door behind him.

She could hear his stern admonitions from the kitchen where she retreated. How dare he intrude on his parents' room without a warning knock? Did the man have no decency or learning in the matter of manners? She was outraged at the way he had treated her; like some low-life beneath his concern. Did this mean she would be booted out and she have to start again at ground zero? She offered up a quick and urgent prayer for calmness and trust. Out loud she murmured, "Whatever is best, Lord, I trust you to work it all out. I'm in your hands now, and so I refuse to worry about it."

With that she finished up her preparation of the pork chops and placed them and the sweet potatoes in the oven and set the timer for one hour. She whipped up a fresh salad and sprinkled diced, hard-boiled eggs on top along with grated Parmesan cheese and toasted pecans. Iced tea was steeping. She set the table nicely with a fresh, clean cloth and napkins. A candle was lit in the middle to add some ambiance. Soon the kitchen was emitting a smell that was so inviting. She was cleaning up her preparation mess, wiping down cutting boards and tossing peelings, when the kitchen door swung open with a bang. The son came barreling in with a scowl on his face.

"I have no idea what got into my father's head, hiring a complete stranger to work for him. What sort of qualifications do you have and where are your references?"

Sadie slowly turned to face him. She grabbed a fresh white kitchen towel and deliberately wiped her hands slowly, all the while looking him right in the eye. "I don't believe we've been formally introduced, so I have no idea what name to call you, although a few do come to mind."

He gasped at her outspokenness but answered, "I am Stephen Shaw, the eldest offspring of the Shaw's. I'll have you know that any decisions that are made in this house will go through me first. I don't like your smug attitude and fresh mouth, so you'd better watch your step. My father insists that you stay. He says that mother has been improving daily since you began working here. So we will let this happen on a trial basis. I will allow you to live in the gatehouse until we can find some other choice. I do not approve of my father spending money repairing and refurbishing that old rattrap of a junk house for a cook. By God, what was he thinking?" He snorted again and cast his eye around the kitchen taking in the neat table and candlelight and finally registering the delicious aroma of supper wafting through the air.

"Will you be staying for supper, Mr. Shaw? I can set another place at the table for you if you like?" Being polite right now was hard for Sadie. Her mouth was eager to lay this buffoon low, but she really wanted to stay with the Shaw's and help them. They were worth taking a little guff. But he'd better not push it.

"I have a dinner date with business partners, so no, I won't be staying. But I will be back to check on things soon. Has my father spoken to you yet of your salary?"

"No. We shall discuss that after I've settled in."

"Well, you must be desperate for work and a place to stay or you wouldn't be coming here on those kinds of terms. I can guarantee you that it won't be much. My parents live on a limited budget."

"Oh, I was under the impression that the Colonel owned this house and property and had a comfortable pension to live on."

"His finances are none of your business, lady! I am in charge of my parents' spending. Someone has to keep a watch over them or they will do just as he's done here: go off on a tangent and hire some . . . . country cook without my knowledge."

"You have a nice evening, Mr. Shaw, and I will see you to the door. I'm sure I shall see you later when you next come for a visit." Sadie's mouth was tight and her eyes narrowed. She would not have been surprised to see steam coming out her ears as she passed by a mirror on the way to the front door. He stormed out of the house. When he was down the walkway heading for the street, she heard the door to the Shaw's room open and she glanced back. She knew her face was red as a beet. Colonel Shaw was peeking around the edge of the door with a worried expression on his face.

"I see you've met him. I apologize for his rudeness. He feels like he has to be tough on us to keep us in line. It is a great responsibility in his eyes to watch after us. I know he means well, but he just wants total control and that is hard for Victoria and me to bear up under."

"Colonel, I want very much to make this work. I will try my best to be polite to him, but if he goes too far with his sharp tongue then I will stand up for myself. I am hoping that you will understand that and forgive me for it in advance."

To her surprise, the Colonel let out a big guffaw of a laugh. He was tickled pink it seemed. He came into the entryway and slapped his thighs with both hands. "By golly, that is just fine and dandy with me. It is about time someone stood up to that bully. I love my son; but as Vicky and I got older and more needy, he got more and more bossy and just took over everything. I've been afraid to stand up to him for fear of upsetting my tenderhearted wife. You just keep on doing whatever you think is right. We'll talk about major choices together, but I'm beginning to trust you with things and it feels good to be on the same wavelength with someone of like mind."

"Is it true that he has full control of your finances and can fire me if he chooses?"

"Not true at all. He wants to have full control; but as yet I have not signed over my assets to him. But I usually do not buck him on anything he decides is best for us. This will be a first, my making this decision to hire you; and by gum, I think it is one of the best decisions I've made yet!"

"I'm glad to hear that. I wouldn't want to be at his mercy; for I fear already that he does not like me much."

"Don't worry about that. I will speak to my lawyer in the morning and set up an account for you to draw from. You can take what you need for keeping up the house, buying groceries, cleaning bills and the upkeep of the truck. Just keep the receipts and make a listing in a bookkeeping book of what you bought and why. I feel somehow that I can trust you young lady."

There it was again, the remark about being a young lady. Now she felt like laughing. "The first thing I will order, then, is a new lock on the door. I noticed that the one you have right now is squeaking and probably is pretty old." She sort of smiled at the Colonel mischievously. "The next time Stephen comes here he will have to knock and wait to come in like everyone else. This is your home and you should have the privacy of such."

The Colonel had a sudden flash of panic on his face. It was replaced almost instantly with a determination and straightening of the shoulders. He took a deep breath and looked deeply into Sadie's eyes. "Sadie, this is a major move toward independence on our part. It will reap repercussions, but so be it. You are right! It is time we stood our around and once again had our own home as a private and secure place. I can't tell you how many times he's barged into our room when we were not ready for company. He won't like this, but he will just have to deal with it."

Sadie sighed a deep satisfying breath of relief. "It shall be done tomorrow, Colonel. I'll call the locksmith today. Now, dinner will be ready in 20 minutes. I'll call you when it is served, or just come into the kitchen whenever you feel like coming. There is no set time. This is your house, your choice!"

"Whatever you've made brings back memories of my youth. What wonderful smells come from your kitchen, Sadie!" the Colonel exclaimed.

"Your kitchen, Colonel, *your* kitchen. I'm only the cook and bottle washer."

Chapter 14

Good End to the Day

Sadie rushed out to see how the cottage was coming. Peter had the paths all raked and clear of last year's refuse. He had covered the widened paths with fresh pinestraw. It smelled so good. She caught up with him as he was taking out the last of the big garbage bags full of weeds and leaves. "Peter, this looks marvelous! And the scent of the pine straw is glorious. Thanks for such a good job."

"You are welcome. I have to admit it feels so good to work and do physical labor. At first I was sore and I tired so easily, but now I feel invigorated and I'll bet I sleep well tonight."

"How is the cottage coming along?"

"Well, last time I looked they had the painting all done and the new floor in. Talk about smelling better. I had my fears that perhaps that old mice nest was not going to be habitable ever!"

"Where there's a will, there's a way. Once I start living there, it will even smell better and be more homey," she responded. "Say, Pete, don't let me forget to pay you for today's work. Your dinner is going to be ready soon, so don't leave till you get it, hear?"

"Lately, I've been thinking more about your food than I should. These past months I've been sort of out of it when it comes to eating. I forgot how it feels to look forward to a nice meal at the end of the day," he offered with a whimsical look on his face. "Got any more work needs doing tomorrow?"

"You bet! This place is massive in acreage. As far as I can tell, no one's bothered with it for ages. If you think you can handle it, I'd like you to explore every corner of this place. If you could map out a tentative plan on what to do with the grounds to make it something worth walking through, that would be great!" Sadie stopped herself short as she considered, "Maybe I'm asking too much of you. I have no idea if you even know about gardens and such."

"Well, I can't say I've ever worked one, but I have first hand knowledge of some fine gardens and I know what to look for and expect," he said cautiously.

Sadie did not question him further. She surmised from what the Colonel had told her that Pete had once been a wealthy man. She supposed that he had gardeners caring for his property. He probably had to oversee their work and tell them what he expected. "Good enough! I certainly would not have the foggiest idea where to start. I only know that I appreciate it so much when a fine garden is accomplished. By the way, Peter, I am choosing the pieces I want for the cottage from all the furniture upstairs. I'm still deciding; but when I'm done, I was hoping you'd be willing to help me bring the pieces down those massive stairs and into the gatehouse. We spoke of this before and you said something about a dolly from the furniture company?"

"Whenever you are ready to move it downstairs, I'll rent that dolly. Maybe I can find someone I know to help with the moving. There are a few guys I know who are down on their luck and would be happy to earn a little extra," Pete said.

Sadie reached into her pocket pulling out a wad of money. She carefully counted out what was due Pete and handed it over. "Here's your pay for today. You can't imagine how good it is to have you here to get all the hard labor done for me. I thank God for you Pete."

Peter Combs turned suddenly and wandered off. She saw him wipe off his face with his sleeve as he reached for the rakes and shovels to put them away. *Perhaps it has been a long time since Pete heard anything nice about himself,* she thought.

Inside the kitchen she could smell the dinner cooking. *Just about finished.* She checked once more the set table for the Shaws and made up a plate for Pete. She knew he would bring back the empty plate and utensils later. She stacked it high with buttery toasted French bread and put some iced tea in a big plastic cup for him. When she took the foil-wrapped package out to him with the fork tucked inside, he nearly lunged for it and had to pull back his enthusiasm of getting to that plate. "Thanks for this. At the bridge I'm being envied by a couple of men who stop by to see what I'm eating."

"Well I'd send more, but it is not my money paying for the food, so I'd better not," Sadie reasoned.

"No worries there. I usually pick up a sack of Krystal burgers for them so they get something to eat as well. But . . . no one's getting any of this. It smells great."

"I'll see you tomorrow morning then. Keep warm tonight. It's getting rather nippy out there now." She could not imagine what it would be like to wrap up in blankets and curl up against the cold wind. But Peter just waved to her and headed off. He didn't look one bit worried. She wished she could politely give him a bar of soap as a hint to wash up. He probably could not smell how much he needed to clean up. Sadie remembered her Daddy, who ran his own barbershop, saying that he was willing to give bums and drifters free haircuts as long as they first went to the river to bathe and wash their hair. He would have bars of soap on hand, just to hand out for that very purpose.

Sadie saw the Shaw's coming into the kitchen, and she decided to eat with them that night. Conversation was easy going and filled the room with warm, caring feelings. Victoria loved to reminisce about the days when her children were young and racing through the house. To her it seemed like just a little while ago.

"I went upstairs today and looked at one wing of the wonderful rooms up there. It is like a treasure land behind every door. I found a good bed I think I'd like to use and some rugs and side tables. And there is a huge chifforobe made of teak that I'd like to use as my closet. Would that be okay with you?" asked Sadie.

Colonel Shaw laid down his napkin and looked at Sadie. "Dear girl, I meant it when I said that you could pick whatever you like from up there. Just like Vicky said, nothing up there is sacred, Besides that, we trust you to take care of anything you choose. Don't we, Vicky?"

Victoria nodded enthusiastically. "I would be so pleased to see that furniture in use again. Will you let me come and see your cottage when you have it all fixed up?"

"As I said before, you'll be the first one invited for a nice cup of tea. Maybe you can give me some pointers on which pieces to pick and use." Sadie wanted Mrs. Shaw to have a say in how her memorable pieces would be used.

"I like to see what a person will configure for themselves. I like to see the style each person deems his or her personal choice. You must create your own space with no help from me. I will come and see it and then I will understand you better. A person's real personality comes forth when they put together a room," offered Victoria.

The Colonel just stared at his wife with his mouth a bit agape. It was as though he was surprised that she could think so clearly and express herself in this way. He slightly shook his head in wonder and then smiled warmly and touched her hand. "It is so good to hear you talk my dear. We do have the best conversations, don't we?" He seemed to be remembering times past and hoping for more times ahead to match them.

Sadie roused herself from staring at the loving old couple. "Well then, let me get these dishes washed up and I'll be on my way. It won't be long now and I will be able to just walk outside and down that path to my own little abode. You can never know how happy I am for this opportunity. I feel like I am being reborn to a new life. It is a little scary, but oh so exciting," Sadie opened up to them.

She checked in on the cottage before she left for the motel. The floor looked so clean and fresh and the freshly painted walls were wonderfully bright and inviting. Sadie was not a visionary like some people. She could not see ahead in her mind's eye what the rooms would look like when she finished filling them with furniture. She mentally took note of what she was dealing with in regard to the size of each room. As far as she could figure, she wouldn't need that many pieces. This cottage would fill up fast and she liked space, not clutter. On the way to Motel 6, she stopped at the five-and-dime store to get some vanilla candles and holders. One thing for sure, she wanted the special scent of fragrant candles to saturate her new place.

Chapter 15

Settling In

And so it went from day to day. The locksmith was called to install the new locks. The heavy, dust-laden drapes were taken to the cleaners, and when returned were hung by Sadie and Gladys a few days later. Oh, they were ever so much better, clean and sweet smelling. Sadie purchased two heavy, fancy corded drape holders, with long fat fringe dangling on each end. She pulled back the heavy, clean drapes and secured them back to each side of each window. Now the light could come flooding in. It was just beautiful.

Sadie loved the old truck from the get go. She even liked the faded paint job on it. She was anxious to use it to explore the area, and become acquainted with the town in which she now lived.

Sadie explored at her leisure the rest of the upstairs sleeping quarters. On the opposite hallway to the west was another bedroom of good size that was very orderly and squared off. It reminded Sadie of an engineer. Nothing was off center. The furniture was elegant but plain, just made for use and not for looks. There were fireplaces in the three bedrooms that belonged to the Shaw children. Sadie knew, of course, that the feminine one with the cream colors and canopy bed belonged to the daughter. The two big bedrooms on opposite sides of the stairway had to belong to the two boys. The more she thought about it the more she was sure that Stephen's room was the no nonsense room with everything orderly and uninteresting. Most of the furniture in that room was not that much to her liking.

In the next bedroom down the west side of the upstairs she found another big oak seaman's chest full of quilts that had been packed carefully with strong-scented mothballs to discourage the pesky moths. She discovered a neat, white free-standing cupboard and a washstand in a big corner bathroom. The cupboard was like a dresser with a marble top that would go perfectly in her simple, sparse bathroom. There was another huge bedroom next to the plain bedroom. It had a closet and its own bathroom. There were two smaller bedrooms with twin beds and just the minimal furnishings. They shared another bathroom. *These must have been for company.* So altogether there were seven bedrooms upstairs and five bathrooms, along with that gorgeous meeting room in the middle. Downstairs, behind the kitchen, was another extra room that looked like it was used as mainly an office, but with a double bed sitting in one corner. This place could house lots of people if need be.

She had stayed nearly a week at the Motel 6 when she finally paid her final bill and hauled her suitcase in the old truck to the cottage. Pete got a buddy from under the bridge to help him move the furniture down from the mansion to her cottage. He also procured the dolly for a meager $10. Sadie told him which pieces to bring down. She marked them with pieces of masking tape. She had chosen the cannonball bed, side tables, the little dark dresser, mirror, the standing dresser and rag rugs. She nearly emptied that favorite room upstairs. Now it was time to haul down the chifforobe. Pete and helper tried to move it, but it would not budge. Pete finally searched inside for evidence of what could be holding it against the wall so tightly. He found some heavy duty screws on both sides that hooked the piece to the wall. "That is very strange," said Peter, "I've never heard of securing one of these to the wall like this. Maybe someone was afraid it would fall over."

"Yeah, maybe it was just too top heavy," offered Sadie.

When Pete found the tools to remove the bolts and screws, the piece moved easily. But what they found behind it was a big surprise: a little door padlocked with a rusty lock. The door was only about five feet high. "What's this?" Pete asked. "A hidden door to where?" He rattled the lock, but it held firm. Sadie looked closely at the back of the chifforobe and discovered that the back panel was really two pieces overlapping each other. She reached inside the cupboard and pressed gently, jiggling the backboards. Suddenly one of them began to slide. It was slow-moving due to lack of use, but it was moving nevertheless. She shoved and cajoled it into opening, and suddenly she was looking at Peter standing at the backside of the piece.

"This used to be a sliding entryway to this little door," she exclaimed. "Whatever this door leads to is a secret place and evidently whatever is in there was precious to whomever hid it so well." She instructed Peter and his helper to carry the piece to her bedroom in the gatehouse. "We'll solve this mystery later. Right now, I don't want to waste a minute of getting moved into my own little place."

Sadie went around to some of the other rooms and chose a cozy loveseat of calico print and an overstuffed sofa in a creamy coffee shade. She would add some colorful pillows to that and a nice quilt throw and it would be entirely inviting. She also chose one of the peach-colored wing-backed chairs and footstool. She rolled up one of the nice oriental rugs for her living room, and chose some standing lamps with creamy silk shades. She marked a few Tiffany lamps for use on side tables in the living room and bedroom. How could she be this lucky to have this treasure trove of old fine furniture from which to pick? It was like letting a kid loose in a candy store.

Sadie discovered the upstairs linen closets full of towels and sheets and blankets. She took what she needed. All of it would have to be washed and dried because they were musty and unused for so long. She took a big box and packed some of the everyday dishes and silverware, of which Mrs. Shaw had a set of twelve. She searched for extra pots and pans and a nice deep cast-iron skillet. She chose some extra utensils from the big crockery pots that held spatulas and spoons and such. She chose a couple of knives which were not sharp enough to cut butter. She found the whetstone and tried to remember how to sharpen a knife. Her dad believed in having a sharp knife. He was a barber during part of his life and kept a long leather strop hanging in the bathroom on which to hone his long razor for shaving. "Always go one way," she remembered. She found an Arkansas whetstone and soon she had those knives sharp as could be. Precaution prompted her to wrap them in extra dishcloths for the walk over to her own kitchen. When she was finished packing up her kitchen items, it didn't look as if she had even touched the bounty in those cupboards.

The Shaw's were enjoying having people around. Mrs. Shaw even began sitting on the front porch on a nice white rattan rocker. Sadie had cushioned it with soft, colorful pillows that she found in the big meeting room upstairs. At first Victoria only stayed out there for a few minutes; but soon she was having her hot tea out there, and enjoying the birdsong and squirrels while watching the people pass by the tiny opening in the wall. Victoria's color was getting better from being out in the fresh air and sunshine. The Colonel was oh so happy with all of it.

Sadie was so relieved when everything was put away and placed just to her liking. She sighed in relief and joy to have it all done. It looked like home to her and almost felt like home. It would take a few weeks to settle in completely and make it her special refuge. She did not have a phone put in. She was enjoying being free from calls. Oh, she remembered all the calls she used to get at the parsonage. She could not even sit down for 10 minutes before the phone was ringing. Someone needed her husband for this or that or just to talk. She took messages like a secretary. Now it was so nice to have no phone ringing in her bungalow. There was no one to call her anyway so why have one? Her own children had no way of getting hold of her right now. She intended to call them periodically (bi-monthly) to catch up and just hear their voices. She purchased a phone card for that convenience. She always drove out of town a ways to use a phone so they could not be pressured into telling anyone where she was.

She hung her clothes in the old teak standing closet that Pete and his buddy had so laboriously carried down the stairs. It had made her feel guilty about requesting that they move that monstrosity; but now that she had it in her room, she was so grateful for it. She had brought so few items of clothing that she had plenty of room leftover. It was amazing on just how little a person could survive. She had left a huge wardrobe at the mansion-like parsonage, a huge walk-in closet full of classy clothes and shoes and purses.

On the first evening of her occupation of the cottage, she had just sat and contemplated what she had there—a quiet harbor with only the birdsong for music. No TV, no CD player, no radio. She knew that eventually she would have to save up and buy something to fill her home with good music, but right now the silence was so appropriate for her. She didn't think she would ever want a TV since most of the programming was tending toward reality TV and she just abhorred all that.

She lit her scented candles and stood on the threshold for a few minutes, looking out at the neat paths and manicured bushes. She was delighted to have the little fireplace. Oh, how she loved a real fire! She would put her winged-back chair right next to it and be so comforted. In the parsonage they'd had two fireplaces and both were gas logs, which did not please her one bit. Sadie enjoyed the fresh woodsy smell of cured wood burning so brightly in the hearth. Her daddy used to find old stumps of pine roots and cut them up into little pieces and called them dynamite sticks. That old wood was saturated with natural turpentine and it would only take a couple of sticks to get a fire going strong. Sadie decided to ask Pete to cut up some dynamite sticks. Life was good.

Tonight Sadie closed the door and sat down on the sofa to pray. How she loved to talk to the Lord and thank Him for how things were working out for her. She told him how much she appreciated his watch care over her. She thanked Him for Pete, and the Shaw's and even Gladys. She even remembered to pray for Cherie and her little baby. It took time to make friends, real friends. She would not be in a rush to let just anyone into the inner circle of her new life. She prayed that the Lord would lead her to do something notable for this area, no matter what it might be. She wanted to make a mark here for good, not just live off all the fine surroundings and bounty here. "Just make a way for me, Lord, and open my eyes to the opportunities you will set before me. I don't want to fail you."

Sadie's first night in the refurbished cottage was a bit strange. She lay awake for most of the night listening to the night sounds. The motel room had that AC going strong all night and it masked any noise outside. Now she heard every snap of twig and rustle of leaves with the scurrying nightlife. Finally, she drifted off to a deep, peaceful sleep.

Chapter 16

Gladys

The next few days went by in a hurry. There was so much to do. Gladys and Sadie liked the results of the dining room drapes being freshly laundered and hung, so they did the same thing to the parlor drapes and then later to the drapes upstairs. It was a lot of work climbing up to the ladder to loosen the dusty drapes. When the fresh drapes were hung back up, Sadie and Gladys both wiped the sweat from their brows and smiled at each other. What an accomplishment they felt. It was like a small bonding between them. Indeed the fine old drapes in the parlor looked so right, tied to the sides like the dining room drapes were meant to be. The big parlor looked grand indeed. Sunlight streamed into a room to reveal every flaw and dust mote, and so they cleaned and scrubbed and polished everything.

As they worked they talked very little at first. Gladys was hesitant about sharing anything about her life. So Sadie talked to her about her own childhood and how she was raised poor but felt so rich. Gladys listened without expression. After several days of this strange, almost silent camaraderie, Gladys finally began telling her own story. She told it in bits and pieces. She had been raised up near Booneville in the Appalachian Mountains. She had seven siblings of which she was the middle child. They were dirt poor and scraped a living from the soil. Her daddy was an alcoholic and her mother was ailing with lung trouble. Gladys worked hard outdoors almost every day. She weeded a huge garden and chopped wood and gathered kindling. She milked the cow and made butter. They had a well-spring house that kept things cool. It was a long time before they received electric services up there in the high hills. A sadness came over Gladys' face and for a minute she sat there stunned and silent. Then she continued her story. When she was seventeen she grabbed the first chance she found to get married so as to remove herself from that rough life. Her husband was a good man. He worked as a mechanic for an Express Oil place. They had no children. She paused again and wiped her eyes with the back of her hand. She told of Stonewall, a big old dog that was nearly too old to be alive. He was like a child to her and she doted on him. She didn't visit her brothers and sisters much even though they were probably just 3 hours away. It seemed to Sadie that Gladys didn't expect much of life. She'd never gotten much out of it and mostly she was merely existing from day to day.

Slowly the whole house was redone. Gladys griped most of the time. However, she was a good worker. Sadie had been taught to find just one good thing about difficult people, focus on that, and brag on that. Gladys was a hard worker, and that was what Sadie pointed out to her and thanked her for. Very slowly this praise began to show in her attitude. Her face was still dour-looking, but she was more polite and would answer Sadie when she talked to her. She also seemed more eager to do whatever was asked of her.

Chapter 17

Stephen Comes Again

The new lock on the door worked smooth as silk. Once a week, while Mrs. Shaw was sitting on the porch getting some much needed sun, Sadie had Gladys clean their sitting room and bathroom. She purchased fresh flowers which Gladys put in the vases in the Shaw's suite.

One morning Sadie was cleaning up breakfast dishes when she heard a man's voice rather huffy and angry. She heard the rattling of the door and the turning of a key, which did not work anymore. She knew that Stephen Shaw had come back for one of his unscheduled, surprise visits.

"Why doesn't this dad-burned door work anymore? Open up in there!! What in tarnation is going on around here? Can't a man get into his own home?"

Sadie quickly went to the door and opened it as far as the chain lock would open. "Oh, Mr. Shaw," she pretended to be surprised, "just let me unlatch this door. We had the locks changed because the old ones were pretty loose and worn. These will give your mother and dad more privacy and safety." She unhooked the door and invited him in formally. He snuffed at her like she was dirt at his feet. He began to stride toward the sitting room. She stood blocking his way to the door and kindly requested that he have a seat in the foyer while she announced that he was there. "I'm not sure they are even ready to have visitors just yet. Let me check."

"What? Not even free to walk around in my own home? What's going on here?"

"Well, as I was raised to believe, 'A man's home is his castle' and this home belongs to Colonel Shaw as well as I can ascertain. You do have your own home don't you, Mr. Shaw? I wouldn't want your folks to be disturbed or surprised if they were not ready for company. Next time you come why don't' you call ahead of time so you will know when it is convenient for them to see you?"

"Who in the . . . . heck are you woman?" he scowled and pushed his chest toward her.

"I'm the new housekeeper as you well know, Mr. Shaw, and it is my duty to protect and provide a safe and comfy place for your folks. I won't have them rudely interrupted without notice. You will kindly wait here until I talk to them and inform them that you are here."

Mr. Shaw was taken aback and huffed and puffed to no avail. He seemed to know that she would not be moving aside without a tussle; and as yet, he'd never physically struggled with a woman. He reluctantly turned his back on her and waited, but he refused to take a seat.

"Just make it quick, woman, I haven't got all day!" he admonished her.

"My name is Sadie Jamison, sir. You can call me by that name or address me as ma'am, but not 'woman' if you please." She turned on her heel and knocked gently on the parlor door. "Colonel Shaw, your son is here for a visit. I'll offer him coffee and a cinnamon roll while you get prepared to see him."

"Thank you Sadie. I had no idea he was coming today. We'll be right out. Thanks for the warning. Be right there, Stephen. Give me a minute."

"Would you like to come into the kitchen for your coffee, sir, or can I bring it out here to you?"

"I don't want any blamed coffee or your old sweet rolls. Just be sure I get a key for that door before I leave," he demanded.

"Well, Mr. Shaw, that will be strictly up to your father's discretion whether or not you get a key to this door. I'm sure he would not mind your having one if you were gracious enough to not barge into their private quarters without knocking." She turned on her heel and went into the kitchen.

The smells coming through that kitchen door were so inviting. The coffee was fresh and the cinnamon rolls were buttery and fragrant. Sadie reckoned that Stephen was quite tempted to give in and request a sampling. He must have been so dumb-founded and angry at this strange ole woman who had just come in here and taken over the house, running it to her own liking. She imagined that he was contemplating that this was not going to be happening and some changes were going to be made very soon.

Sadie stifled a smirk as she swept into the kitchen letting the swinging door flip back in her wake. She knew that the Shaw's would not even consider talk of letting her go. Things were working out too well here. They were happy again and content and thriving under her care. This pompous son would have to work pretty hard to get rid of her. She had no fears there.

Very soon she heard the pleasant greeting of the Colonel welcoming his son into the parlor. "Come on in Stephen. We were just finishing up our breakfast and showers and such. What's up? Everything okay?"

Sadie got busy with her own tasks and mixed up a batch of homemade bread to rise in the warm kitchen. She peered out the window and saw Peter digging up old flowerbeds and preparing them for planting. Some fall ferns and pansies were ready to be planted. Every day that yard was looking more and more inviting. More paths were being raked clear and new ones created. Wayward bushes were being either eliminated totally or were trimmed and shaped. The yard's wide paths, that he created, wound all the way through the grounds exploring even to the farthest corner. She noticed too that Pete no longer reeked of old sweat and dirt. His hair was clean and his clothes although still very worn, were clean as well. She was afraid to ask about his lodging arrangements. She just hoped that he was not still living under the bridge.

Sadie was searching in the cupboard for some spice she needed for supper and heard a rattling of something way back there in the corner. It was a ring of old rusty keys hanging on an old hook in the back corner. She wondered at them and decided to go upstairs and see if one of them would fit that tiny door where the chifforobe had been. As she rushed up the main entrance stairs she could hear Stephen vehemently confronting his parents about locking him out and griping about that 'woman' who had taken over. She smiled to herself and hurried on up the stairs. She liked the impression she'd made on Stephen.

Sadie tried every key on that ring of keys, and none of them fit that little door. Her curiosity was still peaked. Somehow she would find out what was behind that door. She returned to the kitchen.

Stephen shoved open the door to the kitchen as he was getting ready to leave. He walked right through to the back door and barged his way outside. She watched him walk right up to the cottage and open the door and look in. He didn't step inside, but he stared at it for a long moment. Then he stormed off to get in his car and gunned the engine to spew gravel behind him.

That man needs some attention and an attitude change, thought Sadie.

Chapter 18

Exploring the Town

Tomorrow, Saturday, and the next day, Sunday, were Sadie's days off. She was cooking ahead so that the Shaw's could have their supper from the refrigerator and microwave. For Saturday she was making vegetable beef soup with oxtails that she found at the local butchers. And for Sunday she was cooking a small ham and a baking dish of hominy grits soufflé to go with it. She'd made a pineapple upside down cake and put it under glass to be eaten at their desire.

The next morning dawned fresh and bright. It was a perfect day to go exploring. She decided to take the old truck and go search the area a bit to see just what all was surrounding her. She wanted to scope out the local churches too. She needed to find a bank today and start up an account for herself. All her needs were met by the Shaw's, and she was being paid a tidy sum besides. She wanted to save all she could for emergencies and trips to see her children. She might need money to buy things for herself and her loved ones back home.

Sadie almost felt guilty leaving the Shaw's to themselves for a couple days. But as soon as she got into the old truck and started out, she felt exhilarated. It was a whole day to do whatever she wanted: what a treasure! She started driving from street to street, up and down, taking in all the neighborhoods. Finally she drove through the town and explored all of the side streets. She found the First Baptist Church, so she parked and went in. She was glad to see the doors were open allowing her to come inside and stand in the sanctuary in all its quietude. She remembered that the big sanctuary at the church where her husband was pastor was locked at all times when not in scheduled use. It seemed a shame to her that the doors were not open for all to come in to rest and worship quietly whenever they wanted.

The sunshine streamed in through the stained glass windows and made her instantly feel the need to pray. She sat in a back pew and looked up and around her. She prayed a prayer of total thanksgiving and awe at God's care for her. Sadie noticed the baby grand piano up front and felt drawn to it. She glanced around and saw that no one was around. Up the aisle she strode. She sat on the piano bench and placed her hands on the keys. She began to gently play a song that she'd learned from an old record. She sang softly as she played.

> I can get along without riches and I can get along without fame,
> And I can get along without having my share of worldly gain,
> And I can get along without finery and things I can't afford,
> But I can't get along without the Lord.

> The Lord is right beside me, He'll guide me all the way,
> Through the valley deep or on the mountain steep
> He hears me when I pray.
> Oh yes, I've learned now, there's only one way to get along,
> And I can't get along without the Lord.

By the time she had come to the end of the song, her voice was reaching to the highest corners and bouncing back from the upper walls. It felt so wonderful to sing with gusto to the Lord again. When she was finished, she heard someone clapping in the back of the church. It startled her and she stood up quickly looking around.

A middle-aged man dressed casually in khakis and a polo shirt walked down the aisle smiling. "I didn't mean to startle you. I was just drawn from my office when I heard you playing and heard your voice. I'm Craig Harper, the new pastor here. Forgive me if I don't recognize you. I've only been here a few weeks, now."

"It is no wonder that you've never met me. I'm new to the area myself. This is my first time inside the walls of this quaint and delightful edifice. I just meant to stop in and pray a minute and then I saw this piano and was drawn to it. I didn't mean to disturb your contemplation in your office. I'll be going now." Sadie stood up to leave.

"Let me assure you that hearing you playing the piano and singing was no intrusion for me at all. I feel that the walls of a church absorb all the praising of the Lord in song, prayer, preaching, and reading of the Word. The more of that that goes on, the more ingrained this church will be in honoring and worshipping God. That sounds like a sermon, but I feel deeply sincere about this. The first time I walked into this church in view of a call here, I sensed all the years and years of people worshipping here. The place is just saturated with it." He paused to look at her. "If you don't go to this church, where do you attend, if I may be so bold to ask?"

"Well, as it turns out, since I am brand new to this area myself, I haven't even started looking for a church home. I just arrived here a couple weeks back.

Today is my first day to have the opportunity to explore the area to see which church I'd like to try. This one will be first on the list, I can assure you."

"There are several fine churches in this area. The First Methodist is a few blocks from here and they just got a new organ installed with all the bells and whistles. It is just grand to hear. Their pastor has been there for nearly 20 years and is beloved by this town. Let's see, there is an Assembly of God close to the edge of town north of here. It is full of the Spirit and the people there are friendly and welcoming. Just driving by their services you can hear the enthusiasm of their singing—with drums and guitars and the whole bit.

And I guess one of my favorite churches is the Immanuel Baptist Church in the south of town. It is our local black church. The old minister there has two younger preachers helping him out, but he still runs the show there. What a man of God he is! When he preaches he has the congregation in his hands and they respond with 'amens' and encouraging words. By the time his sermon is winding up, he is actually singing his sermon and it is mesmerizing. I love that place and the people there."

"It is so refreshing to hear a minister appreciate the merits of other churches and not just brag on his own church in order to convince someone to come to it. I don't think I've ever heard a minister do what you've just done. I'm truly impressed and moved by it."

"Sounds like you've had some dealings with preachers in your life."

"Yes, you could say that!"

"May I ask your name and what you are doing in our town?"

"My name is Sadie Jamison. I have chosen to be single after 32 years of marriage and I came here to start my freedom. I've always longed to live in these North Carolina mountains. Now I'm giving it a shot. I work as the housekeeper for Colonel Shaw and his wife, Victoria."

"My, how forthright and honest you are! Now *that* is refreshing to me! I know the Colonel's place. I think he attends the Presbyterian Church in town. Depending on your background and how formal you like your services, that is a good choice too," Craig added.

"Well it looks like we are both just starting out here. I tell you what: I'll be coming to church here tomorrow and then I will probably try a few more churches and make my mind up where I feel the most comfortable worshipping. But I thank you for this time to worship alone and also for all the input you gave me on the churches in this fine town. I'll be going now. Thanks for your time." Sadie turned to leave.

"Ms. Jamison, meeting you and knowing this little bit of history about you has been my distinct pleasure. I hope to talk to you further and to watch and see how you adjust to this town. Maybe we can compare notes after a few weeks."

"Jamison is my maiden name. I'm sort of hiding away here and don't want to use my married name. Now I've got you thinking that I may be wanted for a crime. Not so! Just for awhile, I need to get away from people that know me. Eventually when I am sure what I shall do, I will let everyone know where I am. Meanwhile, I just want to have all the strings to my past severed for a bit. You cannot imagine how wonderful this freedom feels," Sadie admitted. "I don't know what it is about you that causes me to open up and share all this with you. I'm usually a more private person than this. Forgive me!"

"Maybe it is because I am a pastor and you trust that I will not betray your confidence. And that is completely the truth, Ms. Sadie. Anytime you need to talk further and just sort things out on a listening ear, I'm your man. You are welcome here anytime."

Sadie shook his hand, which was firm and warm. She was glad that he didn't put his other hand on top of the one shaking hers. Her husband used to do that and sort of twist and bow his head like he was so humbly privileged to shake a person's hand. She knew it was all an act, because she'd seen his actions after he had gone through that charade. She liked this young preacher (young to her age) and his forthrightness and genuineness. "You can count on it Rev. Harper. I'll wave at you from the back row tomorrow. I'm one of those good Baptists who know their place."

Sadie got in the old truck and drove around some more. She found the Methodist church. It was near the park where she had rested the day she met the Colonel. She remembered hearing the church tower's deep resounding bells ringing out the time. She had no luck finding the other churches that he'd mentioned.

She parked near the bank and walked in to open an account for herself. She had to show her driver's license and was questioned as to the change of name. She assured them that it was her maiden name and showed her Social Security Card to verify that. The bank was just happy to have a new account and did not question her further. No checking account for her; just savings. She would draw out cash as she needed it and use the bank money orders if she needed to send away for something. In her estimation, the less trail, the better.

She found the local mall. Though it was small it had a Sears and a JC Penney and some other shops like card shops, shoe stores, a jewelry store, a dollar store, etc. There was a hot dog stand in the middle of the tiny mall that smelled so good. She got a fat Polish hotdog, and when she bit into the hot crispy skin, the juices rolled down her chin. It nearly burned her mouth. *Oh that was so good.* She had onions and sauerkraut and deli mustard, and relish squishing out of it. She had to bend over the little café table and let it all drip onto napkins. It was marvelous.

Sadie left the mall with new tennis shoes, socks, underwear and two pair of slacks, and a new pair of sturdy blue jeans. She found some nice cotton shirts and t-shirts, plus a two sweaters and a sweatshirt for the colder season that was fast approaching. It felt good to get organized and shop for things she needed. She'd always been a shopper who just wanted to drive to the store, get what was needed and get home; none of this browsing shopping for her. Too boring. She knew she was a rare bird and not like the ladies who were normal and loved to shop daily and search through piles of sales items, pushing and shoving to get a good bargain. Not for Sadie. In and out, that is what suited her best.

She found the local library on a side street and went inside to get a card and check out what was offered. Oh that special smell of books always suffused her with the warm, cozy feeling of safety and promised adventure. Ah, to sit down and open up a new novel, that was pure pleasure for her. She loved looking at chapter one and beginning with that single large letter on the first word. Now, that was what she longed for! It was just so astoundingly mesmerizing to settle into a new story. She went up to the counter and asked for a library card. This would be one of her favorite possessions. She checked out a few books. A mystery by the comical Ann George; a historical novel by Ken Follet; and an old favorite, *Oldest Living Confederate Widow Tells All,* by Allan Gurganus. It had been years since she immersed herself in that wonderful tale. These three books would keep her occupied and happy for a couple of weeks. She just could not go to sleep at night without reading for at least 15 minutes. It was the special joy of her day to settle down to her book. Somehow immersing herself in a story helped clear her mind of worries and thoughts of the day, so she could drift off to sleep easily.

How she loved marking in books that belonged to her. She enjoyed making notes in the margin and underlining cleverly worded phrases, finding special truths, which she circled, that expressed her deepest feelings. She would have to find a used bookstore or ask the librarian for the dates of the sale of their discarded books. She liked to *own* books. It was her one and only vice, if you could call it such. The librarian welcomed her to the community and gave her a canvas bag with "Rose Creek Public Library" written on the front. Sadie was indeed grateful for that. She felt like it was Christmas already.

She stopped at a phone booth and called Rebecca. "Hey there, sweet girl. How's it going?" she greeted her daughter.

"Mom, I'm so glad that you called! I've been hoping with every ring of the phone it would be you," her daughter chided. "You need to come home and settle some stuff here. Dad is getting antsy and people are asking too many questions which he cannot comfortably answer. He's desperate to find out where you are. I hope you are ready to tell me where you are. It is like you fell off the end of the earth. All your friends here are worried to death about you."

"Honey, I can't come. I'm just getting my life settled here. I will call your dad, I promise you; or I might write him and let him know I am well and happy. I won't tell him where I live yet because I don't want him making a big dramatic entrance here, trying to do the noble thing so that his congregation will be so impressed about how hard he tried to put this marriage back together. But I will tell you."

Sadie told of her long bus ride to Rose Creek. She went into detail about how she was led by the Lord to meet the Shaw's. She described the miracle of the perfect job and accompanying house, fully furnished. She told of how good she was feeling now that she had talked with God and agonized over all that had happened to her. Becky listened without saying a word. Sadie could just imagine her tender-hearted daughter with tear-filled eyes.

"Oh, Mom, I am so thankful that you are okay. I love that story about how God took care of you and brought you through this hard time. God really is good, isn't He?"

"Yes indeed, precious daughter. My heart is so full of gratitude and joy, that I can hardly describe it." Sadie blew her nose and wiped her eyes. She could hear Becky doing the same on the other end of the line. "By the way, did you go get Wheezer? Did he allow that? But of course he did." Sadie's husband hated animals in the house, and he would never allow her to have a big old dog like she wanted. So Sadie had made do with her fat cat. "I miss that old cat so much. Maybe there will be some way for me to get him soon."

"That is so like you Mom, worrying about hooking up with that old cat before even planning on seeing us. Just kidding of course. Yes I went and got ole Wheezer and he's settled in here just fine. He likes having people around. I took your pillow with me. Just snuck it out, and Wheezer sleeps on it and I can tell he knows that it is yours. But Mom, don't you need your clothes and your personal stuff, like photo albums and jewelry and such? Mom, it seems so strange that you spent 32 years with Dad and do not want anything to remind you of those years. It is like you are abandoning us as well. Don't you love us anymore?" she implored.

Sadie's breath caught in her throat and a little cry escaped from her. "Oh my dearest child, I'm so sorry to put you through this. I guess I was basking in my freedom so much that I bypassed thoughts of what this was doing to you and your brothers. Oh, my heart aches with love for you three. And of course, I would love to have all of the photograph albums. If your dad doesn't want them, then yes indeed, I will be so glad to get them." Sadie stopped to get a breath. "My mind is so full of all the memories of you growing up and becoming independent adults. I'm so very proud of you all. Becky, never doubt that I love you more than life itself." Sadie stopped to ponder how to express what she had to say. "It is just that now that you are out there doing well on your own, I just realized that there was no real reason why I had to stay in that unsatisfying union. I was getting so bitter, satirical, untrusting and hard: all things I did not want to become. I just had to get away from there, Becky dear. I just had to." She stopped to once again blow her nose and clear her eyes. She never dreamed anything could be so painful.

Rebecca interrupted her to clarify that she certainly knew her mother had been very unhappy for many years and that she would not wish her to continue in that at all. She told Sadie that she just felt abandoned and cast aside. "I'm sorry Mom. I'm being selfish and want you here near me. And Treat misses you too. But, don't get me wrong. I support your effort to start afresh. By the way, how's it going?"

Sadie was so relieved to hear the genuine care in her daughter's voice. And she was so wrung out by the realization that her beloved grandson, Treat, missed her. All of a sudden she was so homesick for him, she could not stop the tears from flowing. *I should have brought more tissues*, she thought. "It's only been two weeks now that I've been gone. That is shorter than most vacations. I promise I will come back to see you and will get my cat. Maybe I'll even take some of my stuff, although I dread setting foot in that house of bad memories. And I certainly don't have any desire to see your dad."

"Mom, I have an idea. Maybe I could take the Land Rover and Treat and I could drive with Wheezer to see you."

"On Becky, that is such a tempting thought, my heart is swelling. But if you knew where I am and looked on a map, you would see that where I live now is too far for you to drive. The reason I am insisting on keeping you ignorant of my whereabouts, is because I don't want you to have to lie. It is not your style, dear child, and I feel guilty putting you through that ordeal." Sadie bit her lip and then went on. "Concerning your coming here, I want that as much as you do. Maybe we should wait just a little while longer, however, so that I can get a chance to really settle in here. I'll save up the money and fly you out here." Sadie stopped a second and then went on. "Just trust me that I'm doing well here, and settling in as housekeeper and cook and bottle washer for this wonderful old couple. I have a nice cottage in which to stay and an old pickup truck to drive around. I'm happy and I'm rediscovering myself. I'm experiencing the joys of life once again. Yes, I miss you all so much it hurts, but just consider what it was like for me to let you three go to college and leave home. And yet I wouldn't have had it any other way. You needed to establish yourselves and find your independence. Well, that is what I am trying to do. I don't have that much time left, and I don't intend to live it in resentment and unhappiness. I know you understand that," she explained.

"Oh Mom, it does sound so grand. I'm truly happy for you. Andy and Matt and I have been aware for a decade or more how very unhappy you were. None of us want that for you. And to think you now drive an old pickup. Why that is what you've wanted for as long as I can remember. I recall Dad saying that it was a silly idea, having his elegant wife driving around in an old rattletrap pickup."

"Well, you'd be surprised just how opposite of elegant I am right now," Sadie chuckled. "But the way I am now, suits me so much better. I think you might like the change."

"I already do, Mom. Just keep calling me every once in a while. You should let Dad know you are okay, and not to expect you to come back. And call a couple of your friends at the church. Call the ones who have a tendency to gossip. That way you will get the word spread fast without having to talk to too many."

"You are my personal secretary now? Making lists of all I need to accomplish? I like that! I will take your suggestions and do what you say. I'll have to figure out a way to call without anyone seeing on his or her caller ID where I am. I wonder if there is a way to do that? If not, I will have to take the bus to a town far away and make the calls. Or maybe just write to him and my friends and mail the stamped letters in a big envelope to a some distant post office and ask them to mail them from there." Sadie's mind was figuring all the angles.

"You'd make a great criminal, Mom. You think of all the contingencies. Did anyone ever tell you that you have a devious mind?" Rebecca laughed.

"Well, I'll take that as a compliment although it is far from one, young lady! I'll call you soon. Please keep praying for me and I will do the same for you guys. Call the boys and tell them what is up and assure them I will be in touch soon. Hug my cat for me. Love you so much."

"Bye Mom. I hate to let you go. I miss you terribly. Keep well and happy."

With that they disconnected. Sadie was totally spent from the conversation and needed to rest. So she parked near the fragrant, green park where she had rested only a few days ago. She found a bench and settled down. There seemed to be so many loose ends to tie up and bridges to cross and burn. Sadie closed her eyes and breathed in the fresh pine needle scent.

Chapter 19

Cherie and Joy

As Sadie soaked in the sunshine filtering through the trees, she heard a voice calling out to her. "Hey there! Can't remember your name, but we met in the diner. Can I sit here for a minute with you?"

Sadie was startled to see the young, gum-chewing waitress from the café standing in front of her. She had a little toddler in a cheap stroller. The little girl was sitting up looking at Sadie with interest.

"No problem. Sit down and enjoy this late morning with me. I, too, have completely forgotten your name, if I ever knew it. Tell you what; you tell me yours again and the name of this precious child here, and I will refresh your memory on my name as well."

"You are the generous lady who brightened my day that morning a while back. I think I may have been sort of rude and short with you; and then you responded with kindness and a great tip, and I felt so rotten. Then I got to talk to you again and you seemed so genuinely interested in me. That meant a lot to me. My name is Cherie Strong, and this priceless bundle of energy is my pride and joy. I named her Joy for that very reason. She's 18 months old now." She pondered Sadie for a moment and then added, "I'm not married."

"Yes, now I remember your name and I'm glad to know your baby's name. Your name puts me in mind of an orchard of cherry trees. And your last name reminds me of how strong you are to deal with being a single mother. That cannot be easy, to say the least. By the way, my name is Sadie. Sadie Jamison."

Cherie shook her hand and plopped down on the bench. Joy immediately wanted to be free of the stroller, so Cherie took her out and admonished her to stay close. Joy began waddling away down the path, looking back at her mother now and again. She would go just a little ways and come back to pat her mommy's knee and then be off again in another direction.

Sadie commented, "Kids surely do have a lot of energy when they are at this stage. I remember my three children when they were little. There were times I just wished they were grown up enough to dress themselves, go to the bathroom alone, and feed themselves. It felt so overwhelming at the time to have such responsibility. After my first son was born, I went into a depression, which was so foreign to me. It was because I had been suddenly thrust into the role of being totally responsible for a living being. It was almost too much. It didn't last long though, and soon I was fitting right into the schedules and the duties and finally enjoying all of it." Sadie looked up at the sky and added, "You know, I think the key to adjusting to motherhood is to surrender to it. Of course your life will be changed forever. A new mother needs to realize that and give herself over to it. When that happens, the joy rushes in and the depression fades."

Cherie pondered on this a moment. "You know, I think you are 100% right on that. At first I was so down and felt so sorry for myself. But now I am totally devoted to raising my daughter. It is hard, sure, but I love it." She paused and then asked, "You had three children? Dear me," Cherie remarked. "I just shake with fear to think of taking on more than one of these creatures." Cherie giggled. Then, surprisingly, her eyes welled up with tears as she gazed forlornly at her beautiful little girl.

"Whatever is wrong, dear girl?" Sadie asked. "One minute laughing; the next crying. Do you want to tell me about it?"

"Oh, it is just that I'm having a rough day. No worries. I'll get through this one just like I've gotten through so many like it before. Sometimes the effort of being a single mother just gets to be really heavy. Thanks for listening."

"Well, it doesn't seem to me that you even told me anything yet. But I'm willing to hear all about it, if you care to enlighten me."

Cherie looked deeply into Sadie's eyes and finally said, "Yes, I think you actually would be happy to listen. Maybe that is just what I need right now—a sympathetic listener. I'm not a cry baby or whiner. I just want you to know that. But today I ran out of options, and I just don't know what to do."

"Whatever happened?" Sadie inquired.

"The sweet old lady who watches Joy for me every day while I work is not doing well again today. She can't help it. I don't blame her one bit. She's pretty old and getting a bit feeble and susceptible to aches and pains and such. More and more often, it seems that she is not able to watch Joy. Well, when she is not feeling well, I have to call in to work and tell them that I cannot work that day. They don't like it much when I do that. I'm afraid I may lose my job if I don't figure out another arrangement. I can't afford to take her to a nursery school. All my pay would go to have her taken care of. And I really can't afford to lose another day's pay either," Cherie confided.

"What time are you supposed to be at work? I'm off today and just driving around getting acquainted with the town and area. Maybe I could watch her till you get off work. I know you don't know me from Adam, but you might want to take a chance on me since you are in such a pickle. I love babies. I know I'll be exhausted tonight when my head hits the pillow, but I also know I will have plenty of great memories to ponder when I sleep tonight."

"Oh, I wouldn't dream of saddling you with Joy. That is not why I told you. This is not your problem," exclaimed Cherie.

"I won't insist that you trust me. I just feel so blessed of God right now and it would feel good to pay it back a little by helping someone else. That's all. It's your choice."

"Well, I usually have to work from 7:00 till 3:00 each day. Joy naps about 2 hours in the afternoon. Already it is 11:00, so you would only have to watch her about 2 hours if you don't count her naptime."

"See, you make it sound easy. So what say we stop by your place and get the car seat for Joy and I'll be on my way? You can go and earn your day's pay, or at least part of the day that is left?" Sadie slapped her knee and stood up as if to settle the deal.

"Well how will I get her back? Where will you be?" Cherie seemed to be having second thoughts.

"I'm the new cook and housekeeper for Colonel Shaw and his wife. I live in the little cottage by the big house. There is a driveway into the back right by my house. You could drive in to pick her up, or better yet I could drive her to the Café at 3:00 and deliver her to you." Sadie suddenly realized that Cherie might not have a car.

"No, no, I know where the big house is, and I will bring the stroller and pick her up after work. Thank you so much. You rescued me today," Cherie gratefully said.

And so it was that Sadie got to play the role of grandma again for the day. Joy seemed delighted to be in the front seat of the pickup, riding around with Sadie. Somehow they hooked up a little carseat on the front seat of the pickup. Joy sat up straight and tall and peered out of the window. She wasn't afraid of this strange woman at all. Cherie had rushed back across the street, from her neat, little apartment, to the Café to finish her shift. Sadie drove very slowly and carefully out of town marking in her mind the certain roads and houses as spot checks to find her way back. The countryside was ablaze with color. The leaves were falling all around them like snow. Sadie stopped by the side of the road and got Joy out. They walked in the woods and gathered leaves. Joy was walking really well, but sometimes would topple over in the leaves and laugh at the golden carpet under her. They gathered up a whole bundle of the most lovely, colorful leaves. Then they returned to the truck and continued on through the countryside. Sadie was struck with a deep sense of peace at being in this area. She spotted tiny farmhouses tucked at the end of dirt roads with faded red barns standing behind the houses. Such precious pictures.

Chapter 20

Pastor Noah Brown

Along the way, she came to a little rattletrap church on the side of the road. Immanuel Baptist Church. *This is the church that Pastor Craig mentioned as being one of his favorite churches,* she thought. She pulled into the gravel parking lot, and she got Joy out of the pickup. They walked up to the front stoop. She noticed that the wood was well worn and paint was peeling. The church was in ill repair. She tried the door and it swung open. She called a "Yoo hoo!" No one answered. She pushed their way in. Joy went running down the aisle and crawled up on one of the wooden benches. The atmosphere in the little church was one of closeness to the Spirit. Sadie could feel it even with no one else present. *There must be a lot of real heartfelt worship going on in this place every week,* she thought. She stood at the front behind the pulpit. It was a simple standing podium of pine wood. No frills. She remembered the ornate oak, glass, and marble pulpit in her husband's church back home. How elegant he looked standing up there in all that glory; but to her, there was a quiet dignity to this simple wooden pulpit. She preferred it actually.

Sadie stood in the aisle where she was and began to sing.

"I must tell Jesus . . . all of my trials . . . I cannot bear these burdens alone. If I but ask Him He will deliver. Jesus can help me, Jesus alone. I must tell Jesus . . . . I must tell Jesus. I cannot bear these burdens alone. I must tell Jesus . . . . I must tell Jesus. Jesus can help me. Jesus alone."

When Sadie finished singing, little Joy stood on the wooden bench and clapped her hands. Sadie burst out laughing and rushed down the aisle to grab her up and dance her around while hugging her.

"We 'low dancin' in this church! And singing like that anytime!" came a voice from the back.

Sadie stopped twirling and gasped as she saw that they were not alone. "Oh dear, I am so sorry to be trespassing here. I was admiring your sweet church and just felt led to come inside."

"This is God's house, lady. No trespassing here. All's welcome!" the man replied. "I'm Pastah' Noah Brown."

"Well, I'm Sadie Jamison. Just moved here. I work as the cook and housekeeper for Col. Shaw and his wife. I'm staying in the little cottage out back of the big house. Now why did I tell you all that? I'm not usually this talkative. Forgive me."

"Glad to meet you, Miss Jamison. That there your grand baby?"

"This is Joy, the baby of Cherie, who works at the café in town. I'm just watching her today since her regular caretaker is sick. Isn't she an adorable child?"

"That she is," Pastor Brown smiled. "Your voice sounds like you know your way around a pulpit. I'll wager you have sung many a solo in church. Am I right?" He asked.

"You are indeed right. It's been awhile, though. Sometimes I just feel the need to sing to the Lord. I'll have to come back here one Sunday and see how well you preach. And I'd like to worship with your congregation."

Pastor Noah replied, "You'd be so welcome, Miss. We have a mighty fine time here praising the Lord. Gets kinda rowdy here when the Spirit moves. There be plenty of dancin' in the aisles then. Our services are at 10:30."

"Well, I have one other church I plan to visit, and then I'll be coming here to enjoy yours. Thanks for letting us come in and take in the wonderful feeling in this church. I love it." Sadie shook Noah's dark brown hand. He patted Joy on the head and walked them to the door.

The little pickup carried her back into town. She went to the Clyde's Grocery Store and stocked up on food for the week. She got some soft white cheese squares and crackers for the baby to snack on. In her mind she had planned out the meals for the following week, and so her shopping did not take long. She drove on to the big house and parked. Joy was glad to get outside again and began to toddle down the freshly covered paths of pine straw.

"Hold on a minute Joy," she cried. "Just let me put these groceries away, then you and I will take a walk all through this magnificent park." She scooped Joy up and one sack of groceries, and into the big warm kitchen they went. As soon as she had unloaded all the sacks of groceries from the truck and put everything away into the refrigerator and cupboards of the big house, she took the pickup to her own little parking area by her small gatehouse. Then she and Joy walked hand in hand down the sun-dappled paths. Joy tried picking up pine cones; but the prickles were too sharp, and she would yelp and toss them back onto the ground.

Peter was at the front porch area planting a bed of winter pansies. The purple and white and yellow blossoms made the front of the house cheery. Sitting on the porch was Victoria, rocking gently, with eyes shut.

"Peter, this looks marvelous. And the autumn ferns are gorgeous, too. I think you must have been a gardener somewhere back in the past," she ventured.

"Nah, it's just something I always wanted to put my hand to and never had time. It feels great to get your hands in the soil and make things grow. I love this."

She had never heard Pete speak with such conviction before. It thrilled her to see this happy side of such a serious man.

"Who do you have there, Sadie?" cried Mrs. Shaw, rising from her rocker.

"This is Miss Joy. She is one and a half, and she loves your paths and gardens. Victoria held out her arms and the baby girl climbed up the steps and toddled over holding out her arms. They embraced and the adulation on Victoria's face made tears well up in Sadie's eyes.

"Oh, to feel a child in my arms again. Such pure joy! Wherever did you find her?" Victoria questioned.

"There is a young single mother named Cherie that works at the town café. Rose Vine Café, I think it is called. It's right across the street from the bakery. She was in dire need of a babysitter just for today; so this being my day off, I volunteered."

"Well what a wonderful treat this is for me," offered Victoria. "Let's go inside here sweet girl. I want to show you my collection of Hummel figurines." With that Mrs. Shaw took Joy's hand, and led her into the house.

"But, Victoria, I was just taking her for a walk before her nap. I didn't mean for her to intrude on your rest time this afternoon."

"Nonesense, dear! How often do I get the chance to bask in the presence of such refreshing youth? Come along. Joy, is it? Did she have lunch yet, Sadie?"

Sadie gave a big sigh of resignation and followed them into the house. As Victoria led Joy into her private rooms, Sadie rushed to the kitchen to make some peanut butter and jelly sandwiches. She hurriedly came back with a tray laden with the tiny treats: crustless sandwiches, little glasses of cold milk, along with crispy, chilled grapes. She had a bowl of tiny goldfish crackers and soft, 'moo cow cheese' for spreading. When she arrived in the private parlor of the Shaw's, she had to stop and smile at the scene before her. Joy was kneeling down at the coffee table carefully admiring an array of expensive Hummel figurines. The colorful treasures, collected over years and years, were standing in a row. Victoria was flushed with pleasure at being able to share them with a wonder-eyed child.

"We must be very careful when we touch these," she admonished gently. "We don't want them to break. First eat your lunch, and then I will tell you a little story about each one of them," Mrs. Shaw said. "Sadie, you run along now for about 30 minutes and let me enjoy this delightful child. I'll ring my bell if I need you to come," she added.

'Well, so much for a day off,' pondered Sadie happily. She was truly happy to see the combination of the two opposite spectrums of life: old age and babyhood. What genuine delight they were taking in each other! Sadie watched for a minute as Victoria helped herself to a sandwich and some grapes. 'They are having a veritable tea party, I'd say,' bemused Sadie as she backed out the door.

Sadie busied herself making some hot chocolate chip cookies from cold dough she had in the refrigerator. She took a plate of them to Peter with some cold milk. "Stop for a minute and rest, won't you, Peter?"

They sat on the edge of the porch with their legs dangling down the steps. The day was a perfect combination of coolness and warmth. They sat in silence and just took in the treasure of the afternoon. Sadie suddenly heard the bell ring and jumped up knocking off a cookie into the bushes. She hurried into the parlor and stopped short. There was Victoria sitting on the soft settee with Joy lying beside her. Joy's tiny blond head was in Victoria's lap and the old arthritic fingers of the genteel lady were gently stroking the baby's hair. Victoria's eyes were shining with joyful tears. "This has been the best afternoon for me, Sadie. Do you think there is a chance her mother might let her come back here sometime?"

Sadie carried the sleeping child back down the pine straw path to her cottage. Peter rushed ahead and opened the door for her. She laid down Joy on her bed and stacked up pillows on either side of her in case she might roll around. She covered her with a small colorful quilt of soft and worn cotton.

Now, she had time to just relax and settle the nagging need to write those two letters. She composed the first one to Anthony, her estranged husband. She told him she could not live with him any longer and that she was certain it would not slow him down in the least. She suggested he get some of the ladies of the church to come in to clean and cook for him, or hire someone. She told him that she had been unhappy with their roommate status all these years and had felt stifled and humiliated by his treatment of her. She would not be able to pretend to be a happily married couple anymore. She related to him his betrayal of her at the deacons' meeting, when he had not come to her rescue or defense in any way. "That was the last straw," she wrote. She knew it was the hardening factor that had turned her contemplation to leave into a firm resolve. She told him she was now very happy and was working and earning her own way. She wanted nothing from him except her freedom. She would eventually come there and pick up those things that were precious to her; but not to worry, she would not be stripping his house of furniture or anything else.

She told him that if he was so inclined he could sue for divorce and get on with his life. She would not protest or demand anything. As for herself, divorce was not that important for she never intended to marry again. She wanted him to be reassured that there was no chance of reconciliation. She reminded him that after 32 years of marriage, she knew him well enough to realize that his heart was not broken or even bruised. She knew he would come out of this smelling like a rose, with the admiration and sympathy of all around him. She signed it, "Sincerely happy beyond my wildest dreams, Sadie"

Then she wrote to two ladies in the church who called her friend, but were notorious for spreading rumors and would nearly salivate with the opportunity to do so. She wrote to them she had left her husband for good and that the reasons were her own business. She told them that she was happily living in a far away town and getting along just fine. Sadie was assured in her heart that in order to cover the appalling sin of gossip, these two ladies would introduce their diatribe concerning Sadie with these words. "I hate to say anything about Sadie, bless her heart, but you all need to know what happened, so we all can know how to pray for her."

Sadie stamped the letters and carried them outside to Peter. He looked at her with a slightly, confused look on his face, but he did agree to arrange for those letters to get to another far away town where they could be dropped in a mail slot. Peter knew truck drivers and deliverymen who would be happy to carry them.

Now all she need do was find a time and opportunity to fly back to where her daughter lived, pick up Wheezer, and visit with her precious daughter and sons. She had no doubt that her boys would fly out to Becky's house to see her if they knew she was coming.

Cherie showed up about 3:30 with the stroller. Joy was still asleep, so Sadie made some hot spiced tea and served some of her fresh cookies. Cherie was famished and ate four of them. "What a neat, cozy place you've set up here, Sadie. I just love it. I hope Joy was good for you. Sorry I was a little late, but we had a late afternoon rush and I couldn't leave them in a bind."

"That's no problem, girl. The more you work, the more you earn. It couldn't have been better here with Joy. We gallivanted around town and walked on the wooded paths and collected leaves and she had a tea party with Mrs. Shaw."

"Oh dear, I hope she was not too much trouble!"

"Not at all. As a matter of fact, Mrs. Shaw requested that you let Joy come again whenever you find the need."

Tears welled up in Cherie's eyes as she pondered this gift. "I certainly don't expect to have to do this very often, but it is so good to know I have the option whenever Mrs. Bleu gets sick or has to go to the doctor or something."

Just then a sleepy-eyed baby came toddling into the room rubbing her eyes. Cherie was up in an instant scooping her up to love her and snuggle close to her. Sadie saw them off with a little box holding the beautiful leaves, a nice sack of cookies, and some fruit.

Chapter 21

The Understanding

Sadie kept the housekeeping books. She was given a certain amount for Peter's work, Mrs. Fortenbrau's cleaning, the bills for the cleaners, food, electricity and upkeep and her salary. Since Sadie had no need for money, what with her room and board included as part of her salary, she put most of her earnings in the new savings account she had started. Each week it was encouraging to see that balance increasing. Sadie knew that sooner or later she would have to either get some of her clothes from her former home, or she would have to buy some. She had always hated shopping and trying on things. So she put it off, week after week. Simplifying her life had made her so content. She wondered about the fact that people did not see the joy in having only what was needed.

Peter was wearing nicer work clothes now and sturdy new boots. She noticed that he had a warm new jacket to wear on the cold mornings. The slackness in his gaunt face filled out with her good hearty lunches and take home dinners. She longed to ask him about his sleeping arrangements, but felt it was not her place to pry. He looked clean-shaven and always smelled woodsy and fresh-skinned, so she knew he was taking a bath some place, and she suspected it was not in a cold river. He was still very standoffish when it came to confiding in her or carrying on even the most simple of conversations. So, she did not push it, and allowed him his privacy and space. She hoped that the time would come when he would feel free to actually speak of his past and maybe the hopes for his future. She had no doubt that he was bright as could be and had talents far beyond what he was using at the moment. She also realized that he needed a lot of healing yet in his life, and that took time. Seeing an encouraging smile from him once in awhile was sufficient for the moment.

One day while Sadie was chopping sirloin steaks into cubes to make stew, the doorbell rang and she heard Mrs. Fortenbrau's defensive tone as Stephen, the blustery Shaw son, came pushing his way in rudely. "I have yet to receive my key to this door. Can't a man even walk into his own castle, anymore? I'll tell you one thing, I'm not standing for this. I feel like a stranger here. What are you looking at woman?"

Gladys scurried away with her head down and her hands wringing the dusty polishing rag she was using in the dining room. She braved a quick glance back at the rude son, and the look on her face would have melted steel.

Sadie hurried into the hallway and positioned herself between him and the Shaw's room. "Good afternoon, Mr. Shaw. As I mentioned before, I'm sure that if Colonel Shaw deems it necessary for you to have a key he will arrange that. Please, have a seat and I'll tell your parents that you are here for a visit. Did you try to call and the phone was busy?" She satirically queried.

"I'm sick of this treatment I am given in my own home. Who do you think you are anyway?" Stephen complained.

"As I told you before, Mr. Shaw, I am the new housekeeper and cook, and I am looking after the best interests of your parents. I was told that you have your very own castle, hmm, house in another part of town. This one belongs to your folks and should be regarded as private. You are most welcome, I'm sure, but to boldly barge in unexpected is not acceptable. Didn't we already have this conversation?" Sadie stood there as a firm barrier to him, until he turned and huffed away to sit on the deacons' bench by the stairs.

She gently knocked on the Shaw's door and spoke softly to them. "Colonel and Mrs. Shaw, your son has surprised you with a visit. I shall tell him you are coming out as soon as possible." There was a barely audible response from within. Soon the door opened and Colonel Shaw came rushing out to greet his son warmly.

"Good to see you, Son. Won't you come on in and visit with your mother and I?"

"I don't care who knows it, Father," he spoke loudly glancing Sadie's way, "I am not happy with this woman that you hired to watch over this house. She's impertinent and too bold for her own good. I think you should begin looking for a replacement!"

"That will not be happening Steve, my boy. She is the best thing that has happened to us in years. You must forgive her for trying to teach you some manners, but it is well past time that you learned some." The Colonel ushered the befuddled son into the room and shut the door.

Sadie was upset with herself for letting her tongue loose on that rude man. She knew that she was treading on ground she had no right to pass over; but the demanding aggression of that eldest son was just so irritating. *I can't just stand here and see him treat his parents like that, and not do something, can I?* Well, actually it was none of her business and she realized that. She would apologize to Mr. Shaw the next chance she got, even if she didn't want to.

Sadie retreated to the kitchen to make some Harvest Stew. She browned the cubed sirloin steak and added chopped onions along with garlic. She poured in port wine to simmer and decrease in volume. Then she added beef stock and tomatoes and covered it to simmer an hour. After that she would add cubed sweet potatoes, butternut squash and red potatoes. Finally, in would go the wonderful spices of cinnamon, allspice, chili and cloves. After the stew simmered again for another hour the stew would be succulent and invigorating. The meat would fall apart like butter.

She made homemade bread, filled with cheddar cheese. She took the dough from the bread maker and flattened it out on a big floured board, sprinkled cheeses on it. Then she rolled it back up sealing the edges, and placed it on a greased pan for rising. Oh, that kitchen smelled so good! She decided that for dessert that night she would make a devil's food chocolate trifle. She had some chocolate cake left over and had frozen it. She would place layers of torn cake, vanilla pudding whipped topping, and shaved chocolate bar in clear pudding glasses and then set them in the icebox. Easy as pie. It looked elegant and was light and tasty.

As she was putting together this supper, the kitchen door swung open and Colonel Shaw walked in. "Can I speak with you, Sadie?" he asked. He sat at the table and she poured him a cup of hot tea with honey and sat down across from him.

"Before you say anything, Colonel, I feel I must apologize for my impudence in thinking I had the right to correct your son. I have a way of speaking out when I see something I don't like. I had no right. Please forgive me. I'll try to be better from now on."

Colonel Shaw just looked at her with his mouth slightly open and eyes wide. Then a big smile came across his face; he chuckled once and shook his head. "Dear, dear Sadie, no apology is necessary. We've indulged that boy for too long. Your words gave me backbone to treat him as a son and not as my boss. Of course he is taken aback. He is not used to being confronted and called to the carpet for his rudeness. He thinks he is immune to correction."

He stopped to reach across the table to place his wrinkled hand on top of hers. "Sadie Jamison, we could not be happier with you if you were solid gold. I just thank God for you every day."

Sadie let out the breath she was holding and relaxed her shoulders. "That is so good to hear; nevertheless, it is not my place to correct your son. I'm sure I've sparked some anger in him, and I hope he has not taken it out on you."

"It won't be allowed anymore. You can count on that. I told him I would get him a key to the house since eventually it will be his and his siblings when we are gone. But with the key comes a promise that he will let us know when he wants to come. Then, Vicky and I will figure out when it is convenient for us also. He agreed this was the right way to do things. I will have to squelch his tendency to order me around and try to make my decisions for me. When my wife was so feeble and ill for so long, I was so taken up with her care that I let him make the decisions and depended on him too much. Now he just thinks it is his right to run things, and, of course, he thinks his ways are the best."

Colonel Shaw stopped to sip some hot tea and have a cookie. Sadie waited patiently and quietly for him to gather his thoughts. "Now, I am feeling much stronger and more able to take back my status as head of this family and ruler of this house. My wife is stronger, too, and has some eagerness for life again. What a joy that is to see! I can't thank you enough for the sunlight you've brought into this house. I cringe at the thought of where we would be if you had not shown up. We were going down rapidly."

Sadie could not believe what she was hearing. She knew she didn't deserve such praise, but it felt good to know that the Shaw's felt she had done some good in their lives. Tears filled her eyes and threatened to spill over. She wiped them away with a napkin. "Colonel, it is my privilege to be here and to get to know you. Both you and your wife are pure treasures. I wake up every morning with such purpose and joy. It's been a long time since I experienced that feeling of usefulness."

The Colonel wiped a tear away as well in a blustery sort of motion. "Well enough of all this. Whatever you are cooking for us smells heavenly. By the way, Sadie, if there is any time you need to take off and take care of personal business, we can get by for a while. You just have to promise to come back."

Sadie breathed a deep, lung-filling breath and let it out slowly. "Well, actually you are very astute to recognize that I need to do that very thing. I need to go back home to visit my children. I want to pick up my cat, Wheezer, and tie up some loose ends. Then I can come back free from that burden. If it is all right with you, I shall plan a trip home by bus or plane, and I will box up some stuff and have it shipped back here. Then I'll bring my beloved cat home on the bus with me. You can rest assured that I will be so anxious to get back to my little cottage and to you and Victoria. I will not let you down."

"I know you won't. However, I must insist that you fly there and back so that you not waste so much time on the road. That cat wouldn't appreciate it anyway. And this way we shall have you home a few days sooner. Take as long as you like there with your children. I know they must miss you so much. I shall give you my credit card for purchasing the tickets as you see fit. I trust you completely, Sadie." When he saw that she was beginning to protest he added, "Now, I'll not have you saying a word about it. No thank-you is necessary and no payback either. This is your bonus, okay?"

"You will never know how much this trust and generosity mean to me. I will get Peter and Cherie to come and check up on you. I'll get some food made ahead of time for you to just thaw out and warm up."

"Don't worry about cooking extra food for us. Just get us some of those newfangled frozen entrees that I see advertised. I can open up a can of soup with the best of them, and boil an egg and make toast. We will be fine for a while. When do you think you will be going?" he seemed reluctant to ask.

"Well, now that I know I have your blessing in this, and that I have the means to accomplish it, I shall go as soon as I can arrange for the tickets and for my children to gather together to be with me. Soon I hope." Sadie was revved up with plans and felt a need to hurry. Until then she had been pushing aside the fact that she was homesick for her children. Now all that nostalgic feeling came flooding back. She needed to go now.

Chapter 22

The Trip Home

As soon as possible Sadie cast aside all fear of her location being discovered, and phoned Becky to make plans. Rebecca cried out in happy surprise and started making marks on her calendar. "How long can you stay, Mom? Do you want me to go get some of your things and box them up from the house? I can pick out what I think you might want in the clothes closet and drawers. Just name anything else you want that is personal and important to you. I'll tell Dad I am boxing up some things to send your way whenever you give me an address. It is true in a way. At least I will be boxing things up for shipping to you."

Sadie was filled with warm gratitude at her daughter's eagerness to please her and help her. "Yes, darling, go and pack up what I need, but not too much. I have just realized how wonderful it is to have less. It is so uncluttered and simple. Feng Shui and all that, you know! Choose about four church outfits, but not the really elegant ones. No need for that here. If your dad agrees, we can just put the rest of them out for charity or give them to the church clothes closet. A couple of pairs of sturdy, dressy heels will do. Please include my good coat and another jacket. I'd like to have my white nightgowns and underwear will always be useful. I'd like that precious, little Angel of Freedom that stands on my dresser—the one with the little caged bird ready to fly away. I love that. My digital clock you gave me for Christmas would be nice. Take the jewelry and keep it for yourself. I have no need for it. I left my wedding ring on Dad's dresser when I left."

A little sob broke from her and she quickly stifled it regaining her poise. "I'll take the albums of pictures of all you kids growing up. I need those. Grab some of my favorite books. You know the ones I like the best. They are all gathered together next to my desk. Take the rest of my horde of books and give them to the library. Whatever I need to read I'll get from the library in my town."

"Mom, are you ever going to tell me where you are living?" Rebecca asked.

"Yes dear, when we are all together I shall give you my address so that you can come see me anytime you desire. It will be such a joy to welcome you to my little home anytime you can make it here."

"Mom, give me the number there. Then just hang up and hang on a moment. Wait for me to call you back. I'm going to call my brothers and find out the best possible time for them to come, so that you can see us all when you get here. We can pick you up at the airport. You are flying in, aren't you? It will be so good to hug you again."

"Yes, indeed, I am flying there. The colonel insisted that I not take a bus."

"Oh I am so pleased to hear that. Now, give me the phone number and hang up and wait, okay?" Rebecca ordered.

"Yes ma'am. I will not move from here and hopefully no one will need to use the phone. Keep calling though if the line is busy. I'll be here." Sadie gave the number to Becky and hung up. What a pleasure it was to hear the joyous expectation in Becky's voice. She sounded like a kid waiting for Christmas morning.

It took about 20 minutes of waiting and the phone finally rang. Sadie lunged for the receiver like she was grabbing for a lifeline. "Hello? Becky? What did you figure out?"

The plans were all made. She would be flying out a week from Thursday from Asheville. The plane would leave at 7:00 in the morning and fly west to get there at 3:00 with a stopover in Dallas a couple of hours. The stop and delay couldn't be helped. Peter agreed to drive her to the airport in the Shaw's big Lincoln. The Colonel had insisted they use it instead of the blue pickup.

Pete got the car out of the garage, washed it, checked it all over and s took it for a test drive. It just needed the engine turned over and the oil changed and it was ready to go.

Her two sons, Andrew and Matthew, would be there by the time she arrived. They would be flying in from their separate areas and would arrive at the airport at times close enough that Becky could pick both of them up in one trip. Then, later, Becky would come and get her when she arrived. Sadie's heart was just a'flutter thinking of that reunion. How long had it been since they were all together under one roof? It would be close to Thanksgiving so they would have a traditional big feast.

She would sleep in her grandson's room on his twin bed and he would sleep on the floor next to her. The boys would sleep on the sofas in the living room and family room. Sadie wondered at how her big independent sons would arrange to see their dad while they were there. It was not her concern. She wanted them to continue to have at least some sort of relationship with their dad, even though both Andy and Matt had already chosen a life's path far away from their father.

She wondered if Anthony even missed the relationship he could have had with his sons. She doubted it.

She offered Peter the option of staying in her cottage while she was gone so he could be close by in case the Shaw's needed him. Surprisingly, he accepted. She knew he would be there to pick her up at the airport in Asheville a week later, the following Thursday, at 7:00 at night. Already she was looking forward to that trip home. *Home,* yes, it had become just that to her.

Irrepressible joy flooded her as she walked off the plane through the entryway and saw Treat running up to her. She dropped her carry-on bag and purse and scooped her beloved grandson into her arms. "Oh, man, you are getting heavy," she remarked as she kissed him all over his head hugging him so tight that he squealed in protest. She could not get enough of looking at him. People were impatiently trying to get around her and her abandoned mess on the floor. She apologized and gathered it all up

By this time, her daughter and sons were surrounding her and she was nearly smothered with hugs and kisses. She could not stop the tears from flowing. She could not even speak she was so shaken and full of emotion. They sat down on the waiting room seats and just held hands. Treat was in her lap, Becky by her side and Matt and Andy were squatting down in front of her.

"Oh, Mom, it is so good to see you. You look great! Where have you been—Cancun?" It was Matt teasing her.

"Mom, it's true you look even younger than the last time I saw you," Andy said. "Something must be agreeing with you. I can't wait till you tell us the whole story. It will take us 25 minutes to get back to Becky's house. I think we should just head straight there and not stop at a restaurant or anyplace. We are all too eager to talk to you. Are you too hungry to wait?" Andy inquired.

"Oh, my wonderful children, eating is the farthest thing from my mind right now. Let's get out of here and start this week of reunion right now."

"Besides that, I have a lasagna in the oven and the oven will be turning on in just 20 minutes," Becky said, looking at her watch.

"I'll run and get your bags off the turnstile. What do they look like?" offered Matt.

"Matt, this carry-on bag is all I brought. I don't have much so this is all I needed to bring. Let's just go." She stood and hugged them all again. She held each one tightly, lingering with each one. How precious her children were to her.

As they passed through the automatic doors into the outside air, a member of the church was entering the airport and walked pass them. "Oh Sadie, it's you. You're back! How we've missed you! You look marvelous. Can't wait to talk to you. I'll be back in two weeks. Save some time for me."

Sadie just looked shocked and stood trembling as the woman rushed into the airport. Her hand went to her mouth and she stood staring after the woman.

"It's okay, Mom," Becky said with an arm around her. "You'll be gone before she returns. Hopefully, word won't get around that you are home, uh . . . here, and you can have some peace."

Becky's home was small but neat and warm. Wheezer ran up to Sadie and purred and snuggled next to her on the overstuffed easy chair. Treat wanted to occupy the other side of his grandmother. She cuddled them both close. On the way home she had told them all about what happened to her when she decided to cut and run. She told them the truth from beginning to end. She did not try to make herself into the innocent victim. She wanted her children to know who she really was. No excuses were offered and none required.

She told them about how tangibly the Lord had been in her life from the moment she boarded that bus for North Carolina. She told them where she was living and described her circumstances. They all just sat silently and listened to her tale. She knew questions and advice were coming, but right now it was just nice to sip a cup of hot tea with honey and love on her cat and grandson. How she had missed them. Becky had lasagna bubbling in the oven and a loaf of crusty bread staying warm on top of the stove. Salads were already on the table and iced tea waiting. She had taught her daughter well. Suddenly she was really famished.

She recalled seeing a neat stack of boxes along the wall of the garage. She asked, "Becky, are those boxes in the garage my things?"

"Yes, Mother, they are. Dad was off at a meeting last weekend and I told him I was coming to get some of your things and he didn't protest. He still doesn't know you are coming here. Do you plan to meet with him at all?"

"I'll just have to see about that as the days go on. Does he come here often to see Treat and visit with you?" she asked.

"Not to worry there. Once a month he calls to ask Treat and me to go to breakfast with him. But that is about all there is. I tried for a while to invite him to Sunday dinner, but he mostly declines. He says he has too many offers from church members to take him out and eat somewhere after church, and he cannot say no to them. It's okay though, 'cause Stan can't really abide him for long."

"Do you boys talk to him much on the phone or ever make plans to come visit him?" Sadie inquired.

"Now, Mom," Andy replied, "don't you go planting a guilt trip on us. You know how we stand with Dad. We are a big disappointment to him. Neither one of us chose the religious fields he wanted for us. I am running a couple restaurants that have bars in them, and you know what he thinks about that. So, he surely is not coming to visit me."

Matt added his story. "As for me, I am way too busy finishing up my internship at the hospital to have time for anyone. I'm just lucky someone covered for me this week. It is like a miracle that I got off for this short time. Things will settle down whenever I get into a regular practice, but that will be a couple of years from now," offered Matt. "Besides that, Dad and I are not comfortable talking together. I still have deep resentments about how he chose everyone else over us as we were growing up. I nearly went off the deep end, and in my rebellion, I nearly crossed the line to incarceration. I'm certainly glad I came to my senses and grew up enough to choose something good to put my energies into."

"Man, what a speech. You sure you're not a preacher after all?" Andy teased his brother, grabbing his head and rubbing the top of his skull. They exchanged mock sparring and laughed.

"Okay then, that is the last you'll hear from me for this week," Matt pretended.

"No such luck, I'm sure," replied Andy. Laughter again. "I really think it would be better if Matt and I just kept a low profile this weekend and saw Dad another time. Do you agree?" Andy asked hopefully.

"Well, that is entirely up to you two. When it comes to your relationship with your dad, I've had a hand's off principle with you two for a long time now. You are both adults and can do whatever you choose. I understand any bitterness you may be feeling, believe me. But he is still your dad and I don't want what happened to us to affect your relationship with him, if you can still manage to have one. Someday he is going to turn around and need family. When that time comes and that need hits him, I hope it won't be too late. As much as I do not plan to be there for him, I hope he doesn't end up sad and lonely as an old man."

They ate the delicious meal. Stan arrived home late and greeted her warmly. He sat down to a late dinner and they all joined him gathering around the table again for dessert and coffee. Sadie was so relieved to finally get into bed and settle down to sleep. Treat was beside her on a thick soft pallet on the floor. It all seemed like a big adventure to him. She held his hand as they lay side by side until she could feel that he had fallen asleep. Wheezer was purring loudly at her side. She felt safe and loved.

As she lay there, she prayed to the Lord, *"Dear God in heaven, why are you so good to me? I know in my heart I do not deserve any of the many blessings I enjoy. Today has been such a good day. To be surrounded by my children and feel the love of them and my grandson; it is nearly too much to take in. Please, Lord, be with me during this week and help me to face whatever lies in my path with grace and dignity. Protect me from evil and hurt and help me to be a blessing to those I am with. Put the right words in my mouth and the right actions in my doings. Above all else, I want to make You glad in me and I want to be a blessing and honor to Your name."*

With those words spoken in her mind, Sadie drew the covers around her chin and turned onto her side, and fell deeply into sweet sleep.

The week flew by. Sadie basked in the love and fellowship of her children. Laughter seemed to raise the roof. Sadie shipped off the boxes by UPS to Rose Creek. She called there to tell the Colonel that her things were arriving and to have them placed in the cottage for her return. They all went to a good movie, sneaking in popcorn and cokes and candy bars. All this brought back good memories of raising her children.

She loved hearing all about Andy's restaurants and how people in the town knew Andy's name and respected him. He was determined to provide for his customers memorable times of eating out: good atmosphere and terrific food; friendly and excellent service. Andy always remembered names and treated everyone special. It had been rare for Sadie to fly out and see her son, the chef. But oh, how she loved being treated like royalty every time she ate in his restaurant. He would brag to the customers that this and that on the menu was his mom's recipe. It wasn't. It was so much better than hers, but it was nice to be recognized that way.

Sadie was proud of Matt, too. He had worked so hard to become a doctor. His specialty was going to be putting broken people back together again, resetting broken bones, cracked elbows, popped tendons and pulled and torn ligaments. He was usually so exhausted from hours and hours of being on duty as an intern, that this week at Becky's was mostly spent napping and snoring in a comfy recliner. Good color returned to his cheeks as he rested so deeply.

Sadie tried to imagine what it would be like to live in the same town with all her children. She kept reminding herself that families normally were scattered and just got together for special occasions. But, oh, it would be so wonderful to be within driving distance of each other. This long distance visiting was hard, but she would have to make the most of the precious time she had with them.

When they were younger and at home she had always made sure that at least once a week she spent time with each one alone. Whether it was for a walk, or a bike ride, going to get a hamburger or just lying in bed reading a story. Sadie had always realized how important 'one-on-one' time was to her children. She got the chance to listen and to encourage each in turn and to talk to them about their dreams hopes, and their relationships with friends. She remembered talking to Andy about his future as a chef. Andy was just sure that he would never marry, for his job took so much time and evenings were the busiest time for him. He had some girlfriends that he dated, but nothing serious going on there.

"I guess I'll just never get married, Mom. Who would want this life?"

"Never say never, Andy! Someday you may find just the right girl and fall for her like a ton of bricks. If she knows what she is getting into, she will adjust her life and expectations to suit your job. You'll work it out. Nothing is impossible," Sadie offered hopefully.

Matt had pretty much fallen for a nurse from the hospital where he worked. She was smart and comical and committed to medicine, just like him. Marriage, as yet, was not talked about. Time would tell how things worked out. Sadie was just happy for him and even though she knew he was exhausted so much of the time, she could tell he loved what he was doing and would have it no other way.

Chapter 23

Confrontation

Two days before she was scheduled to fly back to North Carolina, the doorbell rang. Sadie, seeing that Rebecca was busy in the kitchen, went to the door. Her heart nearly stopped when she saw who it was. Anthony stood before her all spiffy in a tailored, wheat colored, sports coat and chocolate colored slacks. He looked handsome as ever. His eyes bored into hers letting her know that he knew she was there and that he had come to see her. She stepped back and let him into the house.

"Well, I waited long enough and finally decided that you really were going to come all this way and not see me. Am I right?" he asked impatiently.

"Right as rain," Sadie replied unapologetically.

"Do you really hate me that much, Sadie? You run off without a word, not telling me where you've gone or what you are doing. I'm worried sick and don't have a clue what to tell the parishioners or deacons. The house is so lonely and empty. Have you lost your mind, woman? What do you think this looks like to the church? A pastor without a wife. How selfish can you be?" Anthony stood with his chest heaving and his cheeks all puffed out and red.

About this time her sons came rushing into the room and stood beside her. "Hold on a minute, Dad," chided Andy. "Don't you come in here accusing our mother of hurting you! You hypocrite! How dare you bawl her out?"

"Oh I expected as much! You two boys have been Mama's boys for so long now. Here you are sneaking into town behind my back to commiserate with your poor, hurt mother and to stand against me, your father!"

Sadie placed her hands on Andy's arm. "Boys! Wait! I appreciate you running to my defense, but you know what? I think I can handle this one on my own. Why don't you both give me just a few minutes alone with your father? One thing I really don't want here is to create an ugly scene where everyone is accusing everyone else. There's no need for that. Can you two just let me talk to him for a little while?" Sadie requested.

With serious stares at their father, full of warning, Matt and Andy retreated. Becky, who was standing in the kitchen doorway, pulled back too.

"Okay, Sadie, let's hear it. This ought to be good. Did you have some other guy waiting in the wings beside poor Jacob? He's still recovering from your affair with him. The music program has suffered poorly from his lack of concentration. We are doing our best to pull him through this terrible time."

Sadie walked to the easy chair and sat down. She crossed her arms in front of her and settled down, taking her time to answer. Anthony stood in the middle of the room like a raging Viking. He liked being tall and towering over her. "If you are going to talk to me, Tony, you will sit and get down to my level."

"I will never stoop to your level, wife. You've gone just as low as you can get."

But he sat finally, putting both fists on his thighs and bending forward menacingly.

"Tony, let me first tell you that I am sorry to have hurt you by doing this."

A satisfied smirk came over his face and a look of pending victory washed over him. He bobbed his head and chuckled. "I knew you would come to your senses. You've embarrassed me big time; but if you try very hard, I think we might be able to work things out."

"Anthony!! I want you to . . . . well . . . . shut up for a minute!" Sadie spoke firmly and softly.

Her husband gasped a bit and sat straight up with his eyes wide in surprise.

"Since I left you, which by the way took great courage and greater wisdom, I have felt so happy and free. I forgot how wonderful freedom feels. I am no longer burdened down by your stifling, non-caring presence. I should have left you years ago, but I suppose I was buying in to all the propaganda I'd heard over the years in your church. A marriage was sacred and a woman had to bend to the will of her husband and not question him or kick against the pricks. Oh that is a funny word."

"How dare you . . . . ," Anthony started and she quickly held up her hand to shush him and say her piece.

"Anthony, you have spent years and years building up your own self-esteem and your place in this church. You are adored and admired, and I truly believe that is enough for you. Having a family was just part of the package. It presented a lovely picture of consistency and normalcy. It was what the church expected, but truthfully, I'm convinced that deep down in your heart you couldn't have cared less about us. All these lonely years I tried to get you to see what we all needed from you, but it was no use. Your own children ran far away from you and your coldness." Sadie stopped to take a breath and wipe her eyes that were getting moist.

Tony, seeing his opening, jumped in, "Oh yeah, here we go again. Whine, whine, whine! 'You don't give me enough attention. I'm lonely. Don't you care about us? Whah, whah, whah!' Give me a break! I'm a pastor, for crying out loud. I'm God's man for the season. My main focus had to be on God's people. A pastor's wife should understand that and be able to sacrifice her own needs and wants for the good of the Lord's work. You never did learn that truth."

Sadie lowered her head and shook it slowly back and forth. Her mouth was in a grim, tight bite. Tony, seeing what he interpreted as cowering, stood up and came close to her, empowered by his dominance over her.

"Tony," she replied calmly, "just once, could you yield the floor and let me say my piece? Please give me that much respect. It won't take too much of your time I assure you."

Anthony sighed heavily and looked up to the ceiling as if he were sorely impatient to get through this muddle. He blew out his cheeks and shook his head. Then he sat down in the nearest easy chair and folded his arms in front of him, cocking his head in an arrogant way as if to say, "I'm listening, get on with it!"

Sadie continued, "When I finally turned to the loving nature of Jacob and felt happiness in his attentions, you were outraged and turned on me. You never once thought of standing up for me, your wife, against the false accusations of your deacon board. You let them assume I was an adulterous wife. I think you knew that I never let things go that far. Sure, it was wrong for me to even show affection for Jacob. I've repented of that and the Lord has forgiven me completely. I think I was so thirsty for love that I just abandoned my good sense of propriety. If it makes you feel more justified in divorcing me and starting over, then go ahead and accuse me of whatever you want. I won't protest; because in my heart, I will know the truth of who I am. You can't hurt me anymore."

Tony leaned way forward and glowered at her. "You want to know what *I* think? I think you are not a Christian after all. I've been reading in the Bible how God allows men to cast aside their wives if those wives have turned to other men and were not saved in the first place. I do believe that you are not, nor were you ever, a Christian." Anthony spat out.

Sadie stifled a laugh. "Well, well. There you go. You figured it out all by yourself, didn't you? Now you can be free too. That's wonderful. Now you are free to pick and choose someone else to stand beside you. The church will think how brave you were to go through such hell with your cheating wife, the pagan. It works out so neatly. Who cares that my reputation goes down the toilet as long as yours ascends to the heights," Sadie paused and looked upward raising her right arm in a dramatic gesture.

"You brought this all on yourself, Lady Sadie. I can't help what people will think of you. It is important that the church not be brought down with you."

Then she smiled a satisfied and peaceful smile and stood up. She looked down on her husband and said sincerely, "Good enough! You do what you have to do to settle into a new life without me. I won't protest or take you to court. I won't even ask for anything more than the personal stuff that I have shipped out of here. There are some really precious things in that house that we gathered up over these past 32 years. You can have them all. No, I take that back. I will request that you give me all the quilts that I've collected and sewn over the years. The rest of it I don't care if I ever see again. It would just remind me of you anyway. And above all, you poor deluded man, I will be happy to never see you again."

With that, Sadie walked out of the room. Her sons were waiting in the hallway, having heard her every word. They gave her a big hug and Becky was sobbing and drew her into her arms.

The boys ushered their dad out the door. Matt said to him, "I will be by the house this evening to get those quilts for Mom. I'm sure you have a meeting to attend or a class to teach, so just leave them inside by the front door and I will let myself in and get them. You know what, Dad, you never even asked what her life is like now, nor what she is doing. You'd be so surprised to learn of the fine life she has made for herself. You've never deserved her. I just wish she hadn't wasted so many years on you." With that Matt shut the door in the stunned face of his father. He shut it slowly but firmly.

Anthony Golden walked slowly to his car. He sat in the car for a good long time and then started it up, and drove away.

Sadie sat at the kitchen table with her head in her hands. The dreaded confrontation was over. Sadie had known in her heart that she would have to face him one time or another. She was so relieved it was over, that she broke down and sobbed and sobbed. She cried for all the wasted years of trying to reach out to him. She cried for her failure. She cried at the shame that would follow her name. She cried with feelings of letdown and relief.

Her grandson, Treat, came and put his arm around her neck and said, "It's going to be alright, Grams. You'll be okay, you'll see." With that she hugged him fiercely and excused herself to go to the bedroom and cry some more. Shutting the door, she fell to her knees and could not utter any words. But she prayed, nevertheless—the Spirit prayed for her. She cried out her sorrow and her failure and her disappointment. She cried for joy at the thought of her wonderful, supportive children. After a while she laid her face on the damp covers and fell asleep kneeling there before the Lord. Her sons came in and lifted her onto the bed, covered her up and turned out the light.

She slept like the dead that night, not even moving. The warm morning sunlight streamed in the window and lay gently on her face like a kiss. She felt emptied out and lighter. Stacked along the wall, also on the dresser and the chair were her quilts. They were neatly folded; their colors so vibrant and well-placed and cheerful. She smiled to see them and ran her hands over each one like a treasure long lost and now found.

She could smell the scrambled eggs, toast and bacon cooking. The fragrance of the fresh coffee filled her with resolve. She was done with mourning. Life was new to her now. She washed her face in the bathroom and combed her tousled hair. When she walked into the kitchen, she was greeted by all her children. In unison they stood up to hug her and seat her at the table like a revered guest. She ate ravenously. She hadn't realized how starved she was. Everything tasted so delicious. It nourished her body and soul.

"My dear children," she started, "I'm going back home. Yes, I said home, because my little cottage is now my home. I welcome you to it when you can come. I think you will like it a lot. My heart will be lonely for you until I see you again. How I love you all, more than you could ever imagine. You three and Treat are the only treasures I come away with from this marriage. I would have endured it all again just to have you four. You are my joy. I'm so very proud of every one of you."

Sadie stifled a sob coming up. "No more tears. I'm done with tears!" she exclaimed. "I will call today and confirm my reservations for the trip back. Old Wheezer will ride in the cargo hold in his cat carrier. He'll be fine. Won't like it one bit, but he'll get over it."

Matt and Andy admitted that they, too, were ready to get back to their positions of responsibility. They were planning to leave the next morning. Sadie could see that they were anxious to resume their exciting lives.

That night the whole family ate at a fine restaurant in town. Andy knew just what to order, and he picked up the bill and left a generous tip. They saw several members of the church glancing over furtively at Sadie and whispering. Sadie put up mental blinders and just enjoyed herself immensely and carelessly. She laughed and proclaimed the meal the finest yet. She walked out holding her head high and waving to some of the curious church people, like she had nothing for which to be ashamed.

Chapter 24

Rose Creek Looks Good

The airport personnel took the protesting old Wheezer and secured him below deck. Sadie was assured by the baggage handler that he would be fine there in the nether regions of the plane. He would be very safe and his protestations would not kill him. Nevertheless, Sadie had given the cat half of a tranquilizer to calm him down for the trip. All the goodbyes had been said, over and over. Becky cried to see her mother leave, but promised that she and Treat and maybe Stan, if he could get away, would come and see her in a few months. Maybe around Christmas break.

Flying home, high in the sky, tucked in by a window, Sadie contemplated everything about her life. The fluffy clouds were right below her as the plane flew high and fast. She talked with the Lord, praising Him and thanking Him over and over for forgiveness and for how things had worked out. She could almost see the tapestry of her life being woven into a wonderful story. *I just want to make you happy Lord. I want to be of service to your kingdom. Whatever it is you want from me, just make it plain and guide me. I'm ready to do it all.*

Sadie felt so happy to see Pete waiting for her at the gate where the plane landed. He had on a fresh denim shirt and jeans. His jacket was clean too. He was clean-shaven and even smelled of Old Spice. She patted his arm and thanked him for coming. The Colonel had insisted that he again take the big black Cadillac to pick up Sadie. As he started the purring motor and pulled away from the curb, the warm air coming from the heater felt so comforting.

All the way home to Rose Creek, Peter talked nonstop about what was going on there on the homefront. The yardwork was coming along just fine. There was too much shade to grow anything decently. He was going to talk to the Colonel about culling out some of the big trees and most of the smaller ones to give more space for sunshine to come through. The Colonel could even sell the timber that was cut down on the acreage. He imagined a pretty good sum would come from that. There would be enough to pay for the tree cutting service and even the renovation of the garden.

Winter was just around the corner anyway, so why bother much with planting until spring? He'd get the beds ready anyway. The Colonel and Victoria had done their best to take care of things while Sadie was gone. Even Mrs. Fortenbrau had pitched in and tried to cook some for them. The kitchen still smelled of burnt food clinging to the burners.

Wheezer's tranquilizer had worn off and he was not a happy cat. Cages were not among his favorite things. "How do you like my cat, Pete?" asked Sadie. She hadn't had a chance to get in a word edgewise, and it tickled her to see Pete so animated.

"Well, he's a bruiser, that's for sure. I don't think I've ever seen such a big cat. He will sure be happy to be out and about in that big yard. What a kingdom he will have all to himself!"

"Tell me, Pete, have there been many visits by the Colonel's son, Stephen?" she ventured hesitantly. The thought of that bully of a son, made her cringe.

"Yes, he's been around some. I heard him bellowing about something or other one day. He seems like he's a surefire pain in the . . . . Oh sorry, didn't mean to say that; but he doesn't act like a very respectful son in my book."

"Well, you pegged him right, Pete. I just hope I have the courage to stand up to him and help him see how unfair he treats his folks. It really is none of my business, but all my life I've hated injustice. When I see it I just have to jump in there and do something about it. It will be my undoing someday, I fear." Sadie sighed and reached in the cage to pet the cat. He rewarded her with a hiss and then a wild meow!!!

Peter drove her to her door and unloaded the luggage and cat. He said his goodbyes, parked the big black car, and left for his own home. Her little cottage looked so good. She placed her carryon bag inside the door and let Wheezer out in the living room to begin his exploration of every crevice and cranny. She was glad she'd thought to set up a litter box in one corner so that Wheezer could adjust comfortably in her house until she felt secure enough with his familiarity of the place to let him outside. Then that litter box would go. Hurrying to the kitchen she fixed the cat a plate of food and a bowl of water. She looked around appreciatively, then quickly retreated out the door to head for the big house and the Shaw's. She needed to check in with the colonel and Victoria. She knew they must be anxious to be affirmed of her return. She let herself in and put some hot water on for tea. The kitchen was cleaned up somewhat with only a few dishes in the sink and crumbs on the tabletop. She smiled at the bread wrapper partially open and the eggs still on the counter in their carton. The garbage can was pretty full. She would deal with all that later. She walked through the dining room into the hallway and knocked gently on their door.

"Yes?" came the reply. "Who is it? Sadie!! Is that you?"

"It is indeed, Colonel. I just now arrived home. Thanks for letting Peter come get me in that big comfy car."

The door flew open and Colonel Shaw appeared. His face was full of joy, his mouth was gathered in, and head shaking with emotion. "I've never been so glad to see someone in a long, long time! I'm so glad you decided to return to us. We've missed you something terrible," he let the words spill out.

"You needn't have worried one bit about my return. There was no question there. This is my home now. I'm so glad to be here."

The Colonel and Victoria stood close together, their arms wrapped around each other as they smiled at her. Tears were forming in their eyes. It really felt good to Sadie that they actually cared that much.

"I'm making some tea for you. I'll be sure it is decaffeinated, so you won't have to worry about insomnia tonight. I brought you some cookies that my daughter made for me to share with you. Date-nut cookies; it is a famous family recipe. How have you been getting along? I hope everything went okay while I was gone."

"Oh, it went well enough," replied the Colonel. "We have just been so spoiled by your presence and care that we tended to resent your absence. I'm just so glad you are back. I said that already, didn't I?" The Colonel laughed and turned quickly to swipe up a tissue for his tears.

Sadie served their hot tea with lemon and the cookies. She even brought in some half and half and sugar for the tea, serving it English style. It was a night for indulgences and comfort. "Did anything exciting go on while I was away?" she queried.

"Well, old lady Bleu died suddenly. She's the elderly lady who lives across from the café. You know the one who watches Joy," the Colonel revealed. "She just went to sleep and that was it. Nice way to go if you have to depart the premises."

"That's how I want to go, dear; just slip off to sleep and then on to the next world," remarked Victoria.

"Here now, let's not be talking about death, okay? You and I have plenty of more years together yet. We'll think about that when the time comes," he chided.

"I'm sorry to hear Mrs. Bleu died. I wonder what Cherie and Joy are doing for a babysitter now. I'll have to go talk to her in the morning and find out how she is doing." Sadie gathered up the plates and cups, said her goodnight and slipped on out.

Sadie quickly sparkled up the kitchen, dumping the garbage can, doing all the dishes, wiping the table, and getting things ready for tomorrow's breakfast. She let out a big happy sigh as she leaned against the sink and looked around the kitchen. Yes indeed, she felt like she was home here. She called Becky to let her know all was well and that she had arrived with Wheezer, safe and sound. Then she thought, *I'd better get over to the cottage and see about that traumatized old cat. I wonder what is going through his furry mind?*

Chapter 25

Back to Normal

Life returned to its familiar and welcomed routine. The air was getting colder now and tiny specks of sleet and fine snow would fall every once in awhile. Sadie had a fire going most days in her fireplace to ward off the dampness and give her cottage a warm, cozy glow. She had Peter set up fires in the kitchen hearth and in the Shaws quarters every day. He was good to remove the old ashes when they got to be too much. He used those ashes on the prepared garden soil. Wheezer stayed inside for a couple of days, and then Sadie opened the door. He tentatively stuck his head outside and slowly eased out halfway, looking every which way for danger and ready to challenge anything or anyone. His hair stood up on the back of his neck and a low, ominous rumble emitted from his throat. "Knock it off, you crazy cat! You are king here! Not one creature around here could take you on. Get out there and climb a tree . . . explore!" With that she had eased the cat all the way out and shut the screen door. He looked back at her like she had just offended him royally, and then trotted off along the pinestraw path. It wasn't long until Wheezer, too, had his own routine and his own favorite spots to sleep and from which to watch. Every once in awhile he would kill a bird and lay it at her front stoop like a mighty warrior/provider. She always fed him plenty, so this didn't happen often. She never scolded him or punished him for the killing either. This was just nature's way. A cat was a hunter. The bird population was not altered by much. She fed all the birds and squirrels and chipmunks. Even an old groundhog and her baby showed up to dig up roots and eat carrots she had put out for them.

Sadie had found out what Cherie was doing for a babysitter. She was taking Joy to daycare now and the cost of it was using up too much of her earnings. Another solution would have to be discovered soon. Meanwhile Sadie would slip her forty or fifty bucks every once in a while into her mail box. It wasn't much, but every little bit helped. She wondered what Cherry thought and if she surmised where the money was coming from. Good deeds were always so much more satisfying to the giver, if they were intentionally not recognized and thusly not acknowledged.

The boxes arrived that Sadie had packed up from Becky's place. They mostly contained quilts and some clothes and shoes that Becky had retrieved from her closet. She discovered a little radio/CD player that had been tucked in and some of her favorite CDs: barbershop quartets, American Indian flute, guitar, piano, and birdsongs. Now her little cottage was filled with sweet sounds.

Chapter 26

The Gift of Quilts

Pete showed Sadie all his work on the huge property from wall-to-wall and corner-to-corner. "These high walls just keep out so much sunlight that it is dark and gloomy here, and lovely flowers like roses and such cannot flourish. Being inside here is like being in a prison," he offered with authority. "I wish these walls were gone!"

An idea began to form in Sadie's mind. Just the thought of such an undertaking was dumbfounding and she shook her head to try to clear out the proposition. "Yes, I know what you mean, Pete. Why ever did they build this wall in the first place? Maybe one of the ancestors was just unfriendly and hated people gawking into their area. I don't know. But it surely doesn't seem very friendly to be so shut away like this from the neighborhood. All of your efforts in fixing up this acreage should be appreciated and enjoyed by all the people around here."

This compliment struck home to Peter and he beamed and ducked his head. It was always nice to have your work affirmed by an appreciative word now and again.

"Pete, is it okay if I ask you how you are doing? Are you enjoying your work here, or are you longing for any previous work and connections? You are a very smart cookie, I can sure tell that. I would hate to lose your company and help around here, but if you chose to move on to bigger, and better things, I would surely understand," Sadie reluctantly inquired.

"First, you tell me how great I'm doing and then you try to get rid of me!" Pete joked. "Yeah, I know I could be doing more noteworthy things and could be earning lots of money working, as I use to, in stocks and bonds, etc. But the truth is I've never been more satisfied with work as I am right now. I really do want to stay awhile longer, if that's okay with you," he added sarcastically.

118

"It is more than okay . . . . it is wonderful!" she excitedly proclaimed. "One more thing. Can I please ask where you are living now? You are not still under the bridge are you? I just cannot think of you there without feeling bad."

"No, I'm not under the bridge anymore. With what you pay me, I've rented a little furnished house in the black section of town. I like it there. The folk there are fine to me and they mostly leave me be, but they speak friendly to me when the occasion warrants it. With all the meals you make me, I don't have to cook much, nor buy groceries hardly at all. I walk everywhere I go, unless I'm using the blue pickup to do chores. So all in all I have very few expenses. As a matter of fact, I'm even saving a good bundle."

Sadie knew she had exhausted her right to ask any more questions and so she left it at that. But she was thinking, *I wonder if he has a family somewhere that has given up on him. I wonder if he misses them and his folks. I wonder if he ever plans to go back to them and take up where he left off, or if he'd even have that option.*

"I'm so glad to hear you are sheltered now and doing well. I feel like you were an answer to prayer for these people and for me."

Pete's eyes got big as he stared at her in wonder. "No one's ever described me as an answer to prayer. I'll have to chew on that one awhile."

As they walked back toward the cottage, Sadie said, "Pete, will you allow me to give you something? Please say yes. It didn't cost me anything but time and that was a long ago time. I'd love for you to take a couple of my handmade quilts to use on your bed. What do you say? Will you accept that from me?"

Peter just stared at her with his mouth open. Words would not come to him easily. Finally he slowly attempted to answer her. "As a matter of fact, I could use some warm blankets. The nights are getting a bit nippy." He continued, "Do you have enough to spare me a couple? I'd love to have them," he blurted out. "I've always been a sucker for quilts. Reminds me of when I was a little boy and used to sleep at my grandma's house. Those beds were piled high with quilts." Peter was surprised at his words just spilling out in a quick bunch like that. He was not used to revealing himself in this way. He shut his mouth tightly.

Sadie rushed inside and picked out two heavy, thick quilts of dark hues and reds. They were manly quilts and looked like they belonged in a log cabin. Carrying the quilts in her arms, she walked to Pete. "I have plenty of quilts and will probably be making more as the years go by. These ought to keep you plenty warm this winter."

"May I keep them in the back porch until I leave today? I don't want them to get dusty or rained on. These are going to make my little house look like a home. Thanks!" Peter held the quilts in his arms and looked appreciatively at the fine stitching and colorful patterns. He knew that each quilt represented hours and hours of tedious work. Time was a treasure and these quilts represented a great deal of it. He truly felt rich.

Sadie took them back and promised to put them in a big plastic garbage bag and set it on her back porch. *That Pete! He's a complicated character, and he is slowly peeling away the armor that protects his identity. Maybe I'll get to know him after all. God be with him and help him,* she prayed silently.

As much as Sadie loved her quilts, she wanted to give them to people who would appreciate them. Her three kids had all they could use. s She'd already bestowed on them the ones she had made especially for them. She knew that she could only use three or four. One was thrown on the back of the couch to be used for naps and reading by the light of a cozy lamp. Two for her bed and one extra for just . . . whatever.

So, she chose a really nice one that was feminine and pastel-looking and gave it to Victoria. One would have thought that she had just handed the old lady the moon. She gasped and clapped her hands and reached for it hungrily. "Oh, I just love quilts. My grandmother had them. My mother wanted fancier stuff and would not allow me to have any when I was growing up. I wish I had learned to make quilts, but I never did. I have some of my grandmother's quilts upstairs, but they are getting old and I'm afraid to use most of them for fear of them falling apart."

"I had been using a couple I found upstairs. They must be two of the newer ones. They didn't appear to be so fragile. I will return them upstairs since now I know how precious they are to you," Sadie admitted.

"Don't be silly. Some of those were purchased quilts I bought at fairs and such. They are lovely to look at, but hold no real sentimental value. Not like this one. To think that it is handmade, stitch-by-stitch with your very own hands. This represents so much work. I feel so privileged to have it. Can you help me put it on my bed?" Victoria requested eagerly.

"With great pleasure, dear lady. Your creamy bedspread looks so nice that maybe we can fold it up and lay at the foot of the bed. What do you think?"

"Well, you may be right. However, I do plan to spread it out each night and enjoy it's warmth and cheeriness. Thank you again, Sadie. I love it."

Sadie gave two quilts to Cherie and Joy. They were ones with rainbows of color and fun designs. Once again the gift of those quilts caused a real stir of emotion. Cherie cried tears of delight. Sadie was wondering if she was thinking about the lack of a mom's care for her and longing for more. It felt good to have her handiwork appreciated so much by those that she was coming to love.

Chapter 27

The Secret Room

One morning during mid-December, Sadie was preparing the entrance hall with a tall, fragrant North Carolina spruce. She had dug out the ornaments from the attic and was busy draping strings of colored wooden balls and lights on the branches. She had warned herself to be very careful on the ladder as she reached up and around. Gladys was on the ground helping her wind the strings of lights around the tree from top to bottom. The smell of the fresh green tree was intoxicating. Sadie breathed deeply into her lungs. "Ahhh, I just love Christmas, Gladys," she exclaimed.

"Silly to go to this much here trouble, if you ask me. Just a lot of work for only a few days. And who's going to enjoy it besides you, me and the old folk in there?"

"Gladys, do you have any idea where that little door in the bedroom upstairs goes to? That big armoire was in front of it hiding it. There was a secret sliding door in the back of the chifforobe that led to it. Someone was trying to keep whatever is behind there a secret," Sadie pondered.

"I don't have no idea what it goes to. The reg'lar attic is by the stairway at the end of the hall. Maybe there is another part of the attic we don't know nothing 'bout and another entrance. Maybe that door just goes to a little closet up thar."

"That is very observant, Gladys," replied Sadie. "Maybe we should look into it. We need to find that key. I've looked in all the drawers and cupboards. Even the Colonel has no idea about that door or where the key might be. Let's you and I be diligent to be on the lookout for it, okay?"

"Or . . . if you don't mind spending the money . . . you could just call a locksmith and have him open it," came Gladys's quiet retort.

Sadie got off the ladder and went to the crusty old housekeeper and hugged her tightly. "What a great idea, lady! Why waste time wondering and looking for that key? It couldn't cost too much to solve the puzzle right away." She planted a big kiss on the woman's cheek and went to find the telephone book. Gladys just stood there with her mouth open and her hand to her cheek. The slight start of a smile began forming and then she rubbed her cheek with her apron and commenced to finish the tree decorating.

The locksmith didn't come until the next day. By that time, the front foyer was completely decorated for Christmas. The fragrance of that pine tree filled the area near the front door and welcomed anyone coming in with its promise of a delightful, forthcoming holiday.

The Colonel came upstairs with Sadie and the locksmith to watch as the little man with his tools worked to open that door. "Sure is rusty and hard to turn," he complained.

Finally the door came loose as the lock tumbled open. The smell of stale air, mice droppings and dry mustiness assaulted their nostrils. The locksmith looked curiously up the narrow stairs.

"Thank you for coming, Mr. Robinson. You are swift and accurate. How much do I owe you?" questioned Colonel Shaw.

The locksmith looked very disappointed that he was being dismissed before he found out the end to this mystery. He sighed heavily and put his tools away. "I reckon $20 will cover it," he said.

The Colonel pulled out a twenty and a five and handed it to him. "A man's time and effort are worth a lot. You were quick to respond to my call for help. I'll be recommending you to others, that's for certain."

The old locksmith seemed reasonably satisfied with this, and picked up his toolbox and headed out into the hallway. "I'll just let myself out, if that's okay?" he replied.

Everett and Sadie waited until they heard the workman walk down the stairs and shut the front door; then they turned to the darkened entrance to the secret attic room. "This must be civil war air," reasoned the Colonel. "I'm sure it must have been my great-Grandfather Malcolm Shaw who made this room. He was known as a Yankee supporter and refused to have slaves. He was so grieved over the nation being divided like that. I believe he built that big stone wall around the property for fear of reprisals against his family because of his stand on the war."

"Do you know if anyone tried to hurt this house and family?" asked Sadie.

"As far as I know, he was pretty much ostracized for his views on the war. But I do not think anyone came onto this property and tried to destroy or hurt anything. My grandfather hired guards to see that did not happen." The Colonel brushed away cobwebs and put a handkerchief to his nose as he climbed the narrow stairway up to the small attic room. Sadie shone a flashlight up through the dimly lit, dusty room. One smudged dormer window let in some subdued light. It felt as though they were stepping back in time a 150 years. The musty room was ghostly and pungent with age, rodent droppings, and rotted cloth.

The secret attic room was very small. It was obvious from further examination that the main attic had been portioned off with a wooden wall to make this small, separate space. There was a tiny cot, with a thread-worn blanket and pillow. There was an old, kerosene lantern on a short side table. There were two earthen jugs and a plate on the floor with a tarnished silver fork. In the corner was a wooden chest with a lock on it.

"Someone was hidden up here. I can only imagine it was some Yankee soldier that my great-Grandfather Malcolm was protecting. Look here under the bed. It appears to be soiled bandages with dried up blood soaked in. I must surmise that right here deep on Confederate soil, my great-grandfather, being a devoted Union sympathizer, did all he could to help the war effort."

Sadie shined the light all around from attic beams to windows and every inch of the floor. The light of the flashlight finally settled on the wooden chest. It was the size of a small ottoman.

"Do you think we can handle getting that chest downstairs?" asked Colonel Shaw. "We could use a hammer to knock off that rusty lock. Looks pretty feeble to me."

Sadie went over to try to lift the box. It was way too heavy to maneuver. "We're going to need Pete's help to get this, I'm afraid. It must be full of rocks or very heavy journals. It just won't budge much."

Pete had to lower the chest with a heavy rope. He wound the rope around one of the support beams to lower it slowly and with less stress to himself. He placed a narrow sheet of plywood over the stairs and then slowly let the box slip down the stairs. Even Peter could not lift that chest. "If you like, we can just knock off the lock right here and carry out whatever is inside piece-by-piece. What do you think?" offered Peter.

"Sounds like a plan to me," replied the Colonel.

Pete took a crowbar and pried the lock as far as he could. Then he took an old sledgehammer, and as everyone stood back, he began to swing away at that rusty lock. On the third hit, the lock cracked open and fell to the ground. The Colonel painfully lowered himself to the floor on one knee. He pried open the box. All three in the room gasped at the contents. Eight bars of gold lay side by side in the box. Spread on top were some antique official-looking papers. The Colonel struggled with one bar and lifted it onto the carpet. "Dear God, what have we here? My Great Grandfather Malcolm must have been so afraid of the outcome of that war that he put his treasure here for safekeeping. What else could this be?"

Pete removed the other seven bars and laid them all side-by-side. The shine on the gold was still brilliant. He reached into the box and pulled out the documents. His eyes opened wide in excited surprise.

"Colonel Shaw, do you know what these are? These are gold certificates. They are still viable. This one is for 40 ounces of gold and this one is for 75 ounces. Here's one for 34 ounces and one for 102 ounces. There are several more here besides. Your grandfather must have turned in bags of gold little by little and received back these certificates for the weight of gold tendered. These certificates were bought when gold was about $32 an ounce. Now gold is up to $392 an ounce and these certificates can be cashed in for a fortune. These gold bars are 25 pounds a piece and that is an unbelievable fortune." Pete told him.

The Colonel had to sit down and put his head down between his knees. Sadie ran to get a cold wet cloth to hold against the back of his neck. "You sit here and rest and I'm going to get you a hot cup of tea to fortify you right now." She ran down quickly to heat up the water. She poured a couple cups of coffee for Pete and her. When the water was hot she carried a tray of the hot cups upstairs. The Colonel was sitting up by then and Pete was kneeling next to him with his hand on his knee. Sadie could see that the old man was clearly very upset about this turn of events.

He was breathing heavily and his eyes were wide open. "Dear me, what ever am I going to do with all of this gold? I almost wish I'd never found it. Most people would be so thrilled to find something like this, but it just opens up a can of worms for Victoria and me." With trembling hands he carefully took the cup of hot sweet tea that Sadie offered him. They sat and watched him as he drank of it. Sadie knelt down too to comfort the Colonel in this dilemma.

"Excuse me for asking, Colonel, but why is this such a bad thing for you to find this fortune?" Sadie enquired.

Pete added, "Yes, I'm puzzled by your statement too, Colonel. This money could be used for many wonderful things. How could this be such a curse on you?"

The Colonel set his cup down and took a deep breath. "Who is going to lay claim to this money? The relatives will be coming out of the woodwork to stake their claim. The city itself may feel that this is a civil war historical occurrence and that the gold should belong to the city. My son, and this I have no doubt about, will do all he can to have Victoria and me declared unable to manage our own affairs, and he will do what he's been wanting to do for years now; he will declare power-of-attorney for himself and take over my finances and be able to boss us completely. Our lives will not be our own. We will be managed!"

"Colonel Shaw, look at me!" Sadie ordered. "We shall just have to see that that doesn't happen. We will go slowly and not announce to the world that you are a rich man right off the bat. We'll get some legal advice and financial savvy and even go to another city to open up a bank account for you. After you are all prepared and have your plans, then you can inform your family about this fortune. I will fight tooth and nail to keep you and Victoria independent and viable. You must let yourself relax now. Pete, we must move this gold and certificates to some place that is safe and hidden."

Peter looked very serious as he remarked, "Colonel, I know you don't really know me that well. I've been working for you a few months now, but you don't truly know me nor have any reason to trust me. All I can do is assure you with my word that I will do whatever I can to protect your good fortune here. There will not be a word from my lips to anyone that this has been found." Pete stopped talking and bowed his head and shook it back and forth. "If I were you, it would be hard to trust a homeless, indigent man like me. I used to know money, stocks and investments. I used to be very good at it, until my greed took over and I broke the law. I'm admitting this to you because I learned through experience, and that, indeed, is a dear school."

"Peter, please stop explaining yourself to me; it is not necessary," responded Colonel Shaw. "I've watched you work around here. You are dedicated and determined and you take great pride in your job. You go beyond the call of duty and do way more than is asked of you. That is a measure of a good character in my books. I have to trust someone with a matter of this magnitude. I choose to trust you and Sadie. Now what do you have in mind?"

"Colonel, are you sure you want us to handle this for you? Do you not have a trusted friend and colleague whom you can talk to about all this? We don't want anyone saying we hoodwinked you into letting us handle this affair. Is there a banker you can have confidence in?" Sadie looked at Pete and he nodded vigorously in agreement.

The Colonel shook his white head slowly. "All my good, trusted buddies are no longer here. Many of them are dead and the ones remaining that I would be able to confide in are either moved away, or in rest homes, or just not able to take this magnitude of responsibility. All the bankers and advisors I know now are the ones assigned to me by my son, Stephen. They would report anything like this directly to him. If my son got wind of this, it would be all over for Victoria and me. He would never trust us with anything of this great worth. He's been trying to take over my life and be my legal guardian for a long time now. So far, it has not come to the courts, but if this got out, I would be before the judge in no time flat."

Sadie looked at Pete. "Well, what do we do first, Pete? You know about such things. What is the best thing to do?"

Pete said, "First of all we open four safe deposit boxes and put two of these bars in each one. The boxes should be registered under the Colonel's name and that of his wife. But they need to be in at least four different banks in four different cities. No one will know what is in the boxes. We will carry the gold bars in a satchel and deposit them one at a time." He paused to let that sink in. "In this way, we will be holding them safely somewhere until we decide how to handle them, how and if to cash them in, and who to deal with concerning this. I'll have to check some things out online."

"What about the gold certificates?" asked the Colonel.

"Those can be used to make considerable deposits in banks in your name, but then again it will have to be in other cities. If you are able, we will drive to the cities of your choice and set up those accounts. There will probably be taxes that have to be paid right off the top, but that should not worry you since the total amount will be so much anyway."

"I guess the government can take its share," the Colonel conceded.

Sadie looked at the disturbed old man and sort of wished they had never opened that hidden attic door. She hated to see his peace and congeniality dissipate. "Colonel, why don't you go downstairs and check with Victoria and talk to her? You can tell her whatever you think she can handle. Take these certificates with you and slip them under the mattress until we can get them to a safer place. Pete and I will haul these gold bars into the closet and cover them up with blankets until such time that we can get those safety deposit boxes opened."

Pete helped the Colonel down the stairs. His legs were weakened by all the excitement. He carried the gold certificates in his hand. Sadie promised him she would bring their dinner to their room so they could just remain secluded and cozy in their own quarters for the evening.

After Pete came back upstairs, he and Sadie worked to haul the eight gold bars to the closet and secure them there. Sadie looked at Pete and said, "Just how much money are we talking about here, Pete?"

"Just roughly calculating it up in my head, I'd say that each bar is worth nearly $160,000. That's a total of a little more than $1,280,000. If I remember correctly, the certificates add up to a total of 250 ounces more or less. At just about $400.00 an ounce that would be worth . . . let's see," Pete was staring up at the ceiling as he calculating in his head. "A little more than $98,000," he announced. "The total amount represented here is well over a million dollars. After the government takes a big chunk of it, say about 30%, they will probably have a little over a million left. Looks like the Colonel and his wife won't have any worries for the rest of their lives."

"I'm afraid with Stephen as their calculating son, they may never see any rewards from this discovery," conceded Sadie. "He is a control freak and likes to be in charge of everything that concerns his parents. He does it under the guise of watching out for them, but in truth, I think he is afraid they will diminish his inheritance if they spend without consulting him. It is so sad how binding his actions are toward them. He must love them; but this kind of singular concern just causes tension between them and him, and really doesn't show genuine love. That's just my opinion from what I've observed. I wish things could be different between them. The whole discovery of this treasure will only make it worse for them, I fear."

Pete pressed his lips together and shook his head. "Well, we can delay that revelation for a while till the Shaw's get legal counsel from a trusted attorney. We can be sure that these bars and certificates are safely hidden away, until the Colonel determines what he wants to do with the money it represents. You are so right, Sadie, that money can cause more trouble than it is worth."

Chapter 28

Securing the Gold

Sadie fixed up a plate of chicken and dumplings with a small salad for the Shaws. She gently knocked on the door of their room and was invited in. The Colonel looked at her with wide eyes and barely shook his head at Sadie to indicate that she was not to say a word about the find in the attic. Sadie smiled and nodded perceptively toward him. "It's a nice chilly night to just stay and eat here in your room," she said cheerfully. "Let me get a fire going so you can watch it sparkle and then die down eventually. A dying fire is the most beautiful thing to sit and watch."

"I agree, dear," said Victoria. "Oh this dinner smells heavenly. If I don't quit eating like this, I'm going to be packing on a few pounds," she teased.

"Woman, are you fishing for a compliment? You'd do well to put on some weight. You've been too skinny for too long. Eat up! If there is more of you to hug, I'll be happy as a lark," said the Colonel with mischief in his eyes.

Sadie set up the fire and lit it and hurried out to leave them to their solace. She knew that the Colonel would tell his wife only the part about the treasure that she would be able to handle. He did not want her upset.

The Colonel went with Pete to four different banks in four different nearby towns. They opened up the safety deposit boxes for the bars of gold, and also four savings accounts under the name of Everett and Victoria Shaw. The government would automatically send them notice of how much they owed in inheritance taxes later on. Into each of the four banks, Pete carried two gold bars, one each tucked away in its own satchel. The Colonel vouched for Peter and was given permission to carry the heavy satchels into the vault for the old man. He had to sign a roster in each bank showing he had entered and helped the Colonel set up his boxes.

When those tasks were done, the Colonel relaxed a little and his lined face smoothed out some. "Pete, whatever am I going to do with all that money?" He asked.

"Well sir, I've been pondering that subject some myself. If I were you, I'd make some improvements on the house and grounds. The big mansion needs repair and painting. That front portico and the columns need some refurbishing. The grounds could be made into a wonderful garden so that people of the city could enjoy the beauty of it. This after all is an historic site around these parts. It has a lot of history, too, that would be of interest to people."

"Peter Combs! You have just started my mind working. You are indeed right about the big house. It needs some drains cleaned and repaired, new gutters and new a roof. The driveway and the steps need to be patched. I could make a list of the things needing repair and find a contractor who would give me an estimate. But about the yard; who would ever see it? That high wall around the place blocks out the sunshine and the view. It would be so nice without that wall."

"Well, you could look into knocking it down. Those big old stones in the wall would be worth something to someone. If you get it knocked down, maybe someone will pick up the stone and haul it away for another purpose. That would curtail some of the cost," Pete offered.

The Colonel was getting excited now. "Pete, how would you like to head up this big project of the wall removal and the repairs on the outside of the house? You could run the figures by me and whatever the reasonable costs. Then we could draw up money orders from the deposits we just made to pay for everything. Oh this would be so much fun!"

"If you don't mind my asking, Colonel, what did you tell your wife about all of this?" Pete asked.

"I waited till the appropriate time and I told her that Sadie had found a secret attic room. When we went up there, we found some gold and put it in the bank. I told her that it was something that belonged to my great grandfather from the Civil War days. I told her not to worry her head about it, and that we would figure out something good to do with it. She seemed to take it in stride. She told me to go put another log on the fire. She hasn't mentioned it since."

"What about your son, sir? Are you going to let him know about any of this?"

"Not quite yet. It would do him no good to know. He'd be in a dither to take charge. This is something I'd like to handle myself, and I feel very capable of doing just that," said the Colonel.

Pete and Colonel Shaw rode home in silence after that. Each one seemed to be pondering on the possible repercussions of these events. When they arrived home, Sadie was waiting at the back door wiping her hand on her apron. The smell of fresh baked bread was wafting from the kitchen. "Well, how did it go? Are you both exhausted from travel and excitement?"

"Yes indeed, I am ready for a nice long nap, myself. We had no problems opening the accounts. I just hope no one familiar with my son works at the bank and speaks of this to him." The Colonel slowly went into the kitchen. "Before my nap, however, I want some of that warm bread with your good apple butter on it."

Standing on the outside back stoop, Sadie looked at Pete questioningly. "He's okay, Sadie. That old man has a lot of wisdom in him and is quite capable of handling things of this sort. In his day, he must have been something in the financial field. I just fear that if Stephen finds out about this money and gold, he will try to legally declare the Colonel and his wife incompetent to run their own affairs. He could gain power of attorney from a judge. If he gets a good lawyer to argue the case for him, he may win."

"Isn't there anything we can do to stop something like that from happening? If the Colonel's son takes over, you and I will be out of here on short notice. I've already rubbed him the wrong way and he's eager to take his revenge. Since you were hired by me, you'd experience his wrath also." Sadie worried.

"Let's not open a can of worms right yet, Sadie. Right now the treasure is a secret and it is safe and sound. The Colonel has some good ideas of what to do with the money. His plans would benefit the whole community, and that in itself might prejudice a judge to vote in favor of the Colonel. If the news media ever got hold of the good things the Colonel would like to do to this property and therefore benefit the neighborhood, that information would certainly have great influence on what a judge would rule concerning power of attorney." Pete made a point of breathing in deeply with his eyes shut. Sadie took the hint and invited him in for a glass of cold milk and a couple slices of hot bread and honey.

Pete sat at the table and told Sadie of what he and the Colonel had proposed to do with the money. Sadie was delighted. "I have a good idea what to do with all the big stones that make up that wall," said Sadie. "The old Immanuel Baptist Church on the outskirts of town is really in bad shape. The wood is rotting and the roof is nearly caving in. They could take those big stones and build themselves a new church. What a beautiful edifice it would be and it would stand for centuries."

"That is a terrific idea, Sadie. If the men of that church would hire some heavy-duty dump trucks, they could haul this stone away after it is knocked down. It would cut the cost of the removal of the mess. Why don't you speak to the preacher down there and see what he thinks?" Pete said.

Sadie was stirring a skillet of beef stroganoff. The scents of simmering, tender beef chunks, carrots, onions, and garlic, wafted across the kitchen and made Pete's mouth water. Sadie had flavored the lusty beef stew with a little lemon juice, tawny port and sour cream. She would serve it with wide egg noodles. "I'll speak to Reverend Brown on Sunday when I go there." Sadie had been dividing her attendance between that wonderful black congregation and the First Baptist

Church in town where she was part of the choir and sang solos once in awhile. At the church in town, Sadie even filled in for the pianist when she was out of town or sick. She also taught a Sunday School of young single adults.

The air outside crackled with thunder, and the wind was picking up, making the old pines sway back and forth. Sadie had been one who always enjoyed a good storm. She would stand on the porch and watch the clouds roll in and finally see the lightning bolt across the sky. She would remain there out in the open until the rain lashed across her face. Storms were exciting and powerful. Storms in life were in some ways exciting, too. Sure, they caused havoc and sometimes heartache, but they shook things up and made a humdrum life perk up and get busy. She knew that ahead for this family would be a big storm. She could feel it coming. She took a deep breath and straightened herself up as she contemplated facing the turmoil that would surely ensue. She had confidence in the goodness of God to see all of them through the raging tempest.

Chapter 29

Making Plans

Pete went with Sadie to the black church that next Sunday on the outskirts of town. The men were dressed up in suits, white shirts and colorful ties. The ladies had on flashy, elegant dresses and outfits with big feathery hats and shiny shoes. It was a feast for the eyes for Sadie to look around. So many friendly handshakes and pats on the back and even hugs and kisses were given. Pete endured the hug of a big black woman who planted a big kiss on his cheek and said, "I just want you to know I love you!" Sadie smiled to see Pete's astonished face and how he reached up with his palm to touch his cheek.

The music was loud and raucous, but so Spirit-filled that Sadie got caught up in the clapping and swaying. When prayer was given, the people raised their hands high and commented loudly on the words being offered up to God. It was team effort of worship. The music got so frenzied that some people began to dance in the aisles and speak in tongues. Someone in the congregation made an interpretation of the words spoken. Peter was wide-eyed and stiff and looked like a wild animal ready to bolt. Sadie placed her hand on his arm and smiled up at him assuredly.

The old black preacher began his sermon slowly and deliberately spoke with an intellectual tone like that of a renowned professor. As the sermon got warmed up he began to gesture with his arms and to shout so his voice filled the auditorium with its deep resonance. At the end, he was actually singing his sermon. The congregation caught up in the hypnotic tone of it, and they swayed and nodded their heads and spoke out their concurrence with his proclamations.

"Amen, brother, preach on!"

"You tell it like it is. We with you!"

"God bless him, he's preaching now. Amen!"

"Speak the truth, pastor. Speak the truth!"

The services lasted a good bit longer than the white version of church downtown, and afterwards Sadie and Peter spoke with the Reverend Brown at the front door. Pete told him about the possibility of ripping down the Colonel's wall and donating the huge building rocks to the church. "You could have great, river rock stones for the building of a church here. All your congregation would have to provide would be the muscle to cart off the stone to your property here. We just want to know if there is any interest on your part before we propose this to the Colonel."

Sadie spoke up. "It looks like you have some very young and strong men in this church. Do you think they'd be willing to take on a project of this magnitude?"

"Well I'd like to think they would, but that is something I'll have to discuss with them. I don't know for sure what they will think of this idea. It sounds like a gift to me. I guess I'd have to put the possibility to the congregation and see how they respond.

There would be some sore backs after all that hauling was done. Lordy, would there! It might remind the old people of the slave days and the legends they were told as children. We even have a stonemason in our church. He's retired now, but not handicapped in any way. He's one of the best men with brick and stone that I've ever seen. He could do the instructing on where to pile the stones and how to build up the walls. Oh dear, my mind is just reeling with possibilities. What we really need is a couple of dump trucks and one of those big scooper machines that could lift up the stones and load up the truck." He pondered a minute and then with a satisfied snap of his fingers he said, "Backhoe. That's what it is called. Backhoe. I'm gonna need to pray hard about this. I'll get back to you as soon as I can. Fair enough?" the pastor inquired.

"More than fair. The Colonel still has to decide if this is feasible for him too. This may all be a big pipe dream. But oh what a good dream it would be," offered Sadie.

Peter and Sadie drove home in silence for a while; both staring straight ahead. All of a sudden they both burst out with comments, each one interrupting and talking over the other.

"What are we thinking? This project is enormous! What will the neighbors think of all that machinery and noise?" Sadie worried.

"There must be so many tons of stone in that huge wall. They could build two churches with it. What will the Colonel's son do when he finds out? He is bound to, you know." Pete worried.

"I know, I know! I just hope that the Colonel's heart will be able to take all the pressure and the arguing and the stress. And what about Mrs. Shaw? Victoria is pretty fragile. I would never forgive myself if anything happened to her," was Sadie's response. "Let's stop at the supermarket and get some roasted chickens and fixin's. We are all going to be hungry when we get home and being that it is this late in the afternoon, I won't have the time to fix much of a dinner."

So they stopped and picked up dinner and headed home. Pete hesitantly said, "I liked it when you said that we were heading home. Sometimes that piece of ground feels more like home to me than that little old house I rent."

As soon as they drove into the driveway they saw the Colonel's son had arrived. Parked in the driveway was Stephen's big silver Cadillac. The driver's door was flung open as if he had exited in such a big hurry that he had forgotten to even shut it.

"Uh oh! It is already starting. We'd better get in there and see what is going on," Sadie said.

"I hope I don't have to throw him out on his ear," laughed Pete.

"Don't kid like that, Peter. I'm already nervous enough as it is," Sadie's voice quivered. Pete started to get out of the truck and Sadie reached over and put her hand on his arm. "Pete, this may seem silly to you, but could we please just stop for a second before we go into the melee and pray? I always feel better and more fortified when I face something tough with prayer as my shield."

"It's okay by me. But you'll have to do the talking . . . . er praying. I'm not used to speaking with the Almighty!"

Sadie grabbed Pete's hand. It was the first time she'd ever touched his hand. His hands were rough and callused from all the hard work he was used to doing. She held his hand tightly and eventually he squeezed back a little. "Dear God. I'm so glad you are our Father. We need you right now. We need your protection and we need your strength. Inside this house is a big turmoil going on. We feel that what the Colonel wants to do is the right thing, and we want to feel that you think the same way we do. Could you give us some reassurance? Could you please walk in there with us, and help us to stand up to Stephen. I know the Colonel loves his son, and I'd like to think the feeling is mutual, but oh Lord, it is hard to tell, because that man has issues with controlling everything that goes on. Can you please work a miracle in his heart, Lord. Help us, we pray. If this can bring glory to your name, Lord, then let it be your will. In our Lord Jesus' name we request this, Amen!"

Pete squeezed her hand a little harder and released it. They exited together from the truck and walked into the house through the kitchen. As they entered the house they could hear the screaming. It jolted Sadie's heart to hear it. She took a deep breath and hurried through the dining room and across the foyer. Peter was right behind her.

Stephen was standing in the doorway to his parents' rooms. He turned and saw Sadie approaching. "There you are, you Jezebel! Whatever do you think you are doing trying to keep such a discovery from me. You are only here by my good graces. I'll have you run out of town and your boyfriend with you, by God!" Stephen screamed at her.

Stephen tossed aside a chair and it hit the wall and the chair spilling a favorite curio of Victoria's onto the floor and smashing glass all around.

Peter stepped in front of Sadie to block the wave of anger that was pouring off of that charging bull of a man. "Just hold it right there, Mr. Shaw. You have no cause to attack Sadie concerning this. She did nothing wrong. This is your father's house and the discovery was his. Don't you think that your father has the right to do whatever he wants with whatever is in this house? Sadie had nothing to do with the Colonel's decisions in this matter."

"The hell she didn't! She's wormed her way into my parents' confidence from the get go, and it stops here! My father and mother are feeble and not able to discern what is right to do. I will not allow her to poison their minds against me and lead them to betray me like this."

Sadie was shocked to the core by these accusations. She closed her eyes and breathed deeply. *Now Lord. Now would be a good time for you to step in and calm things down. Help me Lord, I'm drowning here. I can't do this alone. Give me the words to say and the courage to stand.*

"Hold on son," the Colonel stepped in. "Sadie did not tell me what to do with the treasure from the attic. All she did was help me get up there to find it. I planned putting the gold from certificates in banks myself. I was going to tell you about it whenever you got back in town, but you found out from one of your banker friends before I had the chance. I will not allow you to attack Sadie or Pete, either one. You step back now, hear me?"

"Sure, sure. You had no intention of keeping this from me. That's why you traveled miles and miles to hide the money in four different banks. You were hoping I would not find out about it. I'm not dumb, Father!" Stephen pushed his nose into his father's face with fists at his side.

"Stephen, that kind of deposit would have spread through this town like wildfire. I didn't want to deal with that kind of speculation and gossip. And it is true that I didn't want you rushing in here and taking over the plans for this money. You are trying that right now, I'd say. I want to be able to cogitate on this find and decide what needs to be done with it," the Colonel tried to explain calmly.

On the bed behind the Colonel, his frail wife sat with one hand on her heart and the other covering her mouth. Her eyes were widened in fear. "Oh Mrs. Shaw," Sadie ran to her, "don't be upset. Everything will be fine. Don't let this fret you one bit. The men will work it all out. I'm going now to get you a nice cup of tea with lemon. I have your lunch too. I'll bring it a little later. You need to prop up your feet and rest a spell. I'll be right back."

"I didn't even know my husband had found anything. I feel like I'm in a very bad dream. I wish I could pinch myself and just wake up," she cried out.

"See mother, they even hid it from you! Dad has had his mind poisoned against us both. These people are evil. You can't keep them around. You just can't," Stephen bellowed.

Sadie felt a power move in her. She looked up at Stephen and rose from the bed and walked right up to him nose to nose. "Get out of here! You turn right around and march out of this room, you big bully! I'll not stand for you to intimidate your sweet mother. Are you nuts to act like this in front of her? Now move it! Out of here. You men go talk in the kitchen or the dining room or wherever; but not here!"

Stephen just stared at her with his mouth open. Then he turned on his heel and marched out the door with the Colonel and Peter in his wake. Sadie slowly walked to the door and shut it firmly but gently. She turned back to Victoria and helped her sit up in bed with her back propped up with pillows and spread a silky crazy quilt over her legs. "You rest here and I'll be right back with that hot tea. I mean it now; don't you worry your head about this. Men are just noisy and blustery. They will calm down. And if they don't I'll kick them out of the house," she laughed lightly.

Victoria smiled wanly and closed her eyes. Sadie put on a birdsong CD that she had gotten for them. She had picked up a cheap CD player at the local superstore. They enjoyed some nice music that way. She left the room and closed the door softly behind her. She passed through the dining room and saw that the Colonel and his son were facing off on opposite sides of the table. They were still talking heatedly to one another. Pete was nowhere to be seen.

She went into the kitchen and put the kettle on and arranged the finest china cup she could find on a tray with a lacy napkin and put a tiny flower in an old inkbottle. About the time the water began to heat up, the swinging kitchen door flew open and in stepped Stephen. "As soon as tomorrow comes, I want you packed up and out of here. I will personally give you a month's severance pay."

"I'm not going anywhere Mr. Shaw," said Sadie calmly as she finished up the tray. "You are not my boss. I think you should sit down there and listen to me. Where is your father?" asked Sadie.

"He ran to check up on mother. No thanks to you, she is dangerously upset!"

"I think we know who caused that, sir, and it wasn't me. You should be ashamed of yourself. Sit down . . . . now!" Sadie demanded.

Surprisingly Stephen did sit down. He put his head in both hands with his elbows propped up on the table.

Sadie poured the teapot full of the boiling water and put on the lid and let it steep. She set a mug in front of Stephen and he shook his head to indicate that he wanted none of it. "Yes you will have a cup of tea. It will calm you down, and that is what you need. Don't argue with me, Mr. Shaw. I'm feeling quite formidable right now."

Stephen gaped up at her like she was some sort of alien creature that he'd never known existed. She poured his mug full of the sweet aromatic tea and pushed the sugar bowl across to him. He spooned out the sugar and stirred it slowly.

"Now you listen to me and listen good!" Sadie started. "Your father and mother love you very much and they are very proud of you. But you scare them. That's not what you want is it; to scare them? They don't want to do anything to disappoint you or make you mad, so they just go along with whatever you tell them to do. It is a frightening thing for old people to rock the boat. They need that feeling of security and they crave assurance of being loved and cared for." Sadie stopped and took a deep breath.

"Well they used to be that way, that's for sure. I never had any problem with them before you came here!" Stephen loudly responded.

"Your Dad is not feeble in the mind. His joints might be strained and stiff, but his mind is quick and sharp. He's not ready to be put out to pasture just yet. Maybe you just think that they are not capable of deciding for themselves. Maybe you are truly trying to be protective of them, but it just doesn't look right the way you treat them." Sadie poured the cups of tea for the Colonel and his wife. "I'll be right back. Don't go anywhere, okay?"

Stephen nodded and sipped his hot tea. "There's brownies under that glass dome if you want something to eat with that tea," she offered. She slipped out and delivered the tray of tea to the Shaw's. She assured the old couple that she would be back soon with their supper and that they should just relax. Colonel Shaw attempted a feeble smile and patted his wife's hand gently.

Sadie went back to the kitchen. Stephen was still sitting there where she'd left him. "Do you have brothers and sisters, Mr. Shaw?" Sadie inquired. "I seem to recall the Colonel mentioning that he had some children that lived away from here."

Stephen glared up at her, "Not that it is any of your business, cleaning woman! But yes, I have a brother in Georgia who is younger than I, and an older sister who lives in Alabama. They are both married and have families of their own. They don't get back here that often."

"Why not? Those states are not so far away from here. Surely they would like to see their folks now and again." Sadie puzzled.

"There you go pushing your nose into our business again!" he said.

"You're right, sir, it isn't my business. I apologize. The next time I need to know anything about your family I will ask your mother or father. They will be glad to tell me what I'd like to know. The only reason I ask is that your siblings might want to know about this financial discovery too. The whole family could rejoice in this fantastic find."

"They don't need to know anything! You hear me!" He screamed at her.

"Mr. Shaw, my ears are working just fine. No need to raise your voice. I do not ask about your brother and sister so that they can come and help make decisions about the distribution or expenditure of that money; that is totally up to the Colonel alone. I just wondered about them being apprised of this discovery just as you are." Sadie had made her point and waited now for the response she knew would be forthcoming

Stephen pushed back his chair and slowly stood up, still bent over the table. "Listen to me, woman! My father is not at all capable of deciding what to do with that vast amount of money. I will be taking charge of those decisions. You just stay out of it and quit putting ideas into my dad's mind. They were perfectly happy here before you arrived on the scene."

"I really doubt that, Mr. Shaw. Your mother and Dad were living alone with little help in this big house. You seem to have been the only one satisfied with the former situation. I can see now that it is because you had total control of everything regarding your parents. Have you no family of your own to boss around and dominate?" Sadie bravely said.

Stephen's face turned a bright red and his cheeks puffed out. "That does it! I'm out of here. You have crossed the line, lady. You are insulting and cryptic and rude. I don't have to stand here and take this kind of treatment from a servant. I'll be talking to my lawyer tomorrow to gain power of attorney over my father's affairs and then, you . . . you troublemaking woman, you'll be out of here faster than a squashed cockroach." Stephen stormed out of the house and slammed the door so hard the wall shook.

Sadie started to laugh at that last statement. A squashed cockroach! Oh that was just too precious. The man clearly needed a class in how to effectively express himself. She hurried out the back door in time to see Stephen's elegant car zoom away, dust flying behind it. She called out to Peter and finally heard him coming from around the side of her cottage.

"You called, oh brave leader?" He mocked.

"Get in here, Prince Valiant. We have trouble on our hands."

Chapter 30

The Family Dilemma

Peter and Sadie delivered the hot tea and brownies and promised dinner would be coming very soon. The Colonel was sitting up in the bed next to his wife, holding her hand. He was smiling at her and assuring her that all would be well very soon. She didn't look so sure.

Sadie and Pete sat down a minute to talk to them while they enjoyed their tea.

"Your son has gone home. He's still very upset," Sadie calmly said. "But I think we all made your position on this matter pretty clear. He has no jurisdiction here when it comes to your decision on what to do with that money. That is totally up to you, Colonel, and up to you too, Mrs. Shaw."

"Call me Victoria, Sadie. The other is just too formal and cold," said Victoria.

"Sometimes I think it would just be easier to let him take care of the whole thing, Sadie," replied the Colonel. "I just get tired of fighting with him, and he does watch out for us. My other two kids hardly ever set foot in this house anymore."

"I'm glad you mentioned that. Why is that? Are they mad at you? I just can't imagine that," Sadie inquired.

"No, they are not mad at us," the Colonel sadly said. "Stephen had a big falling out with them many years ago. They all had a big blowup about who was going to get what in the will settlement. We were encouraged to make a will, by Stephen, and he wanted to be there when we formed it up with our lawyer. The other kids were living away with their families already and were not included in the negotiations."

"Why were *any* of them included in your decisions?" Sadie puzzled. "A will is your personal decision on what to have done with your properties and monies after you are gone. You have every right to do whatever you choose with

139

your personal things. Even if you chose to give it away to charity, that would be your rightful choice."

"You just have no idea how strong a force Stephen is around here. He has great influence in this town and beyond its borders too. He was voted City Councilman and I do believe he will soon be running for mayor. People do not buck him, that is for sure."

The Colonel bowed his head and shook it back and forth. Victoria put her hand on his back and rubbed his neck. "Now, now, Everett, you stood up to him quite well today and I was so proud of you." She turned to Sadie and said, "I miss my other kids so much. They come once in a blue moon and stay here only a couple days. Longer than that and Stephen gets worried that they are trying to get something from us. They don't want anything, really. They are happy with their own lives and families. How I love to see my grandkids all grown up. I have five great grandkids too, and I never get to see them much. It is such a shame."

Peter spoke up and tentatively said, "I see what is happening here now. I've seen it before. Your son Stephen is afraid that the main portion of inheritance will not be coming to him. Somehow he feels he deserves it more than do your other children. Maybe it is because he chose to stay in this town and keep an eye out for the two of you. Maybe he thinks that gives him the right to control what you do with what belongs to you. The truth of it is, he has no right to do any of that. I'm sure you are grateful to him for keeping an eye out for you and all, but this should be done out of natural love of son for parents and not with the ulterior motive of coming away with the major portion of inheritance." Pete shook his head and said, "When I think of what he is missing out on by being selfish like this, it blows my mind. He could be close to his brother and sister if he was not so worried about money and property. He could be close to his nieces and nephews and great nieces and nephews too. What a big family he would have surrounding him and loving him."

The Colonel looked deeply into Pete's face and saw something there. Tears were forming up in Pete's eyes. The Colonel's eyebrows moved together in a contemplative gesture. "Peter, you are right about all of it. Stephen lost his own wife and family due to his devotion to power and money. He had no time for them and their love just faded off and gravitated to another person and place. He hardly ever sees his own kids anymore. We miss them too."

Something stirred in Sadie's heart. *Why do so many people miss the boat on this one? Can't they see the treasure right in front of their noses? What a waste!* From the looks of things and the way that Peter stated that last statement, he too had chosen wrongly and had lost someone dear to him.

Oh, how Sadie missed her treasures; her sons and daughter and grandson. Life was too short to be away from loved ones for too long. Making an effort to connect with one another was proof positive of love. She knew that from experience.

But oh, it felt so right to be here right now with this old couple. Sadie knew it was not fate that she believed in. She counted on the ordered steps of an all-seeing God. She had always been amazed at watching the years roll by and seeing the future of her children and other young people just form into a beautiful tapestry. It was like God was keeping good on his promise when he said "I have ordered your steps . . . . I have good things planned for your future." Sadie prayed silently, *I believe with all my heart that when a child of yours tries to live for you, Lord, and do his or her best to make you happy and pleased, then you, Lord, will watch out for and open and close doors to lead that child onto the path that is best for him or her. Sure, people often use their own will and choose differently from what You deem best, but even then, Father, you would not push them aside as failures and worthless. I thank you dear God, that you continue to work in your children's lives in one way or another.*

Right now she felt like she had been guided onto a path that was pleasing to God. She planned to do the best she could where she was planted. Then if God chose a new path for her life, she would pick up and move on.

Peter excused himself and left the Colonel and Mrs. Shaw to their dinner. Sadie too, took her leave and gently closed the door behind her. She caught up with Pete in the kitchen. He was putting on his coat.

"Aren't you hungry for dinner tonight, Pete? If you are in a hurry I can pack you a plate to take on home," she gently offered, pretending to be busy at the sink.

"Well . . . I do need to get on out of here," Pete admitted. "I guess I could take home a plate of your dinner, if you are sure there is enough."

Sadie packed up the roasted chicken and potatoes and slaw and baked beans and rolls. She added some brownies also. "Peter, thank you for standing up to Stephen. He is a tough old goat and his bark is pretty loud. We shall just have to wait and see how this all plays out, won't we?"

Pete nodded his head toward her and received the plate of dinner and turned to leave. "I'll be back in the morning after I talk to some construction men about the possibility and cost and time frames of taking down that wall. If we are armed with statistics and know our business well, we can put up a strong front to Stephen."

Sadie kept herself from breathing out a huge sigh of relief. She had been a little afraid that Pete would just turn and run from this mess and from the personal tension it created. She patted him on the back as he exited the house. "Sounds like a plan to me. 'Tomorrow is a brand new day with no mistakes in it', as Anne of Green Gables would say."

Peter left, and Sadie sat at the table and ate some chicken and slaw. She cried and cried as she ate. It felt so good to release that pent up emotion from having to be so under control in front of Stephen Shaw. She finished cleaning up the kitchen after she had gathered the trays from the Colonel's room. The Shaws were watching T.V. and holding hands, their colorful lap quilts spread across their legs. She slipped quietly out of their room and softly bid them a good night.

Sadie's little cottage was indeed welcoming as she entered it. She lit some candles all around the room and started a fire in her fireplace. Wheezer came and sat on her lap in the rocking chair. Contentment rolled over her like a warm blanket. Where were the fear and the worry? Gone. *The peace that passes all understanding.* She knew that is what was descending on her. She smiled to herself and looked up. "Thank you, Father."

Chapter 31

Christmas Is Near

It took a few days, but Stephen did get his lawyer to work up the papers for the power of attorney order. A court date was set for a month from Christmas. The Shaw's chose to concentrate on other things for the moment. They would face up to that challenge of Stephen's when the fateful day came.

Sadie and Peter were studying on the possibilities of counter measures. Sadie got a good, elderly lawyer for the Colonel. They lined up witnesses to the Colonel and Victoria's competency and clearness of mind. Both of the Shaw's went for a physical from a noted town physician. Even a psychiatrist was brought in to talk to them and ponder on the balance of their minds.

They planned their own strategy of influencing the mind of the judge. Sadie wrote an article for the paper about the history of the old walled in garden and Civil War home. She indicated in that article that the Colonel would not be opposed to opening up those barriers and letting the townspeople enjoy that park-like yard and the home as well. She would offer that article to the paper right after Christmas and let the minds of the town's people ponder on that a while. Sadie and Pete concluded that if the townspeople knew that a generous Colonel planned to accomplish all this with his newly found treasure, then it would behoove the judge to cast his judgment in favor of the Shaw's. Then the Colonel and his wife might be able to retain their right to rule their own lives for a while longer. With all those defensive measures in the works, Sadie decided to just not worry about it.

Christmas was nearly here.

Sadie had an idea. Christmas was just a week away. Why not invite the other Shaw children to come and celebrate the season? She broached the subject with the Shaw's as she served their breakfast. She served them steaming oatmeal with melting butter and brown sugar. Alongside that were toasted, buttered, mini bagels with sliced avocado. She made French press, decaf coffee for them. She had gone to a coffee specialty shop in town and had some Amaretto Royale beans ground for the press. The aroma was intoxicating. The Shaw's were very grateful for all her special efforts.

The Colonel's mouth was agape as he commented, "Sadie, you are talking a bunch of people. Our daughter, Susan, is a widow, but she has two sons and they both have young families. Stewart is our youngest and he has a wife and three grown children. Counting the grandkids and great grandkids, you are talking . . . . a total of . . . . help me out here Victoria."

Mrs. Shaw shook her head at him. "I guess it is a lot of people to keep track of, dear." Victoria got up from her chair and walked to an old photo book. She returned to her chair and opened up the book. "Susan is 58. She has two sons, Michael and William. Michael has Sarah and Suzanna, named after my daughter," she looked pleased. "Now William has Philip and Jessie. How many does that make including their wives?"

Sadie figured up in her head, "Uh . . . Nine!"

"Okay then. Now Stewart, our younger son who is 50, has two daughters, Becka and Beth, and one son, Brad. When we named our children, Everett and I stayed with the 'S's. When Stewart named his children he picked names starting with the letter B. Now then, Sadie, how many is that on our youngest son's side?"

Sadie figured again. "Five," she proclaimed.

"Did I mention that Becka is married and has a 5 year old named Julie?" asked Mrs. Shaw.

"No you didn't. So that makes seven including her husband. Add that to nine and we have 16 people. Add Stephen and the two of you and that is only 19. What about Stephen's children? Would they want to come to this?"

The Colonel looked sad. He said, "We can only ask and see what happens. Stephen's wife remarried after their divorce and moved to West Virginia. They divorced when their two children were ten and five. The children's names are: Patrick, who is nearly 30 now, and Melody, who is 25, I'd guess. What lovely children. I try to send them a little something for their birthdays, but how I would love to see them more often. When they were younger, Stephen would go and get them and bring them here to visit for a couple of weeks every summer. I surely do miss them. I miss all my grandkids and great grandkids. The more I think of this idea of Sadie's the more I like it."

Sadie pursed up her lips and squinted her eyes. "So . . . that brings the grand total to twenty-one people."

"Oh, but Sadie, you are talking about a lot of work preparing for this. The rooms upstairs would have to be readied. Just think of all that food that would have to be prepared. It just boggles my mind," worried Victoria. "Can you really see yourself handling all that?"

"We are only talking twenty-one people in all. That's not so many. I've cooked for more than that plenty of times. It will only be three days of cooking; Christmas Eve, Christmas and the Sunday following. My question to you is; what would Stephen say? Would he resent seeing his brother and sister here? Wouldn't he be worried, like you said, about them imposing on his rule and influence here?"

Colonel Shaw stood up and paced the room a couple of times. "I'll talk to Stephen. Our episode here was a terrific jolt to him. He's not used to having anyone oppose his edicts and desires. Perhaps I still have some fatherly influence on him. Maybe I can make him see what a grand and special thing this reunion would be."

Sadie looked up at the ceiling while she figured in her head, "Stephen's kids could stay with him and maybe a couple more of the grandkids could stay at Stephen's house as well. I take it that he has a nice, big roomy home. Am I right?" Sadie queried.

"Oh yes indeed. He has a seven-bedroom mansion and a pool and pool house. Maybe he would agree to let one or two more stay there. Even if he doesn't want anyone else there, we could squeeze plenty of people in the two wings of bedrooms upstairs. Even the attic has a couple of rooms with dormer windows in it. There are some old antiques up there but it is warm and comfy there with at least three twin beds tucked away under the slanting roof," offered the Colonel.

Mrs. Shaw clapped her hands together and then covered her mouth with them. "Oh, dare I hope that this could really come to be?"

Sadie said, "I have the help of Mrs. Fortenbrau and Peter, and I'll get Cherie to help out too. We can make this work. Why don't you write, or better yet call them all and see what they think of the plan? Christmas is on Saturday this year, so they could all come on Friday and we could celebrate Christmas Eve and then they would stay Saturday and Sunday and be off and on their way on Monday; short, but sweet and memorable. What do you say? Should we give it a try?"

"Let's go for it," the Colonel proclaimed. "I'll get on the phone right now and see what I can get accomplished."

The house became a broiling mass of preparations. The invitations were being accepted right and left. It seemed that everyone was willing to forego their own plans to change them to accommodate this new plan to come to North Carolina for a traditional Christmas with the old folks.

After some serious pouting, Stephen even agreed to ask his two children to come. Their mother balked a bit, but then decided that she could give up her grown kids for one Christmas. Patrick and Melody were glad to come for a change of pace. Stephen tried to retain his blustery disapproval of Sadie and Peter. He wandered up and down the stairs giving orders to Cherie. He willingly offered his house to put up Stewart's children, Beth and Brad and his favorite niece, Becka, and her precious five year old daughter Julie. He hired two extra maids to freshen up the bedrooms and the pool house. He had the pool man come and clean the pool even though no one would dare swim in it at this time of year. He wanted it glowing with the underwater lights and he wanted it to sparkle.

Only one bedroom upstairs was devoid of a bed, since Sadie had removed it to her cottage. So Sadie, with the permission of the Colonel, rented a nice king size bed and had it installed. All were all aired out and dusted and floors vacuumed and polished. They re-washed all the stale linen and put clean, freshly sun dried sheets and pillowcases on all the beds. Sadie went to a warehouse store and purchased six dozen roses for a mere $40.00 and made bouquets for every room. She bought fragrant French soaps for the bathrooms and candles to match each scent chosen. Although it was a lot of work, she had not felt this satisfied in a long, long time.

The Colonel and his wife were beside themselves with joy. The huge, decorated Carolina fir lent an intoxicating scent of Christmas. It looked so breathtakingly beautiful standing as a greeting in the foyer. The hundreds of tiny colored lights and new and antique Christmas balls and ornaments hanging from it made it the most gorgeous tree Sadie had ever seen. Peter had wrestled with and planted on top of the tree a billowy, white angel. The white lights underneath it made the gauze like skirt glow.

Another smaller tree, only 7 feet high, was set up in the upstairs family room near the baby grand piano. Cherie and Joy decorated this one with lots of colorful wooden ornaments and bows of red and gold and white lights all around. Presents began appearing under that upstairs tree; beautifully wrapped packages, big and little. Sadie had sat with Victoria to make lists of the presents she wanted to get for her children and grandchildren. Sadie ordered some on rush delivery from catalogues that she showed to Victoria. Others she bought in town and in the nearby malls. She wrapped them all up and Mrs. Shaw worked to tie the silken, colorful bows on each package. Soon the area surrounding the tree was taken up by scores of presents. Stephen added a carload to the pile a few days before Christmas.

As happy as Stephen appeared to be with all this preparation, when he encountered Sadie in the hallways and kitchen, she could not get him to smile at or show any warmth towards her. She just shook her head and smiled. Men were sometimes so tough and stubborn.

Sadie made lists of meals to prepare, and from those lists she made lists of food to procure. Peter was off shopping for her in between all his raking and preparation of the front porch. He had at least 25 bright red poinsettias lining the columned wide porch. Encircling these were strings of tiny white lights. A huge wreath about four feet in diameter hung over the steps leading to the front door. The door itself was aglow with lights and greenery and tiny red sprigs of holly berries were tucked in all the way around. Every front window and bedroom window had electric candles glowing in them.

Sadie began her preparation of the food on Wednesday. She made an Italian Crème Cake of four thin layers soaked in Grand Marnier simple syrup. She made a Mississippi Mud Cake in a sheet pan with fudgy, pecan icing on top. A carrot cake was made from scratch and wrapped in plastic and set aside for emergency dessert. Some desserts would have to be made the day of their serving, but these she could do ahead of time. The refrigerator in her cottage was filled up with the desserts. She made hordes of Christmas cookies that she cut out of buttery dough. These were wrapped up and put in the freezer. She made chocolate covered cherries with stems in tact. Those took forever and Cherie had to help with those. She made date nut cookies from her grandmother's old recipe. On Thursday she made three pecan pies with bourbon in them. Fudge came next. It was always touchy to judge at the soft ball stage of the cooking of fudge. But she got it right, thank goodness. Oh that fudge just melted in her mouth. She liked that version much more than the one with the marshmallows melted in it. She would make a fresh apple pie and a lemon pie with golden meringue when the time came.

The house was all in order and ready for the first arrivals on Friday late afternoon. Carloads of the Shaw relatives began pulling up the long driveway about 3:30. Sadie had fresh brewed coffee, along with hot cider and fragrant tea ready in the big formal parlor. She had laid a plate of iced and decorated cookies and fudge on the side table for snacking.

First arrived Stewart with his sweet wife, Cindy. They had Becka and her husband, Rod, and little Julie was with them. The small child ran into the house with eyes wide with expectation. "It's just like you said it would be, Mommy!" she exclaimed. "Just like a castle in the woods."

Mrs. Fortenbrau was dressed up in a black maid's dress with crisp white apron and cap and black nylons and shoes. She looked very official and proper and surprisingly her demeanor matched her clothes. "Won't you please come in? I'll take your coats and Peter, here, will take your luggage upstairs to your rooms. As I understand it, Miss Becka and family will be staying with Mr. Stephen, so I will leave them suitcases here by the hall closet."

They thanked her cordially and handed over their coats and scarves and gloves. The Shaw's came out with big smiles and open arms. "Oh," exclaimed the Colonel, coming forward behind his wife, "I can't tell you how happy this makes me that you decided to come have Christmas with us. I feel so full of joy I just might explode."

Victoria was speechless and eyes brimming with tears as she hugged and hugged her son and his wife and her grown granddaughter and great granddaughter. "Oh this child is so beautiful!" she rejoiced. "I've missed you all so much. I'm afraid already that the time will just go by too fast for me. I won't ever get enough of you being here."

Stewart too was stuck for words immediately. He had to hug and wipe his eyes and finally they all settled into the Shaw's roomy quarters to sit by the fire and talk. Sadie came in quietly to announce that the big parlor was ready whenever they all wanted to retreat there. She told them there were hot drinks in there and snacks and that dinner would be served as soon as everyone had arrived. She had nearly gotten out the door when the Colonel called to her. "Don't you go sneaking out of here before I properly introduce you, Sadie!" he scolded. "Stewart and Cindy, Becka and Rod, this is the lady who is responsible for all of this reunion. She's the sunshine of this house and has made such a difference in our lives. Come here Sadie and meet my youngest son and family."

Sadie moved forward and shook hands all around. She welcomed them warmly and said that all was ready for them to have the best time ever. She reminded them again that the formal parlor was all freshened from not being used for so many years and was ready and warm for them. She excused herself saying she had lots more preparations to accomplish before dinner was served later on. What a relief it was to get back out into the foyer and slip away to the kitchen. She wished she could just stay out of sight and watch this family reunite from a distance. She was being rewarded plenty and enough just watching the joy being experienced all around. Her one apprehension was that Stephen might come with an attitude and ruin it all. *Oh Lord, please don't allow that to happen,* she prayed silently.

As she passed the dining room she smiled in appreciation for Gladys and her excellent job of setting the table. Both leaves had been put in the table. Now there was plenty of room for the 21 people to sit comfortably in the dining room and eat. The pristine white tablecloth was ironed and crisp. Matching napkins were folded a special way and placed in the crystal water goblets. Fine silverware was all polished and set. There were wine glasses for the adults. Flowers and candles adorned the table and all over the room were glowing candles lending fragrant scents to the atmosphere. The buffet was cleared off for putting the food in silver serving dishes. Warmers were ready to keep things hot.

Sadie pushed through the swinging door to her kitchen and checked under all the pots and into the oven. The fragrant yeasty smell of bread poured out of the oven as she checked to see how brown it was. She had a lemon pie piled high with meringue ready to go in the oven for browning. The chocolate trifle with homemade fudge sauce was cooling in the icebox. Simmering on the stove was a huge pot of her mother's famous Beef Vegetable soup, made with ox tails and six pounds sirloin cubes. She had seasoned it with port wine. She knew the soup was nutritious and delicious. She readied four small bowls of horseradish sauce to serve with the soup.

The water for boiling large shrimp was steaming and all the shrimp were clean and sitting in ice in the sink. *Seven pounds of shrimp should be plenty* she figured. She had a spread of cream cheese with dried beef and pecans ready to heat up in the oven at the last twenty minutes. A crock pot held her notoriously coveted ham and pork meatballs in sweet and sour sauce made with apricot jelly and mustard and catsup. A cold spinach dip had been sitting in the refrigerator since morning. She had special crackers for both dips in Christmas napkin-lined baskets. She also had some cold crispy veggies on a platter ready to serve with the dips.

The doorbell rang and Gladys rushed to answer it. Sadie could hear a woman's voice. *It must be Susan,* she thought. "I just now got in from the airport," she heard the woman say. "I decided to take a cab and not bother anyone to come get me." *That was thoughtful of her,* Sadie decided.

After a little while the bell rang again and this time, there were several voices and a horde of people came stomping in. Sadie could hear the patter of young people's feet exploring around and talking excitedly. Her curiosity got the better of her and she peeked through the swinging door to see two handsome men in their mid thirties. Their wives were being helped to take off their coats and scarves. Gladys led them into the big parlor where a fire was blazing and told them she would let the Shaw's know they had arrived. *These must be Susan's two sons and their families,* thot Sadie. The house was filling up fast. Sadie stood by the dining room entryway and listened.

"Mother we could have picked you up at the airport. It wasn't that far out of the way for us!" exclaimed one of the sons. "Oh but it is so nice to be back here again. The place looks marvelous . . . better than ever!"

"Hello Grandma and Grandpa. I can't believe we all get to come be with you this Christmas. Reminds me of times long past. This is going to be the best time together. Grandma, you smell so good, just like I remembered."

Hugs and welcomes all around were given and the whole group settled into the parlor where there was hot cider and tea and coffee available. Sadie peeked in to see the children standing around the tray of Christmas cookies, each choosing one to eat. "These are super. Look at this one! I think I'll have two of them. Can I Mom?"

The chairs in the refurbished parlor had been arranged in a big circle facing the fire. The adults settled in and the children were happy to explore through the room and point to the vast acreage outside. "Moma, if is snows, can we go out and play in it? It looks like a forest out there. We could play dragon and dragon slayer out there," quipped Philip, William's twelve year old.

"There will be plenty of time to run around out there I'm sure. Those woods are pretty wild though. You'd have to be very careful," responded the mother.

"Well actually it is all quite nice out there now, Jill. I have a gardener, Peter Combs, who has cleared all the paths and raised the canopy of the woods to a decent height. The children will be quite safe out there now," replied the Colonel.

Sadie walked to the stairway on pretense of adjusting the Christmas tree and saw that all the adults were milling around the spread of good food she had set up in there.

They were enjoying the hot pecan dip with crackers and the spinach dip with veggies and they were oohing and ahhing over the crock pot of hot meatballs. "Good grief, I'm going to weigh a ton when I finish with this visit. This food is marvelous!"

"Children, don't eat too much. Dinner will be served pretty soon and you need to save some room for that, too," advised one of the mothers.

Sadie retreated to the kitchen with a satisfied grin on her face. How pathetic was it that her major source of self-confidence and gratification came from watching people enjoy her food. She just loved to cook for people and see them relish it. Somehow, experiencing that made her feel worthwhile and successful. *I need to be in the restaurant business,* she thought.

The doorbell rang again and this time Stewart ran to answer it. In trooped Stephen and his two grown children, Melody and Patrick. The two Shaw brothers gripped hands instead offering hugs. Gladys took their coats and seemed cowed by Stephen's blustery presence.

"It is good to see you Stephen," said Stewart. "How long has it been? A couple of years anyway. Melody and Patrick, you both look great! I will be anxious to catch up with all your news of your lives. How is your mother doing?"

Stephen's grown children warmly hugged their Uncle Stewart and began chatting with him animatedly. Stephen sort of smirked and snuffed a little. He pushed his way into the parlor and the warmth of the room dipped a bit.

Dinner was served at 6:00. The steaming bowls of hot oxtail and beef soup were carried in and placed before each person. Fragrant hot bread was sliced at each end of the table. Sweet ice tea or iced water was offered and milk for the children. The dips and meatballs and veggie platter and crackers were transferred back to one side of the buffet table and the family rose to help themselves from the array. The iced down shrimp were sitting in bowls along the length of the table. Sadie had made her own horseradish shrimp sauce to go along with it. Sadie announced that the blue bowls were bullet bowls.

"What does she mean, Moma . . . where do we get bullets?"

The mother looked inquiringly at Sadie and she explained. "In olden days when a father went out to shoot the meat for dinner, some of the buckshot would still be in the meat. If someone bit down on it they would spit it out and put it in the bullet bowl. These 'bullet bowls' here are for your shrimp shells and for any oxtail bones you wish to drop in there."

Sadie busied herself in the kitchen washing up the dishes and peeping in now and again to see that everyone had what they needed. She could hear snippets of conversation now and again when the swinging door to the kitchen would open and close with Cherie and Gladys going back and forth. It seemed that things were going quite well. No harsh words or raised voices were heard.

Finally dinner was over and several members of the family slipped into the kitchen to congratulate Sadie and her helpers for the marvelous repast. Stewart's wife, Cindy and her oldest daughter, Becka, rushed to the sink to give her a warm hug. "It was a marvelous dinner: just what we all needed on this cold night after a long trip here. Thank you so much."

Sadie told them to just make themselves at home and she would be serving their dessert and decaf coffee and hot chocolate in the parlor soon. So they left the kitchen and Sadie breathed a sigh of relief. Cooking for a big bunch of people never bothered her, and she had been sure of herself to know she could pull it off. But having to accept people's gratitude made her nervous. She just wanted things to appear like magic before them so they would not have to be polite to her and thank her. But even so, it did feel good to be thanked and especially hugged. Those hugs made her miss her daughter and grandson so much. Next Christmas she would definitely be with them.

Sadie thrust her hands into the warm, soapy water once more and felt the peace of it. She loved washing dishes and making things clean and right again. The door swung open again and Sadie expected it was Cherie or Gladys bringing in more dirty dishes. She didn't turn to acknowledge the person. Then, right beside her stood a young teenage girl with her hands on the sink peering out the window into the black night.

"I wish I lived here," she said whimsically. "I have such good memories of this house and yard. It makes me so sad to think how many holidays we've missed here in the past years. I just wish everyone would get along and be nice to each other. I want to come here all the time."

"You must be Suzanna," Sadie responded. "Your great grandmother told me how pretty you are, and she is definitely right. You are lovely."

"That is so nice of you to say. But no I'm not really pretty! I'm fat! My sister, Sarah, is the pretty one. She's so tiny and looks so good in her clothes. But I just hate diets. I love eating so much. Wish I had a magic pill I could take and wake up in the morning looking like a model."

"Didn't you know? Models are not real people. They are just showpieces that are used to sell things. To have figures like that, they have to suffer and deprive themselves of regular living. Most of them are very unhappy. But they make pretty good money and so they stick with it till their youth fades. Then they become regular people, like us, again."

Suzanna laughed. Then she sobered and said, "But why then, does everyone try to be just like them? And . . . the boys all admire girls who are stick thin. I feel like a big lumbering teddy bear when I stand next to one of the 'in' crowd."

"That's because you are comparing yourself to them. Instead you should feel sorry for those girls who don't get to enjoy a nice ice cream sundae, or a hot off the grill hamburger dripping with juices. I always taught my daughter to just be herself. Everyone has his or her own special persona. To try to be someone beside who you are is unnatural, difficult, and phony. Most of those girls you envy are wondering how to act and are actually losing the special person they could be, by imitating someone else. Just be you."

Suzanna began to help rinse the dishes. They were silent a moment and then Suzanna said, "Yeah I'd like to do that. When I think about who I am, I like myself. But I'm afraid no one else will like me, so I just try to be like everyone else."

"Big mistake! Why deprive the world of the uniqueness of you? God made you to be one of a kind. It would make Him very sad to think you were trying to change his perfect plan."

"I feel like I just had a visit with the Dhali Lama," Suzanna giggled. "But truth is, I do need to lose some of this . . . chubbiness."

"Well then, if that would make you feel better, do it. You will have to change your way of eating and stick with it for the long term. Just make it a daily habit. Once you devise a plan of eating right and get into it, then you will be uncomfortable eating any other way. It takes time and determination to change the pattern of your eating, but you'd be healthier, that's for sure. I should talk. I eat lots of things with fat in them and cook the same way. I do not stick with just healthy things. Old habits are hard to break. That's why it would be good for you to start now and set the pattern while you are young."

The door swung open and Suzanna's mother, Mary, came bursting in. "There you are Suzanna. What are you doing? I hope you are not bothering the cook."

Sadie glanced back with her hands still in the sink and replied, "She is not bothering me at all. We were just having a nice visit. You've got a great girl here."

"Come, Suzanna, the family is gathering upstairs to open one present for Christmas Eve. You need to pick one to open." With that she flounced out the door.

"Sorry about my mother. She is a little rude sometimes."

"No problem. I think she is just excited to be with the whole family, and she surely doesn't want you to miss out on anything going on in there. Thanks for the help, Suzanna. It was so good to talk to you."

Suzanna stood a moment and looked deeply into Sadie's eyes. Then she abruptly threw her arms around Sadie and gave her a tight, side hug. With that she rushed out the door nearly running into Cherie carrying in a piled-up tray of more soiled dishes.

"I sure wish we had a dishwasher, don't you?" Cherie asked.

"We do have one . . . . me!" Sadie replied with a chuckle.

Sadie prepared trays with lemon pies hot and fresh out from the oven. The meringue was perfect with tall golden peaks. It was like a dessert caravan. She carried in the lemon pies and Cherie carried in the chocolate trifle and fudge sauce along with the dessert plates and forks. Peter and Gladys brought in the cups and hot drinks and fixin's. Sadie could see that everyone in the Shaw family had picked out a present to open. They were all gathered around the room and fireplace. The children were getting antsy to get on with it. Little Julie was looking rather sleepy and was holding her soft, silky blanket close to her face. Colonel Shaw's two sons and daughter had nothing next to them.

"Grandma Susan! You are supposed to pick out a present to open tonight," said Suzanna.

"Well I was searching around the tree doing that very thing, and Great Grandpa Shaw told me to not bother with it. He told me he had some special Christmas Eve present for me and for your great uncles to give to us later. So I have no idea what is going on," Susan offered.

Sadie hurried back to the kitchen wondering what that old man had up his sleeve. Most of the gifts under the tree had been wrapped by her and Gladys. She thought she already knew what gifts everyone was getting from the Shaw's. *I guess he's got a surprise or two up his sleeve,* she thought.

The sounds of happiness floated across the foyer and into the kitchen. Paper being ripped and squeals of surprise and delight and expressions of gratitude wafted on the fragrant air. Sadie's heart was full to bursting. How great to see this big family finally get together again. Oh, indeed, what treasure family was.

"Sadie," the Colonel called from the kitchen doorway. "I was hoping you would come upstairs and lead us in some Christmas carols. That big ole grand up there is just itching to be played. It would just put the icing on the cake if you'd come on up and play piano and lead us. Will you?"

How could she say no to that. Cherie and Peter assured her they could finish up the kitchen. Gladys was already setting the table for the Christmas breakfast buffet.

"Okay I will. Are you sure your family won't mind having a stranger joining in on their Christmas Eve celebration?" Sadie worried.

"Not at all. I've been bragging on you all night. They should pretty much know you by now." He led the way to the foyer. Sadie was wiping her hands dry on a bar towel. The two Shaw boys were carrying their frail, delicate mother up the sweeping stairs with their arms folded and forming a chair. Victoria was squealing delightedly and the children were clapping their hands at the frivolity of it all.

"All right children, settle down. Before we start the singing let's read the Christmas story from Luke. Where did I put my Bible?" The Colonel was searching around, looking on shelves and into drawers. "I guess I need to use that book more so I'll know where it is when I need it," he fidgeted around. The mood of the room began to drop a little seeing the frustration of the head of the clan.

Sadie stepped up and said, "In my family we always quote the Christmas Story like this. If you like, I'll just say it for you. I know it by heart."

"Great! Okay kids, settle down. I want to hear a pin drop," he held up his two fingers pretending to have an actual pin ready to drop to the floor.

The children and adults sat in family groups together. The room was ablaze with soft, warm light and the candles were glowing. The smaller tree in the corner was lovely and bright and fragrant. Sadie had a feeling of deep joy in her heart. She opened her mouth and the Christmas story poured out word for word. "And it came to pass in those days . . . ." Sadie put her whole heart into that story. She used her hands and voice to convey the fear of the shepherds and the wonder of the angels and the quiet unceremonious birth of the baby, Jesus. "Be not afraid, for I bring you good tidings of great joy which shall be to all people; for unto you is born this day, in the city of David, a Savior, which is Christ the Lord."

Sadie's eyes filled with tears as she saw the wonder sparkling in the eyes of the young people before her. They were rapt with attention. ". . . . and Mary kept all these things and pondered them in her heart."

"Do it again! Please!" cried Jessie Susan's nine year old granddaughter. Everyone laughed.

The Colonel stepped in to take charge. "Okay now, it is getting late and we will have a few of Christmas Carols and then the children will get settled in their rooms and the rest of us can talk as long as we like."

A chorus of groans came from the children who did not want to be told to go to bed. Little Julie was already laying her head on her mother, Becka's knee. There would be no argument there anyway.

Sadie went to the piano and played 'Joy to the World' and 'Silent Night'. 'Oh Come All Ye Faithful' was next. The family knew a goodly part of the songs and Sadie's voice carried strong to cover the words they missed. Then Sadie led them in Jingle Bells and Winter Wonderland and Rudolph the Red-Nosed Reindeer. By the time those songs were completed, the whole room was full of laughter.

Chapter 32

The Big Mistake

Sadie rose to leave the room, and the Colonel stopped her with a hand. "Sadie, you need to be here for this next part. Since you are the reason it is happening," declared the Colonel with a warm smile. "I have a special gift to give to each of my three children. It is a surprise. A good one. Stephen, Stewart and Susan, go to that tree yonder and you'll find three identical shoeboxes wrapped up underneath it. Bring them out here and open them." The Colonel was full of anticipation like a child pulling a prank.

The three siblings walked to the tree and reached down to each pick up one present. "Whoa! This is heavy! What in the world is in this shoebox? Gold?" laughed Stewart.

Sadie's heart took a leap of fear. *Oh no, not now, Colonel. Not here. Things were going so well. What have you done old timer?* She began to ease backward toward the door, but the Colonel stopped her with a motion of his arm. "Sadie, no you don't. You are part of this. We have another story to tell. Get back over here!"

The sick feeling in her stomach lurched and made her knees buckle. But she stepped forward a bit and waited for the inevitable. The two younger siblings tore open their boxes and discovered a bar of shining gold. Their mouths dropped open and they slowly looked up at their Dad. "Is this a joke, Dad? What is going on here?" inquired Stewart with a worried look on his face.

Stephen finished unwrapping his gold bar and a gleeful, vindictive smile appeared on his reddening face. "Yeah, Pop, tell us another story. I'd like to hear what you have to say."

The Colonel was taken aback by their response. He sat down and looked alarmed at their reaction. Sadie was sure that his intention was to surprise each of them with this bountiful treasure. He wanted to share his good fortune with them and somehow things had turned around on him. His eyes looked stricken. "Sadie, help me out here won't you? Tell them our story please. I seem to have lost my voice."

Sadie stepped forward placing her hand reassuringly on the Colonel's shoulder. "A wonderful thing happened here a while back. We discovered a secret and unused attic room that had been for years covered up with that old chiffarobe in Stewart's old room."

"That old armoire was not in my room," said Stewart. "That was Stephen's room. I always wondered why that ancient piece of furniture would never move," offered Stewart.

"It was bolted to the wall is why," replied Sadie. "Behind it was a short door leading to a stairway and up into a hidden, small room in the attic. We discovered an old bed and oil lamp on a side table and there beside the bed was a big wooden chest. We dragged it down the stairs little by little and forced it open. Inside were these gold bars."

"What else was in there?" Stephen loudly demanded. "Why don't you tell the whole story of your deceit and cover up, Dad? Tell them about the gold certificates. Tell them how you took those valuable treasury bonds and spread them out to three banks around the county. Tell them how you felt it necessary to keep it all a secret from your loved ones! Tell them how this conniving woman here convinced you to horde away the rightful treasure that belongs to all of us."

Susan and Stewart's mouths just would not close. "Dad," said Susan, "what's going on?"

The Colonel's shoulders were bent a bit as he seemingly cowered under the harsh words of his son. He began to explain. "Susan dear, the money and gold must have been something your great grandfather hid away. He was always a proponent of the north and rumor had it that he helped the Yankees as much as he could. That's why he built that formidable wall around this place . . . for protection. There were lots of people in this town who would have been glad to lynch him had they found the proof of his loyalties to the North. I'm just guessing that this was part of a contribution that he was planning to give to the Union. There were old soiled bandages up there. We are guessing that a Union soldier was hidden there and he was doctored until he was able to carry away some of the gold."

"That's a fine fairy tale Dad. We don't really care about the hows and whys. We just want to be sure we all get our portion of the treasure. This piddly gold bar is just a part of it. Where is the rest of it, old man?" yelled Stephen.

Colonel Shaw was visibly shaken now. Victoria was crying behind all the people. Sadie took charge. "Okay everyone. It's time to get your grandmother downstairs to bed and Colonel, I think the rest of the story can wait till tomorrow. How about you Michael and William, can you lend your grandfather a hand down the stairs?"

Stephen bolted forward with his fists balled up. "There you go again, woman—stepping in and ordering people around. Who do you think you are? What kind of voodoo hold do you have on my folks?"

Sadie walked right up to Stephen and put her face right up to his. Her voice was soft and terrible at the same time. "You . . . . go . . . now!" she said, pointing her finger at the door. "You've done enough to ruin this beautiful evening with your yapping and complaining and whining. You are the eldest son here, and you are acting like a spoiled child. Your father was trying to do something great and generous for each of you. He wanted to surprise you with this special gift. You have taken it and trod all over it with ingratitude. You should be ashamed of yourself. Now march your carcass out of here before I get mad."

There were a few snickers and more than a few intakes of breath as she laid down the law to Stephen. He was blustery and shook his head glaring at her with hatred. "You are going to find yourself on the street, woman!" he screamed. "I'm taking charge here. From now on any decisions regarding the distribution of wealth from this family are going to be mine. You have no rights here. Get out of my way, you pariah!"

Sadie stepped aside quietly and watched as Stephen, with shoebox of gold bar in his hands, strode out of the room past his shocked parents and bounded down the stairs and slammed the door on his way out.

Stephen's children, Patrick and Melody, were so embarrassed by their rampaging father. "He'll calm down," said Patrick. "Why don't we get our things and go on home. Can we ride with you three, Becka? Are you all ready to go? Looks like little Julie here is a gonner," he said trying to lighten things up. Julie's father Rod was holding his daughter who was fast asleep. Beth and Brad rushed to get ready to leave also. Stewart's children were all staying with Stephen in his big mansion.

Michael and William helped their grandfather down the stairs and then came up to get Victoria. Peter gathered up the suitcases for those who were staying at Stephen's house and helped them all get in their cars for the journey over there.

Sadie announced as they were leaving, that breakfast would be a buffet affair and everyone could come at their leisure in the morning and eat. Afterwards they could all gather in the parlor to open the presents. She did not mention anything about Stephen. It was as if he was just a side aggravation that had been dealt with. But inside, Sadie was fuming with indignation and disgust. She ushered the traumatized Shaw's into their room and helped them settle in. Susan was in the bathroom there, gently helping her mother change into her nightgown. Medications were issued and warm cups of milk were brought in. Stewart sat with his father by the little fire in their suite. They talked softly together. The Colonel was staring into the fire and shaking his head back and forth. "It wasn't how I meant it to go. We were all having such a good time. How did it all go wrong?"

Peter took Cherie and Gladys home in the old truck. He would keep the truck at his place until tomorrow and then bring it on back, picking up Cherie and Gladys on his way.

Sadie turned off the lights in the kitchen and slipped out the back door and off down the path to her own refuge. How she loved this little refurbished cottage. It was her personal space and hers alone. She never was lonely there; never scared of shadows and strange noises. Sadie removed her clothes and slipped into one of her long white cotton nightgowns. She had always loved nightgowns made of soft, pristine, white cotton. The cat came to sit on her lap in the big wing-backed chair. Sadie had revived the banked coals, adding a few sticks of fire starter and some scraps of wood and a tiny log. The small fire was cheerful and sparkling. Sadie gathered up Wheezer in her arms and tucked her feet up under herself. As she pet her purring cat, Sadie began to ponder on the evening.

Whatever had happened tonight? She thought. *Things were going so well. Even Stephen was having a good time laughing with his nieces and nephews and talking animatedly with his siblings. It must have been just the thought of his father taking charge of something so important as money and treasure without confiding in him and asking his advice. Maybe he didn't like being excluded in such matters. It was so preposterous how he blew up all of a sudden. He had verbally attacked the Colonel and her. It was so unprovoked and yet there it was to deal with.*

Sadie decided to just pray about it. She set the cat down and got to her knees by the chair. For a while she just knelt there quietly, waiting and patient. Then she began praying out loud to the Lord. "Lord, I can't thank you enough for giving me enough energy to pull this reunion off. I thank you for Gladys, and Peter and Cherie and all the hard work they did without complaint. I am so glad I got to meet the whole Shaw family and to see the joy in their reunion. I pray that somehow you would take this sticky situation and help smooth things out and bring contrition and forgiveness to Stephen. Help us all to understand him and help him. Lord, I only want good to come out of this. I want you to be glorified through the whole experience. I hope and pray that these young people will see what God's love is, and will seek it out as they grow up. Be with me and tame my quick tongue. Give me compassion and mercy to deal with Stephen. Forgive me for being such a 'take charge' person. I really only want to do what makes you happy. I pray all this in my precious Jesus' name. Amen."

Chapter 33

Christmas Day

Christmas day went off without a hitch. Breakfast was a richly laden buffet of eggs, sausages and hash brown casserole. There were slices of bacon and ham and hot grits with butter. A tray of colorful, juicy fruits was offered. Biscuits and sausage gravy along with apple pecan muffins and several special jams and honey butter were set in a prominent place in the dining room. All these things were kept nicely warm and people came and went helping themselves and either eating at the set table or carrying their plates to the parlor or to the Shaw's suite or upstairs to the big family room. Music was playing. Christmas music. The day was divine. About 9:00 Stephen's children arrived along with Stewart's children and grandchild, Julie. Stephen was not with them. They all behaved as though nothing was wrong and joined in the celebration of the day.

Soon the noise of Christmas wrapping being ripped off packages could be heard from way down in the kitchen. Laughter and loud talking filled the house.

Sadie had the turkey in the oven stuffed with her mother's famous cornbread and bacon stuffing. Cherie was peeling the potatoes for mashed potatoes. The hominy grit souffle was ready for the oven as was the extra container of dressing. The giblets were simmering on the stove for gravy later on. Bread dough had been separated into yeast rolls which were lying under flour sacking to rise in the corner. The baked ham was scored and pitted with cloves and pineapple, brown sugar, mustard topping. It would go into the oven very soon too. The smell of the place was divine. Sadie had Gladys making a fruit salad. Green beans were simmering on the stove with tiny onions bobbing among them. Deviled eggs were neatly arrayed on a colorful platter and covered with plastic wrap in the refrigerator. The tray of several kinds of olives and tiny gherkins, carrot sticks and celery filled with special cream cheese filling were ready for early

159

snacking. Sadie had crusty, golden bruschetta slices ready with fresh tomato basil pesto to spread on top.

Sadie had a sudden notion, and she knew without a doubt that it was the Lord leading her. "Cherie, Gladys, I need you to hold down the fort for me. Set the snacks out for the family in the parlor so they will be able to eat a little before the big meal is served. Keep an eye on things here and don't let anything burn. I have somewhere I have to go. I'll be back very soon. Sadie rushed upstairs and slipped into the room where all the excitement was going on. She sidled up to Patrick, Stephen's son, and asked him to step outside on the landing with her.

With Patrick's map in hand and instructions on how to get there, Peter and Sadie drove the rattletrap pickup to Stephen's house. Peter stayed in the vehicle and Sadie walked up the walkway praying the whole way. *Please, Lord, speak through me. Let it be Your words, Your love, Your miracle.* The door was opened by a disheveled Stephen. He still had on his robe and slippers and pajamas. His face was unshaven and his hair standing up on end. Sadie's heart went out to him.

"What in the hell are you doing here, woman?" he rudely exclaimed. "Haven't you ruined things enough for me without making it worse?" Stephen turned on his heel and went into the house leaving the door open. Sadie stood there, shaken, and finally decided that the open door was her invitation to come in. She signaled to Peter to wait for a minute. She left the door open for him.

"Mr. Shaw, Stephen, please let me speak to you. I am feeling rather terrible about how I spoke to you last night. I feel that I spoke hastily in response to your tirade."

Stephen turned suddenly and glared at her. His face was ferocious and frightening. Sadie began to think that maybe Peter should have come in after all.

She continued hesitantly, "You are the eldest son and I believe that you clearly love your mother and father," Sadie began. Stephen's severe face softened a little and he turned to sit in a big leather chair, putting his feet up on an ottoman. Sadie, continued to stand. She took courage and continued. "Your folks love you so much and are very proud of you. I've heard them bragging about your position in this town and about how smart you are. They appreciate how you watch out for them and check up on them to be sure they have all they need. I think you really do worry about them and want what is best for them." Sadie stopped and took a reading of Stephen's face. He was staring out the window at his lush garden and pool out back. His fist came up to his mouth. He was silent.

Sadie continued. "But the fact of the matter is, your father is still quite capable of making his own decisions about their life together. He may be somewhat up there in years, but his mind is sharp as a tack. When you come in like a charging bull and act like you are going to run their lives before it is time to do so, it frightens them and puts them in a peculiar spot of trying to please you and at the same time trying to stand up for their own independence at the same time." Sadie took a deep breath and prayed in her head, *help me Lord!* "Everything your father has belongs to you and your brother and sister. All of it. I have no designs on any part of it. I'm only here to take care of them for a while and carry on with my own simple life. Please believe that."

Stephen took his fist down and turned to look at her. She was still standing awkwardly in the middle of the room. His eyes were still menacing, but not quite so volcanic. He finally ventured to speak. "It is a big chore, no . . . responsibility, to look after them. I worry about them all alone there. I invited them to live here with me, but they refused. That's their dad-burned 'independence' notion." He hurried on, "I have so much to do with my job and financial business, that I don't have that much time to check up on them. I never know when I can get by there, so I just, as you say, bluster right in whenever I can."

Sadie could tell that Stephen was making a point of explaining why he would come unannounced and in a hurry. "I am afraid that my father will eventually do something or decide something that will put his estate in jeopardy. He is always trying to help people, and that is fine, but people can take advantage of his good nature and sympathetic ways. I was sure that you were one of those people." He looked straight at Sadie. "Maybe I was wrong there."

Sadie was tired of standing and decided to sit without an invitation. "Yes you were very wrong there. You do not know my circumstances, but I assure you, I'm not interested in getting wealthy. Been there, done that! I just want to quietly live my life right now without lots of pressure. I only demand a veritable amount of privacy and peace. I have that there in that little cottage. I have grown to absolutely love your folks. They are such special people. I suggested this Christmas reunion so that it would bring joy to them." Sadie saw that Stephen's eyes had softened somewhat and that he was really listening to her. "That is why I've come here this morning. I do so want you to be part of this great time. It will be over tomorrow and who knows when you will all get together again. Can't you just set this contention you have with your father aside for just another day? Won't you please come over for dinner and join in the good family time. Life is too short to season it with bitterness."

Stephen visibly started with a sudden jerk of his head, and then he stood up. Sadie turned to see what he was looking at. Peter had come into the house and stood with his hat in his hands. His face was not humble or apologetic. It was formidable in its own way. Sadie was sure that he was ready to defend her against this big bad wolf of a man. *God bless him,* she thought.

Sadie stood up also and turned to Peter. "Peter, thanks for coming in for me. I do indeed need to get back to my dinner preparations." She turned back to Stephen. "I hope that you will consider joining us today. Dinner is at 2:00. Come sooner if you can. Everyone will be so pleased."

With that Sadie turned on her heels and left with Peter closing the door behind them. "Whatever did you say to him," Peter inquired.

"I hardly remember. However, I do think some of the anger went out of him. I hope he can see his way to come and be civil. This matter of the treasure and distribution of it is not over by a long shot. I just hope he can be man enough to set it aside for a while and not ruin the reunion."

Cherie and Gladys had kept the kitchen running well. Nothing was burned and everything was nearly ready. She hugged them both. Joy was in the playpen enjoying a set of measuring cups and spoons. Sadie reached down to kiss her on the head. "Oh, it is such a healing thing to see a baby and know there are still uncomplicated souls and innocence in the world."

Philip and Jessie were running outside playing cowboys and Indians. A bit of snow was falling outside. The tiny flurry was just enough to make it picturesque and exciting. Music was being played on the piano upstairs; simple recital fare with cheering going on. *It must be Sarah playing for everyone,* Sadie thought, smiling. Sadie set the yeast rolls in the oven. She was just about ready to make the gravy out of the giblets, when the kitchen door swung open and Suzanna came in. She rushed right up to Sadie and hugged her.

"I've had the best time here. I don't want it to end. I'm already getting sad to think we have to leave tomorrow."

"Well, I'm glad to hear it. There's nothing stopping you from coming back and staying a bit longer. You are a young lady now, and I suspect your folks would allow you to come here and stay on your own sometime," Sadie offered.

"Oh, do you really think I could? I'd love to be here. I love that room here behind the kitchen. I've felt so grown up all weekend being farther away from my little sister and those rowdy cousins of mine. Thank you for assigning me that room."

"You are so welcome. You need to go on outdoors and walk over to my cottage and see how you like that. My cat needs letting out anyway," Sadie prompted.

Suzanna leapt toward the back porch with a little shout and was gone.

"Doesn't take much to please that 'un, I reckon," said Gladys.

"Young people just like to be trusted with things and given their privacy," explained Sadie.

The doorbell rang. Sadie thought, w*ho could that be on Christmas Day, for crying out loud?* She hadn't let herself even hope it would be Stephen. Besides that, he would just open the door and make himself at home. Gladys went to answer the door and came back into the kitchen with her mouth open and eyes wide. "It was Mister Stephen," she remarked. "All dressed up and smelling good. He was polite as could be too. Handed me his coat, hat and scarf, and nodded a sort of thank-you to me and walked up the stairs to join the others. Don't that beat all?"

Sadie didn't mind any of the clean up chores. She loved hearing all the talking and laughter and singing going on in the next rooms.

At one point the Colonel came into the kitchen and patted her on the back with affection and thanks. "He came back, Sadie. He came back. It is like a miracle."

Sadie would never think of telling the Colonel that she had gone to convince Stephen to come back for dinner. It was way better that Colonel Shaw determine in his mind that his son wanted to be there, and had swallowed his pride and come.

It was about 4:00 when Peter took Cherie and Joy home. Gladys got a lift from her husband, Ned. They were going to have Christmas later that evening. Gladys was very glad to work on Christmas day and earn the extra money. Besides, Ned had to work that morning anyway as a security guard. That was his extra job.

Sadie was reviewing the day in her mind. While the family had eaten their feast in the dining room, Sadie had set the table for her workers in the kitchen with candles and all the crystal and fine china and silver. She handed out the presents she had wrapped up for them. Practical things that she knew they could use. She had always had trouble buying frivolous gifts even when she could afford to be spontaneous and silly. She got a gift card for Cherie for the local Walmart for $100. For Joy she purchased a satin edged baby blue, thick and soft, flannel blanket and a medium sized grey teddy bear with the sweetest face and a pink ribbon. Since Joy was the smallest and most precious person at the table, Sadie had splurged and made up a big wicker basket full of packages. There were new clothes for Joy and books, and many little toys in colorful wrappings. For Gladys she wrapped up a warm winter hat and scarf to match. She gave her a $100 gift certificate for the local Target Store. Peter was given a nice warm work coat that was light but very protective in black and yellow. That way she could spot him in the yard wherever he was working. She got him two pair of work gloves too. In the pocket of the coat was $50 worth of movie tickets to encourage him to go and have some fun once in a while. Her gifts were nothing to write home about, but she wanted her friends and workers to know she cared.

Sadie had sent presents to her grandson, Treat; a big cardboard box full of presents, in fact. She bought a cashmere sweater in apricot for her dark haired Rebekah. She also included the promise of free tickets to fly out and visit. She got Stan a gift certificate from Lowes for $75.00. For her two sons she bought the brand new version of the Message. It was the whole Bible translated by a real Biblical scholar in the modern vernacular. The verses were not numbered and so it was like reading a novel. She also bought each of them a palm pilot to keep records of appointments and schedules written down and in their pockets. How Sadie would have liked to spend Christmas with her own family. But that was just not possible this year.

She had packed up leftover dinners for all three of her loyal staff and sent them off with a big thank-you and hug. Even Peter got a hug and gave one back. "You all take Monday off now. We'll tackle all the rooms and put things back in order on Tuesday. I can handle breakfast for this crew by myself, and they can see themselves to their cars. No problem. There is no way all this reunion could have been accomplished without all your help."

The truth was that Sadie needed some time to herself. She was sorely tired of talking and being around people. She would have made an excellent hermit.

Chapter 34

Coming Up With a Plan

Stephen was kind enough to let his folks rest a few days before approaching them on the subject of the treasure, its use, and distribution. But approach them he did. He was not finished with this deal by a long shot. Sadie could hear the banter back and forth. Sometimes the voices got a little louder, but mostly they stayed civil. She wanted so to be a little mouse in there so she could view it all and hear it all. As soon as Stephen left the house, the Colonel came into the kitchen where Sadie was making a couple of little turkey pot pies. She had always believed in using up leftovers wherever possible.

"Well Sadie, looks like we may have to go to court after all. Stephen wants to have the judge declare me unfit to run my own affairs. He wants to have the power of attorney over my estate and financial business. He says that I am too old to know what is best to do anymore." The Colonel looked defeated and tired. "Maybe he's right. Do you think he's right, Sadie?"

"Poppycock! He's not right! Not for a long, long time yet. I'm no expert, but I firmly believe that you are perfectly capable of making your own decisions on money matters. When I think of how many years of hard work and carefully made decisions you've made to accumulate and protect this estate, I can only conclude that you are still the man to handle those affairs. I see no evidence of senility in you whatever. Let me add, however, that I personally think Stephen is stepping in like this because he truly thinks he is doing the right thing. He does care for you both so much and just wants to not worry so much about you." Sadie stopped for a breath and continued, "But, Colonel, you are just going to have to fight this thing and prove to him that you are still capable to be in charge. Don't give up without a good hard struggle."

"But how? It is his word against ours and he is so well respected in this community that I can't imagine a judge in town that would go against his wishes."

Sadie set two cups on the table and poured hot brewed tea. The Colonel sat down wearily. "Let me think about this," she said. They sat in silence for a while. The Colonel had a warm tiny cinnamon roll and quietly waited for her to ponder things.

"Here's what we will do," she offered. "You spoke about tearing down this impregnable, restrictive stone wall and opening up this property to the neighborhood to enjoy and see. Do you still want to do that?" Sadie asked.

"It would be a hefty project, but it would be my final legacy to this town. This wall has been up way too long. It shuts us away from people and shuts them out of our lives. Peter is making such a park out of this property that I'd love to watch other people enjoy it too. My wife would so enjoy sitting on the porch seeing the people walk by. She might even feel free to greet a few of them. It would be good for her."

"You say that you would do this for the town. That is a very good point," Sadie was quiet again. Her mind was working swiftly through all the possibilities. Finally she spoke. "Here's what we could do, if you want. This is just a suggestion, and it must be your choice," she added. "We can easily get character witnesses for you who will testify to your capabilities and brightness of mind and establish your right to be free from Stephen's ruling hand. Then we can make an announcement to the paper that you've decided to open up your property, so the city can enjoy your park acreage. If the mayor and powers that be know that you have chosen this, they will put pressure on any judge who hears your case that might think of siding with Stephen. After all if you are incompetent to decide something of that magnitude, then the town will not get the benefit of your gift."

"I have an even better idea," piped in the Colonel. "All of my children have their own homes and plenty of money of their own to live comfortably without my inheritance. I propose that I announce that this big mansion and this acreage will go to the city when Victoria and I are gone. They can make an historic museum of it with tours. That story about the hidden attic room and the treasure found there will bring in a lot of curious tourists. I imagine that story will grow into some sort of legend." The Colonel was beaming now. "By golly, that should do it!" The Colonel was actually chuckling.

"I'm sure the Immanuel Baptist Church would appreciate the donation of all those huge stones that make up the wall. I venture to say they'd even be willing to come and haul them away for you. The pastor, Rev. Noah Brown, told me that the congregation could use those stones to build themselves a new sanctuary. They even have a master brick builder, albeit retired, that could head up the project." Sadie was getting into the swing of things now, too.

"You know Sadie, tearing that wall down is going to be noisy and messy. We might need to go door to door to all the neighbors surrounding these three blocks of property and get them to sign a paper agreeing to the inconvenience it might cause them. It will take a while to get that wall down; weeks and even maybe a month or two. Think of the traffic and dust and noise. We'd have to take into consideration whether the neighbors would be upset about it or not."

"See, there is proof once again that you are fully capable of reasoning things out." Sadie bragged on him. "I'll get some young adults from the First Baptist Church to volunteer to take a petition around from door to door. I teach one of their classes in Sunday School and I'm sure I can convince them of the advantages of such a project. We will have those teams of two deliver a box of cookies to each house, as they tell the folks about the proposed plans for the neighborhood. If the households around the wall realize what all the removal of this wall entails and can be convinced that the end result will be the best thing for the neighborhood, and yes, the community, then . . . . your neighbors might be more willing to put up with those inconveniences for a while." Sadie gulped in a deep breath. She wasn't used to making such a long speech.

The Colonel grinned from ear to ear. "By George, let's do it. I'll call the newspaper about our proposed plan. But first I'll get a hold of Rev. Brown to be sure that his congregation approves of all that work. If they vote yes, then I'll run my plans by the mayor and his council. I'm sure they will think it a grand idea. For a while this project will put Rose Creek on the map. They'd love all that media attention." He paused to ponder his next words. "I'll have to contact some contractors and get bids on how much they would charge to take down the wall. It may take most of those certificates from the attic to get the job done."

Sadie had tears in her eyes as she contemplated the determination of this very fine old gentleman. "And don't forget, you must get your lawyer to line up character witnesses in your favor, so you can beat Stephen's argument to declare you unfit to run your own affairs."

"Oh yes, that! I'll call my lawyer right now and go there for a meeting. I'm sure he will do all he can to see that power of attorney remains with me." The Colonel turned on his heel like a dedicated soldier and marched back to his suite.

Chapter 35

Stephen's Day In Court

The hearing was held within two weeks. Stephen came to it all sure of himself. Sadie could see it in his step and haughty manner. He stopped to pat his father on the back in a sort of conciliatory way. Victoria had been encouraged to stay home and wait for the Colonel's return. Sadie had figured that things might get a little ugly and didn't really want her upset by any of it. There were hardly any visitors in the courtroom. Sadie sat behind the Shaw's courtroom table along with Peter, Gladys and Cherie.

"All rise!" the bailiff ordered. "Judge Huntington presiding."

Everyone stood immediately to his or her feet. In walked an attractive woman in the clerical black robe. She was about Stephen's age. She searched the room quickly and her eyes rested on Stephen for a second. Her mouth formed a lopsided, though slight grin.

Uh oh, thought Sadie, *I think this courtroom is rigged.* She exchanged glances with her house staff companions. Their raised eyebrows and Gladys' opened mouth told her that this was the summation of the lot of them.

Stephen proceeded with his witnesses. Three bankers came forward to testify that the Colonel had indeed come in to deposit the cash certificates with little explanation as to why he had come to the bank of three different towns rather than his own bank in Rose Creek. They thought it "quite odd, to say the least." A doctor came up to explain what happens to the brain at this age, and how confusion can color decisions.

Blah, blah, blah, thought Sadie.

After Stephen had exhausted his list of 'witnesses', the judge then looked to the Colonel's lawyer and said, "Mr. Holcomb, are you prepared to defend your position regarding your client?"

"Yes your honor, we are. The defense calls in the editor of the newspaper, Mr. Ed Biggins."

Mr. Biggins came forward from outside. The judge looked at Stephen and he shrugged his shoulders slightly.

"Mr. Biggins, have you had any dealings with Colonel Shaw recently? And if so, could you tell us about it."

"Yes sir, I sure have. Mr . . . . er Colonel Shaw there, came into my newspaper office a couple of weeks ago with a story he thought I might want to print. It was a tale about Civil War treasure, including deceit, a wounded Union soldier and a secret attic room in his house. I went there to see it for myself. I'm getting ready to print this story. I can guarantee this story is going to become a major part of our city's history, your honor. This man wants to tell his story for all to read."

"Did Colonel Shaw seem confused or feeble of mind to you in any way?"

"Not at all. He was spry as I am. His mind was working like a fine tuned clock. He asked me to hold the story until after this hearing. I'm sure anxious to print it. Hope this hearing is finished up soon."

The next witness was the Colonel's own doctor who testified of the Colonel's keen mind and good health for his age. "There is absolutely no sign whatever of dementia in this man. He is an avid reader and holds a very intelligent conversation. His memory is top notch."

Next came Reverend Brown, who marched up to the witness chair with purpose and not a little chagrin. "The Colonel here is a generous man. He's a kind and honorable soul. He has offered to help us build a new church with the stones that make up that wall around his home."

A gasp came from Stephen and he stood halfway up. His lawyer gently pulled him down. "What the heck? What's that about the wall?"

The judge had to quiet Stephen down. "Stephen . . . . I mean, Mr. Shaw, you will have to remain quiet and sit down. Proceed with the defense witnesses."

"The defense calls in the Mayor of Rose Creek. Mrs. Ivy Bridges."

The back doors opened and in came the mayor and her entourage. Newspaper photographers came in with her and they were snapping pictures right and left. The flashes of their cameras made the judge flinch. "Stop that flashing; do you hear me?" She shouted while banging her gavel. The entourage with the Mayor settled down in the seats nearly filling the place. The mayor dressed in a fine, wool violet tailored suit with white ruffled collar came forward and sat down.

"You honor," began the lawyer. Both the judge and the mayor turned their eyes to him as if to answer. Judge Huntington, realizing that she was not the only 'your honor' in the room, cleared her throat and adjusted things on her desk. "Mayor Bridges, do you know the defendant, Colonel Everett Shaw personally?"

"Indeed I do. This sweet man came to me with a very generous offer."

"And what exactly was the nature of that offer, your honor?"

"Colonel Shaw owns a sizeable piece of property near the center of town. On it is a grand old mansion from the Civil War days. I understand that just recently a treasure was found there and there is a story to go along with that discovery that will bring many tourists to our town in the future. Many people will come and want to see that small secret attic room and tour such a fine old house."

"You say, tour? How could they tour his private abode?"

"This wonderful man intends to improve our little city with the future gift of his mansion and acreage surrounding it. He plans to tear down that hideous monstrosity of a wall and make a park of his land. It will benefit the community and make that neighborhood a truly lovely place to walk and relax."

Stephen was irate. He beat his fists on the table and stood up straining against his lawyer to get to his father. The Colonel sat stoically facing the front. His eyes never wavered right or left.

"Mr. Shaw, I must ask you to be seated and stop that ranting," the judge begged him. "I have to have order in this court. Any more outbursts like this and you will be removed from the courtroom. Do you understand?"

Stephen slowly lowered himself to his seat and glared at his dad and then at Sadie and then he foolishly included the judge in his reproachful looks. It was more than she could bear. "Mr. Shaw, if I hear one more word from your mouth and one more unruly gesture, you will be held in contempt of court. This is my last word," the judge admonished him.

After that, every effort of the Stephen's lawyer fell flat. The judge quickly ruled that Colonel Shaw was in fine mental health and could indeed manage his own affairs. Stephen stormed out of the courtroom. The rest of the people in the room cheered and rushed forward to congratulate the Colonel and ask him question after question about the legend and the treasure. They probed him for details concerning the benevolent future gift of his property to the city.

Colonel Shaw was visibly shaken. His victory was a bitter one. He loved his son so much. He hated to push Stephen to the wall where hatred and rejection were his only recourse. He slumped forward a little as Peter and his lawyer led him out of the courtroom and to the car. Sadie followed close behind. The drive home was a silent one. No rejoicing over the victory. Sweet Victoria was waiting at the front door for him with open arms. Whatever the outcome, she was ready to console her man. He moved into her frail arms and they retreated into the suite. Sadie quickly fixed them hot lemon tea with honey and carried in fresh chicken soup and egg salad sandwiches. *A little rest and privacy will do wonders for them.* She thought again of how brave the Colonel was to buck up against his powerful son.

Chapter 36

Tackling the Project

The next day the story about the hidden Confederate treasure and the gift of the house and property to the city appeared in the newspaper. Nothing was mentioned about how Stephen had taken his father to court to try to assume control of his finances. This had been one of the Colonel's requests. Eventually by word of mouth the truth would leak out, but Colonel Shaw did not want it announced in the paper along side the good news of his gift to the city. After that, photographers from magazines and newspapers came to take pictures of the property and the secret, attic room. For a while the house was like a depot of people coming and going.

Sadie recruited three pairs of singles to canvas the adjoining neighborhood. She baked an assortment of cookies and layered them neatly in cake boxes and sent them with a hand written note to each occupant. There were twelve houses in all surrounding the Colonel's plot of land. The young people were cordial and friendly and presented a copy of the sketches Sadie had drawn of how nice the land would look without that thick, gray wall. The cookies were appreciated. To Sadie's surprise every one of the owners of those dozen houses agreed that although it would be a noisy and dusty time, the end result would be wonderful. Signatures were gathered at all the addresses. Now Peter said they were ready to roll.

The Colonel had sought the advice and estimate of a contractor about tearing down the wall. The price was pretty formidable. The rental of the huge crane and ball to do the initial breaking up of the wall took a lot of their budget. They looked into the hiring of three backhoe drivers to break up and scoop up rocks and debris and fill up the pickups that would be coming to carry it all away.

Peter and the Colonel discussed how it would be much way more efficient to rent dump trucks to load up the stones and deliver them to the church.

One evening after supper, Sadie and the Colonel sat at the kitchen table with Peter, trying to figure out how to make the money from the certificates and two of the gold bars cover the cost of everything.

"We've come this far. We can't turn back now. I didn't realize how expensive it would be to get this wall down," said the Colonel. "After I gave those three gold bars to the kids it whittled the amount we have to work with down to about $400,000. Is that right Peter?"

"Good figuring Colonel Shaw. When you consider all the repairs you need to do on the house and driveway and garden, well that pretty much eats up that part. How did that treasure suddenly seem like so small an amount?" Peter asked.

"I still think it was right for me to give those three gold bars to the kids. We still have three held back for emergency use and investments. If we have to, we'll just dig into that surplus and get this job done. My daughter and sons can use their money for their grandchildren's college educations. Susan can put that in a fund for her four grandchildren: Suzanna and Sarah, Philip and Jessie. That should help to cover the cost of their education. Well at least $36,000 a piece. Right now, my son, Stewart only has one grandchild, Julie. But that doesn't mean there won't be more coming. Beth and Brad haven't even gotten married yet. So I'm sure more will be coming. Then there's Stephen. He has no grandkids as yet, but his two kids, Patrick and Melody might just surprise him some day. Yeah, I was right to give them those bars of gold," reasoned the Colonel.

"Let's work these figures again and this time we'll delete the dump trucks. Maybe the church will have enough pickup trucks and men available to drive them and unload them. The backhoes can scoop up the stones and lay them in the trucks. I wonder who would be willing to let their truck take that kind of abuse. Yikes!" queried Peter.

At that moment the phone rang. Sadie answered it. As she listened her eyes got very wide and her mouth stretched into an incredulous grin. She listened intently for a few minutes and then said, "Yes ma'am, that would be wonderful. We were just sitting around trying to figure out how to cover the cost. Let me let you talk to the Colonel," Sadie handed the phone to the puzzled old gentleman.

Peter looked at Sadie and signaled "What?" with his hands. She put her finger to her lips, shushing him, and gave him the thumbs up signal and crossed her fingers. She bit her lip as she watched the Colonel's face.

The Colonel was staring at the floor nodding his head and saying over and over, "Uh huh, uh huh, okay. Are you sure?" Finally the conversation was finished and he hung up the phone. He stood there dumbfounded for a moment and then seemed to notice Peter and Sadie standing eagerly with their hands clasped together at their chests.

He turned to the table and sat down. "You are not going to believe this! I am still reeling with the improbable prospect of it. That was Mayor Bridges. She's received so many inquiries about the house and treasure story that she has been sort of pressured into making this historic project happen. She wants for the city to have a part in this renovation. She says that if the city will reap the rewards for years to come, then it definitely should help finance the work. Evidently she had a meeting with her council and they checked their financial capabilities." He stopped for a breath. Sadie went quickly to get him a glass of water. He gulped it down and continued. "Offers have been coming in from contractors and even individual heavy equipment operators that they would be willing to give their time to get this job done. The city has come up with a plan that they will provide the equipment and the dump trucks, if the city's manpower will volunteer the work." He looked up at Sadie and Peter, who spontaneously hugged each other tightly in celebration.

"God is good. He is so good." Sadie spouted. "I love to see miracles like this unfold. It just boosts my faith."

Peter shuffled his feet and made a sort of unrecognizable sound. Sadie knew he was still struggling with any faith in God at all. He still thought that whatever happened to people was of their own doing. In Peter's estimation, people made their own luck, not God. She smiled at him and patted his shoulder. "There, there, Peter. I didn't mean to shake up your determination to deny the Lord any glory in this," she teased him. "But you have to admit, it does sound pretty miraculous. So I'll just choose to give Him thanks for it, okay?"

The Colonel nodded and said, "Me too. This has to be a miracle. The Lord must be in this whole project. Now, I just wish I could get back in the good graces of my son," he said.

"Looks to me like your son should be the one trying to get back into **your** good graces, Colonel," Sadie retorted gently. "You are not the one who went on the attack. You just defended yourself and proceeded with your plans. I don't think you have anything to be apologetic about."

"Well, it feels terribly disrupting to my soul, this being separated from my eldest son like this. He must be miserable. I know I am."

"If I may inquire, what have you heard from Susan and Stewart? Surely they have read about this venture. It's been in several newspapers," asked Sadie.

"I've spoken with both of them on the phone. They both think it is a marvelous idea. Neither one of them has any desire to inherit this big mansion. They would just like the privilege of coming and staying here in a couple of the private rooms upstairs whenever they feel like coming into town. For old times' sake, you know. I spoke to the mayor about that stipulation, and she said there would be absolutely no problem with it; just as long as it didn't include the room where the hidden attic is located. That room will be needed for the tours. So, when my children come to town, those two big bedrooms will be set aside as off limits to tourists. It would only be once in a blue moon anyway." The Colonel sighed. He stood up and excused himself to spend the rest of the evening with Victoria.

Pete shook his head and said, "That old man is hurting. How good it would be to have his son come around to his way of thinking. If Stephen would just stand up for this idea and help his dad accomplish it, then this victory, and admitted miracle," he grinned with eyebrows raised, "would be ever so sweet."

Sadie smiled at Peter for his concession to the miracle and patted his arm. "Pete, you are so right about that. I'm afraid all the Colonel's joy in this great undertaking has been drained out by the fact that Stephen is so distant and angry. How I hope and pray he comes around. It seems like a fat chance; but God can work in hard hearts."

"You'd have made a preacher, woman!" Pete turned on his heel and left.

After the coldest part of winter had passed, around the end of February, things began moving very fast. The street was blocked off as a huge crane came with a hanging wrecking ball to begin the initial knocking down of the wall. A crowd of officials gathered for pictures and newspaper and T.V. coverage as the Mayor issued the order for the first swing of that destructive steel ball. A big cheer went up. In the crowd were some of the black congregants and their pastor. The neighbors had come to their front porches to watch and clap. The sound was terrible. *It must be like the sounds of a war zone*, thought Sadie. The diesel trucks were roaring back and forth with their loads of rocks. The backhoes were scraping and gathering the stones. Whenever a load of rocks was dumped in a truck, the screeching noise made Sadie jump. She wanted to stuff her ears with cotton. The work was endless, it seemed.

The dust from the destroyed cement and stones filled the air and wafted into the house covering everything with a fine powder. Gladys was kept busy trying to keep the house from being overtaken by the dust. "I've had a coughing fit for days now," she griped.

The Colonel noticed that Victoria too was suffering with labored breathing. He decided that she would be better off at Susan's house for a good spell. He decided to drive her there and stay a while himself. Sadie thought it was a great idea.

Wheezer seemed to enjoy the whole mess. He would climb a tree and sit out on a branch and watch all the activity. When the day's work was completed, he would descend easily to the ground and trot to the cottage to settle in for a nice long nap.

Peter would wait till the machines had finished with one section of wall and then he would move in to clean up the debris and left over stones. The best leftover stones he would pile in his construction pile for future park projects. He would shovel up the chunks of abandoned old cement and mortar and shovel it into the old pickup truck. Several times a day he would haul his load to the dump. Peter's arms were getting very filled out with muscle. He told Sadie that he'd never worked so hard in all his life. She gave him a raise. If he were in charge of what was to become a city park, he deserved more money. He would need the freedom to hire workers to help him when necessary. When Spring came around, there would be a lot of preparation for planting. Pete had plans for fountains and streams and fishponds. He wanted to build little cubby-holed stone planters all around the area. Sadie approved of this, for to her, little hideaways and alcoves of privacy were what made places so inviting. His plans for the acreage were sketched on paper and Sadie found that, in fact, she approved of every idea he came up with.

Chapter 37

Becky's Visit

During the six weeks after the trial, when deep winter kept the work crews from starting the wall project, Sadie had once again gone back home to see her daughter and grandson, Treat. They had kept the visit quiet and mostly she had stayed at home talking and getting caught up. Rebecca had given her mother a nice camera with which to take pictures of the places she talked about. Sadie made it a point to talk to her daughter once a week on the phone. She would keep in touch once a month with her sons, who were too busy anyway to be bothered by their mom. She also wrote once a week to Rebecca and sent her pictures of the cottage and garden. She included snapshots of the mansion and the town. She included portraits of Peter, Cherie and Joy, Gladys, Victoria and the Colonel.

Now that Victoria and the Colonel were gone for a spell to avoid the noise and mess of the project, Sadie wanted Rebecca and family to come and see her. She had saved up her wages, having very little to spend it on, and she sent them the money to buy plane tickets. Becky's husband, Stan, decided he could use this time alone to catch up on things, so he declined the invitation to join his wife and son on this escapade. Sadie was not surprised. She had never been able to get close to Stan. There was an underlying resentment there. Sadie could feel it, but for the life of her, she could not explain it.

Her big sons were invited too. Andrew and Matt wanted to come and even tried to work out their schedules to make it happen. But in the long run, there was no way they could pull away from all their responsibilities at the restaurant and hospital. Sadie was sorry about it, but completely understood.

The day of Becky and Treat's arrival had come. Peter had worked on the old truck to make sure it would be able to make the trip to Asheville and back.

Their plane arrived fairly early in the day. It felt so good to see her daughter and grandson come walking through the gates and into her arms. How she loved them and missed them. Sadie was like a child with a toy she wanted to share. She could hardly wait to get them to her little home and to let them see her new life. Treat absolutely loved the old truck. Peter had rigged a couple of seat belts for them to use, since the truck was so old it hadn't come with any. Sadie had taken the precaution of purchasing a toddler's booster seat for Treat to sit on.

But before they headed for Rose Creek, Sadie took them by the fabulous Biltmore estate and mansion. They parked and Sadie piled the luggage in the cab of the truck and locked the doors. Sadie paid the extravagant fees for them to tour the huge grounds and house, no, castle. Treat was overcome with curiosity and awe. He could not believe that anyone had ever lived in such a place. The rooms had ridiculously high ceilings. There were huge halls for dancing and eating. They saw classical scenes, like the ones from

Renaissance times, painted right on the walls and ceilings. The mansion had formidable gargoyles set on the parapets outside to greet visitors and scare away evil spirits. Treat didn't' like them much. He loved rubbing his little hands over the marble banisters and smooth, polished wood. They held him up on the wide, long porches where he could see the scenic views of the manicured acreage and magnificently, giant trees. Sadie found out that the Biltmore family had the right of occupancy in some of the private rooms on the third floor. She smiled to herself thinking of how small in comparison the old Shaw mansion was to this, but that the Shaw family wanted the same rights in that old house of theirs.

They had lunch at a little quaint teashop near the gift shops down by the front of the mansion. Treat got a strawberry ice cream cone, which he greedily gobbled up while walking back to the pickup. On the way home, he fell fast asleep laying his head on his grandmother's arm. She tried to guide the truck with her left arm so as not to disturb him. What a joy that boy was.

"How are things going, dear?" She asked Becky. "You seem sort of pensive. Maybe you are just tired after the trip."

"Actually, I'm not tired at all. I'm just elated to be here with you. Thanks so much for getting us the tickets so we could come. Stan is always so tight with his money. He is determined to save for a rainy day."

"I'm sorry Stan couldn't get away and come too. It might have been good for him. And as far as 'saving for a rainy day', well that is just good practice. You never know when one of those messy deluges might descend on you," her mother said encouragingly.

"Oh Mom, I'm tired of worrying about things that never happen. I just want to live life with abandon once in a while. Is it such a crime to want to be happy, and spontaneous? Stan is such an engineer! I never see that humor that attracted me to him in the first place. All his energy goes toward building up his career or saving more money." Rebecca began to cry. She was disgusted with herself for losing it like this, but the pent up turmoil in her heart just bubbled over when she was with her mother. "I do this every time I see you. I fall apart. Why is that? You just trigger that in me."

"Hush, now daughter. I'm your moma. You can feel free to let everything out when you are with me. I'm here to listen, and I'm on your side. You know that, and you can release it all now. It will make you feel so much better to get it off your chest. Let's hear it," demanded Sadie.

And they talked, or at least Rebecca talked and Sadie listened. By the time they got to Rose Creek, Becky was petered out and ready for a break in her mini-tirade. "Here it is," Sadie offered. "Here is where I live. This is now my town, Rose Creek."

Becky rolled down the window and breathed in the air and looked at the neat squared off little town with old-fashioned storefronts and window boxes with flowers. She noticed that a few of the sidewalks were made of old brick. There were only two streetlights on the whole of Main Street.

"Oh mother, the light is going, but I can still see the charm of this place. It looks like a Robert Kinkaide painting with all the lights in the windows. I'm afraid it will be hard for us to go home," admitted Becky.

"I do hope you like it. When you see the rubble around the mansion where they are taking down that wall, you may not like it so much," she admitted. They drove on for just a little ways and she pulled into the darkened yard and parked near her cottage. The lights in the little house were all on and it was a welcoming sight. Peter was standing at the door holding Wheezer.

"I see that your gentleman is also your welcoming committee," Becky teased.

Sadie gasped a little and said firmly, "First of all, he is not *my* gentleman, although he is indeed a gentleman. I think Peter just wanted to be sure we made it safely home in this old truck, and he probably didn't want us coming into sheer darkness." She got out of the truck and turned to scoop the sleeping boy into her arms. She placed Treat's head to the one side and laid it on her shoulder.

"Here let me take him for you," offered Peter. "I'm so glad you made it home safely. That old truck is a pretty good one, but all the way to Asheville was a little chancy."

"Peter, thank you for having the lights on for us. You are the best," she said as she handed over the sleeping child. Peter carried Treat into the house and laid him on the bed they had set up for him in the corner of Sadie's room. Peter had hauled down a twin bed from one of the room's upstairs and Sadie had made it up with her quilts and a soft feather pillow. She had brought down a little side table with a cheery tiffany lamp on it. The whole scene was very welcoming. Peter covered the boy up with a lap quilt and then exited the house.

Peter walked up to Becky. "Nice to meet you. My name is Peter Combs. You must be Rebecca." He offered his hand to greet Becky.

"Yes, I've heard so much about you. I'm so glad to meet you and see you in person. You are like a legend to me after all my Mom's told me about you," Becky timidly remarked.

Peter looked quickly at Sadie in a bit of a panic. "Well, I don't know what she's told you about me. I don't really think she knows that much about me, come to think of it."

"I know all I need to know about you, Peter. I know you are the hardest worker I've ever known. I know you finish a job when you start it. I know that you do way more than is expected of you. I know you are creative and have great joy in life. But, you are correct; I hardly know anything about your past life. Maybe some day you'll be more confident to share that with me. When and if that time comes, I will be eager to listen and learn 'the rest of the story' about you." Sadie finished her long speech and then put her hand over her mouth as surprised as he was that she had said all of that.

Becky just stood there with her eyes wide and her mouth parted a bit. Her mother was verbose at times, but this was a bit unexpected.

"Mr. Combs, I only meant that my mother has bragged about all you've done around here and what a help you are to her, and . . . . what a friend too."

Pete took the luggage and deposited it in the bedroom, then quickly responded. "Well, I'd better get going. It is so nice to have you here, Rebecca. What fun it will be to have your young son around to enjoy all this property. Tell him he can help me whenever he feels like it. Hope you brought some nice heavy coats to wear. It is still very nippy around here." Peter got in the pickup and drove away slowly. And now they were alone.

Peter had built a nice fire and the room was warm and cozy. Becky checked on Treat. She got out her pajamas and robe and slippers and after putting them on she settled on the comfy, quilt-covered couch in front of the fire. Wheezer seemed glad to see Becky again, because he jumped up and turned around in a circle and settled next to her side. "Oh Mom, this is so nice. It's very small, but I just feel so at home here. All of your colorful touches are here. Simple but elegant, that's what it is."

"You'll be able to see it better in the morning. There is just enough room here for me to feel at ease. More room and I'd feel lost." Sadie went to the back porch and got some milk out of the refrigerator. She quickly warmed some in a pan and made steaming hot chocolate with tiny marshmallows floating on top. "Here you go, sweet daughter. Drink up and you'll sleep well tonight." They sat in silence a while just watching the flames. The only sounds were the crackling of the fire and the sipping of the cocoa. Becky's head began to nod. Sadie went in to open the bed she would be sharing with her daughter. It was plenty big enough for both of them. She put on one of her white cotton nightgowns and then led Becky, all wobbly, to the bathroom and then the bed.

"Mom, we'd better make sure Treat uses the bathroom too. He's trying very hard to quit wetting the bed, and I know he would be embarrassed to do that in front of you."

"You tuck yourself in there, Becky. Let me take care of Treat and the bathroom duties. I raised two boys and I remember this part well."

Sadie gently uncovered her precious grandson and pulled him out of the bed leading him slowly to the toilet. The boy never even opened his eyes. He did his business, and she led him back to the soft bed and tucked him in, kissing his forehead and turning out the colorful lamp. Then Sadie wandered back to the fire and sat there finishing up her chocolate. *Life is so good. Thank you Lord. I certainly don't deserve all these blessings, but I'm so glad to have them. Help our visit together to be memorable and sweet. Thank you Lord, thank you Lord,* Sadie entreated. After a good while Sadie's eyes began to slip shut and she gave it up and went to bed. Wheezer settled down at the foot of the bed. Sadie couldn't resist gently touching the sleeping head of her daughter. She just wanted to be sure that all this was not a dream.

The visit was indeed sweet and much more. The noise of the trucks and wrecking ball and backhoes was formidable, but Becky soon got used to it, and Treat just loved every minute of it. He would sit on the front porch of the big mansion, holding Wheezer, and he would watch with rapt attention as all the commotion went on before his eyes. Pete made sure that Treat never got anywhere near the danger zone. Some of the time, Treat would help Pete pick up the good stones and carry them to the wheelbarrow and then dump them on the 'good rock construction pile'. At the end of these workdays, Peter would pay Treat a couple of dollars and brag on his hard work. Becky and Sadie even agreed to let Treat ride with Pete to the dumping area to get rid of the chunks of cement and rubble left behind.

Rebecca loved the big mansion and went through every room. She helped Gladys with the dusting and swept off the front porch. Sadie took Becky and Treat on walks to the town, where they had lunch at the Rose Vine Café and visited the bakery for a confectionary delight. Becky enjoyed becoming friends with Cherie. They took Joy home with them a couple of the days and Treat enjoyed playing with her and letting her nap on his bed. One night Sadie babysat for both children while Cherie and Becky went out to eat and see a movie. It was so good for both of them.

On Sunday they went to the First Baptist Church and Becky and Sadie sang a duet while Sadie played the piano. People came up to Becky after the services to speak to her and welcome her. Becky noticed how well accepted her mother was. The people of the church and Pastor Craig had no idea who this Sadie Jamison used to be. They didn't realize all the responsibilities she'd had in her former life at church. They didn't know about her notorious departure from the church either.

While the Colonel and his wife were gone, Sadie cooked her meals in the cottage. She loved using the old wood burning stove. Treat was intrigued with it. He loved looking at the glow of the hot, red coals when Sadie would lift one of the circles of iron to add more wood. Sadie swore that the food tasted so much better fixed on that old stove. The coffee, the bacon and eggs and even the biscuits had a smoky, light flavor. Becky had to agree. Sadie would mix up soft butter and honey and whip it together to go on those golden brown biscuits. That taste was heavenly.

At lunchtime Peter would come inside for lunch since it was cold outside. Sadie always made sure that when his work day was over he would carry a plate of food home with him for dinner. He would always return it clean as a whistle the next morning. Becky grew to have great respect for the man as she watched him work so hard.

The week went by too fast. Two days before she was scheduled to go back home, Becky began getting depressed and sullen.

"Now don't you start this! You'll waste the last two days we have together. I don't want you to go either, but you have your home and husband to go back to, and go back you must!" Sadie gently chided.

"I know, I know, Mom. But this has been the best time. Now that I've seen it all, and I can picture for myself your life here, I will miss you even more. I wish Treat and I lived here too."

This statement shocked Sadie a bit. Becky had not mentioned Stan in her wish to stay in Rose Creek. "Well, who knows, maybe some day Stan can get a job back this way and we can be closer. I'm sure there are plenty of engineer spots open around Asheville or surrounding areas. His skills are universal, after all."

"If Stan moved away from his job, he'd lose his vested interest status. He'd have to start all over again building up a retirement with another company. Stan is way too practical for that kind of choice. No, I'm afraid there is no chance of him moving here."

"Well then, you'll just have to buck up and make the best of things. Stan is a good man, Becky. Right now you consider him to be sort of boring. You see, he is too focused on his career and in amassing material things. I think he considers it his responsibility to provide a good life for you and Treat and to also prepare for a bright future. Being a father and husband is an awesome commitment. Try to look through his eyes and see where he is coming from." Sadie stopped and grabbed Becky and hugged her close, rocking her back and forth like she used to do when her daughter was a young girl. "Just try to go back there with a loving attitude and a heart full of thankfulness for him. Open yourself up to the love of God. Let that magic love fill you. It will give you so much joy, and that love will bubble over to cover Stan too. You will be amazed at how the Lord can work miracles in stagnant marriages. I've seen it happen so often. It is just a matter of surrendering bitterness and disappointment and sincerely seeking for the good in the other person."

Becky began to cry then. Pretty soon her sobs became hiccups. Sadie got her a drink of water. "I know what I should be doing, Mom. Your advice is all too perfect and I know it is what I need to adhere to. It's just that now you are gone, I just miss you so much and haven't anyone to turn to. I need to vent all these feelings and resentments."

"I know dear. But you can call me anytime when things get sort of burdensome and hard to bear. I'll listen to your complaints. You can rant and rave all you like. Sometimes just doing that can make one feel so much better," Sadie lamely offered.

"I guess I just want our marriage to be like it used to be when we first got together. Back then we couldn't wait to get together at the end of the day. We had so much to talk about. We couldn't keep our hands off each other." Becky's words got caught in her throat. "I want to get that back again. I want the Stan that I married."

"I just wonder how many women are out there who feel this way. It seems to be an almost universal problem. How do we keep the freshness in marriage? Is it even possible?" Sadie sincerely wondered.

"I don't know if it is or isn't Mom. I just know that I don't want to be like you and spend 32 years of my life finding out I made a big mistake and wasted all my time and devotion on a dead end relationship," Becky admitted.

"Now, stop that! Don't you dare start comparing your woes with Stan to the circumstances of my marriage with your father. I won't be used as an excuse for you to give up on your marriage. You have to give your connection with Stan a fighting chance," Sadie softened somewhat. "I think that all marriages go through dry spells of disinterest or side-tracked purposes. I truly believe that most marriages go up and down in the passion level. And I'm not talking just weeks or months, but years. If a couple can get through those dry patches, then the union they have is even better afterwards. I've seen it so many times, and talked couples through times like these quite often." Sadie drew her daughter to her and again hugged her tight. "Please don't use me as your example. Go back and fight for Stan. Wake him up. Cover him with care and tenderness and love and appreciation."

"How do I do that when he acts like he could care less?" Becky exclaimed.

"If I were you, I'd set aside a special time for just the two of you. Say, a special dinner that you make with candles and flowers and leave Treat at the babysitters. Tell Stan that you want to talk about some things in your marriage. Tell him that it means so much to you that you are going to insist that he listen and respond."

"Yeah, that'll work!" Becky responded sarcastically. "He'll just sigh and look away like I'm leading him to a torture chamber."

"Just carry on no matter how he acts. Do not accuse or scold or whine about things. Just tell him how you miss being close to him. Tell him what you remember about the way you were in the beginning. And don't forget to mention how much you appreciate all he does to keep you and Treat so well cared for. Ask him if you two could just set aside one day a week when you spend at least an hour or two together; just the two of you. It doesn't have to always be something special. You could just drive around somewhere, or sit and watch a sunset, or read books together, or nap together. Tell him you love him and are proud of him. Try to build him up."

"What about me? I work hard too. Can't he appreciate what I do? I'm not just sitting at home twiddling my thumbs all day waiting for the master to come home from his hard days' work, you know!" Becky was miffed.

"Becky, do you really want this to work, or do you just want to have a pity party and make the whole thing about you?" Sadie spoke bluntly.

"Why didn't you try all of these things you are suggesting to me? Maybe you could have saved your own failing marriage," Becky cried out cruelly.

Sadie just stared at her miserable daughter. Then she turned and grabbed her coat and slipped outside. Becky came after her and pulled on her sleeve. "Oh Mother, I'm so sorry. I, above all people, know how hard you tried with Father. You didn't give up for so long. You tried and tried and tried. Please forgive me for saying that."

Sadie stopped and heaved a big sigh. "Oh, Becky! I do so want you to be happy. I'd do anything I could to see that come to be. But the one thing I don't want you to do is give up on your marriage before giving it a fighting chance. Give it your best shot. Don't give up so quickly. You owe it to Stan to at least see what is going on with him and why he is acting this way. It could be that there is some hurt he's experienced. Maybe he is afraid to talk about it. Get down to the core of it, no matter how long it takes. Keep on loving him no matter what. Please try to save your marriage. Won't you just try?" Sadie begged.

Becky fell into her mother's open arms and was wrapped up in the big coat Sadie was wearing. She cried and cried. "Okay, that's enough tears. I will go back and do what you said, Mom. I'll see if God's love can shine through me. Feeling sorry for myself has sort of blocked out that light. I'll try Mom, I really will."

At the airport while they were waiting for the plane, Sadie told Treat that she knew about a grand camping place where they would go next time he came during the warm weather. "It is not far from here. It is called Moonshine Creek. It is up in the mountains and there is a stream for fishing. We'll camp out in a tent and have a big fire with rocks all around it. I'll tell you ghost stories if your Mom will let me. We'll cook outside and we'll hike and even ride horses. How does that sound?"

"Oh Grandma, that sounds like the best thing ever. You promise? Mom, can we come again? Can we?"

"But of course dear. And next time we will insist that your daddy come with us. He'd love it here." Becky replied. "Mom, be sure to thank Peter for all he did to make our stay fun. I can't wait to see that wall completely down and all the plans Peter has made for that property come true. Give him a hug for me, won't you?" She asked with a twinkle in her eye.

"Now Rebecca, none of that!" Sadie squinted at Becky's mischievousness. "Peter sure did enjoy being with you, Treat." She looked at Becky, "I think he taught him to work hard and not quit." Then she turned back to her grandson, "I'm proud of you Treat," she said, hugging him like she would never let him go.

As they walked away from her, she felt a sort of loss sink into her soul. She did truly miss them so much. She watched them until she could see them no more. They waved and waved until the last possible moment. The drive home was so lonely and Sadie was pensive and sad of heart. She decided it was a good time to pray.

Lord, I guess you can tell I'm sort of down right now. I'll start off by saying thank you for this wonderful visit. I love my daughter so much. Lord, I want her to be fulfilled and happy in her marriage. I pray you will soften the heart of Stan. Renew his mind to the times and memories that brought them together in the first place. Please Lord, revive their love for each other. Keep my grandson safe if you will. Assign him the strongest guardian angel you have. I think he's going need it.

This time Peter was not waiting for her with a fire glowing in the fireplace. Wheezer was asleep on the couch, however, and Sadie collapsed near him and covered herself with a lap quilt. There was so much to be done. So many plans that needed accomplishing. No time for sadness or melancholy. "Well, old cat, let's get to bed. We'll need lots of rest to face what is coming."

Chapter 38

Stephen Sees the Light

Spring finally began to show it's fresh face. Tiny crocuses popped out close to the ground with their purple blossoms. Then the daffodils came forth. Sadie gathered arms full to grace the mansion in every room they used downstairs. The kitchen was glowing with them in the windowsill catching the sunlight that streamed in. The foyer had a huge pitcher of them. Sadie worried a bit about using them all up, but the property had so many, there was no worry. Peter assured her that come next Fall he planned to plant hundreds of bulbs to add to the next glorious awakening. Next came the tulips in brilliant reds, yellows and pinks. The yard was pretty much cleaned up from the rubble, but the grounds where the stone wall used to be, was raw with mud and dug up dirt. There was still a lot of labor needed to make it all neat and manicured. And Peter was up to the task.

Sadie often drove over to the Immanuel Baptist Church to check on the progress of the new church that was being built of the old stones from the wall. The master brick layer was always at hand instructing his protégés and apprentices how to do the job, showing them which stone to put where, and how to seal it tight. Even at his advanced age, the old man enjoyed mixing up the mortar and placing stones in strategic places. At his instruction, the stones had been organized into piles according to size and shape. It was certainly easier to find the perfect stone at that rate. The new chapel was very roomy and taking shape nicely. Men from the church would come when time permitted. They would come after their day of work. Some gave time early and some late. Some of the young men, who were in high school would come after school and work a few hours each day. But there were at least three full time, paid workers who were there all day long. So the progress was excellent. Sadie noticed today that the wooden beams and rafters were being set into place.

She noticed Pastor Noah standing on the side admiring the progression of work on his church. He was beaming. "The Lord bless you Sister Sadie. Isn't it grand? What do you think of it?"

Sadie shaded her eyes with her hand to look at the steeple being built. "It is *so* grand that I feel like a dwarf standing here beside it. This is so exciting. I see you are out here again watching over the workers. You'll never get a sermon prepared doing this," Sadie laughed teasingly.

"Now missy, just seeing this church being built inspires me to preach a sermon. I was just making plans for the inside as well as the outside." The old, black pastor smiled and shook his head in wonderment. This project had solidified his congregation. Having a common goal and cause was just as binding to his people as that cement was to the stones. His church was united and growing.

The Shaw's returned home. It was quiet once again since the wall was down and most of the stone had been hauled away. Sadie was oh so glad to have them home. They had enjoyed their stay with Susan, but longed for the familiar things of their own home.

One morning in early Spring, Sadie was working in the kitchen, cleaning up from breakfast. Cherie's little girl was spending the day with her. She was playing on the floor with a set of old pots and pans. She had a wooden spoon and was happily beating out a tune. The doorbell rang. "Now what!" Sadie complained. She hoped it was not another newspaper man wanting pictures. The hordes of media people were a tiresome bunch. Most of them were rude and pushy. It had been a tedious time to put up with them for the last couple of months.

Gladys was not at work today. So Sadie set down her dishrag, patted Joy on the head and told her to "be good", and pushed through the swinging door to answer the big front door.

It was Stephen standing there all dressed to the nines, and smiling. "Morning Miss Sadie. Isn't this a fine day all right? May I come in for a few minutes?"

Sadie sort of shook her head in confusion. Did Stephen have a twin? This friendly sort could not be the Master Stephen she had grown to dread. "Well . . . yes indeed it is a grand day, Mr. Shaw. Come in, come in. The air still has a biting chill to it. Step in here and get warm."

She stood aside and shut the door behind him after he walked in. "I'll just see if the Shaw's are ready to see you yet. They just finished their breakfast."

"No, no. It's you I wanted to see today," Stephen sounded apologetic. "I know, I should have called, but I wanted it to be a surprise and frankly I don't want to talk to dad about it before I speak to you."

Now Sadie was really intrigued. "Come into the kitchen, won't you? I have a fresh pot of coffee and you can sit and have some." She led the way through the dining room and into the kitchen. The scents of fresh cinnamon toast lingered in the air and coffee was percolating in an old tin pot she had found at an antique store. Joy looked up from her pots and waved at Stephen.

"What's this? Are we turning this place into a nursery now?"

Ah . . . there was the old Stephen she recognized. "No, no plans for a nursery yet. This is Cherie's little girl. I watch her some days when her Moma has a hard time getting a babysitter. She's a joy to this house. In fact that is her name, Joy. Your mother loves to be with her and in fact she sometimes asks me to go get her and keep her." She picked up Joy and carried her away from the noisy pots and sat her in the playpen. Joy stood up and stared at Stephen and smiled. He couldn't help smiling back.

"Now, Stephen, how can I help you?" Sadie wanted to get on with whatever this meeting was about.

"I know, I know. I'm keeping you from some important work, aren't I?" He sniggered a little and looked around. "You surely do make this kitchen a nice place to be in. I'll give you that. I will take some of that coffee if the offer still holds."

Sadie brought him a mug and filled it with coffee. "Cream and sugar?" she inquired.

"No, thanks. I just take mine plain and strong like a man should."

Sadie leaned against the sink and folded her arms in front of herself and waited. This man was so exasperating. He wanted so badly to fit in and be clever and funny and yet all his efforts turned out wrong. He came across belligerent and cocky and disdainful.

Stephen glanced at Sadie and noticing her impatient position said, "Well, since you want to get right to it, I'll tell you why I've come. I've had a change of attitude. There I've said it!" He softly banged his hand on the table and sat up a little straighter. Sadie could tell it had been a real struggle for him to admit that. "I've been watching all this frantic work around here. I drive by daily to see the progress. I am amazed at how much has gotten done and at how good it is looking. I guess I never imagined what this place would be like without that monstrous wall around it." He stopped for a second and took a swallow of coffee.

Sadie waited.

"I feel it is about time that I made it up with my folks. I know they are not comfortable with us being at odds with each other. Dad always was one for peace and harmony. I'm sure they would like it if I came around again to visit and see to their needs."

Sadie reflected on that egotistical statement. "Yes, Stephen, you are right about that. Colonel Shaw and your mother are pretty miserable because of this strife going on between you. I think it has cost your father many sleepless nights. It is because he loves you so much that he is restless and fitful because of your disagreements. And yes, I think he would enjoy having a close relationship with you again." She paused and bit her bottom lip. She continued bravely and boldly, "What's in it for you?"

"What? How dare you say that to me. Do you think that I always have an ulterior motive whenever I do anything? That was a rude statement!"

"Yes it was. I apologize. It is just that I don't want to see your folks beleaguered by any more dissention. They have a few more good years and I want those years to be happy and free of conflict. In my observation of you, I see that mostly you seem to have a personal agenda whenever you do anything. It has to be of some profit to you monetarily or politically for you to want to put much effort in it."

Stephen stood up so fast the chair fell back behind him. Joy gasped and began to whimper.

"There, there, Joy. It is alright. The big bad man is not going to hurt you. He's just mad a me." She settled Joy down with a sippy cup of milk and a cookie. "Sit down Stephen. I apologize again. My sharp tongue will be the death of me yet," she admitted.

Stephen finally sat with his mouth open and his eyes wide and expectant like a child after a good scolding. "I probably deserved that after all. No apology necessary. It's just my blustery manner. I come across as . . . pushy and overbearing. Let me start again." He stood up slowly this time and carried his coffee with him as he paced around the kitchen. "This coffee is great, by the way. Must be that old fashioned percolator you have. I haven't seen one of those since I was a little boy."

"Yes there is something about an old-time pot on the stove, just bubbling away that makes coffee what it was meant to be," Sadie admitted. "Here let me warm that up for you." She filled his cup.

"Okay, here's the deal. Dadgum it! There I go again. This isn't a deal. It isn't anything like that. Let me word it another way." Stephen looked so chagrinned at himself. Sadie had to stifle a grin as she watched him struggle with his bullish nature. "I want to make up with my folks, but I want to do it in a special way. I'd like to have a nice dinner with them here, just the four of us."

Sadie was taken aback and sort of jerked backwards a notch. "The four of us?"

"Yes the four of us. You have to be included in this. Could you make a really nice intimate dinner for us with flowers and fancy dishes and all and even candlelight if you like? I'll show up and we can sort this whole thing out. Would you do that if I promised you that I would come in with a recalcitrant attitude, acknowledging my failings and showing how much I want to make it up to them?"

Sadie put her hands in her apron pockets. "Stephen, this all sounds too good to be true. My mind is reeling with the possibilities of peace and happiness on the horizon here. But, forgive me if I have some reservations about your motives. There I go again, questioning your reasons for doing something like this. It is just that I have become very protective of your folks and I certainly do not want to see them plunged into any more grief and heartache. They are just too precious to me."

"I assure you that I have no alternative motives, Sadie. Truth is that I miss them. I'm so proud of my father for sticking to his guns and doing this tremendous task in the face of such opposition that I posed for him. I admire him so much and I want to tell him so. I want to apologize for being such a big oaf and domineering son." Stephen stopped a minute and turned his back to her. He gazed out the window and took some deep breaths. "You have no idea how hard this is for me. It is against my nature to grovel and admit wrong doing." He turned back to her.

"Stephen, if this is for real, I must tell you that I don't interpret what you are doing here as groveling or as demeaning yourself in front of me. As a matter of fact, what you have done here today, is just about the most attractive thing you've done since I met you. It is becoming to see a man admit a mistake and have the courage to try and right it. You know what? I'm proud of you, too."

Stephen sniffed a little and shook his head. "Now you make me feel like a little boy being buoyed up by his mother after a confrontation." He finished up his coffee and said, "So if that is okay with you, just name the time and day and I'll be here. I'll even send the flowers for the table."

"What do I tell your folks about the plans for that evening?" Sadie questioned.

"Tell them that I contacted you and wanted this dinner so we can sort all our differences out and become a family again . . . or something like that. Don't make it too mushy or they won't believe it came from me."

Sadie laughed in spite of her reservations. "Okay. How about Friday at 6:30? I'll make you a dinner that will knock your socks off. And I will join you at the table even though I'll feel sort of strange doing it."

"And one more thing, Sadie, let's have it in here and not in that big dining room. I like it in here better." With that he placed the empty cup in the sink and turned around and left on his own. He slipped out the front door with his folks none the wiser about his visit.

The Shaw's were rattled by the announcement and Victoria had to be reassured that it would not be an unpleasant time. Sadie spent the next few days getting ready for this special occasion. She got the finest beef roast she could buy. A big sirloin tip. She soaked it in brine of salt and vinegar and sugar and lemon juice. Three days it sat in the refrigerator in this smelly mixture. She would turn it several times a day. She was making Svitskova for dinner. Her Czech nature was going to shine out. This was what her grandmother, from the old-country, always made once a year when Sadie was a girl. Her mouth watered just thinking about it.

The flowers arrived on Friday morning. They were beautiful. There were big, sweet smelling lilies with pink streaks in them and pale, blush pink roses and baby's breath and fern. She made one nice sized bouquet of them and set them on the little, side table in the kitchen. She also made two little bouquets in small white pitchers to reside on the window sill and countertop. She used the finest linen and silver and crystal and dinnerware. Candles adorned the room. She filled crystal votives with vanilla candles. Some were on the windowsill, some on the counter and several on the table. She had given the Shaw's specific instructions not to come into the kitchen that day. She wanted it all to be a surprise. They were like children waiting for a birthday party.

The brine was poured off the roast with just a little kept inside the pan. She pan sautéed onions and carrots and a little celery and whole mushrooms in some olive oil and added some butter at the end and finally port wine. This combination was added to the roasting pan along with some cut up lemons. The roast was cooked slowly in the oven. Soon the house was filled with the stringent and beguiling scents of roasted beef this old world way.

She boiled potatoes in the skin and peeled them while they were hot and grated them. From this she made potato dumplings by adding egg and flour and salt and pepper. She tried to keep them light by not mixing them too much. She knew they were good ones when she rolled them into balls and sprinkled them with flour. They felt soft and pliable and she knew they would boil up in the salt water to buoyant perfection. She made red cabbage at her house with a little clove spice. She didn't want to smell up the kitchen in the big house with the smell of cabbage cooking. She had cucumbers thinly sliced and soaked in salt and then rinsed and patted dry. She put them in a combination of mayonnaise and wine vinegar and salt and sugar. These masurated in the refrigerator for a few hours and were crispy and tasty. She served this little cold salad in tiny dishes to the side of the plates.

For dessert she made plum dumplings, another of her grandmother's famous recipes. She was lucky that the season for prune plums was in and she was able to find some of the oblong purple plums in the store. She split them open just enough to get the seed out and filled each with a cube of sugar. Then she rolled rounds of thin potato dough around each plum and sealed it. She set these aside with a cloth over the top. She would boil them in salted water just before serving them. Cooking them only took a few minutes. When they floated to the top they were done. For the topping, she had to take a rolling pin and crush a bowl full of graham crackers to which she added sugar and cinnamon. A little pan of melted butter was on the back of the stove keeping warm.

When the roast was done to tenderness, she drained some of the juices and discarded the veggies except for the mushrooms which she kept around the roast. She made a sour-cream gravy out of the drippings and seasoned it to taste. Now everything was ready to go. The potato dumplings for the Svitskova would be boiled after Stephen had arrived and while they all were being seated. The timing had to be perfect or the dumplings would be rubbery if they sat around too long. She had thought twice about making two kinds of dumplings for this dinner, but reasoned that they were light and completely different in taste.

The doorbell rang and Colonel Shaw answered it. Sadie could hear the warm welcoming sounds of the doorway greetings. Victoria was heard to say, "Oh Stephen, these flowers are lovely. You shouldn't have done that, dear." Soon the swinging door opened and in came Victoria with the extravagant bouquet of pale cream roses and white day lilies and baby's breath and fern. The flowers were oh so fragrant. It almost overwhelmed the cooking smells. Sadie found a vase and helped Mrs. Shaw arrange them. It really was the loveliest grouping of flowers and probably cost a mint. But where to put them? The table was too small. No one would see around them or over them to converse. Finally she pulled out a small table with two sides folded down. She put on it a crisp white eyelet cloth. The bouquet looked lovely there with a candle glowing next to it. She put the teacups and dessert dishes there too. It fit in perfectly and graced the table to the side.

Stephen and his parents stayed in the formal parlor until she called them to dinner. She really wished that the young Mr. Shaw had not insisted she join them. It just seemed awkward. But she knew that any protestations she made would seem falsely humble, so she decided to refrain from expressing her reservations. When they walked in, the Colonel and Stephen actually gasped at the table. In the midst of such a homespun kitchen, this table shone out like a bright jewel under a spotlight. The shining crystal glasses and silverware, complimented the exquisite china that Sadie had found tucked way in the back of the bureau. The napkins were ironed and starched and folded just so in an artistic spiky pattern. In front of each plate was a votive candle lit and glowing pearly white. Set beside the candles were tiny three inch vases of sprigs of wild flowers that she got from the florist. Every place setting had its own tiny crystal containers of salt and pepper. Beside each plate was a little bread plate with two pats of butter, each molded into a pattern of a flower. In the middle of the table was a steaming, fragrant loaf of just baked bread with a bread knife sitting on the bread board reading for cutting.

Stephen closed his eyes and stood there in the kitchen doorway drawing in the scents of the food through his nose. "Oooh! That is the most delicious smell. Tangy and beefy and sort of foreign. What in the world did you make, Sadie?"

"You all be seated, please. Stephen you can sit at that end and the Colonel can sit at the head of the table. Victoria, this is your place. Let me help you."

But Stephen was too quick for her. He pulled out his mother's chair and gingerly helped her be seated. He then stood by Sadie's chair, but she said, "Even though I have the privilege of eating with you three tonight, I am still the cook and server. So I will be getting up and down during this meal and I would feel very uncomfortable if you had to get up and down with me to help me be seated." Stephen shrugged with raised eyebrows and a sort of lopsided smile. He sat down.

"Today we are having my grandmother's signature meal which I used to get but once a year when I was a little girl. It is the same as the German Sauerbraten, but in Czechoslovakia it was called Svitskova. I shall start you out with a little cucumber salad." Sadie handed out the salads and cut the bread. She offered iced tea and water. And the meal began. Next she served the dumplings with the sliced beef and mushrooms and the dark, sour gravy. She gathered up the salad dishes and replace them with little dishes full of red cabbage cooked with sugar and vinegar. They all seemed to be enjoying the food so much. Stephen had to have seconds which pleased Sadie very much. Finally, after she had cleared the table of dinner dishes, she made the fresh brewed coffee which she had ground that morning and served the plum dumplings. She Had her hot salted water boiling and dropped the six dumplings in gently. They took no more than 7 minutes to float to the top and she scooped them out and drained them on paper. Then she placed a hot, fresh light dumpling in a little bowl and split it open with a knife. The wine red juices poured out. She sprinkled a generous amount of the graham crackers and sugar mixture on top and then dribbled melted butter over that. It was steaming when she placed each dumpling in front of each person. She placed a little pitcher of the hot butter on the table along with the rest of the cracker mixture. Again, Stephen wanted seconds. Sadie knew then that her dinner had been a success.

All through dinner the talk had been of the weather and the nieces and nephews and Stephen's children and job related stories. The Colonel talked about the wall coming down and the park that was being created out there now. When dessert was finished and tummies were patted indicating satisfaction and fullness, Stephen pushed back his chair a bit and stood up.

"I arranged for this dinner for a special reason. I wish to formally apologize for my stubbornness and pig-headed bullying."

The Colonel and Victoria exchanged glances and their eyes got wide with expectation. *What are you up to now, Stephen,* thought Sadie. *Please don't ruin this wonderful time we've had together.*

But Stephen was serious. Even though it was hard for him to put on the appearance of humility and repentance, he was truly telling what his heart was feeling. "I've been so wrong in the manner that I have treated you two. I'm sort of a 'take charge' person, and being the eldest of your children, I felt it my duty to watch over you and be sure that you were well cared for. I guess I just assumed that because you are old and grey, Father, that you were also getting senile. How wrong I was! I realize now that you are still as bright as a penny. I am so sorry for putting you through such heart-wrenching trials. I'm glad you proved me wrong."

The Shaw's were dumbfounded. Their mouths were open a bit and they kept exchanging glances at one another with incredulous reaction. "Son, you have no idea what your saying all this means to your mother and I," the Colonel started. "Life for us has been tainted by the separation we have had from you. How we've missed you. We are both so proud of you and your accomplishments. We want you to know that we recognize that a lot of what you did was because of your genuine care of us. We know that you love us, and we hope you realize just how much we love you."

Victoria, who usually kept to herself and let her husband speak for her, added, "Dear Stephen. You've always been so special to me. My first son; so big and strong and noble. I must admit that my heart was broken when you withdrew from us. I can feel it healing up as we sit here together. It feels so good."

This time Stephen did show some real emotion. He reached over to shoulder hug his mother and hold her hand. He kissed her on the top of the head. "I know what you mean, Mother. Something tight and painful is loosening up inside of me as I sit here and confess to you. I have felt so lost during all this time. It is just not natural to be at odds with your folks. I hope you will forgive me. And if you do, I will promise to try hard to never again pull any stunts like that. For your sake and mine too. I've been miserable."

"Stephen," added the Colonel, "no matter what happens in the future, we shall always come back to this special moment when you expressed this love for us. We will always love you no matter what. Maybe in the future you will lose it with us again, but we shall all be reminded of our harmony and oneness by remembering this dinner together. We will be all right, no matter what happens."

Sadie excused herself and went to the pantry. She wiped her eyes and stayed there to let the Shaw family finish off their reconciliation alone. *Lord, how wonderful this has been. I've seen a miracle here, Lord. I'm so glad I got to be a part of it. Thank-you Lord.*

"Sadie, are you in here?" It was the voice of Stephen. "I know that you left to give us time alone. But you are the biggest part of this, you know."

"What do you mean?" Sadie asked wiping her tears away.

"The truth is . . . I've never had a woman talk to me the way you have done. At first I was so dumbfounded and angry I could not think straight. I just wanted you out of my sight and life."

"Yeah, I pretty much got that message from you." Sadie smiled lopsidedly.

"But you were just what the doctor ordered, let me tell you. I was a punk and arrogant bully. I guess I thought that no one had the right to oppose me, let alone a woman. Oh the nights I spent cussing you and ranting and pacing the floor trying to find a way to get back at you . . . to get rid of you." Stephen paused and turned toward the back porch. It took him a while to rearrange his face and clear up his voice. "Sadie, I just want to thank you for not letting me get away with the things I did and said. Thanks so much for telling me the truth. You were not afraid of me. I think that was the most surprising thing of all. I'm used to people who are fearful of my responses. Most people make a path for me and get out of my way and do not dare aggravate me or disagree with me. But not you. You stood up to me, face to face, and told me how it really was. I could not bear it. It took me this long to come to grips with the truth of it all."

Stephen turned suddenly and grabbed Sadie into a big bear hug. She was aghast at this personal touch. She gently pushed away from him. He grabbed her hand and drew it to his lips and kissed it. His eyes bore into hers and she knew that she had to stop this train right now.

She pulled her hand away slowly and backed up toward the kitchen entrance. "Mr. Shaw, you are being too kind. I'm glad you made up your mind to do all of this and get things sorted out and right with your folks. That was so very honorable and brave and I respect you for this. But the truth is I was too forward and didn't even try to hold my tongue. I hope you will forgive me for being so bold and hurting you so much. I just seem to get carried away with administering justice even when it is none of my business."

Sadie walked into the kitchen. The Shaw's had retreated to the parlor or their suite, she knew not which. But gone they were. She almost panicked. She started toward the sink and grabbed her apron to put it on. But Stephen was not to be deterred. He came up behind her and put his hands on her shoulders and turned her around.

"Sadie, maybe this isn't the time, but I want you to know that I'd like you and I to become good friends and maybe even more than friends."

Sadie's eyes got wide with apprehension. She put her hands on his chest gingerly pushing him away. She smiled up at him and said, "Mr. Shaw . . . . Stephen. I am so flattered by your reaction to me. Yes, indeed I would welcome the chance to become your friend." She stopped and looked down at the floor and then boldly up to him again. "But anything other than that will not be happening."

Stephen was taken aback and dropped his hands from her shoulders.

Sadie hurried to say, "There you go reacting in a hard way. Don't turn away, please. Let me finish." Sadie laid her hand on his turned away shoulder and he responded by turning back to her

"You see, I just came away from a failed marriage. A long marriage that I had determined would go on forever. I have to admit I am embittered somewhat and definitely not the least bit interested in starting up a close relationship with any man. It's not you at all. I just need lots of time to get my life in order and to heal from the scars I bear. Being here in this house and especially in my little cottage has done me a world of good. Please don't be offended by my response. You know me by now. Honesty works for me. It may be uncomfortable at first, but it deletes any future pain."

Stephen sat down at the table and she poured him another cup of coffee. "You beat all, Sadie. I have never met anyone like you. Most women in this town would be so flattered that I even gave them the time of day. I'm a real catch around these parts, you know." He shook his head and laughed. "People consider me the most eligible bachelor around." He laughed again at his own egotistical attitude. Sadie laughed with him.

"I have no doubt on that subject," she offered. "I'm sure that some day when you find just the right lady, she will fall for you like a ton of bricks. You are indeed very special and have great promise as a partner in life."

"You really think so? You are not just saying that?"

"Well, I may be saying it to somewhat appease you, but truly I think that under that self-centered, pompous attitude, is a very gentle, loving man, who would really like to be close to someone and grow old with someone in joy and loyalty. Am I right?"

"I hope to goodness you are right. Sometimes I wonder about myself. I think maybe that I put on airs of being so self-assured and always right, because deep down inside I feel pretty insecure and unlovable. Good grief, why am I telling you all this? You are not my psychologist." Stephen laughed a little nervously. "I hope you can keep all this to yourself."

"One thing I am very good at Stephen is keeping secrets. I just pray that you grow into the man God intended you to be. And that you find the happiness that God has planned for you. You can find it, really, if you seek it the right way."

"Here it comes again; you with all that religious stuff. What are you a preacher or something?" Stephen chuckled.

"Not far off the mark, my friend. I used to be married to one."

Stephen was taken aback. "Really? Wow! That sort of explains a lot of things about you. It would take a very brave woman to leave a preacher and face the disdain of the congregation."

"Why do you assume that I left my husband? Maybe he got tired of me and dumped me." Sadie offered.

"No way! A man would be the world's greatest fool to let you go. It had to be your dissatisfaction with him. And I can imagine it was going on for years and years before you finally ditched him. What was it? Was he unfaithful to you with his secretary?"

"Well Stephen, we are already acting like close friends with your personal questions about my life. You are very perceptive in some ways. But my husband was not unfaithful in the normal sense of the word. He was just in love with the adoration of his flock to the exclusion of his family. It is a common thing among ministers. Another woman might have endured it and gone on suffering in silence. But me, I'm not ready to give up on life that easily."

"Sadie, I apologize for getting into your personal life. I had no right. Forgive me. I surely have been doing a lot of apologizing tonight. I'd better stop before I put my foot in my mouth again. Friends?" He put out his hand and she took it.

"Friends," she agreed.

After that dinner with the Shaw's, Stephen felt very at home in her kitchen. She wasn't sure she liked his becoming so close to her, but he was like a new kid on the block who'd just made a good friend. She couldn't discourage that, could she?

Peter noticed that budding closeness and frequency with which Stephen showed up at the house to visit. Sadie watched his reactions from the kitchen window as Stephen would drive up and walk to the house without giving Peter even a recognition nod.

He still considers himself above most people, Sadie thought. *How sad for him. He's missing out on another good friendship with Peter.*

Peter was curt and cool with her now. She could read it in his eyes. He figured she had given in to the desire to be on the side of the rich. He kept his distance and was very formal in his responses to her.

"Miss Sadie, I was wondering if there is money in the budget to hire a backhoe to come and load the scrabble and extra stones for taking to the dump. That old blue pickup is wearing out fast. We will need a big dump truck in which to load the final bunch of refuse stones. It would help me out so much. These short trips to the dump with me loading the odd scraps of stone is just taking up too much of my time."

"Peter, come into my kitchen for a minute and have a cup of coffee with me."

"I'm really pretty busy right now, Miss Sadie. I need to get back to my work."

"No you don't. And quit calling me Miss Sadie. You'd think we live on an old time plantation in the old south. You are not my slave, you know." Sadie scolded. "Get in here, Peter."

Reluctantly he came inside her cottage and hung up his coat and hat on the hooks by the door. He looked uncomfortable and just stood there waiting for further instructions.

"Sit!" Sadie gestured to a seat at the table. She served up a cup of steaming coffee for both of them and a nice sized piece of pecan pie with a scoop of ice cream on top.

"Are you trying to make me fat?" he retorted.

"Yeah, that is my goal in life. To make you fat. Like that would ever happen anyway. You work too hard as it is. We couldn't get enough calories in you to make you fat."

"Man, this is so good. What's up? To what do I owe this special attention?" He asked pointedly.

"What's with you Peter? You are acting so put out with me. Am I just exaggerating or have I done something to offend you lately?"

Peter took another bite of pie and a gulp of coffee. He looked around the room and then at Sadie and started in, "I don't know. Things just seem different now. It used to be you and me against the establishment and now you are hobnobbing with the powers that be. I sort of feel like a hired hand again."

Sadie could hardly help smiling at the 'little boy face' that Peter was revealing. "Are you speaking about Stephen's change of attitude and coming her all the time to visit?"

"Yeah, I guess that is what I'm talking about. When I say it out loud it seems so petty and stupid. But I have to admit, I don't like him around here all the time, taking up your time. Used to be me that you talked to, and now it is him."

"Peter, Stephen has made a hard turnabout and it is all so new to him. He's trying hard to be a good son and not be repulsive, which is normally his nature. I like the new him and I'm just trying to help him get there." Sadie stopped and sighed.

"Well that is all well and good, but he comes here and never even acknowledges that I am part of the scenery. I'm not used to being treated like a dirty, hired hand. I guess I just resent him, and then I resent you for being so close to that son of a . . . ." Stephen stopped short of the bad language. "I'm so sorry. I shouldn't even be thinking like that. But he irks me so much. I'd just like to say to him, 'What makes you think you are such hot stuff?'" Peter laughed at himself and then said, "Good Lord, I sound like a discarded high school sweetheart, all jealous of a new suitor to his girl. Where am I getting this? It is crazy."

"I don't know, but it is funny that you are so upset with him. I can assure you that my interest in him is purely friendship. I'm a hired hand here too, remember that!"

"Not that I'm implying that you are my girl, but you are my good buddy and I don't like to see you getting so close to the likes of him." Peter turned away.

"What do you know about the likes of him?" Sadie inquired. "Let's just say that in my past I was around people like him every day. It was my job to deal with people of his caliber. Those memories just leave a bad taste in my mouth."

"Peter, this is the first thing you've ever told me about who you were before here. I wish that you felt free to tell me more."

"Well, I could say the same thing about you, mysterious lady," Peter responded. "I know very little about your former life too. I can tell that you haven't been a cook and bottle washer before, although you are mighty good at it. There is just something classical and elegant about you that you can't hide behind that apron."

Sadie looked at Peter with new eyes. She put down her coffee cup and reached across the table for his hand. He responded by reaching for hers. They sat that way for a while just looking into each others eyes. "Peter, one of these days you and I are going to have to come clean and tell our stories to one another. I guess I'm afraid you will not think much of me when I tell you the truth, and I suspect that you feel the same way about me finding out the true story of your past. Maybe one of these days we shall trust each other enough to spill it all out. I think it would be good for us."

Right then there was a knock on Sadie's door. She broke the hold she and Peter had on each other and went to the door. It was Stephen wondering if she was coming to the house soon. "I have to leave pretty soon and I just wanted to talk to you a minute before I left." He looked past her shoulder into the house and spotted Peter there finishing off his pie. "I see you have company. I guess you and the gardener are planning the rest of the park outside."

"Peter . . . . and I are just having a cup of coffee and a piece of pie together. We have been far too busy lately and I have missed out on this camaraderie."

Peter turned suddenly to look at her and a wry smile developed on his mouth. "I've got to get back to work, Sadie. Thanks for the pie. I needed that. Excuse me Mr. Shaw, I'll be getting back to work now." Peter exited the room with Stephen not giving an inch. Peter had to nearly shove him forward to get out the door.

"Well, I can see you are busy, so I'll just head on too," Stephen said with hurt in his voice. "I'll talk to you later, Sadie."

"Sure thing." Sadie said innocently. "Let me wrap you up a piece of this pie to take home with you." She turned to complete that small task. "How are things going for you Stephen? How is your family? Did you hear from them lately?" She turned to hand him the pie.

"Oh they are doing fine. They call every now and then. I wish it were more often." He turned to go and then just as suddenly turned back to ask, "Are you close to that gardener?"

"Oh yes. Peter and I are good friends. I've always thought it very interesting to have male friends. They are so forthright and honest and have few hidden agendas and no jealousies and petty grievances like women do. It is refreshing to have a male friend. I have you too and I count that a blessing as well." She smiled guilelessly at him.

"Okay, I was just wondering. I'll talk to you later." With that Stephen left. Sadie stood there amazed at these two men in her life. They were both just trying to be her friend but both of them were a little bit possessive and chagrined at the other.

Chapter 39

Word Leaks Out

It was astonishing to watch as the gardens, paths, fountains and ponds formed. Peter had hired two local landscapers to help him make the plans for the park. Those talented landscaping architects even helped him with the work, or at least assigned their own workers to get the jobs done. It seemed that every day the scenery improved and something new was added. The town's people would drive out their way to pass by slowly in order to keep up on the progress. Some would take their daily walks to include that area. Local newspapers did stories on the new city park. The articles would always include the local legend of the hidden attic room, with the blood and the chest of gold.

It must have been a slow week for the national media, because Good Morning America decided to send a crew to film and do a story on the treasure of the Shaw mansion and the little known town of Rose Creek. The film crew came in what appeared to be droves. Cameramen and makeup people and reporters descended on the Shaw property. Peter was photographed as he was working on a stunning fountain. Colonel Shaw was interviewed in front of the mansion and as he took a walk along the newly manicured paths. The bricked walkways were graced with an assortment of spring flowers that were freshly blooming. Daffodils and tulips lent splashes of color in mounds and along pathways. The promise of roses and honeysuckle were seen on quaint-looking wooden fences and gates.

The Colonel seemed delighted to relate the story of his past relatives who occupied the mansion during the Civil War. He told about the huge wall that was built so long ago. He included the story of the new church that was built out of the torn down stones. He showed the video crew the secret attic room and the tiny door in the antique chiffarobe that led to the attics. Sadie had had to give up that chiffarobe. It was carried back to its original spot.

Everyone seemed very intrigued. The story included the Mayor's perspective, and mentioned the whole town's involvement and cooperation in the making of this park. It was a most heartwarming story. Just the kind of spread that morning news programs craved.

As the Colonel was walking the video crew and reporters through the house they passed through the kitchen, where Sadie was cooking. She kept her back to the camera, but the Colonel called her forward to introduce her as the housekeeper who had discovered the treasure. That portion of the interview was a short time span, but it made Sadie very nervous. She liked her new life where no recognition or notoriety was included. She feared that someone from her former world would see her on T.V. She knew that if perchance they did include this portion of the interview on national T.V., that the word of her whereabouts would spread. The inquiring minds from her former cathedral-like church, and also those of the religious leaders that knew her pastor-husband would now know what had become of 'that woman'. They could discuss amongst themselves the 'ignoble' course her life had taken. "A cook and cleaning lady, living in a little side cottage. Can you imagine?" She could just hear the tongues clacking away and self-righteously whispering, "Oh poor pastor Golden's wife. Look what she's become. It must be so hard and sad for him to see where his wife ended up. That's what comes when someone gives into adultery."

When finally the story aired one Wednesday morning, Sadie was indeed on the television screen. But more important than her story was the exposure of Peter Combs. He was seen on screen talking about how much work it entailed to make that park. He was ruggedly dressed in flannel coat and Levi's and boots with a black skull cap on his head. His face was shadowed by three day's growth. He looked like a lumberjack. On screen, Peter, like Sadie, appeared reticent to talk to the reporters. She knew that he hadn't wanted to appear sullen and uncooperative, so he had agreed to speak to the reporter. He had kept trying to turn his face away from the cameras as he spoke.

After that story aired, it seemed that everything just hit the fan. Peter was recognized as the man who years ago had fallen from grace in the major financial markets. He had been influential in some shady stock sales and purchases involving insider trading. The story included his stint of two years in prison. It told of his past, opulent lifestyle including pictures of his beautiful, former wife and children. Their pictures were splashed all over the screen. This was a real human interest story for the world to slice up and have for breakfast. "See what can happen to a greedy, high-falutin', rich man? He lost it all by being selfish and cheating the public. See there, his poor wife and children? What shame he brought upon them." Sadie could just hear the speculations abounding.

Finally they added her story as well. "Nationally prominent pastor's wife who had been caught in adultery and removed from the church, runs away to oblivion and is discovered near Asheville doing the work of a housekeeper."

They had Pastor Anthony Golden, looking very sadly at the camera, saying, "I've been heartbroken by this sudden and unwarranted separation. Even though I did not know where she had gone, I've prayed daily that the Lord would protect her and help her find her way back to grace. Her family here has missed her and been torn up as well." True to form, Anthony had come out of this smelling like a rose and had endeared himself to millions of people with his forgiving nature.

Letters of castigation poured into her mailbox from her former church member acquaintances and from strangers across the nation who just felt it their duty to speak their mind on the subject of her unfaithfulness and desertion.

The Mayor and Town Council of Rose Creek had had the air let out of their balloon. The national coverage was supposed to be about this wonderful, generous town and a legendary historic event. Now it was discolored by the seedy, dirty secrets harbored by these two people who had figured prominently in this story. The opinion of the whole town was split concerning Sadie and Peter.

There were some people who voiced their strong opinions. "How embarrassing and demeaning it is to have these two in our midst. We surely were hood-winked. I remember when Peter was just an old homeless bum on the street. I knew there was something unsavory about that man."

"Can you picture that woman being the noted wife of that great preacher? What a shame that she chose our town to settle in. She surely had us all fooled. Went to church and sang solos and everything. God protect us."

Sadie shook her head at such statements. Gladys had told her about what people were saying in the stores and places of business. Sad quit reading the mail and just tossed it into the fireplace. She would like to have thought that after all this time she would be immune to such a thoughtless diatribe. But the truth was that all these opinions did hurt her. No one enjoyed being judged or despised and ridiculed. She kept a low profile and quit going to town so often or even to church. Both ministers came to talk to her and pray with her.

Reverend Harper came and assured her that the congregation on the whole was not upset with her, and that many people missed her and wanted her to come back. "I always say that just because two people decide to get married and walk down an aisle and say vows in front of people, doesn't mean that God has joined them together. You've never talked to me about this, but just knowing you brings me to some conclusions. It seems to me that you must have tried your best. After all you were married for a very long time to the man. Looks to me like the great Preacher Golden has a different personality when he is not behind his ministerial badge of honor."

Sadie, who had been so stoic through all this, burst into tears and covered her face with her hands. "It is so good of you to stand by me like this. I really don't deserve it. There really was fault on both sides of this, but you are right about one thing. I did try very hard to make it work. I'm just not strong enough to live a married life without love. I'd rather be alone. I know one thing for sure. The Lord has graciously forgiven me and that's all that really counts with me."

Pastor Brown from the newly made stone church came by and they walked the paths of the property and talked.

"Miss Sadie, I don't rightly know what happened between you and your husband, but whatever it was, God is big enough to forgive it. His grace has covered up much greater sins than we are talking about here. Just try to be strong under all this criticism. And please know that we love you and are holding you up in prayer."

Sadie was so touched by these kind words from her two pastors. She vowed to once again start back to church and just let the chips fall where they might. She missed worshipping in the church and singing praises to God with fellow believers. Sure there would be a few who would look askance at her and whisper things in her presence. But after all, what was the church for? It was not a country club for the righteous. It was a hospital for the sinners. Jesus himself had said, "I have come to seek and to save that which is lost."

Sadie was warmed by the reaction of Colonel and Mrs. Shaw. She had Victoria over for one of their 'high teas' and they talked about it. Victoria just 'tsk tsked' the whole affair and told Sadie to just ignore it. "People always need someone to look down upon. It makes them feel better about themselves. Don't pay them any mind. This will be a passing interest. Soon everyone will just forget about it."

The Colonel was indignant about the whole reaction from the nation and town. He sent a scathing letter to the editor of the newspaper in which he spoke up for Sadie and Peter. He told certain members of the town that he considered them downright hypocrites for attacking these two good people in this manner. "Rose Creek citizens need to stand up for and stand by their own. Miss Jamison and Mr. Combs are part of us. They've proven that very well."

Stephen Shaw made himself scarce. His frequent visits stopped abruptly. Sadie knew it was because he was afraid of public opinion and was concerned about protecting his high place among the better known and admired people of the town. And the truth was, it was just fine with her. She didn't really miss seeing him on a regular basis.

Sadie called her daughter and heard the news from that end. "How are you dear? Are you bearing up under all this uproar? How is Treat? I feel so far away from you all." Sadie greeted Rebecca.

"We are fine Mom. I mostly just stay home and only go out when I have to. Stan picks up the groceries for me. The weather has been a little blustery, so Treat doesn't mind staying in. Sometimes I take him for an outing, but in a place far from here. We've gone to the zoo and to the nearby parks for hikes. So we are doing okay. This will blow over soon, I hope."

"My dear daughter, you are being so brave and coping so well. Do you know how much I love you? I never meant for any of this to hurt you or affect your life. If I could protect you from this barrage of opinions I would. I'm so sorry." Sadie wiped her eyes blew into her handkerchief.

"Don't worry about it Mom. This has actually caused Stan and I to get closer. He is standing up for you and it makes me love him so much. We commiserate together about things and even laugh at the responses of people and especially at Dad's actions and words. Sometimes it is so ridiculous that you just have to laugh instead of cry."

Sadie said, "I never listen to the news. I don't even have a T.V. It is kind of nice, I've discovered. So what is really happening out there? What is your dad's reaction to all this?"

"Oh Dad is glorying in all this. Don't worry about him. This will only make him more popular when people see him as the victim. He has told the media that he tried so hard to keep you from leaving. He wanted to make the marriage work, but he could only do so much. He asked for the people's forgiveness for being part of bringing shame on the name of Christianity. He said that he is going to seek a divorce based on the Biblical principles that you are not truly a Christian and that you two are unequally yoked. He says that he is ready to go on with his life."

Sadie could not help but utter a nervous and sad laugh. "Oh that's Golden for you. I'll just bet that news made all the single women happy. He won't be alone for long, you can count on that."

"Well, from what I hear from my church sources, the ladies are lining up for review. He is getting so many covered dishes and cakes and pies, that his pantry is clogging up. It is almost embarrassing. No . . . it is embarrassing!"

"So I am assuming that pretty soon I shall receive divorce papers for my signature. You know, I never wanted anything from your dad when I left, but now that he is instigating divorce on the evidence of my adultery and abandonment, I feel that it would be right for me to get some recompense for all the years I put in with him. After all I was his wife for 31 years. That should count for something." Sadie stopped and gasped at what she'd said. "Oh, Becky, I sound like a gold digger. I can't believe I said that. But I did just run off without anything from our joint accounts. If I think about it, just about half of what we had together is mine. Why do I feel so selfish saying that?"

Becky interrupted her, "Mom, stop it. You are the most unselfish person I know. Money and riches have never had that much allure for you. I think that is exactly what dad is counting on; your distain for wealth. Has he ever even offered you one thing to help you get set up there and live?"

"Well . . . no, he hasn't."

"Why do you think that is, Mom? Is he hurting for money and just can't spare any? Of course not! He wanted to punish you, I think. Now that the dust has settled he is happily surprised that you haven't asked for anything. I'll bet he hopes to keep it that way."

"I really am getting by just fine, you know. It doesn't take much to live when you cut back on a lot," Sadie mused. "You'd think that after the luxury I lived in with Tony, I'd be missing all that extravagance, but I really don't. Simple is just fine with me."

"You do what you is feel right, Mom. I won't try to persuade you. But my brothers and I would really admire you if you would stand up for yourself and get what is due you. After all, you never know how long the Colonel and his wife will live and need you. Then what will you do?"

Sadie was quiet a minute just contemplating what Becky had just said, "Well that was pretty strong persuasion right there, girl." Sadie gently admonished. "But as I think on it, you are right. The Colonel and Victoria are getting up there in age. My living here and earning my own way is decidedly dependent on them needing me here."

"That's what I'm saying, Mom. You need a backup plan. A little nest egg from Dad's accumulated wealth would help you set up some sort of business. You are so smart and clever and creative, you could have your own little shop or something." Becky was getting excited now.

"Becky, you've got me to thinking and my mind is racing around all the possibilities. You are the dearest daughter. I have pretty much always lived in the present, thinking that tomorrow would take care of itself. But you are so right, my dear. I need to be thinking of what I will do when there is no more job here; when I no longer have to cook and clean for the Shaw's. By golly, I am going to petition the courts, during this divorce, to settle upon me what I need. It's not like it would break your father to part with some of his accumulation."

"Now you're talking Mom. I know you are doing fine without anything from him, but it would be right to get something on which to start your new life. I'm sure Dad will be congenial about that. Just tell him what you expect," Becky responded.

"I have no idea whatever what I expect or even can hope for. I guess I never in a million years thought I would be in this situation, and just didn't consider settlements and all that."

"Get some legal advice, Mom. There are people out there who know what is fair and just. They will make these decisions easier for you." Becky intoned. "Mom, get yourself a lawyer. Dad has a team of them working for him. If he wants a divorce this fast, then there must be something or someone spurring him on. I do remember him saying to the press that he does not like to live alone, and that a pastor really needs a wife at his side to help in the ministry. So whatever you ask for, I'll just bet he will comply with your wishes."

"Maybe you are right. I will try to get some legal counsel about this. I'm not in need of anything right now. Life is good. Oh why can't things just move along gently when life is going well. That just never happens, because life is always changing and throwing us new curves." Sadie laughed out loud. "Golly, Becky, I'm beginning to sound like an inspirational speaker."

"That's what you used to be, Mom. Don't you remember all the women in the state who hung on your every word. You used to be in demand and booked for months on end. We all know that you are full of wisdom. So now use some it on yourself. Get out there and get going, okay?" Becky encouraged her.

Chapter 40

Peter Faces the Music

The next day Sadie approached the Colonel and asked for the name of a good lawyer. "I need one to figure out the arrangements and settlements for a divorce," she explained.

"Well, I'd say it is about time, dear woman." The Colonel got up from his chair and went to his desk and pulled out an old leather address book. "Here's just the man for the job. He used to be in Asheville doing major cases of this sort. But the quiet, country life appealed to him and so now he is living here with his elderly wife just working a case now and again. He sort of picks and chooses what he will take one."

"Oh, then he might not want to mess with this case," Sadie worried.

"Nonsense! He'll do it for me if nothing else. But I think he would enjoy working on this one, when he gets all the facts," the Colonel smiled warmly.

So Sadie gave the lawyer a call and thus started the process of her negotiations with Reverent Golden. As Sadie expected, the divorce papers arrived for her signature and she handed the whole thing over to Mr. Trinity to handle. And handle it he did. Anthony's lawyers never knew what hit them. He had their legal experts tied up in knots and after just a few days they were scrambling to meet her demands and requests.

At first Anthony had responded by mail with threats that he would just come out and confront her in person. He thought she was being outrageously unfair to expect a settlement, when she is the one who abandoned him. Sadie told him to come on out and they would talk it over. But his was just an idle threat. Coming out to North Carolina was the last thing he really wanted to do. Reverend Golden wanted no part of such a public debacle. Sadie was relieved that he had no backbone to confront her personally.

In the end, she received a very healthy and generous settlement. Her lawyer took his cut and that was the end of it. Now, sitting in the bank was a nice little nest egg with her name on it. She'd just let it sit there. She didn't need it right now. The divorce papers had been mailed back to Anthony so she was once again waiting for them to arrive for her approval and signature.

Sadie wondered if that was the end of seeing Anthony Golden. She certainly hoped it was. But he was still her children's father and there would come a time when they would have to meet again. She sincerely wished him well in whatever marital venture he decided to take on. She hoped he would find a wife that would adore him and uphold him; a trophy pastor's wife. Maybe a woman would come along who didn't really care about her personal relationship with him and would be just content in the status of being his wife. She wished him no ill thoughts. After all, bitterness and revenge just poisoned the one holding them. So she just dropped all the resentment and let it be. Anthony was in God's hands.

Meanwhile, Peter was having his own problems. His past came on him in a rush and tossed him around like a ship on a stormy sea. He tried to keep up with his gardening and plans for the park area. But pretty soon he had to tend to the business at hand. There were authorities to answer to and old clients who wanted their pound of flesh. Peter had served most of his time, but on being paroled had slipped off to Rose Creek, far away from the maddening crowds of Atlanta. He was still wanted by the law for breaking parole.

Pete took a leave of absence from the job as property manager. Colonel Shaw said that he would keep that job open for him as long as he could. Victoria hugged him and told him he was like a part of her family. Tears formed in the corners of her sad eyes as she patted him on the back.

Sadie knew she was going to worry about him and miss him so much. She invited him over for a last supper before he left the next day. She made his favorite dinner; fried chicken, mashed potatoes and gravy and biscuits with apple crisp for dessert. As he ate, she sat silently watching him. Their conversation was light and touched on unimportant things. They had remembrances together of their meeting and getting acquainted. She wanted so badly to know more about him, but she sensed that that was forbidden ground and she was not about to insist on hearing it.

"Sadie, you outdid yourself tonight. The memory of this dinner will have to hold me for quite a while. I'll be eating in restaurants and fast food places and old diners for a good while; at least till I clear up all this stuff."

The Spring weather here in the low mountains was still nippy at night. Pete sat back on the couch in front of the warming, crackling fire and sipped his dark, strong coffee. He stretched out his legs toward the fire and let out a big sigh of resignation or pleasure. Sadie did not know which one it was.

"I can't even imagine life here without you here to pick on," Sadie teased. "This property is so beautiful now. I think back on what it looked like not even a year ago with bushes and limbs all thrown around and weeds. It was a mess. Now look at it. Everything is trim and manicured. There are paths and benches and color everywhere. Did you really learn all this just being here and working on it?" Sadie asked tentatively.

"I've always loved a neat yard, I guess. I used to use some of my rare leisure time to plant beds of flowers, and I did read up on some gardening books. But most of it, yes, I just learned as I went along. Truth is that in my high flying days, I had gardeners who took care of everything for me. I was working long hours everyday worrying about everyone's stocks and bonds and money, so I paid someone else to do what would have given me the most joy. It's funny how life is like that. What do people work so hard for anyway?"

Sadie looked at his serious face as he stared at the flames. "I don't know, Pete. I've often wondered about that myself. I've seen it so often: frantic efforts to accumulate wealth and prestige and then no energy or time left to really live. It doesn't make sense to me either."

"I'm thinking of trying to see my kids too. That is really worrying me. Did you know I have two daughters. I got started a little late in life with forming up a family, so my girls are still in High School. Emily is a senior and Ellie is a sophomore. I don't even know if they want to see me again; probably not. I've been no kind of father anyone could brag about, that's for sure."

"Have you seen them at all since you left, or written to them?" Sadie asked before she could think straight. "Oh, Pete, I'm sorry. I have no right to ask that. Forgive me."

Sadie reached out her hand toward Peter as a token of her repentance for the question. She just touched the top of his hand and just that quickly, he took her hand in his and held it there between them. Sadie felt such a lightning bolt of pleasure from that gesture that she had to stifle a shuddering gasp. There was just something chemically exciting about his touch. *What am I? A silly teenager hungry for someone's touch? Snap out of it Sadie.*

But Sadie could not pull her hand away. And Peter was not about to let it go. They sat there is congenial silence. Then Peter spoke.

"I know I've been so close-mouthed about my past. But right now I just want to let it all out; but only to you. You are my best friend. Best one ever, come to think of it." Peter pondered. He didn't look at her. He just kept his eyes on the fire. Sadie was grateful for that. If he had looked at her right now, he would have been shocked by the love in her eyes.

"I have all the time in the world, Peter. Let's hear it." Sadie tried to relax. It was hard because her focus was on that little space where their hands held together tightly.

"My ex-wife, Sandra, and I were married about 15 years when I made a stupid decision. I had a chance to make a killing on the market. Someone told me some inside information that I knew would give me a head's up on some stocks that were about to be worth a lot of money. I struggled with that knowledge for a good while. We were content enough, I guess. What I'm about to say sounds like a cop out, but I don't mean it that way. My wife had her heart set on a new home in the hills where the ritzy people lived. Our existing home was fine, comfy and medium sized. We had gardeners and house maids and even a cook. But this new home my wife found was luxurious. She toured it with a realtor, and took the girls along. They were always jumping from one house to the next dreaming of living higher up. The new home had a view of the valley. There was a pool and sunroom. She and the girls were crazy about it. It definitely was out of my price range. So their longing for that home might have factored into my decision to use this insider information and run with it. But I could have said no and gotten on with my life as it was." Peter stopped, pulled his hand away and sat up with his hands on his knees.

Sadie's heart fell like a thud when his hand left hers. It felt like she had just been left out in the cold rain. She pulled in her hand and held her hands together on her lap. She was just going to have to stop being so silly. She remained quiet.

"So I told some of my active investors about the stock and the pounced on it. My commission on their killings paid for the house. My wife and daughters were ecstatic." Peter stopped and stood up. He backed up to the fire and looked at Sadie for the first time since this conversation had started. "Sadie, I cheated and broke the law. Somehow word got out that I knew about the merger before the public announcement. I was hauled into court and humiliated and accused. Sandra was in tears and so ashamed of me. My girls were ridiculed in school as having a cheat for a father. We lost the house, of course, and the fines I had to pay along with the lawyer fees left my family with little recourse but to go live with her folks. You can imagine my standing there. When the trial was over, I was given 3 years time to spend in jail. My family had to take care of themselves."

Peter caught his breath, put one hand over his mouth tightly and one hand on his hip. He looked like a man trying to stop the floodgates of his words from coming out.

Sadie looked up at him. She stood and stepped forward to him. "Go on, Peter. I don't know why but I think this is good for you. I'm listening."

Peter put his hand across the front of his brow and paced away, around the couch and coming to stand in front of it again. He finally sat down and put his hands on his head and elbows on his knees. Sadie took her poker and rearranged the logs adding another small one on top. Then she too sat down not to far from Peter.

Pete continued, "While I was in prison, I received divorce papers from Sandra. She had hooked up with an old high school sweetheart and wanted to be free. She had never visited me in prison and had kept my daughters away too. It was a very lonely time there. I kept writing to them every week, and once in a while I would get a letter from Ellie, but nothing at all from Emily. I read and worked in the prison library. I taught computer skills to the prisoners. I worked out. The days were pretty boring compared to the life I had been used to living. The months dragged by. It was not pleasant, but I got through it. My parole finally came up and I found myself walking the streets of Chicago once again."

Peter turned to Sadie, "Are you sure you want to hear all of this? I just wonder if you will still want to be my friend after you realize who I really am." He looked worried and apprehensive.

"Peter," Sadie answered him, "I don't think there is anything you could do or say that would negate my friendship for you. People make mistakes. We all do. I made a mess of my life too. But we both went on and managed. I don't think God ever gives up on us, so why would I give up on you." She touched his shoulder and left her hand there to comfort him.

He stared at her a moment longer like he was trying to really figure out who she was. He finally broke the stare and looked back at the fire. He continued. "I was assigned a parole officer and a little apartment. Actually it was one room with a shared bathroom down the hall. Not much different than what I was used to in prison. I was given a job as a grocery clerk in a nearby market. I was supposed to report to my parole officer every two weeks and give him $150.00 every time I saw him. It was almost more than I could afford. $300.00 a month. There was not much leftover for food and lodging. I've never understood why the law enforcement organization has to demand so much from rehabilitated prisoners who are just trying to make ends meet. I always wondered where that money goes. Maybe to pay the salary of the parole officer?"

Sadie took her hand down from his shoulder and laid it on her lap. "What happened then? Were your folks not close by to help you?"

My parents had passed away ten years before in a car accident. I wondered if I would ever recover from that loss. My brother lives in California and struggles to make ends meet himself. All I really wanted was to see my daughters. So I called them up. Ellie was so excited to finally get to see me. Her mother got on the phone and discouraged me from getting involved in their lives. She said that they were content with their new family. She had had a new baby with this new husband." Peter stopped and bit his lips and rumpled his hair in consternation.

"I insisted on seeing them. So she brought them to a little café nearby. She was carrying the new baby in a baby seat. I remember how cute he was. Emily, who was fourteen at that time, kept her head down and looked away. She barely endured my light hug. Ellie, on the other hand, rushed into my arms and hugged me tightly. Oh Lord, that felt so good. I held onto her like a drowning man with a lifeline. Sandra finally pulled her away and we sat down. After a little small talk with me asking the girls about their lives, Sandra informed me that I was not to approach them again. She had obtained a restraining order prohibiting me from getting within a hundred yards of my own children. I must have snapped, because I jumped up, knocking over the table and spilling all the plates. The baby was crying and Emily rushed outside. Sandra just glowered at me and marched out too. Ellie was crying and held onto me. 'Please daddy, don't forget me, okay? I love you.' Then she too was gone."

Peter was quiet and contemplative for several minutes. Sadie got up and brought over fresh coffee to fill his cup. The steam came up from the cup and seemed to pull Peter out of his reverie.

"What happened then, Peter?" Sadie asked.

"Well then I became what you found on the streets of Rose Creek," Peter admitted, drinking his coffee. "A bum and scoundrel. A drunkard. A lazy, no good, two bit, flea ridden excuse for a man. I didn't care anymore. I just gave up. Isn't that just so admirable? I just gave up, darn it! I ran from my parole officer and hitchhiked all the way to this little town and stopped."

Sadie spoke to him softly, "The first time I saw you, you were soaking up the morning sunshine, dozing against a building on Main Street. It looked like it felt good there with the sun streaming onto you. I almost wanted to join you." Sadie tried to lighten things up a bit. "What a pair we make, Peter. We both ran from heartache and failure and ended up in the same place. What are the chances of that?"

Peter chuckled a little. His effort was feeble and short lived. "I can't say that I've been miserable since I started working here. I haven't. In fact I've experienced the most satisfaction I've had in a very long time. Just making things grow and making order out of chaos has been enough for me." He looked at her and reached for her hand. Again the pleasant current rushed through her making her breath catch.

"I remember the first glimpse I had of you. You walked by me and dropped a dollar in my cup."

"It was five dollars, which I could not afford, by the way." Sadie laughed.

"I remember how resentful I was of you, looking down on me and offering me a job. Who did you think you were? I just wanted you to go away and leave me alone."

"Your sign said, 'Will work for food.'" Sadie teased.

Pete looked at her and took her hand in both of his. "Sadie, you were my salvation. I don't know what I would have done if you hadn't come along. I guess I should apologize for my abrasive behavior when first we met and worked together. You probably wondered what in the world you were getting into when you asked me to help you clear out the filthy gatehouse." He gestured around to her cozy abode with all its color and cleanness and just shook his head. "How things have changed."

"I remember how hungry you were and how you tried hard to hide your need for that old coat we found in the gatehouse. But you came back. When I saw that, I knew there was hope for you. I think I sort of liked you from the start." Sadie admitted.

Peter dropped her hands and reached for his coffee. "I don't know how long I will be gone. Will you be here when I get back?"

"Far as I know, I will be. I have no plans to the contrary," Sadie said. "Tell me, Peter. Do you know what you are going to do? Are you going to try to see your daughters again? Will you be allowed to try?"

"I am going to face up to my legal obligations first. It may mean some more prison time. Then I will face the people I disappointed so badly. I just feel that I owe that to them. The company I worked for was shamed by my actions. After that I will appeal to the court to let me see my daughters. The mayor and Colonel Shaw have given me some commendable letters that might convince the judge that I am harmless and that I live with purpose now. I can only hope."

"Oh Pete, I will pray so hard that your efforts to mend your fences will be successful and that you will get to see your daughters. Sounds like little Ellie will be so very happy to see you again."

"Since I worked for you and the Colonel, I've been saving money each month toward college for both my girls. I have an account for each of them. It isn't much, but someday when I get back on my feet financially I can add to it and maybe help them out a bit. I have sort of given up on Emily ever coming around to loving me again. But I will do what I can."

Sadie got up and went to the cookie jar. She didn't keep her cookies in there. She had cash there for emergency situations. She pulled out all of it in one big bundle. "Peter, quit shaking your head now. I want you to have this for your trip. It is my investment in you. I have no need for it right now. When I do, you can pay it back. And one other thing, when you get back, I want you to take my little nest egg I received from my divorce and I want you to guide me on how to invest it. I have confidence in you and I know that it will be better to have it out there in the market rather than sitting in the bank accruing a piddly amount of interest. Am I right?"

Peter looked at her with such love, she nearly melted. "Yes, you are right, dear Sadie. Your confidence in me is like the water of life. Thank you so much."

"There's only one 'water of life' and that is Jesus. And don't you forget it, mister." Sadie punched him in the arm and he grabbed her and held her tightly. Her head rested on his shoulder and she let out her breath and relaxed into his embrace. *Good Lord, it felt so right and so good to be hugged by this man. Get a hold of yourself, Sadie. Don't be a fool. He's only being a friend, and after all that is all you want right now.*

Peter reluctantly pulled away. "I'd better get going. My bus leaves early in the morning. I'm going to miss you so much, Sadie. I'll try to write once in a while, since you have no phone, crazy lady."

He turned and walked toward the door. She followed him and touched his shoulder. "I want you to know that I love you, Peter Combs. You take care of yourself and don't you dare get discouraged ever again. There's a whole band of people here that are pulling for you. Okay?" She reached out to hug him again and he planted a firm, warm kiss on her cheek. She kissed him back on his cheek. Then he turned and was gone.

Sadie thought about getting up early the next morning and seeing Peter off at the bus depot. She even planned on baking some fresh cookies for his trip. But after she thought about it a while, she knew it would not be the right thing to do. Goodbyes were hard, and last night they had already endured that one. It was better to leave well enough alone. So instead of going to the depot, she woke up and knelt by her bed to pray for him. Sadie didn't always kneel when she prayed. She prayed wherever and whenever she could. But somehow she knew that it honored God to kneel before him, and she definitely wanted to honor the Lord with this request for watching after and guiding Peter Combs.

"Dear Lord," she prayed out loud, "please be with my good friend, Peter, as he tries to right some wrongs. It will be hard for him. It will take courage. Brace him up with what he needs, I pray. Help him to find receptive responses from former co-workers and from friends. I pray especially that when he faces the judge, that he will find mercy. I pray that the letters of recommendation from all these important and notable people here will count for something. Please let the powers that be understand that Peter Combs already suffered enough for his indiscretion. I pray that he will be released free and clear and not even have to answer to a parole officer or pay the monthly fees. And pleas, dear Father, let a miracle occur with his girls. May they be receptive of the love he extends to them. Heal his heart Lord, I pray, so that he may be emotionally whole again. I know I've asked so much here, Lord, but just one more thing. I guess this is the most important request of all. Please have the Holy Spirit work on Peter's heart to soften it. I would love to see him come to a faith in Jesus Christ and a healing of his soul. I so appreciate your listening to my prayers. I love you. Amen."

Chapter 41

Moonshine Creek Campground

Sadie kept herself busy. She was trying not to worry about Peter. A letter finally came three weeks after he had left. It was an encouraging letter about his meeting with his former company and employees and co-workers. They had talked things through and he had profusely apologized for dragging them all down and putting the company name through the mud. A few still held the grudge, but most of them wished him well and the bitterness seemed to have dissipated.

His court hearing was set for the next month. Meanwhile he was back with a parole officer. He was working at a café, waiting tables and washing dishes. The judge had temporarily placed a collar on his ankle and he had to limit his area of travel to work and the small, seedy apartment he had rented. It was not pleasant, but Pete was not really complaining.

As far as Peter's girls were concerned, he found out where they were living and wrote them each a letter. The letters were not returned, so he assumed they had arrived. He checked his post office box daily in hopes of finding word from them.

Sadie wrote him right away and sent him pictures of the fresh growing flowers on the acreage. She told him about all that was going on and kept him up to date on the Colonel and Victoria, Cherie and Joy.

The Colonel had hired two Mexican workers to continue the work on the park. They followed Peter's plan. He had left it all written up and drawn out in simple instructive drawings. What talent those young Mexicans had with stone. They constructed two fountains which were not hooked up with water as yet. Now they were working on three seating areas with benches and little walls. Peter had asked them to hold off on forming up the stream. He wanted that little

214

gurgling brook to run through the property from fountain to fountain. That was a job that he wanted to do himself, if ever he got back there.

The two Mexican men were very respectful and grateful for the kindnesses Sadie showed them. She made sure they had good food to eat. She didn't know where they were staying, but felt it must be a very cheap and humble abode. She tried to use some of her acquired Spanish on them, but usually it was for naught. She did ascertain that they both had wives and children back in Mexico and that they were working hard on their temporary work permits in order to send money back to the families to make their lives better there. Their real dream was to finally and legally bring their families to this wonderful, America. Sadie arranged for Pastor Brown to come see the proof of their expertise with stone. Sure enough, when the pastor saw it, he wanted those men to come help him with some of the decorative work with rocks and masonry on the new stone church. This extra work they did on their own time and made even more money to send home. Sadie was so glad to have them.

"Pablo and Samuel, this looks so good. Es muy bien. Mucho grande. Muy bonito. Gracias por su . . . . uh . . . . trabajo?" Sadie ended her statements of approval with a questioning lilt to her voice. She shook her head in frustration. But the two men laughed amicably and seemed to understand that she was complimenting their hard work and telling them that it was lovely. Now she wished she'd taken her study of Spanish in college more seriously. Sometimes she would tuck in an extra $20 or $40 bucks in their pay envelopes just to encourage them. This came from her own money, but she felt good about giving it to them

Spring came in a rush and was so lush it nearly took Sadie's breath away. It seemed a fine time, in Sadie's estimation, for that promised trip to the campground in the Appalachians that she had promised Treat a while back. She okayed the trip with the Shaw's. They seemed so happy to release her from her duties there. They assured her that they would be just fine warming up all the dinners she had already prepared and put in the freezer.

Sadie called Becky and proposed the idea. It was approved wholeheartedly. She dared to suggest that Stan come also. And after a couple of days of conferring, she was happily surprised by his acceptance. *Hurrah!* She thought. *This will be so good for him and for all of us together. Please Lord, let us somehow get closer to each other. I need that.*

She insisted on sending them the money to pay for their air flights. Stan protested some, but Sadie convinced him that she had been saving most of her earnings and had nothing better to do with it. She made it sound so casual and like he would be doing her a favor to accept it. Sadie knew that the expense of a trip like that would be a burden on their budget. She was just so happy that Becky was able to stay home and care for Treat. Soon enough he would be in school all day and then she could think about getting a job. They lived very frugally, but it seemed to work for them.

Stan rented a car and drove the family from Asheville to Rose Creek. Sadie had sent them a detailed map on how to get there. Becky had done it before so she had a pretty good idea where they were headed.

Sadie greeted them in the driveway. She had prepared the house just for them. She had cinnamon candles going and the smell of freshly baked cookies permeated the air. The bedroom was all ready for them. There was a neat little corner twin bed fixed up for Treat. Flowers filled the cottage. The Shaw's had given permission for Sadie to stay in their mansion in the room behind the kitchen.

There were hugs all around. Stan seemed a little stiff but endured her hug as best he could. They carried in their bags and settled into the bedroom.

"We won't be here but for a day or two, and then it is the wilderness for us," said Sadie ominously.

Treat knew she was teasing and ran to get his wooden toy rifle out of his suitcase. "Don't worry Grandma, I'll protect you," he laughed.

Treat did the honors and gave his daddy a tour of the yard. He felt very important to be in charge and dragged his dad around all the paths and showed him all of the fountains.

Sadie had made stuffed manicotti for dinner. They ate in the mansion with the Shaw's. What a happy evening of conversation that was. The Colonel seemed so genuinely interested in learning about Stan and their life. After a dessert of apple pie and icecream, Sadie walked the Shaw's to their little suite and bade them goodnight.

Becky and Sadie talked and caught up while they did the dishes. When the dishes were done, Stan got a tour of the place.

"I really like the Colonel and his wife. They seem so gracious and welcoming to us. No wonder you like to work for them."

Stan loved that big house and was amazed at all the rooms and how kept up it all was. "This is like a dream house to me," he remarked. "There is something about the big old houses that gets to me. I don't know what it is. But I feel safe and solid when I am in one of them."

"I feel the exact, same way, Stan," admitted Sadie. "I'm always dreaming about a big old mansion just stuffed full of furniture all piled up in so many rooms. In my dreams it is like a storehouse of furniture, and I'm trying to organize the rooms and make them habitable. I am always so excited about the possibilities and yet frustrated that there is so much to do." She stopped and sighed. "Those dreams are partly like a nightmare, and yet I look forward to them so much, and I wish that I could go back to them at will."

"I can't believe you said that," said Stan. "I have nearly that same dream. Always it is the same place, but I just happen upon it in my dreams. Some of the rooms are so strange with high and low levels and corner tubs as big as a small swimming pool. I've never told anyone about the dreams before. In the dream I have there is even a theater area with lots of seats and a stage. It is down a steep set of stairs in the bottom under the house. I can never get enough of looking through the rooms. And I always wake up way before I am ready."

"I know, I know," agreed Sadie. "And you are left with that empty feeling of having been dragged away from a place you want to be. So strange."

"Okay, you two. That's enough of that. You are both 'weirding' me out. How come you never told me about these dreams, Stan? I would have loved to hear about them," Becky sounded hurt.

"I don't know why I never told you. Maybe we are just in too big a hurry when we get up. Rushing around to get ready for work and eat. Maybe I didn't think you would be interested in my silly dreams," Stan replied.

"Stan, my dear man, I am interested in anything and everything that concerns you," Becky responded. "From now on I want to hear about your interesting dreams. I just wish I had some good dreams to share with you. My dreams are dull and uneventful."

"I should be so lucky," offered Sadie. "Sometimes my dreams scare me to death Sometimes I feel like I've worked so hard in my dreams, that I wake up exhausted."

Treat tugged on his Dad's shirt. "Daddy, can we go for one more walk outside? Grandma has a flashlight; a big one that we can use to see the path."

Stan looked to Sadie for permission.

"Go ahead, you two. Becky and I will go turn down the beds and get a fire started. We will go through the attic and the extra secret attic room tomorrow. Treat can show you where to get into it. He knows the whole story too."

Treat looked so proud of himself. "Yeah, Dad, I'll show you where it is and tell you what happened here a long, long time ago."

Sadie and Becky watched as father and son grabbed up the flashlights and headed out the door. Sadie put away the last dish and draped the dish towel over the wire drying rack. "It is so good to see Stan and Treat enjoying each other so much," Sadie commented.

"This is good for both of them. Stan usually comes home so tired and upset from work that he hasn't the time or patience for Treat's chattering and needs." Becky sighed and hugged her Mom. "Why is it that everything seems to be all better when we are with you, Mom?"

A warm rush of gratitude washed over Sadie. *What a wonderful thing for her to say to me,* thought Sadie. "Maybe it is just the change of routine and the fact that Stan has no work to go to tomorrow. What do you say we go camping in a couple days? I have to keep my promise to Treat. This weather is just perfect, and . . . . we'd have a big strong man to help us with all the details of camping."

"That sounds great. Treat is looking forward to it so much. Are you sure you can get away?"

"Certainly I can. Cherry and Joy are coming to stay in the cottage and watch Wheezer. I've already prepared ahead. When I make a big dinner I always make a little more than is necessary and freeze it up in containers for when I have to be gone and for the weekends when I don't work. The Shaw's can warm up their meals while I'm gone. Where I plan to take you is that wonderful little place north of here. I've heard about it, and I think that it would be perfect."

"That's just about all Treat talks about. Moonshine Creek. He's told all his buddies at nursery school about it. They think he is going into the wild."

"Well truth be told, it is the wilds. But it is a campground taken care of by rangers and they will not only protect us, but will be good tour guides if we need them."

"Treat doesn't forget a thing you say, Mom. He always says, 'Remember what Grandma said about this or that . . . . ?' I can guarantee that you have a great influence on him, Mom. You are like a hero to him. Or should I say heroine?"

"I can't think of myself as a hero to anyone. A hero is someone who saves people from dire consequences or death. It's someone who gives their life for another's well being, or someone who gives up something precious for the love of someone else. I've done none of those things," Sadie reasoned.

"Well, little boys have a whole different judgment on what a hero is. Just accept it, Mom, you are his hero." Becky gave her Mom a quick hug.

"I have a great idea, dear daughter," Sadie added excitedly. "As a matter of fact, I just thought of it. Don't know why it didn't occur to me before." Sadie paused and swallowed, "For the duration of your stay here I request permission to take Treat with me to my bed and give you both the cottage to yourselves."

"Mom, you don't have to do that. We don't mind Treat being in there with us," Becky responded.

"Well maybe I just want to have a few nights of slumber party with my hero worshiper. Did you ever think of that?" Sadie laughed. "Come on sweetheart. I'd have fun . . . . you'd have fun. Let's do it."

"I know he'd love it for real," said Becky. "But he's a squirmer and you'd have to leave a little light on somewhere so when he wakes in the night, he can see where he is."

"Done! My grandson and I will have hot chocolate in the big kitchen before we go to bed, and we'll plan our camping trip and talk about all the fun we are about to have in the next few days. I need this bonding time with my grandson."

Sadie and Becky walked out of the big house and over to the cottage. Sadie began packing up her pajamas and toothbrush and toothpaste that she would need across the way. "Just throw in Treat's sleeping gear and favorite pillow, which I assume you brought."

"Wouldn't leave home without it," assured Becky.

When Stan and Treat finally got home from their night time trek, it was obvious that Treat was ready to call it a day. Sadie told him the plans and he got so excited. He began jumping up and down.

"Calm down, son," said Stan as he looked to his wife questioningly. Becky smiled alluringly at her husband and then he understood. He had the grace to blush a little and turn his head. "Here let me help you carry over your stuff. Give me a big hug, little guy. We are really going to have a good time while we are at Grandma's aren't we?" Stan looked over at Becky and winked. Now she had the grace to blush too.

Treat went to sleep after a quick cup of hot marshmallow topped chocolate. His head was nodding as he leaned over the table on his elbows and tried to sip the steaming brew.

". . . and if you want," finished up Sadie, "we can ride horses into the woods, too. It will be a fun time of camping out. You wait and see."

She led him to the turned down bed and tucked him in. "You coming too?" he asked.

"Of course I am. Just let me turn off the lights." Treat started to protest and Sadie assured him, "I will leave one small light on in the hallway so you can see around you when you wake up." Sadie rushed to do those little last minute chores. When she got back Treat was still sleepily waiting for her. She crawled into bed and he moved close to her.

"Can you just rub my back a little, Grandma?"

"You bet. Turn over and I'll rub your back while we pray."

Treat rolled over and settled deep into his pillow. As she rubbed his tiny back, Sadie began to pray. "Dear Father in heaven, I can't tell you how happy it makes me to have my Treat here with me. I pray that you will fill his sleep with the sweetest dreams. And I pray that his time here with me will be full of great adventures that can become our best memories. We love you so much, Jesus. Be with Mommy and Daddy too. Let them have a good rest too. Amen."

Sadie snuggled close to Treat and in just a minute he was breathing quietly and not moving at all. She lay there and thought about all her blessings. *Father, may I add that I feel very complete tonight. How you have blessed me. I cannot even name all of them. My life is full. Thank you. Be with my precious daughter and her husband right now. May they grow very close and renew the vigor of young love. May they rekindle the tenderness and freshness of their relationship as man and wife. Please, please assign one of your strongest guardian angels to watch over Treat as he grows up. Keep him from harm and from evil. And Lord, would you please be with Peter up north. He's dealing with a lot. I pray your will be done in his life, and all this so you can be glorified and your name praised. Amen.* Sadie settled into sleep swiftly, too. Life was good.

The next day was a whirlwind of happy activity. Stan and Becky could be seen through out the day, draping their arms around each other and giving each other little nibbly kisses. Their eyes exchanged sweet remembrances and tender love. Sadie loved to see it.

Sadie took them all over town letting Stan experience the bakery, the café, the library. "This is so much fun to actually see in person all the things and places that Becky and Treat told me about. I visualized them a certain way and now I get to see for myself."

The Sunday after they had arrived, she took them to the two churches she loved so much. Sunday morning was the Baptist church and Sunday night was the Immanuel Baptist Church. Sadie and Rebecca sang together, 'Follow Me' one of their old favorites while Sadie played the piano. Everyone loved it. Stan admired the solid and artfully done masonry with all the stone that he was assured used to be the rock wall around the property.

On Monday they had Joy and Cherie over for a picnic on the estate grounds. She spread a big quilt and they invited the Shaw's to come too. Two folding chairs were brought out for them. Treat proved once again what a fine boy he was by playing with Joy and leading her along the paths. The weather held nicely. All they needed even on the coolest of evenings was a sweater.

They rented a pop up camper right outside of town. Stan's rental car was big enough to pull it and had a towing hitch on the back just for that purpose. Becky and Sadie planned the meals for two nights and three days. They stocked up the little cupboards in the camper. Cherie and Joy came to stay in the cottage with Wheezer. The meals for the Shaw's were all prepared and ready for warm-up. Cherie promised she would check up on them to be sure their needs were met. But the Colonel waved that suggestion off enthusiastically saying, "We aren't invalids yet. We will be fine. You all go and have fun. Be sure to tell us all about it when you get back."

Early on Wednesday morning they took off. Traveling songs were sung. 'Over the River and Through the Woods' and 'You Are My Sunshine' and 'This Little Light of Mine'. The list went on and on. With the windows down to let in the fresh morning air, the sound of their laughter and songs could be heard by the people in the houses along the way.

Moonshine Creek campground proved to be all that Treat expected. They found a spot for the camper right by the stream. There were big flat stones to sit on. The rented a couple of fishing rods and bought some worms. Sadie took pictures of Stan and Treat sitting side by side waiting for a fish to bite the line. There were horses too and they were each one assigned one to ride. Treat got a small horse that was so gentle and was led by the guide. A horse named Hellfire was given to Stan and his eyes got so big; Sadie thought he might have a stroke. They rode through the mountainous woods and it was a fabulous time. Treat was sure now that he was a real cowboy and should be able to get a job on a ranch herding cattle.

The very first night Sadie made hobo stew in cleaned out silvery, tin cans. She put layers of potatoes, onions, corn, peas, chopped beef and beef broth. On top she placed a canned biscuit. Then she wrapped each can in tinfoil and snuggled them under the red hot coals to cook slowly. Oh the smells that came from that meal. It was so delicious.

"I thin I'd like to be a hobo," offered Treat enthusiastically.

"Me too, son," exclaimed his father. "no rent, no worries, no property to take care of."

"Dad, don't you think we could just live here. We could hunt for food and fish in the stream and grow our own garden. Just like the pioneers did in the old days. Can we dad? Can we?"

Stan grabbed up his son and swung him around and around. "Oh boy, Treat. That is a big order there. I think it would be fun; a big adventure. But it would be such hard work. We'd have to cut down trees and build a cabin. We'd have to haul water, cut wood to keep us warm. We'd have to wear our clothes till they had holes in them." He looked at Becky. "And I'm not too sure that Mama knows how to sew very well."

Becky frowned at him in a teasing way and put her hands on her hips. Treat laughed out loud. "I could do all that, Dad. I'm strong," Treat promised.

"Wed have to go to the bathroom behind the trees. There would be no ice cream, no hamburgers and French fries. We'd be so poor." His dad ruffled his hair.

"But Daddy, I don't feel poor right now. I feel rich!"

For one of their breakfasts, Sadie made steak and fried eggs and potatoes. Many of the campers wandered close by to see what was cooking. Sadie could almost see their mouths watering. Another morning she made bacon and pancakes. The maple syrup warming on the fire smelled so good. Again . . . the campers were envious.

On the second night they made steaks on the outside grill over an open campfire. The baking potatoes were wrapped in heavy foil and place right in the hot coals to get steamy soft. She took an old antique pot and brewed a pot of coffee. The fragrance of that coffee filled the mountain air. As they were roasting marshmallows around the embers, Sadie told a ghost story. She made sure it was not too frightening, just scary enough to make Treat shiver a bit. He loved it and begged for another. But his eyes betrayed him and kept drooping shut. So off to bed he went and was tucked in. He could look right out the screened in window and see them sitting around the fire. There was no fear there. He could hear them talking softly. They all three sat and spoke of past memories and laughed at the antics of the family as they had grown up. Reminiscing was such a rewarding thing. The fact that they had golden memories to recall was like opening a forgotten treasure chest. Sadie knew that Stan and Becky were filling up their own personal box with priceless memories.

Soon Sadie too got sleepy and excused herself. She walked the long walk to the privy area and washed her face and brushed her teeth. The night was so black there with the stars shining in bunches above. She breathed in deeply the cozy smell of campfires and coffee and she could hear the soft laugher coming from campsites all around. She slipped into the camper and settled beside Treat. As she drifted off to sleep, she could hear Becky and Stan talking softly. She heard, "I love you so much," and "Ditto right back atcha."

Their last full day there, they cleaned up camp after breakfast, packed a nice lunch and hiked to a nearby falls and had a picnic there later. The vistas were magnificent and they watched as people repelled down the cliff walls. The sun felt so good kissing Sadie's face. She turned up her face toward the sun and closed her eyes. Life could be so good.

When they got back to the campsite, Stan and Treat found a few video games to play in the camp store. While they were gone Sadie and Becky got the chance to talk. Becky was so full of happiness that it warmed Sadie's heart to see it. "Mom, I love it here. I wish I could stay here forever. I wouldn't mind being poor and living like a gypsy if it could be like this," she remarked. "I didn't think I'd ever see Stan like this again. Mom, he's so different when he gets away from that dreaded job."

"As young as the two of you are, it might be a good idea if Stan seriously thought about switching jobs. Would you be willing to work outside the home if push came to shove?" Sadie queried. "Treat will be in school next year and maybe that could work out."

"Mom, I'd be willing to do anything to have my husband back the way he used to be. This just proves to me that the real Stan is still under there somewhere. And he wants to get out," Becky laughed warily.

"Well, just pray about it and broach the subject with Stan. Assure him that you are game to live more simply and still be happy. Tell him you don't want to waste any of the years you two have together with just the hard effort of acquiring stuff and being more secure. Tell him you are willing to struggle if it means that you two can have more times like this. He might just go for it too."

They talked more about the boys. Becky missed her big brothers and tried to keep in touch with them both by phone and letters. Sadie longed to see them again too.

Stan and Treat walked into the campsite with tempting ice cream bars dipped in thick chocolate and pecans. "Yum," said Becky. "How did you know I was craving one of these? Hand it over!"

Stan was sweet to Sadie on that trip. He was affectionate, giving her hugs and pats on the back. Once they were sitting by the stream in their folding chairs. Becky and Treat had taken a short walk to the shower room for a quick bath.

Her son-in-law started the conversation. "Sadie, Mom," he added hesitantly, If I could, I'd move us all out here in a heartbeat. It's hard back there. My job is so stressful that when I get home, a lot of the times, I'm a bear to live with. I feel sorry for Becky. She deserves better."

Sadie, who had been thrilled to be called, 'Mom' by Stan, just nodded and kept looking at the stream.

Stan started up again, "Becky misses you so much. We have friend, and the church, and we do have some good times. But Treat and Becky need you."

"I miss you all too, Stan. How I wish we could all live close together. We could make years of growing up memories together." Sadie stopped and considered her next words carefully. She added, "but Stan, we sometimes have to make do with the cards that we are dealt. We have to play our hand." *No why did you say that Sadie? That sounded like something Andy would say to her. Him and his gambling terms.*

"Stan, I take that back!" She sat up straight. "Why should you have to settle for the situation you are in? You can make choices and do what you want. I know of a family of four that decided to sell their house and buy a nice sized schooner with galley and beds. They dared to travel the seas for one year. They had a ball and the kids learned so much from the people and places they visited. When they got home, they sold the boat and purchased another house and started up working again. It was just a whole year of reprieve from the ordinary. Who's to say you can't do something daring and risky." Sadie looked at Stan and he was sitting there wide-eyed and open mouthed looking at her. She went on, "You and Becky are so young. You have expertise in what you do and I'm sure there are jobs that you could fill right around here. You should consider the possibility of changing your lifestyle. Be a pioneer, Stan. It might be so good for you three."

Stan was silent for a while and they both just sat there in the peaceful, evening light and thought quietly.

Becky and Treat came racing back carrying their soap and wet towels. Treat's hair was still damp from his shower and he smelled so fresh and soapy.

Stan looked at Sadie and shook his head ever so slightly so that she would know not to mention what they had just spoken about. She just shut her eyes and smiled and nodded a tiny bit. Now the two of them had a secret, and that was bonding too.

Chapter 42

Peter Needs Help

The next morning they broke camp. It was sad to pack up everything and tuck it away inside the camper. They cleaned up the campsite, locked everything up and went for another hike. They all agreed that they just had to have one last glimpse of this wonderful, practically unknown campground. When they got back all they had to do was pull away from the campsite. Treat kept his nose pressed to the window as he looked longingly back to where they had stayed. "I want to come back here again, someday, okay?" He asked.

"Yes, and right to this very same spot, I reckon," answered his dad. That seemed to satisfy Treat and off they drove, down the mountains toward Rose Creek. They were all silent, pondering on the simple, rich memories they had made there.

It was a bitter, sweet moment to say goodbye to this precious family. She would miss them so much. The longing for them would be more acute now that she had been with them for a while. However, Sadie was a loner at heart, and she had missed her periods of solitude. When they drove away a sort of relief welled up in her. *I'm so glad they came and I would not trade one second away that I had with them. But oh it feels so good to just sit here with Wheezer and not have to talk or even think.* She brewed herself a cup of mint tea and settled down in front of her fireplace. *Life is so good here,* she thought. She snuggled down on the couch and covered up with a quilt. Soon she was fast asleep. Her dreams were ragged and disturbing. Peter and Stephen were pushing to get into the doorway at the same time; both of them stuck and bickering back and forth. She knew that she had to make dinner for a horde of strangers who had shown up at her door. Her house was a mess, with mud on the floor and trash thrown around. The refrigerator had nothing worth eating, and the cupboards were all but bare. She grabbed some stale bread and an old jar of peanut butter and began frantically making sandwiches. She heard screams and looked up to see the floor alive with rattlesnakes. All of her guests were climbing the furniture, afraid for their lives. She ran out the back door and confronted a huge black bull. He was snorting and dragging his front feet back and back kicking up the dust. She began to run through the paths of the park. The bull was right on her heels. She climbed a tree and sat on a high limb. The bull was still at the base of the tree kicking, rearing and butting his head against the trunk.

She woke with a start and was gasping for breath. *What was that?* She thought. *If dreams have meanings then that one is a doozy*, she pondered. She shook herself fully awake and washed her face with a very hot washcloth. Yawning and breathing deeply, she looked around her at the peaceful setting. The floor was clean and everything was tidy. The refrigerator had a sufficient amount of fresh food, and the cupboards were anything but bare. The dream had been so real that she glanced outside the back door just to be sure. She had to laugh at herself. *Why are big, black bulls so prominent in my dreams?* Again she had to laugh at herself.

She tidied herself up and put on fresh makeup and went on over to see the Shaw's. They had been so nice to require nothing of her for the week's visit with her family. She had seen them and visited with them throughout the week, but they had not expected anything from her and had taken care of themselves just fine. Cherie and Joy had been there just in case they needed help. It was good to know that she could get away and feel free to do so. She was grateful for that. Now she just wanted to check back in their snug corner and be assured that all was well.

I've certainly become so close to those two. I'll have to admit that they are as priceless to me as my own children, she thought. The Colonel and Victoria were both so happy to welcome her home. They had been reading together. She quickly stoked up the fire and carried in some more wood for them. The March air was still a bit chilly. The Colonel had picked a vase full of cheery daffodils and had set it on the coffee table. "The place looks so nice. I don't think you two need me after all," she feigned a pout.

"Nonsense and all that young lady," huffed the Colonel. "We've missed you like nobody's business, haven't we Victoria?" He turned to his fragile wife and she nodded enthusiastically. "Besides, it was Joy who picked the flowers for us. Some are tall and some short, but together they made a nice bouquet, don't you think?"

Sadie sat down for a few minutes to tell them all about her camping trip with Becky and family. She had them laughing over parts of the adventures they had had. They seemed genuinely interested.

After her visit she went into the kitchen and took stock of what was there. She made a list of all she would need for the next week's menus, and off she went to the grocery store. The little Green Cove grocery store, which she preferred to the big super market east of town, was alluring and intoxicating with the sweet smell of hickory smoked bacon and fresh fruit. There was the unmistakable earthy scent of potatoes and onions and celery. The grocer, Mr. Mackabee, kept a popcorn machine near the front door and was always making fresh popcorn. The smell of it drifted out to the street and beckoned people inside. The popcorn was free to all who wanted it. People could just reach in and get a bag of it. It wasn't just for customers. Anyone could get a bag. Mack made sure there were at least fifteen bags lined up at all times.

She recognized a lot of folk there and they all spoke to her kindly. "How was the visit with your daughter?" asked one lady.

"Is that town park coming along? Will it be ready for dedication soon?" queried another.

Sadie was warmed by their recognition of her and by their friendliness. It took time to meld into a town. She was just getting started here. It seemed like the media frenzy and all their resultant backlash, was about to be laid to rest. She was glad. She wanted nothing more than to just be inconsequential here; just one of the townspeople.

Sadie was not one to jump into friendships quickly. She took her time and when she finally settled upon a few, chosen ones, she was a friend for life. She had lots of acquaintances, but just a few really good friends. Friends took a lot of time and effort to maintain. It was necessary to keep in touch and do special things with and for them. After all, anything worth having was worth spending ones time and effort on. Sadie was plagued with guilt at not keeping up her correspondence with the best friends she did have. She made a vow to write to them and maybe even call them, although talking on the phone was just not among her favorite things to do. Maybe she was a little shy of telling her friends what she'd done. What if they didn't approve of her anymore? What if they decided to dump the friendship? *Well it couldn't be any worse than it is right now*, she thought. *Right now you only have the Shaw's and Cherry and Peter as very good friends. If you lost some of your past friends it wouldn't kill you. It would be sad, but you'd survive*, she chided herself. She made up her mind to get in touch with those few that she longed to hook up with again. *Let the chips fall where they will*, she reasoned.

She stocked up on eggs and milk and butter, along with the meats she would need, and fresh veggies. She even treated herself to a store bought cake and some blueberry muffins that looked delicious. The bagger boy carried her groceries out to the parking lot and neatly packed them in the back end of the truck. Sadie loved her little beat up blue truck. *Submit your ways to the Lord and he will give you the desires of your heart*, she pondered on that promise in Psalms. She had always had a hankering for an old truck with curvy fenders. And now she had one to at her disposal. She was glad that she had the mechanic service "Little Blue" and bring it up to par. She wanted that little vehicle running like a top.

In the morning-mail was a letter for her from Pete. She tore it open hastily and sat on the big winding stairs to read it.

Dear Sadie,

I'm hanging in here trying hard to keep my spirits up. Most people do not know me and could care less. But there are a few who remember what I did and how I ran away to escape the parole restrictions. Those that recall my past are downright rude and difficult to be around. I guess I can't blame them. I am getting what I deserve, so I shouldn't be surprised.

The main thing I am trying to do is convince the Judge that I've changed and that I am very sorry for what happened in the past.

I must somehow convince him of this. I had already served the time required in prison and the thing I did wrong was running away from the rules of staying in state until I was fully released from my parole. I had felt so hopeless there, and like I told you, I had descended to a state of feeling sorry for myself. I guess I was just so desperate that I ran away from everything. What coward that makes me. A good for nothing loser.

I can just hear you now. "Snap out of it!" You know what? I feel like I've grown up so much. If I had to do it over again, I know, I would stay and complete my legal and penal obligation. After a person has been in the pits, everything else seems easier and brighter.

I called my ex wife and she finally agreed to meet me at the city park. She looked good and prosperous. So at least I know that what I did hasn't kept her from succeeding like she always wanted. We talked about the girls and she showed me pictures of them growing up during the time I was gone. Oh Sadie, they are beautiful. I'm ashamed to say I wept openly when I saw them. I'm afraid it made Sandra very uncomfortable. Did I ever tell you my wife's name is Sandra. Ex wife, I meant to say.

I had purchased some silver necklaces for the girls. I searched until I found the diamond cut silver links that shine so nicely. I had a silver disc engraved for each girl with their initials on it. I tried to give the necklaces to Sandra, but she hesitated and then said that I could give them to my daughters in person. I nearly cried again. What a wimp I am becoming.

So now I must meet with them next week at a little café near here. Did I mention that I am working in a nice, small, family café

228 Peter Needs Help

on a little side street of the town where I live. The elderly couple
who own it and run it are so nice. They have a little apartment above
their garage. After a few weeks of me working there as a waiter and
dishwasher, they had me move into that garage apartment. It is so
much more quiet and comfy than my fourth floor, walk up, one room
apartment in the city. Here I am, a man who slept under a bridge,
and that place was too sleezy for me. Go figure.

My final hearing comes up on Thursday, the 14th. The judge
(his name is Judge Winston Herald) had to study on my case some
more before deciding my fate. You know what Sadie, I'm not worried.
Somehow I have peace about it. Whatever happens I will go through
it with dignity and I won't fall into the maze of depression this time.
I know who I am, and I decided that I sort of like myself. I guess you
are freaking out to be getting a letter from me so long and detailed.
When I was there I was pretty close mouthed and stingy with my
rhetoric. Sometimes I write better than I talk. Just something you
didn't know about me, I guess

So hang in there. Keep praying for me. That request is another
shocker, I'm sure. You probably didn't expect me to ever crave prayer.
I will let you know how everything turns out.

Your friend,
Pete

Sadie could hardly see the words because her eyes misted up and tears
rolled out and down her cheeks. She held the letter to her breast and closed
her eyes. She began to pray aloud.

*Oh my father in heaven, hear my prayer. Peter Combs is changing, Lord.
His letter shows that he is changing. How grateful I am for this. Please God, let
your Holy Spirit draw him to a decision about accepting Jesus Christ into his
heart. He is ready. I can tell it, Lord. Please let a good number of the people he
meets and deals with be Christians so that they can influence his life with hearts
of divine love. Cause him to hunger and thirst after righteousness. Help him find
his way, I pray thee.*

*And Lord, if you think it is the right thing, please help that judge to decide
in Peter's favor. Let him understand that Peter has changed and is recalcitrant
and ready to make a good, honest life now. Let him be free of this troublesome
time and loosed from the bonds of the law.*

*And Lord, one more thing. When he meets those daughters that he hasn't
seen in so long, please let them be nice to their dad. May this special reunion
be blessed with your gentle touch. I love you Lord. I love to see how you work in*

lives and change them for the better. In Jesus' name I pray these things and also that you might be glorified in the results. Amen!

Sadie thought about whether Peter considered this letter totally private or if she might share the news in it with the Shaw's. She finally came to a decision. She knocked on the Shaw's door and went in to share the letter with them. Victoria cried openly. Even the Colonel was wiping his sleeve across his eyes once in a while as she read it to them.

"Well, something has to be done. That's all there is to it," exclaimed the Colonel. "I am going to find out the address of this judge and send him vouchers from all the distinguished folk here at Rose Creek. I'll have them all notorized and if I have to, I'll deliver them in person." He was getting worked up.

"I'll go too," shouted Victoria. The Colonel laughed then and softened some.

"Oh, you dear, sweet wife. You would do that wouldn't you?" he said.

"Of course, dear. Peter is an honest fellow and he deserves a break. I think I can make it up that far, as long as I can come back soon enough." She smiled her brave, sweet smile. Sadie was so touched by that gesture of good faith. Talk about love being poured out on someone. Here was a good example of it. She wished that Pete could see it and know about it.

"Then let's all go! The three of us! Sadie can drive the big black car and we will travel in style and comfort. I'll get on the task of collecting those affidavits right now. Where is the phone?" he queried.

"Right where it always is, dear. Calm down. Sadie you must help me pack. I must look elegant but not showy." Victoria rose from her chair and headed for the closet. Sadie got a glimpse of the strong woman that Victoria used to be.

"Wait a cotton-pickin' minute here. Stop!" Sadie held up her hands with her head down. "Let's think about this carefully. That is a long, long trip. We have to be sure that Victoria is up to it. You could just send the letters and affidavits up there for the judge to look at."

The Colonel came close to Sadie and smiled. He put his hands on her shoulders and looked her right in the eyes. "Dear, dear Sadie. You are rightfully looking after our best interest, and thank you. But this is a time for drastic effort. Our presence there will make all the difference in the world. Letters are cold and impersonal. Flesh and blood speak of real feelings."

Sadie just stood there with her mouth open. The Shaw's were both moving around the room with purpose. She decided not to reason this thing out. It was too wonderful to see new life in their faces. They had a purpose and goal, now. She had to admit that they both looked years younger.

Chapter 43

The Trip

And so it was that they gathered together letters and vouchers from the Mayor, two pastors, construction foremen, bankers, and a myriad of townspeople. The word had spread and it seemed that a great number of people wanted a hand in helping this man, (once the town bum), make good again. The letters were all notarized and placed in a nice black leather folder.

Sadie had called ahead to the Chicago area to make reservations for accommodations in one of the finest hotels. The Colonel had called around until he found the courthouse where Peter had been placed on the docket. Peter had given them the name of the judge in his letter. Sadie sent a letter to Peter telling him what was going on. She just hoped he had received it and wouldn't be blindsided by their appearance. They didn't wait for a response; they just took off.

It was early on Monday morning, the 11th, just three days before Peter's hearing, that they tucked Victoria into the back of the big black Lincoln. She had feather pillows and a down comforter tucked around her. Sadie was to drive. Cherry and Joy showed up early, Joy still sleepy in her mother's arms. Once again they were to stay at the cottage and watch out for Wheezer and keep an eye on the house. Mrs. Fortenbrau was given the week off. She took the time to go visit her maiden sister in Bryson. Sadie ran through the big house and checked all the burners and fireplaces and sealed up the front door.

As they were pulling out of the driveway the path was suddenly blocked by an incoming car. It was Stephen. He stormed out of the car and rushed to the passenger side to talk to his father.

"Father, I can't believe you are going through with this. This trip will kill mother. I hope you know that." He entreated. "Mom, come, get out of the car and come back into the house."

Sadie got out of the car and stood glaring at Stephen. She was ready to step in and confront him if she had to. *Oh that man exasperates me so much,* she thought. *One day all friendly and sweet and considerate and the next ranting and raving and demanding things.*

Colonel Shaw slowly got out of the car and guided Stephen away from the car. He was far enough away that their conversation would not upset the Colonel's wife, but Sadie could still hear what they were saying.

"Son, I am really touched by your concern for our health. I know you love us. But you know what? Your Mom and I are up for an adventure. We have Sadie with us, and I'm not decrepit yet. But the most important thing of all is that we need to try to help Peter Combs. He made a mistake."

"He darn well did. He's a crook. How can you even trust him after what he did? He might try to talk you into letting him invest your money and then you will feel obligated to show your trust in him. You could end up with nothing. You have to be careful, Dad. I'm only trying to protect you," Stephen offered.

"I know that, and I appreciate your motive, son. And I know that Pete's mistake was a big one. But, Stephen, I believe in restoration and forgiveness. I want to help this man. Don't you see? I have to help him. Doing this gives me purpose again. Can't you see that I need that, Stephen?"

Stephen turned to look at Sadie. He stormed over to stand in front of her. "This is all your fault. Once again you are disrupting this family with your schemes and hair-brained ideas. I wish you'd never come here," he shouted.

And there it was. The real truth in the heart of Stephen. He still didn't want her around. Sadie opened her mouth to defend herself but was cut short by the Colonel's intervention.

"Stephen, stop this right now! Sadie had nothing to do with this whole thing. She has only consented to help us get there by driving a lot of the way. In fact she tried to talk me out of going there in person. She told me that if I wanted to get those letters to the judge, I could just mail them. I didn't have to go there. She advised me against it."

Stephen looked at his dad and then back at Sadie. "Well, I'm sorry, I guess. Once again I jumped to conclusions."

Sadie just stood there with her eyes open wide in an expression that said *I'm not surprised at all.* Stephen read her face and turned away, ashamed. "Dad, do you want me to go with you. I can take off work and drive you up there. I can have my secretary move stuff around and postpone some conference calls and all."

"Stephen it warms my heart to hear you say that. And I know you really mean it too, and that means so much to me. But son, there is no need. Sadie has our trip all mapped out and our reservations for accommodations all set. I have plenty of money and actually, your mother and I are as excited as children to do this. We will be fine. I'll keep you informed of what is going on. I'll call you every afternoon. We'll only be gone a few days." The Colonel reached out to grasp the shoulders of his tall son with both arms. "Just keep an eye on the place. Check on my workers as they continue planting and building areas of rest. They seem to be very good workers, but it would make me feel better to know that someone was checking up on them now and again."

"I'll do it, Dad." He hugged his dad firmly. Then he walked over to the car and opened the back door. He knelt down and reached in to kiss his mother's tissue paper cheek. "You always smell so good, mother," he remarked lovingly. "You take care now. I'll hear all about it when you get home. I love you."

Victoria hugged him warmly and pulled him down to kiss him on the top of his head. "Son, have I told you lately how proud I am of you. You've really grown to be a wonderful, strong man."

Stephen looked at her with wide-opened eyes and his nostrils flared a little as he controlled his facial response. He said nothing. Sadie could tell that he dared not speak. He just kissed her hand and looked at her tenderly. Then he shut the door.

Then the biggest surprise of all, Stephen walked to Sadie's door and opened it. "I need a hug!" he demanded.

Sadie was so surprised that she actually got out of the car and hugged him warmly. He didn't seem to want to let her go. "I hope you can forgive me once again for my outrageous outburst. Once again, I blew it. The truth is, I'm so glad you came here. You've made a big difference around here. Thanks for everything." He pulled away and patted her on the back as she returned to the driver's seat.

"We'll be back before you know it, Stephen. Don't worry. I'll take good care of them." She started the engine again and waited for Stephen to get back in his car and back out. Then they were finally on their way. Cherie and Joy were standing in the door of the cottage waving them off.

The trip was beautiful. They traveled up to Knoxville and picked up Highway 75 and headed north through Kentucky and north toward Illinois. They planned to go straight up to Toledo right at Lake Erie. They would then make an abrupt left on 76 all the way into Chicago. The simpler route, the better. That was Sadie's assumption. Spring was unfolding in glorious array. May's colors were stunning. They stopped often and let Victoria and the Colonel stretch their legs. The picnic lunch was eaten by a sunny lake. A picnic table was available and they sat there taking in the view and eating the delightful repast that Sadie had packed for them. As evening approached and the sun was fading off in the west, Sadie found a quaint little café called Jess's Grille, where they had a nice dinner.

"This guy cooks almost as well as you do, Sadie," the Colonel teased.

They finished up their chicken and dumplings and homemade applesauce. Jess, the cook, came out wiping his hands on his stained white apron. His belly protruded over the apron, and he had a toothpick in his mouth. On his head was a little, sagging short chef hat. *He is a portrait I'd like to photograph,* she decided. Sadie thanked him warmly for the good food and commended him on the menu. He blushed some and said that he was glad they'd stopped in and to come again. *Small towns are just so fun to be in,* thought Sadie. She really didn't much like traveling the giant, wide highways. But sometimes they were the best choice: safer and faster. But the country roads were where one really got a taste for the land and the people.

It was nearly time to stop for the night. Sadie had made reservations at a well recommended bed and breakfast out in the country just north of Dayton, Ohio. The directions were easy to follow and they found their way easily. The owner of the Inn gave them a warm welcome and showed them to their two rooms. Victoria and the Colonel had a room on the ground floor and Sadie had a high-ceilinged room upstairs. She settled the old couple in and opened the door to the little private patio that overlooked some cow fields. The air was redolent with scents of cut grass and wisteria and lilacs. The Inn keeper brought them honey-lemon tea and some butter wafers. The room had a Bennington pottery bowl full of grapes and Braeburn apples. Victoria was thrilled with it all. She settled into a comfy padded patio chair to watch the sunset and sip her tea.

When Sadie finally retreated to her own small room, she sighed with pure relief. She threw herself on the comfy, high bed and sank back into the down pillows. *Ahhh! Sweet rest,* she thought. *I'd love to run one of these places. I love to see people enjoy themselves and relax and eat well.* Sadie's room had a small balcony with one big wing-backed chair and ottoman there for her use. There was a small, colorful lap quilt lying on the chair and Sadie settled in with her own cup of tea and cookies. *Life can be very good.*

Sadie began to pray for Peter Combs. *Lord God. Father. Thanks for making this trip so easy and enjoyable. Your world is so beautiful. Life is meant to be enjoyed. But life is also meant for service and purpose. That's why we are making this trip. Dear Father, we want so very much to be able to help Pete find a way through this dilemma. Guide us and give us the words and the opportunities to speak those words. Make straight the way for us to travel. If we do come upon hindrances, please show us the way through or around them. We love you, Lord and praise your holy name.*

That night Sadie dreamed of the big house full of furniture again. She was delightedly wandering all through the different rooms. Then she spotted Pete just disappearing around a corner. She took off chasing after him. Every time she caught a glimpse of him, he would slip around another door frame into another room. She called to him. She was frantically racing and jumping over the furniture. The rooms became more and more cluttered as she strove to reach him. Finally she came to a room that had no exit. She searched and searched for a way out and then she saw an old rickety ladder going up into the eaves. She climbed up and peered over the edge into a messy attic room. There was little room to stand and she crouched over trying to keep her head from bumping into the eaves. On the floor were all sorts of bedding, strewn here and there. People were sleeping on that mess, and some were crouching against walls whispering together. It was a seedy lot, and looking at them all made Sadie feel exposed and scared. Some of them began to rise and move toward her. She headed for the ladder, but more were climbing up toward her. Their faces had sores and their hair was thin and plucked out as if they'd just suffered through chemo. There was a vacant, bruised-eyed stare on their faces. Sadie saw a dormer window and rushed to open it. She jumped through it onto the steep roof. Hands were reaching out and grabbing for her foot and her clothing. She ripped the cloth out of their hands. Then she saw the gorgeous sunset and she felt free and light. She spread her arms wide and began to run down the slope of roof. All of a sudden she began to float and the feeling was heavenly. She used her arms to steer and she went up over the trees and looked down at the lazy stream and colorful houses below. She could do this all day and never tire of it. This feeling of freedom was intoxicating and Sadie never wanted to stop.

But stop she did. She woke with a start and her heart was pounding. There was a faint light through the window and Sadie rose up to check the time. It was nearly sunrise.

That special and rare dream stayed with her throughout the day. She would find herself slipping back to the memory of it and relishing the euphoria of flying. *Snap out of it, girl.* She castigated herself. That day's trip went smoothly as they traveled north and then west. The air got colder as they neared the Great Lakes. Victoria would tire easily and she would lie herself down in the back, resting on the comfy bed Sadie had made for her there.

Sadie took a little side trip to Benton Harbor, which was right across the lower tip of Lake Michigan from Chicago. They had clam chowder and sourdough bread along with a plate of hot fried clams. The place was a bleached white, pine-covered diner near the water. The wind was pretty fierce, so they stayed indoors, although there were neat, wooden tables outside that could have been used. Sadie could tell that Victoria, who did not complain in the least, was getting tired of riding in the car.

"We are nearly there, Victoria. You've been a marvelous traveler. I will get you two settled into your hotel and then, tomorrow, Wednesday, I'll scope out the area and find the best route to the courthouse for Thursday's hearing," Sadie told her.

"Honey, I'm fine. It's just been a very long time since I went on an adventure like this. I'm not worried, because I know that you and Everett are in charge. Just lead the way and I will follow," Victoria replied. "The truth is I'm having a very good time."

"This clam chowder is so tasty and hot," commented the Colonel. "How did you know to stop here, Sadie?"

Sadie pondered that a moment and then answered. "Colonel, I don't know this area at all. I just looked on the map and found this little town off the main highway and the thought came to me that it would be a nice stop for us. Guess I just got lucky. No, that's not right. The truth of it is I prayed that the Lord would guide us to a good place to stop and eat, and here it is." Sadie truly believed that the Lord dealt with His children in the smallest details of life. Like a good father, he loved pouring out his blessings on His children. She just knew that God's hand was on this trip, and that they could trust Him to lead them where they needed to go.

The Colonel looked at her questioningly with his mouth pursed into a smile. Then he nodded and said, "You know what, Sadie, I believe you are right. Yes ma'am, I believe you are dead right."

She motioned for the waiter to come and bring them some tapioca pudding she'd seen behind the glass cooler doors. It was delicious and just the thing to top off their lunch. Sadie got a steaming cup of coffee too. She would need it to keep her mind sharp for the harrowing entrance into the wild Chicago area. She studied her map again and imprinted it on her mind.

It got a little hectic when they finally reached the Chicago area. So many main highways merged there and surrounded the city. It was a good thing that Sadie had memorized the directions to the Marriot Courtyard Inn where they had a reservation. Surprisingly, they found their way with little effort. *Take exit 44, turn right at the signal. Go under the overpass and turn left. Go 3 miles and turn right on Harbor Blvd, the hotel is 2 miles down on the right.* It felt so good to finally be parked and breathe a sigh of relief. Sadie went inside to register them for two adjoining rooms she'd secured on the phone. The place was newly renovated and was all done up in hunter greens and browns with lots of varnished mahogany and nice thick carpet. The smell of the place was pleasant too. In the lobby fresh bouquets of flowers graced the rounded tables and lamp stands. She was so glad that she had chosen this place. She could see hot coffee offered at the reception area and plates of cookies and bowls of fruit.

She got their room keys (or rather computer cards) and went out to summon the Shaw's inside. A doorman helped them get the suitcases inside. They only had two small ones and a carry on satchel. He pointed them to the elevators. Victoria had to take it slow and was huffing and puffing when they reached the rooms. *I shall have to watch her carefully. She hasn't the stamina for too much of this,* thought Sadie.

The rooms were lush and comfy. Victoria breathed a sigh of relief and sat down on a comfy wing-backed chair and took off her shoes. "Why don't you two lie down and take a nice nap, while I go and find some information on the whereabouts of the courthouse and the routes we need to get there. I'm sure there are parking places nearby so that there will be a limited amount of walking." Sadie took a breath and went on. "If you'd like I'll arrange for a wheelchair to be at the courthouse for you Victoria. It might be a good idea."

Victoria looked at her like she'd been slapped. "Nonsense, dear, I am perfectly capable of walking from the parking lot to the courthouse. I'm not an invalid, you know!"

Sadie glanced at the Colonel who shrugged and rolled up his eyes a bit. Sadie decided right then that she would arrange for that wheelchair just in case. Victoria had a vital, young spirit, but her body just couldn't keep pace with her intentions.

After the Shaw's were settled in and cold drinks had been procured for them, Sadie went down to the desk and asked for directions. The clerk pulled up map quest directions from the computer and printed them out for her. It showed her exactly the route to take from the hotel. The desk clerk circled the parking lot where she could park. She decided that tomorrow early she would drive down there anyway, just to make a trial run there and back. The fewer surprises the better.

Chapter 44

Peter's Hearing

The next morning, the traffic was horrendous. Going so early was probably not such a good idea. Everyone was rushing to work. It was 'every man for himself'. Horns were honking and fists were waving. The faces of the people were either frustrated and frantic, or calm and settled into the routine of every day ritual.

She finally found the entrance to the parking lot after her second trip down that side street. She drove round and round, up and up until she found a parking space. Thank goodness there was an elevator that took her to the street level.

What must it be like to live here in this hustling, bustling city? No one looks at anyone else. Everyone is rushing around like someone is chasing him. So very busy! The scents of the city were so like any other big city. Sadie could breathe in the bus fumes and the cigarette and cigar smoke, There was a faint wafting of garbage smells coming from the sewer openings and alley garbage cans. There were delicious smells of pastries and popcorn and coffee. On one corner was a wide cart full of bouquets of flowers. They were so colorful and tempting.

She spotted the courthouse. It was huge; made of white granite. It reminded her of the elegance of Washington D.C. The formidable stance of the building looked so intimidating and authoritative. She approached the front entrance and walked up the long row of steps. This would be a problem for Victoria. Even she was huffing and puffing when she reached the top step. She would have to find a better alternative.

Inside the courthouse in the foyer, she had to lay down her purse and her watch and walk through a metal detector. While she recovered her things, she asked the attendant if there was a way for wheelchair people to get in. The chubby, short woman was so nice and pointed to a side door. Sadie went back out through the gate and over to check it out. There was a ramp along side the building that led right down to the street in front of the courthouse. Again she approached someone who looked like they were in charge and requested information on how to get a wheelchair for the next day. She had to go to a little room on the ground floor to sign up for one. She could pick it up tomorrow morning when they arrived. All she had to do was go get it and run it out to Victoria and push her up and into the courthouse. *Good! That is done. No surprises tomorrow.* Sadie felt good that she'd come early to arrange this right now.

She checked in her purse for the courtroom number where Peter's hearing would be held. *Let's see her, room 512. Fifth floor. Where's the elevator?* Sadie found her way and finally came upon the formidable room. She pushed open the swinging door and peered in. The room was empty at the moment and the lights were off. The room was dim, lit only by the filtered, morning sunlight coming in the high windows. Sadie looked around the hallway and saw no one, so she slipped inside. She marched to the front and sat right behind the defendant's chair and began to pray out loud.

"Lord God, here we are. We made it. Thanks for your guidance and help in getting us here. Be with the Colonel and sweet Victoria as they have put so much effort to come here and honor this man. Lord, please, if it be your will, help the judge to see the change in Peter. Tomorrow, be with the people who make this decision concerning Pete's life; may they be full of compassion and wisdom. Help them to see Peter's determination to live a good life, an honest life. Help them to see his genuine repentance. Lord, please let him have a chance again to live a normal life. Relieve him from any fear, dear Lord, and let him place his trust in you. You are my source of courage. In you alone I rely. Be my refuge in this matter, my tower of strength. How I love you, Lord. You are the best Father." Sadie bowed her head and just sat quietly.

"You there! What do you think you are doing here? This is not a place to come and pray and contemplate life. This is a courtroom!" The man who spoke to her was old and gruff looking. He had a head of white hair that stood up on ends and a wrinkled and craggy face. White hairs protruded from his ears. Low on his nose was a pair of Benjamin Franklin style reading glasses. He had on an old grey, baggy sweater and old loafers.

Sadie stood up and looked at him. "I'm sorry sir, if I've imposed on you. I know this is a courtroom, but it was empty and tomorrow a big decision will be made here, and I just wanted to speak to the Lord about the outcome." Sadie stopped and took a breath. "And I respectfully disagree with you on the matter about this not being a place to contemplate life. It seems a perfect place to do just that. The decisions made here are ones that will affect the life of the man I pray for. Forgive me for bothering you." Sadie turned on her heel and walked out of the room. The old man just stood there and watched her leave.

Sadie stopped at a restaurant that looked good to her on the way back to the hotel. She ordered three different choices of meals to go. She made an educated guess at what she thought the Shaw's would enjoy. And she was right. They loved her choices. When she had entered the lobby, she had asked for and procured three sets of silverware and three real plates. How she disliked eating on plastic dinnerware and using plastic forks and knives.

In the Shaw's room, they sat around the small round table by the bed and ate their lunch contentedly. The Colonel would reach over with his fork and jab something off his wife's plate. She would, in turn, reach over and get a bite of Sadie's food. Sadie did the same. It was a fun meal. She gathered up the plates and utensils and took them away. She took her leave of the old couple and went through the adjoining door to her own room. For some strange reason she was exhausted and it was only early afternoon. She peered around the adjoining door and said, "You just call me if you need me for anything, hear?" She smiled at them and stepped through to her own room.

It felt so good to be alone. She stretched out on the bed and kicked off her shoes. *Ahhhhh, peace and quiet at last.* She started to watch a little T.V., but everything offered was so stupid and so tinged with worldliness. Even the good old programs she had once enjoyed were now compromised by the writers' insistence that the audience accept all the immoral premises of the world's view. Professional women, even those in the police force and CSI investigations, had to wear skin tight, low cut blouses and show plenty of cleavage. *What a farce.* She thought. *As if any decent organization would put up with a professional woman dressing like that. Give me a break!*

She turned off the T.V. and stripped down out of her clothes. She caught a glimpse of herself in the mirror. *Oh boy,* she pondered as she perused herself in the mirror, *maybe you are just jealous that you no longer look like some of those young, loose women,* she chuckled. She had to admit that she didn't look half bad for her age. Her tummy was protruding a little, but that was just normal for women her age who had delivered three kids. She was so unused to staring at herself in the mirror that she did a close up discretionary search of her skin. She had wrinkles around her eyes and some on her mouth. But generally she looked okay. *I wouldn't win any beauty contests, but I don't look too bad. If I look as beautiful as Victoria when I reach her age, I will be happy.*

Sadie stepped into the hot shower and stayed there a bit longer than usual letting the steamy water flow over her with delicious warmth. Whatever would they do with the day ahead? She was indeed glad that they hadn't come up a day later. She knew that for them to rush to the courthouse the day after they arrived would have been too much for the Shaw's. She found a brochure on the side lamp table and it told of interesting things to see in Chicago.

She checked in with the Shaws to see if they might be interested in sightseeing, and like she supposed, they were not in the least bit interested. The Colonel said that just the thought of being out there wandering around sight seeing, was exhausting. They were perfectly fine just sitting in their room and wandering down to the lush and elaborate lobby. Besides that they had both been to Chicago years ago and didn't care to repeat the adventure.

"You go Sadie. We'll be fine here. Take the whole day and explore to your heart's content." The Colonel guided her to her room. "Off with you, now. Victoria and I are going to have a little honeymoon," he said with a twinkle in his eye.

Victoria gasped and shook her head at him. "You old coot, whatever are you talking about? Honeymoon? We've had so many honeymoons I could write a book. You and I are going to just read and rest."

"We'll see about that," he teased her. She blushed smiled at him.

Sadie asked at the desk about where to go and what to see. She stepped out into the blustery air, but the sun was shining now and her scarf and jacket were sufficient. She did as she was instructed and waited for a certain numbered bus to pick her up. She had to be sure to get the right one. It wove around the streets amongst the tall sky scrapers. The sun had not a chance to get in there. The buildings cast shadows on everything. It was sort of an ominous sight. The city was so noisy and smelled of petrol and steam and garbage. Sadie sat back and just enjoyed watching the people as they hurried through their daily routines. They walked fast and miraculously didn't seem to bump into each other: some hurrying this direction and some going the opposite direction just barely missing each other as they passed by. She saw the elegantly dressed business people and model type women. She saw the poor and shabby, the worried, down-trodden folk The self-confident ones walked with arrogance and purpose. They seemed assured that life would be good to them from that moment on. The world was so full of people in need. Even the rich ones driven to and fro in their limousines had need. Sadie felt a deep burden for them all of a sudden.

Sadie toured Chicago's Sears Tower Building. She called Rebecca from the very top. "Oh Becky, I wish you were here. This building is so tall and I am looking out over the city and the Lake. The sun is streaming through white billowy clouds and across the sparkling water. It is so beautiful. I want so badly to share it with you."

"I wish that too, Mom. Maybe one of these days we can share stuff like that. Andy and Matt both called this week. They wanted to know all about our camping trip and what Stan thought of the whole thing. Andy actually got him on the phone to talk to him about it. I guess they don't trust my view of things, since they think I am prejudiced toward anything you decide to do."

"Well . . . . what did Stan tell them?" Sadie was seriously curious.

"He told them that your life there was ideal. It was simple and stress free and that you were loved by many in the town. He bragged and bragged about the camping trip and told the guys that he wanted to move there and was going to seriously contemplate that possibility. Oh Mama, that made me so happy."

Sadie spoke to Treat for a minute also. When she hung up, she gazed over the fabulous scene for a while. *This must be what it was like on the Tower of Babel when God brought it tumbling down and scattered the people. Man surely has reached for the stars and the moon. I'll bet God is proud of his creation being so creative. He probably sits there wondering what man will try to do next.*

Sadie walked the long walk on the wide sidewalk near the lake. She had a cup of coffee and a slice of coffee cake and sat on the benches watching people again. *Oh how I long to see the whole country here in the good ole U.S. There is so much variation from state to state and I want to see it all. I want to eat all the food they offer from place to place, hear the different language variations, eExperience the cultures. What a rich, interesting country we have. Every type of terrain and peoples from all over the world living here. It is a big hodgepodge of people. I love it.*

In the downtown area, Sadie found a marvel. It was a magnificent, self-contained living area where there were apartments in a huge complex that included, schools, churches, grocery stores, department stores, post office, restaurants, banks. It was all included in the complex. People need only walk out of their doors to do their business and shop and play. No cars were needed to go from place to place. She searched through and found bowling alleys and swimming pools, beauty parlors, barbers, cleaners and a movie theater. There was even a police station and library. It was like being in a space movie where the whole world could be in ruins but that one area was alive and functioning on its own.

The next morning dawned cloudy and threatened rain. The wind was blowing and it had that cold, dampness carried from the lake. Sadie ushered the Shaws' to the lobby area where a good breakfast from the generous breakfast bar was offered.

Back up in the room, Sadie suggested that Victoria dress very warmly for the day's trip. "That wind out there can be a doozy. Make sure your ears are covered. I think cold air holds fast here even in springtime."

"Maybe you should just stay here and wait for us to return, dear," suggested her caring husband.

"Everett! It's very seldom I get upset with you, but right now, I'm ready to crown you. I didn't come all this way in that car to sit in a hotel room and wait things out. Don't even suggest that I stay here. I'm going!" Victoria rose up and stormed into the bathroom, slamming the door.

The Colonel rose too quickly and had to stand with his hand on his head until his blood quit draining from his head. When he was steady again, he went to the bathroom door to assure her that she was going and that he would have it no other way. He told her that her presence there would give Peter such encouragement. "And it will help me too to have you by my side," he added.

The bathroom door opened slowly and Victoria slipped out and into his arms. "I'm sorry I yelled at you, dear," she explained. "I just want so badly to be useful and have purpose again. This is my chance to be part of something meaningful and worthwhile."

"I know, sweet woman," the Colonel responded. "It is rather a grand adventure, isn't it?" He kissed the top of her head and smiled as he held her tightly.

The trip downtown was so slow. Sadie had factored in that eventuality when she planned the time they should depart from the hotel. So they took their time and didn't worry. She parked on the 3rd floor of the parking building and they walked slowly to the elevator. The air was cruel and biting. The wind whipped their coats. The Colonel had to hold on to his wife so that she could keep her balance. They stopped ever so often to let her catch her breath.

"Whoa," she exclaimed, "this is a little harder than I expected. Hold on a minute. We aren't late are we?"

Sadie smiled down on her and put her arm around her as well. "No problem. We started early enough that we shall be there in plenty of time. By the way, Colonel, does Peter know we are coming? I wrote a letter, but I'm not sure he received it yet. Did you get to speak to him on the phone at all?"

"Me? No, I didn't talk to him. I just assumed you'd written and told him we were driving up." The Colonel looked worried.

"Oh boy, he is going to be very surprised. I hope our presence won't rattle him," worried Victoria.

"Too late to worry about that now," mused Sadie. "Let's just go in and pray for the best!" They walked to the ramp by the side of the courthouse. Sadie rushed up and entered the building. Soon she came back with the reserved wheelchair.

"Now, wait a minute. I thought I said I didn't need a wheelchair," scolded Victoria. She was huffing and puffing due to her walk from the parking garage.

"Now, Vicky, you do this for me, okay? I will feel better about taking you here if you will just allow us to push you into the courthouse. You can walk into the courtroom on your own, I promise," the Colonel pleaded.

She narrowed her eyes at her husband and squeezed her mouth down tightly. Finally she said, "Alright then. I will let you push me in, but as soon as we reach the courtroom, I'm getting up and walking. I'm not a total invalid, you know," she chided with a wicked glare.

They settled her in and Sadie pushed her easily up the ramp and into the building. She had to stand and walk through the gate. Sadie could tell she felt very important in that aspect. Sadie led them to the elevator. She was glad that she had made a trial run here. It gave her confidence. Easily they found their way to the assigned room for Peter's hearing.

The smell of the courtroom created a reverential atmosphere. The scent of leather and polished wood always correlated with ostentatious ambiance. The place exuded history and years of anticipation. There were only a few people in the audience seats. Sadie was sure that most of them were just sightseers or interested observers. They walked up to the left front and sat behind the defense chair. "See, I told you we would get here in plenty of time. Maybe I timed it out a little too generously. I wonder how long we will have to wait. Do you think they will start on schedule?" Sadie nervously talked on and on.

The colonel stared at her in a bemused manner. "Well Sadie, if I didn't know better, I'd guess you were really anxious for this moment and a bit apprehensive as well. Don't you worry! It's going to be alright. He will be so glad to see you, and delighted and surprised to know you came all this way to support him."

"What if he is upset with us for surprising him like this? Maybe he wants to face this without an audience. Maybe there is too much shame involved for him," Sadie asked him. "I just hope the judge recognizes that Peter has good friends that are standing by him. That's all I want for him; a fair chance at a new life." Sadie lowered her head and said a quick prayer. *Oh Lord, our Father, hear our prayer. We think this is very important. We want Peter to be free of the stain of his former life and transgressions. You are a God of forgiveness and mercy; a giver of grace. Please impress upon the judge that mercy is appropriate here. I pray this with all my heart in the name of Jesus Christ and for His glory alone.*" She raised her head to see the Colonel and Victoria looking at her. She smiled wanly at them and clutched her hands together in her lap. A big sigh burst forth from her. The Colonel patted her hands and Victoria reached over to touch her knee.

"There, there, girl, it's going to be fine. Just you wait and see," Victoria assured her.

They waited another fifteen minutes before anything started to happen. More people came in and sat down. Then down the aisle walked a very well dressed man with a black leather briefcase. He appeared to be full of himself and cocky. His hair was perfect and his tie was an Italian job that Sadie recognized as most expensive. He sat in the prosecutor's chair.

A side door opened and in walked Peter with his defense attorney. Peter was in a neatly pressed suit. He probably had purchased it off the rack of a thrift store, but he looked great in it. He had on polished shoes. There were no handcuffs. *Thank goodness* thought Sadie. Pete had his head down as he walked in. Just as he reached to pull back the chair, his eyes caught sight of them and he stopped dead in his tracks. His mouth opened and he took in a deep breath. His eyes got wide and his forehead puckered up in astonishment.

"Hello there, Peter," said the Colonel standing up and reaching out his hand for a warm two handed shake. "We just decided we wanted to be here when you went through this trying ordeal. We wanted you to know, we love you and want you back with us."

Tears welled up in Peter's eyes and he wiped them quickly away with his left hand. Victoria stepped close to the railing and reached for him. He gently put his arms around her and patted her on the back. "You're going to be fine, young man, just fine," she encouraged him.

Then Peter put all of his attention on Sadie. She stood there not knowing how to proceed. She waved a tiny wave and they stood looking at each other. Then Sadie's eyes too filled with tears and Peter took a step toward her. She returned the favor and stepped eagerly up to the bar that separated them. They fit into each others arms like two puzzle pieces. She laid her head on his shoulder and said not a word. There was nothing that needed saying. He held her tightly and then kissed the top of her head.

Right then the door next to the bench opened and they all parted and took their seats. The bailiff stood erect and at attention and called out in a loud voice, "All rise! The honorable Judge Winston Herald, presiding!" Everyone rose as one to join Sadie and Pete and the Colonel that were already standing.

To Sadie's utter amazement, in walked the funny old codger that had been there yesterday. This time he was not wearing the old grey sweater, but instead was outfitted with a crisp white shirt and black tie and his silky black robe billowed out around him as he walked. He still had the tufts of hair protruding from his ears and still had on the granny glasses. He glared at the courtroom taking in the visitors. He looked formidable as he ascended to the judge's perch. Sadie stood there with her mouth open. *Oh dear, what will this mean to the case? Surely he will remember seeing me here and he will wonder what is going on. Oh Lord, I pray that I haven't done anything to jeopardize Peter's chances here.*

The court officer said loudly, "You may be seated!"

Sadie continued to stand with her mouth open staring at the funny little judge. The Colonel reached up and tugged her jacket. "Sit down Sadie. What is the matter with you?"

Just then the judge made eye contact with her and smiled a crooked little smile and tipped his head to her almost like he was waving to her. She just stared at him and then nodded quickly.

The prosecutor got up to plead his case against Peter. As he started his soliloquy, the back doors banged open and a rush of people came quickly forward.

"What is this, pray tell," the judge ordered. "Who are you people? This is a courtroom, not a stage."

Sadie turned to look, and there, to her amazement was the mayor of Rose Creek along with her entourage of city councilmen and some reporters. "Excuse me your honor. My name is Ivy Bridges. I'm the mayor of Rose Creek, where Peter Combs lived and worked for the betterment of our city. We meant to be here on time, but our plane was delayed due to weather, and the traffic in Chicago is horrendous. We are the leaders of the town of Rose Creek, North Carolina, and we've come here today to show our support for this fellow citizen, Peter

Combs. We hope that our presence here will signify our confidence that this man is worthy of release from his bonds and punishments."

"Your honor, I protest! This disturbance has messed up my rhythm and confounded my presentation," complained the prosecutor.

"If it please the court we shall be seated now." With that the mayor sat down as did her people.

Judge Winston Herald tried to stifle a smile pressing his lips together and lowering his head. "I understand your dilemma, Mr. Jackson. Why don't you start over. Let's just hope you can resume your rhythm," offered the judge with a barely masked smirk.

The prosecutor made a good case against Peter. He stated that the crime he committed was a very serious one and that people were harmed by it. Some people lost money and others were misled. He said that just because time had lapsed and this man had not gotten into any more trouble, did not excuse him nor give him the right to have his sentence cancelled. "If he cannot be trusted to report to a parole officer and keep the rules of his probation, then he needs to be made an example of and returned to prison to serve the rest of his sentence."

Sadie's heart sank. She knew that the prosecutor was right. Peter had done harm to people and society with his insider trading. He was guilty as charged. Normally she would nod an approval to such a verdict. However, in this case she knew the accused personally. She had witnessed his heart and seen his soul thaw out. *Oh dear Lord, here I go again. But please hear my prayer. Please soften the heart of Judge Herald. Help him remember other times that he too was guilty of something and was sorry. Help him see that in this circumstance, mercy would be appropriate. Oh Lord, let it happen, I pray.*

There was nothing more to do, but wait and hope. When the prosecutor rested his case, the judge called a recess until 10:30. Everyone stood as the judge left his high seat. Immediately Peter turned and sought Sadie's eyes.

"Whatever were you thinking dragging these people up here to watch this trial? I have to admit that I'm thrilled to see you. It has made my trepidation drain away just to know you are behind me. But I never expected it of you. This is too much." Peter shook his head and his brow furrowed and he turned his head to see Mayor Wheeler and her entourage coming forward for a chat.

Sadie slowly backed away to give room to the crowd that gathered around Peter. The flash of photography brightened up the room, until the bailiff yelled firmly, "No photos in this courtroom please."

Victoria had to use the restroom so Sadie led her out of the courtroom and found one nearby. She was so anxious to get back to where Peter was. It was as though a giant, powerful magnet was pulling her. She thought, *Hurry Victoria, hurry. I don't want to waste a minute. I have to be with him. He needs me.*

The Colonel met them outside the bathroom. "I'm taking Vicky downstairs to find something to snack on. She has to eat every few hours to keep up her blood levels. Sadie, are you coming with us?" he asked. Sadie begged off and said that she would go back and see if Peter was available to talk. The Colonel pushed his wife in the wheelchair down the hall to find some refreshments. Coffee and sodas and sweets were served on the main floor from coin dispensed machines.

Sadie hurried into the courtroom. She got there just in time to see Peter ushered out the side door where he would have to wait in a holding cell until the time came to resume the hearing. He glanced up as he was exiting the room and waved at her and smiled so warmly that Sadie thought her heart would melt.

"Miss Jamison," Mayor Bridges rushed over to talk to her, "we have spoken to the defending attorney and he is going to let us take the stand for Peter's defense."

"Oh that is wonderful. I'm so grateful that you came. Did all of you fly here this morning?" She dumbly inquired. "Of course you did, sorry. I heard you say that to the judge. I guess I'm just nervous about this is all."

"As well you should be," replied the boisterous Ivy Bridges. She was dressed in a fine wool suit of sage green. It fit her to a 't'. She looked very impressive with a silk white blouse. On her feet were alligator heels of the finest quality. There was no shabbiness here. "Just a few members of the counsel could make it. We arranged for the photographers to meet us here. They are eager to cover this as an extension of the national story about our confederate mystery and transformed park in Rose Creek. For some reason the nation is interested in our little corner of the world. Just a good human interest story, I guess." The mayor looked around to smile for the camera. "Anyway, this may put some pressure on the judge to be lenient. When he sees how important Peter is to all of us and recognizes that he will have to deal with the response of a disappointed nation if he rules otherwise, maybe he will rule in Peter's favor."

"I hope and pray you are right." Sadie responded. "He certainly has a better chance with you being here." She was so pleased that the Mayor had come. She knew that deep down the publicity that Mayor Bridges would receive on this matter was probably the major motivation for this trip, but if it worked in Peter's favor, then, good enough.

The Colonel and Victoria arrived back in the courtroom and slowly made their way to be seated next to Sadie. Just a few minutes later, Peter came back in with his counsel and then the judge arrived once more. He looked perturbed and in a hurry. A frown creased his brow as he took his seat and hit the gavel denoting the starting up of the procedure again. "Defense? Are you ready to proceed? Let's get going on this!"

Peter had drawn a public defender who took the case seriously. The pro bono work fell, this time, to a lawyer who knew his stuff. He was neither pushy nor tentative. He was deliberate and forthright. His diction was good and he wasted not a word, but came right to the point.

"Your honor, this man is guilty. We concede that point. He ran away from his obligation to the law. All this is punishable, we agree. But Peter Combs is an exceptional man and in my opinion deserves special judgment."

The judge's eyebrows rose in surprise. "Are you trying to tell me how to do my job Counselor?" The judge raised his chin and stared at the lawyer.

"Not at all, your honor. We recognize your wisdom and fairness," he countered. "I will continue my defense to explain that after Peter Combs left the jurisdiction of this court without permission, he hid away in a small mountain town in North Carolina. He became a homeless wanderer there and took odd jobs to exist. He slept where he could, mostly under bridges. He mourned the loss of his wife and children. His decadent life from before was no longer important to him."

The lawyer turned to Peter and put his hand on Peter's shoulder in an attitude of sympathy. "He was totally depressed and I would venture to submit, was mentally altered for a good long while. After a year of this, he took on a handyman, yardwork job at an historical mansion in the town. He slowly earned enough money to clean himself up and procure a small room in which to live. His work in Rose Creek was exemplary and added so much to the community. His depression slowly lifted as he gave his energies to this project." The lawyer took a breath and turned to the Mayor. "If your honor allows, I'd like to call up Mayor Ivy Bridges from Rose Creek, North Carolina to testify to Peter's contribution to society there."

And so it went. The mayor got up to tell of how much Peter had done for Rose Creek and that he was needed there to finish the job on the park. The Colonel was called up to testify to Peter's loyalty and honesty and good work ethic. Finally Sadie was called to the stand. She rose slowly and walked forward. Her heart was pounding and her hands were shaking.

Peter's lawyer said, "State your name, please."

Sadie took a deep breath and said, "My name is Sadie Jamison"

"Miss Jamison, how is that you came to know Peter, and what is your relationship to him?"

"I work for Colonel and Mrs. Shaw as their housekeeper and cook. When I moved into the little cottage that serves as my quarters next to the mansion, I needed some clean up work to be done on the place before I could move in. I asked Mr. Combs if he would be willing to take the project on."

"Where was he when you made that proposal of employment?"

Sadie looked at Peter and grimaced a little. The judge turned to her and said, "Miss Jamison, please just answer the question and let's get on with this."

Sadie looked at the judge and their eyes locked. She could see the recognition there and feel a surprisingly gentle nature in this otherwise brusque man.

"Forgive me, your honor, I just didn't want to show Peter Combs in a disagreeable light." She cleared her throat and went on, "I met Peter on the streets of Rose Creek He was sitting on the sidewalk in the sun with a sign at his side that read, 'Will work for food'." Sadie stopped and bowed her head just a moment, swallowed and went on. "I was moved to ask him if he wanted to earn some money by helping me."

"Weren't you afraid to approach a dirty bum of disputable reputation?" The defense attorney inquired.

"I was not afraid. He looked miserable and alone and I wanted to help him if I could."

"Like a good Samaritan?"

"No, not like that." She thought *I just knew what it felt to be alone and sort of lost and I wondered if he could use a hand.* "I needed help and he looked strong enough to handle the work. It was just a short job and he was available." Sadie sat up straight like she was ready for a challenge.

"How did it happen that Peter Combs came to be a regular employee of the Shaw's?"

"Well, as it turned out he did a fine job clearing out the little gate house for me. Then we discovered more and more things that he could help with. Yard work became his primary occupation. The acreage around the mansion had been neglected for a long time and the Colonel got it in his head to get it straightened up. Peter was a good worker; quiet, steady and on time. We just naturally asked him to stay on."

"So, would you say that Peter Combs became a valuable asset to the restoration of the mansion and grounds?"

"Yes indeed." Sadie smiled at Peter and he gave her a tentative smile back.

The prosecuting attorney rose and cleared his throat. "Your honor, I have a question for Miss Jamison."

"Proceed, Counselor." The judge readjusted his seating position as though he was in arthritic pain.

"Miss Jamison? That is your name isn't it? Jamison?"

"Yes it is my name . . . . now."

"What do you mean . . . now?"

"When I was married, it was Golden," Sadie offered reluctantly. *Where is this going? S*he thought.

"You wouldn't be the infamous wife of the Reverend Anthony Golden would you?"

"Why yes, I would; although 'infamous' seems a rather extreme term to me. I don't see that that information has any relativity to this case," countered Sadie.

The judge intervened, since the defense attorney sat stunned and silent. "What is your point Counselor? Why did you bring that up? Her picture has been on the news and we all know who she is." The judge was getting irritated.

"Well, your honor, I was just pointing out that one runaway was trying desperately to help another runaway. Her testimony is prejudiced for sure. I'm not sure there isn't some romantic involvement here that is coloring Mrs. Golden's view of things."

Sadie laughed. She couldn't help herself. The judge looked at her as though she had lost her mind. "What, may I ask, is so comical, Miss Jamison?"

"I'm sorry your honor. The tension of being on this stand must have gotten to me. I didn't mean to be rude. It's just that the thought of taking on a romantic venture at this time is just a ridiculous notion to me. I've just ended thirty-two years of so called romance. That's enough to last me a good long while. Peter Combs and I are just coworkers and friends. That's all."

"I think you've exhausted my good graces, Phil," said the judge to the prosecutor. 'That will be all. You may step down Ms. Jamison." With that the judge asked if there were any more witnesses for the plaintiff.

"None, your honor. The defense rests." Peter's lawyer sat down.

After that, the prosecutor called up two very well dressed men who testified that Peter Combs had cost them money by his insider trading. They had lost some investments and been caught up in the discoloration of the affair. Their reputations had been sullied and they had had to work hard to overcome the stigma. They looked arrogant and annoyed to even have to give their time for this frivolous affair. Sadie thought, *this is the clientele that Peter worked with . . . these stuffy, Italian suited men whose main goal in life was to get more money and power no matter what the cost.* She was certain that they had put so much pressure on Peter that he succumbed to choosing the wrong thing.

The judge looked at Peter and studied his face. Peter looked right back at him without arrogance but with humility. "Mr. Combs, you have been silent during all of this. Would you like to come up here and defend yourself?"

Peter looked shocked and then a little panicky.

"Your honor, I will come up there, but I cannot defend myself. I am guilty as charged. I was caught up in the excitement of pleasing my clients. This insider information came to me unexpectedly and I knew it was wrong to act on it. I chose the wrong way. With all my heart I wish I had chosen correctly and honorably. If I could go back and choose again, I would definitely do the right thing. I am so sorry for all the inconvenience I've caused these men and for breaking the rules of stock market conduct. I will gladly accept whatever judgment you bestow upon me. I will not feel cheated or bitter." With that Peter sat down and bowed his head with his hands clasped in his lap.

"One more question, Mr. Combs. You had already done your time and were paroled for a year. Why did you run away and take on the lifestyle of a bum?"

Peter stood back up, and slowly looked up at the judge. "That is a hard one to answer, your honor. I can only explain it by saying that I was devastated to have lost my family. My wife divorced me and remarried almost immediately to a very wealthy man. My two daughters were not allowed, or didn't want, to see me any more. It felt as if life was not worth living. I never had intentions of suicide, but I just wanted to disappear and not be a reminder to those around me that I was such a loser and failure. So I hitchhiked down to North Carolina and stopped in Rose Creek. I'm afraid that my depression overtook me there and I became the lowest of scum."

"That will be all, Mr. Combs. You may be seated." With that, the judge sat silently for a good long while. He pursed his lips and worked with his pencil. It looked as though he was drawing cartoons. The courtroom was silent. A few people cleared their throats or sighed, but otherwise it was dead silent.

Finally the judge spoke. "I'm afraid I need a little more time on this one. I will have to ponder on all the facts and testimonies and will render my decision tomorrow morning at 10:00. Meanwhile, I am releasing Mr. Combs from custody on his own recognizance. I expect you to be here bright and early for this sentencing, is that clear, Mr. Combs?"

"Yes, your honor," both Peter and his attorney chimed in.

The prosecuting attorney was incensed. "Your honor, this is highly unorthodox. This man is a risk for running away. How can you release him at a time like this?"

"I do it just like this," said the judge with a sneer. He banged the gavel hard on the high desk. "Court dismissed."

What a thrill it was to walk with Peter out of the courtroom. The Mayor and her entourage met him in the outside hallway. Pictures were being flashed right and left and reporters were asking him questions. He seemed overwhelmed by it all.

The colonel stepped forward and held up his hands. "Your honor, Mayor Bridges, and gentlemen, what say we let Mr. Combs have a little respite from all this drama? Can we meet you back here tomorrow morning at 8:30? Then you can interview him and ask all the questions you like. Is that alright with you Peter?"

Ivy Bridges shook her head, "I'm afraid we are flying back home this afternoon late. We won't be here for the rendering of the decision. Be sure someone calls and informs us of the outcome. We will be so eager to hear."

Peter looked up grateful for the Colone's suggestion, and said, "I'll tell you what. I'll go ahead and face this interview right now, so I won't have to think about it all night long." He looked at the Colonel and his wife and at Sadie and said pleadingly, "If you could just wait for me at those benches over there, I'll be with you in a few minutes."

Then he turned to the Mayor and her group and said calmly, "I am so honored that you flew out all this way to support me in my bid for freedom. I feel very unworthy of such a gift." To the reporters he said, "What is it you want to know? I will answer it all," he offered graciously.

The Colonel, Victoria and Sadie reluctantly walked off leaving him to the clamoring questions and flashing pictures. They sat on the hard mahogany benches. Mrs. Shaw was looking a little peaked. Sadie searched in her bag and pulled out a small candy bar and a bottle of water. "Here, Victoria, chew on this a little and soon we will find a good place in which to eat." The Colonel took a candy bar too. They sat silently watching the frenzied scene before them. Sooner than they expected, Peter turned and slipped toward them waving his hand at the reporters.

"Let's get out of here. I know a special little café close by that will suit our needs just fine."

"That's right, you know Chicago, don't you," replied Sadie. "Lead on!"

Peter flagged down a cab and helped Victoria into the front seat. "This will be easier for you to get in and out of," he explained. The rest of them got into the back seat with Sadie in the middle. Peter told the cabby, "Pappy's Hole in the Wall, please. It's over on 4th and Vine."

"I know where it is," said the cab driver in a friendly manner. "Not many people know about that little place. You must be a native of Chicago."

"I've lived here a while, yes, you're right," said Peter. "These folk have never been to Pappy's and I thought it would be a real treat for them."

"You right about that. If somebody don't like Pappy's, then they's somethin' wrong with 'em. It's the best place to eat in the city." He masterly drove them in and out of traffic, swiftly and expertly weaving his way between cars and getting them to their destination in very little time.

When they got to the alleyway, Peter paid and generously tipped the driver and helped Victoria out of the car. They all looked around as the cab pulled away from the alleyway. All they could see were stores and tall buildings. Not a restaurant in sight.

"This way. Follow me," he announced with delight in his voice. Sadie knew that he liked the way they had been stupefied to see the area. "I'm taking you to one of the little known treasures in Chicago."

They headed down the bricked alley. It was clean. The brick walls had been power-washed. No trash was stacked on either side. The red brick walls looked very old and parts of them were crumbling and were covered in climbing vine. An ivy of some sort clung to the bricks and worked a pattern up the side of the wall. Sadie noticed a potted tree and some other plants in heavy cast iron urns sat along the way. It appeared that the alley got very little sunlight, and Sadie wondered how anything could grow in the dark here. Very soon they came to two cast iron lantern stands. On the tops were glass lanterns with live gas flames burning brightly. The steady flame cast a welcoming, warm glow over the area. In between the two lanterns was a recessed doorway with a big, heavy, dark wood door. No sign was visible announcing what there was there. No sample menu was hanging in a glass case out front. Nothing.

"How do they get business with no sign announcing what is here?" asked Sadie. "Someone just walking along here would think this was just someone's home."

"That's the idea," explained Pete. "Only those who already know about this place come here. If they tell someone else about it that person finds it and starts coming too. This restaurant has no lack of customers, believe me. Their way of advertising is word of mouth."

He held the door open for Victoria and the Colonel to go through. He stopped Sadie as she started to slip pass him. "Sadie, I want this to be my treat. I've saved enough of my earnings in that little restaurant to pay for this. Please go along with me on this, so I won't be embarrassed."

"Of course Peter. It is so kind of you to treat us like this. We certainly didn't expect it, but we will accept it gladly." She gave him a warm smile and touched his arm as she walked on past him.

The place was a marvel of simplicity and class. The walls were of forest green wall paper with dark wood wainscoting and crown molding trim above and below. The dining area was made up of little private booths with soft leather backed benches. Each table was shut off from the other by the high backed seats that extended up several feet. This allowed for veritable privacy. There were antique mirrors and lovely Renaissance pictures in heavy dark frames gracing the walls. Someone came up to them immediately and the maitre'd looked surprised and said, "Mr. Combs, it has been entirely too long since you graced our establishment. Come in, come in. I happen to have your favorite table available. Welcome."

"Thank you Stanley. It is good to see you again too. These people are my very good friends from North Carolina. I couldn't let them get away from here without having this fine dining experience."

"Certainly not, Mr. Combs. Come this way."

He led them to a corner booth for four. The table had a white linen cloth on it, set with crystal and silverware and a finely decorated charger china plate. There was a bud vase with two pale pink roses in it. And a protected candle sat in the middle next to the flowers. Two tiny, stone ware containers were placed at each place setting: one holding fresh ground pepper and one holding kosher salt. They sat down and made themselves comfortable.

"Oh these seats feel so good on my back," sighed Victoria. "Those hard benches in the courtroom are okay, but after a while they just wear on the bones."

"Oh Peter, this is so wonderful. I feel like I've stepped into a fairyland cavern: a secret cave of riches. It smells so good in here. Fine dining always has its own scent. I love it." Sadie was beaming and taking it all in with her eyes.

The waiter came quickly and asked if they wanted menus. Peter said to his guests. "You can order from the menu, or you can allow me to order for you. Whichever you like will be fine."

The Colonel piped in, "I'd like to see one menu, but I will trust in my good friend to order for us. I just want to see what is offered here for my own amazement."

"That sounds perfect to me also," said Sadie.

So the waiter brought them menus and they studied them proclaiming now and again how varied the menu was. They enthusiastically remarked on all the wonderful options available.

Peter began his order. "We'll start out with small maple, walnut, cranberry spinach salads. Please bring a little container of the maple dressing to use if we need extra."

"Very well, sir," said the waiter. He was standing with his hands behind his back taking in their order with his mind only.

"And we'll have a basket of your three choices of hot bread, also," continued Peter. "After that we will have a platter of seared tuna with the wasabi dip and seaweed salad. Please add a few slices of buffalo mozzarella and tomato slices with fresh basil and balsamic vinagrette. Then bring us some petite bowls of French onion soup."

Sadie's mouth was watering by this time. "Oh that sounds marvelous," she couldn't help but remark.

"I think we will have four different entrees and we will all get a chance to taste each one. Let's see . . ." he pondered. "How about one of your famous bourbon filet mignon steaks with garlic mashed potatoes and asparagus? Add to that the salmon steak with lemon buer blanc." Peter took a breath and continued, "We will also have your almond crusted rainbow trout with orzo and crisp green beans. And the last one will be chicken and dumplings with collard greens and corn muffins."

That last order surprised them all. Peter quickly explained, "They have the best chicken and dumplings the north can offer. It is a standard on the menu." He looked back at the waiter. "These people love sweet tea, so let's have those all around. And if you could, I'd appreciate you bringing a little stack of bread plates so we can sample each other's entrees."

The waiter nodded and didn't seem perturbed at all by this unusual request. "Right away sir," he responded. "Will there be any wine needed for lunch?"

Peter looked inquisitively at his guests, and they all shook their heads no. "I think that will be all for right now, thank you." The waiter bowed slightly and backed away, finally turning to go to the kitchen with their order.

"How can he remember all that without writing it down," queried Mrs. Shaw. "I can't even remember what I went into a room to get." She laughed.

Lunch was just too marvelous for words. They took their time and savored each course. Sadie coveted the recipe for that maple salad dressing. But of course it was a secret. *I know that if my Andy tasted it he could duplicate it perfectly,* she thought proudly. They dipped the seared tuna in two special sauces, one creamy and one vinegrette with wasabi for heat. The taste of that strong, green horseradish made Sadie shake her head with the blast of it. The seaweed salad was crunchy and soft at the same time. It almost squeaked in their mouths as they chewed it. The bread was fresh baked right on the premises. Little molded mounds of butter were served at each plate. Sadie could tell that the soup was made from real beef bone stock, boiled down slowly for hours on the back of the stove. The onion soup was beautifully presented from the broiler with golden gruyere cheese melted on top. Sadie was so glad that Peter had ordered the petite portions. There was no joy in stuffing more and more food down to an already full stomach

When the entrees arrived they felt like children having a tea party. The little plates were passed from entrée to entrée so that each person received a portion of each choice. Sadie forced herself to eat slowly and savor every bite. The chicken and dumplings were indeed good, but not even comparable to Sadie's. She felt a quiet pride in knowing that something she made outdid this fine cuisine.

Peter asked them about the park and how it was coming along. "I miss that place so much. I think I realigned my life by working there. I got my priorities straight. Are the Mexican workers doing a good job? Describe to me how it now looks."

The Colonel responded first. "Peter, it is coming along nicely. All the plans for the stonework and benches and ponds and little streams are being done just as you invisioned them. I don't know how these immigrants from Mexico know how to do such fine workmanship with stone, but they are masters at it. You'd be proud."

Peter was happy and sad at the same time. "I'm glad to hear that, but I'm a little jealous that I didn't get to be the one to make it happen. Maybe I'll get to try my hand at that one day soon."

Finally, after all the food and plates were cleared away, Peter ordered coffee for the Colonel, Sadie and himself, and ordered mint tea for Victoria. "To settle your stomach," he explained. "And please bring us two crème brulees and a hot, molten chocolate torte with sliced strawberries macerated in sweet liqueur with whipped cream. We will share all that too."

The meal was a smash hit. They all were groaning with pleasure and fullness when it was done. "Peter, that was marvelous, just marvelous!" said the Colonel. "This will be one our all time favorite memories. It was worth the trip just to get to eat here."

"What was worth the trip for me," admonished Victoria, "was to get to see Peter, here, and root him on. You are mighty special to me Peter Combs."

"I second that," said Sadie. She paused and considered something and then spoke out. "I was just wondering if you would all like to hold hands for just a minute and pray for Peter and the outcome of this judgment." She fully expected

Peter to wince and give a big sigh, but he did not. He grabbed Victoria's hand and her hand and bowed his head.

"Whose going to pray?" asked the Colonel. "Is this a silent thing or does somebody actually speak out?"

"Well, since it was Sadie's idea," offered Peter, "I vote she does the petitioning."

"I second that," said the Colonel. Mrs. Shaw just nodded with her eyes already closed and head bowed.

"Dearest Father in heaven, we have come a far ways to get here and sit here together. Thank you for already being with us to get us safely to this point. God above, we love Peter Combs," Sadie prayed. She could suddenly feel his hand tighten on hers as if in a jolt of surprise. She continued, "We sit here at this table knowing what we'd like to have done in this matter of Peter's trial. We all want him to be set free, Lord, but the prayer that never fails is that your will be done here. That is the best we can pray for. We know what we'd like to have happen. We'd love to see Peter exonerated, forgiven his debt and set free to go on with his life. We feel he deserves this second chance, Lord. We'd love to continue to have Peter in our lives. But it is your will we crave, Father. Be with all of us as the judgment comes down. Be with the judge who renders it. May he think with mercy and compassion. We accept whatever decision you surprise us with, God. We know you are a fair and just God. In our priceless Savior's name we pray, Amen."

Peter continued to hold Sadie's hand for a few seconds after the prayer was finished. His head remained bowed and his lips were pursed tightly shut. He swallowed hard. "Thank you Sadie for that. And thank you all for coming all this way to show your support for me. You have no idea what it has meant to me."

"Where are you staying, Peter?" asked the Colonel.

"Oh I have a very comfy little spot to stay during this short time of trial," said Pete. "Don't you worry about me."

The bill came and Peter took care of it with adept smoothness. It must have taken all he had, but he paid it graciously and with an authoritative air. Sadie knew this was the old Peter that used to shine here in the money world of Chicago. In that moment she got a glimpse of how easy it was for him to fit into this kind of life. He seemed so sure of himself, so in charge. She wasn't sure she could get used to this Peter. She longed for the days when he worked on the park and showed up at her door to receive his plate of dinner to take home. The gentle, humble Pete was more appealing to her than this suave man.

They exited the snug hideaway restaurant amidst bows and handshakes from the staff. "We've all missed seeing you, Mr. Combs. We hope this will become a standard practice of yours once again."

Standing on the street, Peter watched for a taxi and hailed one. The air was cooling down considerably. The nearby Lake Michigan worked like a giant air conditioner. A storm seemed to be brewing and dark clouds were gathering.

"Well, it looks like we need to hunker down for the night," he remarked glibly. "Will I be seeing you all tomorrow at the conclusion to this hearing?"

"Son, it is why we came. To give you support and to hear the judge's ruling. We'll be there with bells on," answered the Colonel.

Mrs. Shaw was clearly exhausted when Sadie left them at their hotel room. "Just ring me up, or knock on my door if you need anything. I'll be there in a jiffy. Try to get some rest, Victoria. You were a real champ today. I'm so glad you wanted to come."

"Honey, I wouldn't have missed this for the world. It might be my last hurrah, but it will be a good one," the old lady smiled.

"Don't talk about last hurrahs to me, woman," chided the Colonel. "We have a lot more where this one came from, waiting in the wings, and don't you doubt it." He hugged her.

Back in her own room, Sadie felt so tired she could barely remove her clothes and step into her nightgown. *Why in the world am I so tired. It is just the end of the afternoon.* Sadie knew that it was the emotional strain of seeing to the Shaw's and watching Peter face such a procedure. Being on the stand and testifying was very taxing. *I am surely a wimp if I can't take any more than this,* she castigated herself. She lay down and watched a little T.V. *Ahh . . .* that bed felt so good. It seemed so strange to her to see television again. She had grown so accustomed to living without it. Tonight she was just mesmerized by it and couldn't pull herself away from it. She flipped through the channels and was shocked at how many more reality shows had been added to the roster. *Good grief,* she thought, *who wants to take their leisure time and watch someone eat worms and throw up? You've got to be kidding.*

Sadie finally turned the television off and grabbed up her latest novel that she was reading. Oh how she loved a good book in which to lose herself at the end of the day. Sadie hardly ever went anywhere without a book at hand. It helped to endure long lines or to sit out a long wait at a doctor's office. But tonight as usual, reading at the end of a long day for more than fifteen minutes was hard. Her eyes involuntarily closed and her mind slipped into semi-consciousness. She finally gave it up and set the book aside and turned off the light. *Blissful rest . . . ahhhhhh.*

Chapter 45

The Outcome

The next morning dawned stormy with high winds. Sadie showered and dressed quickly and checked in with the Shaw's.

"Oh, this weather is terrible," she declared. "Why would it have to be like this on a day when we needed to be at court? I hate to take you out in this stuff," she stated.

"Well dear," said Victoria graciously, "you won't need to. I'm going to stay put here in this fine, comfy room. You all go and hear the good news, which I am counting on, and bring me back a big, juicy hamburger. I'm feeling frivolous today."

That brought a laugh from the Colonel and Sadie smiled wanly. The Colonel said, "I believe I shall sit this one out too, and we shall let Sadie be our representative, courier and fetcher. She can pick us both up a nice hamburger and we will celebrate the hopefully good news when she gets back. How does that sound, Sadie, dear?"

"It sounds smart, that's what it sounds like," admitted Sadie.

She went with them down to the breakfast area. The smells of toast and muffins and fruit and hot coffee made their mouths water. They had a leisurely time eating and talking. Afterwards, Sadie settled them both into their room and kissed them both lightly on their cheeks. "I'll be back as soon as I can. Can we just have a prayer before I go?"

The Colonel stood up and helped Victoria to her feet. They stood in a triangle and held hands. The Colonel started the prayer, "Lord God, we trust your wisdom and judgment and plan for Peter. Of course we are all very concerned and personally want him to be released from his sentence. We all agree on that, and we remember in the Bible how it says that if two or three get together and agree on something, it will happen. Please Lord, let this happen. We want Peter back with us."

Victoria added, "Oh Father, I'm just an old, frail woman and I don't know much about trials and such, but if there is a way for the judge to release Peter under the law, please let that judge find a way to do it and give the judge the heart to do it also."

Sadie prayed, "I agree with what has been requested here, Jesus. We think that Peter is worth receiving a second chance. Help us to accept whatever is decided upon. Sometimes your ways are not our ways and we won't even see how it was a better decision until much later on." Sadie stopped and squeezed their hands. "So we pray these petitions in our Savior's name and we rest in peace knowing that you are in charge and have all of our best interests at heart."

They all hugged each other and then Sadie rushed off to catch the bus downtown. She didn't want to worry about having a car to park. Weaving through early morning Chicago traffic on her own was not something she wanted to do. Now that the Shaw's were remaining behind, she felt free to hop on the buses and work her way to the courthouse. She was amazed at how easy it was. The drivers were helpful and directed her how and where to change buses.

Sadie arrived back at the courthouse about forty five minutes before the case was to be reviewed and decided upon. The assigned courtroom was being used for another case at that time, so she wandered around the vast, high-ceilinged hallways and noted the dark mahogany, carved wood and fancy, marble pillars holding up the building. Courthouses were indeed so regal looking and demanded respect. The place echoed with footsteps and talk. Finally, when the previous case was over and the courtroom was emptied, she entered the room and sat near the front on the left side. She had forgotten her book, but she wanted to just pray and think about things anyway.

She heard the door by the judge's high podium desk open and she glanced up to see the judge who would be deciding on Pete's case walk in. He was headed up the steps to his desk and was looking around agitatedly. She sat very still so as not to disturb his searching. His eyes finally found the pair of glasses that he had left there, and as he turned to go, he noticed Sadie sitting there.

"Well, you are an eager beaver this morning, miss." He remarked.

"Yes sir," Sadie ventured to answer. "The weather was so bad this morning that I had to leave the Shaw's at the hotel room and come alone. I didn't want to take the chance of being late so I took the bus as early as I could in order to get here on time." She smiled a tenuous smile at the judge.

"You all came a long way to cheer this man on, didn't you?"

"We would have come twice as far. He is worth encouraging."

The judge stood still for a second or two and stared at Sadie. Then he roused himself out of his slight reverie and stepped down to the door. He glanced back at Sadie, "Well, it will all be over very soon," he offered and went out the door.

Soon the courtroom began to pull in more people. They were mostly there for the case scheduled to take place after Peter's but had arrived early like

Sadie. Finally the prosecutor arrived, walking down the center aisle. Then Peter entered in from a side door along with his assigned, pro bono lawyer. Peter noticed Sadie at once and rushed over to hug her. He looked a bit raggedy with his hair blown in tufts and the collar of his suit jacket folded inward. She reached up to straighten up his coat and tie. *This is the old Peter we all grew to love,* she admitted in her mind. *He's vulnerable and a little unsure of himself; slightly scared and eager at the same time.* She smiled at him and said, "Don't you worry, Peter. It will all work out the way it is supposed to."

He looked at her with a questioning eye and turned to take his seat. He glanced back at her and nodded with a wan smile. "Where are the Colonel and Mrs. Shaw? Not sick are they?"

"The weather was too blustery for them. They send their love and prayers."

"All rise," the bailiff demanded, "The honorable Judge Winston Herald presiding."

The judge entered quickly and took his seat. The bailiff seated the people and stood aside. Judge Herald pushed some papers around in preparation and then opened a bright red leathery folder. "Ahemmm!" he started. "We are here today to make a decision concerning the former sentence of one Peter Combs. I have taken into consideration how this man ran from his parole obligation. He was required to complete his punishment for his unlawful actions of several years ago when he engaged in insider trading. This is a serious offense and must be approached as such."

Sadie's heart sunk. The prosecuting attorney took a deep breath of satisfaction and sat back in his seat with his arms folded in front of him. Peter bowed his head and shut his eyes. His lips were pinched tight and he was shaking his head slightly back and forth. *Don't give up Peter, don't give up!* Sadie pushed her thoughts toward him.

The judge continued, looking right at Peter. "Mr. Combs, please stand up for this sentencing."

Peter stood immediately and straightened his shoulders and held his head tall.

The Judge continued, "You made a big mistake running from the law. Your offense was a serious one. The law must be satisfied. I know that an example was made of you when this case first came to trial. The court was trying to send a message to all the eager and ambitious stock market wizards in this city. The laws will be obeyed or else." The judge cleared his throat and looked up at the ceiling. "I have pondered on this case a good while now, and I see a man who made a terrible mistake for whatever reason. And I see real shame and remorse in him. He served a good part of his sentence already and when he ran he inadvertently served an even more severe punishment when he chose to live the life of a homeless man. He lost his family, his friends, his money."

Sadie's heart began to hope. *Oh Lord, please!* Peter was looking up with a hesitant, eager contemplation at the judge.

"The extenuating circumstances after his homeless trek, when he became a real asset to the community where he lived, are impressive to me. His work was selfless and determined, as witnessed to the court by that city's mayor and city council. We heard from the man who hired him, a Colonel Everett Shaw. He testified that he had watched Mr. Combs live honorably in a humble setting. The community of Rose Creek has need of him. This is an unusual case. I normally decide straight for the law, straight down the line, but I am led to consider this case differently."

Sadie's hands were so clinched together that her nails were cutting into her flesh. Peter's eyes were wide with wonder. The prosecutor sat forward with his mouth open with incredulity. "I am therefore ruling that Peter Combs be released from his obligation to serve out his two year jail sentence here in Chicago. He may stay here, if he likes and be reinstated with a parole officer to complete his six month obligation, or he may move to Rose Creek and serve out his parole sentencing there reporting to an assigned member of the law enforcement. He may not ever again do any stock trading, but must focus his earning ability in some other way. It will be acceptable to the court if he chooses to be a financial consultant, but trading is not an option. If any of these obligations and agreements is not followed, Mr. Combs will be remanded back to Chicago to serve out his sentence in the prison here with no parole available. It is so ordered. Court adjourned." The judge rapped his heavy gavel on the desk and rose with a stern glance at Peter and a swift and warm look and tentative smile at Sadie. He exited the courtroom swiftly.

Everyone but Sadie was standing as he left the room. Sadie could not find the strength in her legs to stand. Her face was in her hands and her head bowed. The judge had ruled so that both sides were satisfied. The law was appeased and the freedom of Peter was agreed upon. It was a just decision. She said over and over in her mind, *Thank you Jesus, thank you Lord.*

Peter was allowed to come and meet with her a minute before he had to go with his lawyer and take care of the paperwork and arrangements. He stood before her with his arms on her shoulders and his eyes brimming with shining moisture. He just stood and shook his head back and forth. His lips were pursed and he could not speak for fear of his voice breaking.

Sadie stood transfixed with her arms at her sides. She did not try to stop the tears from flowing, but let them fall. The countenance on her face was one of complete awe. She too shook her head back and forth slowly. Then without even thinking about what it must look like, she leaned forward and rested her head on his shoulder. His arms went around her in a comforting hug. She returned the gesture with her arms going behind him and holding him tightly. Nary a word was spoken. They just stood like that slowly rocking back and forth. Finally Peter put his hands back on her shoulders and gently separated them.

"Dear Sadie, I feel like your presence here made all the difference in the outcome of this hearing. I don't know why, but I think that judge was taken with you and respected you quite a bit. Did the two of you ever speak?" he asked.

"Well, as a matter of fact we inadvertently did speak a few words to one another. I had come in here early on the day of our arrival. I had made a trial run here to be sure that the three of us would not be confused when the actual morning of the hearing rolled around and started. I was sitting in here taking in the legal ambiance. I believe that I was praying about the trial, or hearing, or whatever you call it. Right then this hyper old man walked in. He spoke gruffly to me about not hanging around in the courtroom. I had no idea who he was and I spoke up to him defending myself." Sadie smiled to think of the dismayed look on that old Judge's face as she had stood up to him. Then she continued, "Then today I was again sitting here praying and thinking and he came rushing in. This time, he was looking for his glasses on the judge's bench. He was agitated and in a hurry. He seemed very surprised to once again see me sitting there quietly. We spoke a few minutes and then he left."

Sadie stopped and looked at Peter closely. "Why would you think that I had anything to do with his decision to let you go?" she inquired.

"Oh Sadie, you have no idea what a miracle occurred here today. That Judge, Winston Herald, is the toughest and most straight-lined judge there is. When I heard that I had drawn him to hear my case, my heart just sank. I knew that there was no way I would get any leniency from him. Yesterday at lunch, I was so disheartened and I was trying hard to appear suave and confident."

"I noticed that you were not being yourself yesterday. Or at least not the self that I had grown to uh . . . . appreciate," Sadie corrected what her mind almost said. "You seemed so comfortable with the elegant restaurant and the setting and service. It was almost like you were showing us where you came from and what life used to be for you."

"I'm ashamed to say that I was doing that exact thing. I wanted you three to see that I had once been a part of the rich crowd and that the circles I had once run with were made up of the top-notch people." Peter bowed his head and shook it back and forth. "What a phony I am. I'm so sorry I did that to you. I'll bet you were so disappointed in me."

"Not at all. That time in your life was exciting and fast and privileged. I'm sure there was so much of it that you came to love and expect as your entitlement." Sadie stopped and considered her next words carefully. "The Peter we came to be acquainted with down in Rose Creek, was humbled and desperate and needy. He was so quiet and mysterious. I really liked that man. But that doesn't mean that you have to stay in that realm of life. The judge just gave you an incredible gift. You are free now to choose whatever you want to be. I now am very aware that you are indeed clever and smart and can probably make a really good life for yourself here in the big city. You need to take stock of what you want in life, Peter. To be close here to your daughters on the chance that they might want to be close to you again, is a great opportunity. I'm sure you still have many friends here who would seek out your advice on money matters and investments."

Sadie was not used to making such a long speech. She paused now to take a breath. Peter broke in to say his piece. "Sadie, I am confused right now as to what I should do. As you said, I have the opportunity now to try to get my daughters to visit with me and for me to be a part of their lives. It would be slow going to get back in the swing of things here. I have to consider how familiar I am with the city and the people here. But I think about North Carolina and those quiet, safe mountains, and I can't even bear the thought of not living there, or of not seeing you . . . . and the Shaw's," he added quickly.

Sadie grabbed his elbows and straightened her arms standing back from him and looking up at him. "Peter, you need time to think and cogitate on this most important matter. The whole rest of your life depends on what you decide now." She gathered up her purse and coat and took a deep breath. "You must be careful of your choice, Peter. I'm going now to be with the Shaw's. We will be heading out tomorrow morning to go back home." She thought, *Home! Yes indeed, it does feel like home to me. I am looking forward to going back home.* She smiled up at Peter. When you decide, just let us know, will you? We will be praying for you and hoping for the best to happen to you. You are a very good man, Peter. I know the Lord will guide you and help you find the right path to take." She reached up and pecked his cheek with a slight kiss. Then she turned on her heel and headed for the door. Glancing back she said, "Good bye Peter. I'm glad we got to be a part of this adventure. You are surely worth it."

She almost got to the door and was grabbed from behind. She was turned around swiftly and Peter had her in his arms again. He felt so warm and smelled so good. She settled into his embrace and felt safe.

Peter spoke softly to her, "Miss Sadie, I am so very grateful that you made the effort to come here. I know it was a great effort. I am so glad I was privileged to know you. You've helped me so much to get straightened out and to find hope again. When you first offered me work and dropped a dollar in my dirty coffee cup, I resented you so much. But that little gesture was the turning point in my life. Thank you, Sadie. Thank you so much. You mean a great deal to me."

Sadie's heart was dropping. She could hear the finality in his voice: the settling of accounts. This was going to be their final goodbye. Her lips quivered in disappointment, but she gathered her courage together and stood tall and smiled at him. "And you to me, dear Peter. Your life will not be wasted, I'm sure. Just know that I will be praying for you daily. Let us hear from you once in a while so we too can rejoice in your new life."

With that she turned abruptly and left the courtroom. She could hear Peter's lawyer calling to him to hurry so they could conclude the day's paperwork. She stifled a sob trying to break out as she hurried out of the courthouse.

On the way back to the hotel where the Shaw's sat patiently waiting, she spotted a shiny railroad car-like café and pulled the cord so the bus would stop and she could exit. As she was leaving the bus, she asked the bus driver how she could get back on a bus and finish the trip to the hotel. He pointed to a bus stop about fifty yards away and told her to take Bus number 42.

The little diner was just as her mind had pictured it. It was busy and noisy and full of delectable smells. She realized just how hungry she was. Everything looked so tantalizing. She walked to the counter and stood waiting for a person to come take her order. She ordered three fully loaded hamburgers and an order of fries; a big order. As she stood there watching the drama of a small diner unfold before her, she had a definite urge to step behind the counter and get busy. *I could run one of these*, she thought. *I could make it so homey and comfy and welcoming that the place would be full all the time. When I didn't feel like working, I'd just hang a sign up that said, 'Gone fishing!' People would know me and know that I was just in need of some time away. They wouldn't get mad, but would be happy for me. And when I finally opened again in a few days, they would come back issuing their gripes but in a kidding manner.*

Sadie was smiling as she waited. Being in this café was good for her right now. She needed something unique to take her mind off of Peter and his words that conveyed the notion that he planned on staying in Chicago to make a new life for himself. She knew in her heart that it was the answer for him. It was the right thing to do. After all, his girls were here and he had lots of friends and business acquaintances still here. If Martha Stewart could go to jail and come home and make a new life, so could Peter. She tried hard to be happy for him and wondered at herself when those benevolent feelings would not come forth easily.

The Shaw's were so happy to see her come back and they too were hungry. They placed the lunch on the table, but would not dig in until Sadie spilled the news of the hearing.

"Tell us, tell us. What happened? Oh I hope it is good news," cried the Colonel.

"Yes, Sadie. Spill it!" Victoria was so sincere in her command that Sadie nearly laughed.

"Okay. There is really good news and a bit of bad news, or really not so bad if you actually think about it." Sadie turned to pluck some icy drinks out of the little refrigerator. *Heck with the added cost*, she thought.

They all sat down at the little round table to eat. Victoria handed over her pickles and onions to the Colonel who split them with Sadie. The hamburgers were so delicious that Sadie was tempted to just sit and eat and talk later.

But the two of them kept staring insistently at her, and so she told them the whole story.

". . . . and so, as happy as I was that he was released from the hard part of his sentence, I was stunned when I thought of his pending decision on where to spend his parole time. I truly think he would love to come back to be near us and finish up his beloved park. But he honestly would like to make amends with his daughters, and I can't blame him for that, can you?"

They both shook their heads, sadly. The Colonel spoke up, "I guess we were all just expecting he would want to come back to Rose Creek. Why couldn't I see this coming? Of course he has to stay and see if he can work out his relationship with his daughters." The Colonel set his hamburger down and stared out the window.

Victoria, who had also stopped eating, laid a hand on his arm and said, "There, there, dear, everything will work out the way it is suppose to. Let's just be happy for him in the decision of the judge to release him from further obligation. It could have been so much worse, don't you think?"

She was right, of course. The Colonel and Sadie looked at each other across the table and nodded. They both reached out to touch Victoria's arms.

Chapter 46

Homecoming

It was decided that they get up very early and head out. Sadie went out to scope out the area and found a nice little restaurant where they could eat dinner that night. As the Shaw's took a nap and watched T.V., she took advantage of the time in Chicago to do a little more sight seeing. This time the ride to the Sears Tower was easy. She knew what she was doing. She took the elevator all the way to the top. Sadie knew that Rebecca would be waiting to hear the outcome of the hearing, so she called her. She reversed the charges and knew that it would be okay. She could pay Becky later for the call.

Becky accepted the call and quickly asked, "Mom, Mom, are you alright? How did it all turn out? Is he free? Was the judge nice after all? Tell me, Mom!"

"Calm down, dear. Everything is fine, or just about," she added. "I am calling you again from the top of the Sears Tower in Chicago."

"Have you decided you want to make a new life there now, Mom," Becky said teasingly. "If you decide to move there, you'll be running the Sears Tower in no time."

"Not on your life, my girl. The Shaw's and I drove up here to attend the hearing on Peter's case and that is the end of it. We are going back home as quickly tomorrow morning as we can. It's been quite an experience. I won't go into all of it right now. When I see you next, we shall sit with a cup of coffee and I'll regale you with the adventure." Sadie looked around, astounded once again at the sight of that sprawling city from so high up. Lake Michigan was so vast it looked like a sea. The sun had finally come out and was shining brightly on the water. Millions of diamonds were dancing on the water.

"Mom, how did it turn out? Is it over?" Rebecca asked.

"Yes, dear, it is over. The news is wonderful. It is like a miracle really. The judge is a hard man and noted for his rigid judgments, so we had little hope of his releasing Peter. And yet it turned out okay. The judge must have seen something in Peter's broken spirit and revised attitude to render a merciful decision. He released him from further imprisonment and actually excused his running away. But he did reinstate his parole obligation. And believe it or not, he has given him the choice of fulfilling the time in either Chicago or Rose Creek."

While Sadie took a breath, Rebecca jumped in, "Well surely he is coming back to North Carolina. There's no doubt about that, right?"

"There is a great deal of doubt about just that. You remember that his two estranged daughters have grown up here without his input or support for the last three years, and he feels so guilty about that. I'm sure he will want to do all he can to make things right with them. At least he has to try, don't you think?" Sadie asked tentatively.

The line was silent for a while and Sadie thought maybe they had been disconnected. "Becky, are you still there?" She asked.

"Yes, Mom, I'm here. I just feel sort of let down for some reason. I hate to think of Peter up there where he is not wanted, trying to make amends. Do you think that will really work?"

"If it were me, I would try my hardest to make it work, Becky. And so would you, I venture to say. Peter Combs lost himself in grief and disappointment back those few years ago. He made some big mistakes. But now his mind is set right again. I know he must love his girls and desire a relationship with them. I'm sure he will try all he can to get back in their good graces at least partially." Sadie stopped and blew her nose. *The air is a little chilly up here.* "We shall just have to pray that he is successful and that his life can take a good turn again."

"But Mom, you are going to miss him so much, aren't you?"

"No doubt dear, no doubt. But right is right. I would not try to dissuade him, and neither would you. I'd better get going. We are heading back in the morning. I'll call again when I get home and let you know we made it safely. The Shaw's are such troopers. You should see Victoria. I think she is enjoying all this, although she is getting mighty tired. I need to get her back in her own safe abode."

"Bye, Mom. Thanks for calling. We all three send our love to you. We can't wait to see you next."

Their trip home was uneventful. Victoria rested on the bed in the back seat almost the whole way home. It took two days to make it back since they didn't want Victoria to get too cramped and tired.

That little cottage looked like a palace to Sadie. She sat on the floor and held the purring Wheezer in her lap. The cat kept rubbing his head back and forth on her. He was once again staking his claim. He was saying, "This lady belongs to me."

Sadie hugged Cherie and Joy and looked around. The place was pristinely clean and neat. Cherie, knowing Sadie's love of flowers, had put several little vases full of wild flowers all around the house.

"It has been such a joy staying in your home, Sadie. It sort of seems like your spirit is still here even when you are gone. I love it here." Cherie looked around fondly. "We'd best be getting back to our own little apartment. Joy is tired. We walked the park today and she wanted to run and run. Come on sweet girl, let's get in the stroller and get out of Miss Sadie's hair." Cherie turned to Sadie and said, "We will get caught up on the whole story tomorrow. I'll drop by after work and we can talk about it, okay?"

"Sounds good to me," said Sadie rising up and giving her a hug. "Plan on coming for dinner. And Cherie, thanks so much for watching my cat and taking such good care of my little home. I love you for that, you know." Sadie reached down to lift up Joy and hug her too. "I'll tell you this much. Peter is free now. He just has to report to the parole officer for another six months. I'll tell you the rest of the story tomorrow. You are right, I am exhausted."

After Cherie had left, Sadie plopped down on the couch and the cat joined her. She began to cry. *What am I doing?* She thought. *I must be way more tired than I realize. This is silly. I should be so happy for Peter and for me to be safely home again.* She cried a little more and reached for a tissue and wiped her eyes and nose. *Enough of that!* She demanded of herself. *Get up and get going, girl.* But her body would not obey. So she cried some more and stretched out on the couch and fell fast asleep.

She woke to a knocking on the door. It was a soft knock as though whoever was there didn't really want to disturb her. Sadie rose up slowly and patted Wheezer. "I'm coming. Just a minute."

It was the Colonel and he was checking up on her and wondering about supper. "If you are too tired I shall just warm up a can of chicken noodle soup." He offered.

"What time is it anyway," said Sadie checking her watch. "Oh dear, I have slept five hours. How can that be?" She felt so disoriented like she was going through jet lag.

They had arrived home about 1:00 on the second day of travel. Sadie had helped them inside and gotten Victoria squared away in her room for a good long nap. The Colonel assured her that he was going to join his wife and that eating was the last thing on their minds. Now it was 7:00 at night. She was in a dither.

"You don't worry about a thing. It will be good for me to get up and get going. I won't be able to sleep tonight if I don't get up and do something," Sadie insisted. The Colonel nodded and headed out the door. Sadie went to splash water on her face and to comb her hair. She decided to change clothes and get out of those crumpled travel clothes.

She fixed them a simple fare of bacon, lettuce and tomato sandwiches on toast. They had only been gone for 5 days and yet it felt like months to Sadie. She made them the chicken noodle soup too and all three of them sat quietly at the kitchen table. There didn't seem much to say after being together 24/7 for so many days.

The phone rang. They all three jumped in their seats. "I'll get it Sadie, you just sit there," said the Colonel. "Hello? Yes we are finally back. Yes it was a good trip. Sadie is a great driver and we had good weather most of the time." The Colonel waited and listened a while and then said, "Well, yes, I think it was a good thing we went. Somehow I think our presence and support for Peter was good for the judge to see. The mayor and her entourage were there the first day to vouch for him too. The judge was truly amazed." Again the Colonel waited for his chance to speak. "Well, he did have a good verdict from the hearing. He is free of any more jail time and only has to finish up his parole time. We think he is going to do that in Chicago. But he can come here if he chooses." The Colonel rolled his eyes and gave out a big sigh. "Okay then, we'll talk more about this tomorrow. Thanks for calling Stephen. It was good of you." He hung up the phone.

"That was Stephen in case you didn't catch that," he offered. "He said someone called him to say they saw the big black Lincoln coming through town."

"Well that was good of him to call and find out what had happened," offered Sadie sincerely. "Was he happy to hear the outcome of the hearing?"

"I really could not tell how he felt about it. He just sort of grunted and said, 'Oh . . . that must have made you all very happy.' I should have called him as soon as we arrived. I promised him I would. I was just too tired to do anything but take that nap."

Life got back to normal after that. The routine of breakfast, lunch and dinner started up again. Gladys Fortenbrau came again to dust and mop and vacuum the place. She was surly as ever, but it didn't bother Sadie. She truly felt God's love filling her heart for the housekeeper. She always treated Gladys kindly and with real joy upon seeing her arrive. "Oh Gladys, it's so good to see you. How have you been? I know we were only gone five days, but it seemed like a long time to me."

"Seemed like a coon's age to me, too," complained the housekeeper. "I read in the paper that Combs' hearing got a good ruling from the judge up there."

"Yes, indeed it did," replied Sadie. "We were very happy for Peter. He's a good man and now he has a chance to make a new life."

"Well, if you ask me, I think he should come back here and finish up his job." Gladys huffed and walked off to grab the dust cloths.

My sentiments exactly, smiled Sadie. She knew that Peter was doing the right thing and she truthfully was proud of him, but missed him so much.

The divorce papers finally came through. Sadie signed the papers before the bank's notary public and they were sent post haste by registered mail back to Anthony's lawyers. It was a mixed bag of feelings when she signed those papers. Thirty-two years of marriage up in smoke. How sad and yet how relieved she felt at the same time. That night she celebrated quietly in front of the fire with a fresh warm crème brulee and a cup of Irish Cream coffee. She smiled and cried at the same time.

She was glad that her capable lawyer had requested a healthy settlement. She was satisfied with the goodly amount she had received to have as a backup for the rest of her life. She had no real earnings for Soc Security benefits and no pension, so what she had received was indeed welcome. She would have to be careful from now on with her earnings. She was, after all, getting up there in age, and life could take a turn for the worse soon enough. She shook herself and said out loud, "Sadie Jamison, stop that right now! Why are you worried? You are a child of the King. You will be fine."

With that she settled down and finished off her dessert. "Yum!" she offered up her estimation of the evening.

Sadie toured the park grounds. She couldn't even imagine the wall that used to surround this place. The acreage looked so open and inviting now. People were walking along the sidewalk and looking over at the big white house. Some ventured hesitantly onto the paths and slowly walked along the way through the gardens. She saw a couple sitting on one of the wooden benches having coffee and muffins. *As time goes by, more people will get over the strangeness of being able to come into these sacred grounds. They will make themselves at home here,* Sadie pondered with a satisfied smile on her face.

It was Sadie's job to oversee the workmen and keep the plans going that Peter had laid out as much as she could. Sadie remained amazed at the Mexican workers. They were artists with stone and grout; everyday something new was formed up by their talented hands. And each new piece was like a work of art. There labor was noisy, but oh, the results were wonderful. At lunch time they would get out their Spanish guitars and play and sing the harmonic songs from their own country. She knew that many of them were separated from family so they could earn a good living and send the money back for their loved ones' survival.

The landscape architect, who had been hired by the city to follow Peter's plans, had come and consulted with the city council as to what plan of action was best for the streams and fountains in the park. The workers were digging the stream beds and lining them with plastic and rock.

Sometimes a news crew would come through, taking videos and pictures to keep up on what was happening here. Sadie figured that when it was all completed, they would have quite a documentary to show on T.V. The story would show the transformation of an historic, private, wildly wooded area into a public park to be enjoyed by all. It made Sadie feel good about herself to know she had a hand in this venture.

The Colonel came to Sadie's door one night to tell her that they had received a call from Peter. She perked up noticeably and invited Colonel Shaw inside. When he was seated he began. "Peter is wondering how things are going here. He is trying to get a good job up there in financing as a consultant. He says that his effort with his daughters is a slow process and he is still trying to gain their trust and become part of their lives." The Colonel stopped and looked around. "You know, I love this little place. You've really made a decent home out of it. I don't suppose you'd ever consider moving into the big house with us, would you?"

Sadie smiled warmly at him. "Thank you, but no. I actually love this little cottage more than any place I've ever lived. I am so very content here. I feel safe and happy."

"It's kind of lonely here isn't it?" he queried.

"Not at all. I've always been a person who is not afraid of being alone. I actually crave it. I guess you could say I like my own company," Sadie explained.

"Maybe you should get a phone. Peter really wanted to talk to you, you know."

"There again, I have no desire for a phone. The ringing of a phone was always so disturbing and intrusive to me. If I need to call someone, I can use the phone in the mansion or a pay phone. I'm doing fine like this," replied Sadie. "I would have enjoyed hearing Pete's voice though, I have to admit that," she sighed.

He stood to leave. "It is sort of late for us old people, so I'd better get back to my sweetheart."

"How is Victoria doing tonight? She didn't seem that perky today. I hope she is not coming down with anything," said Sadie. Just the thought of Victoria failing in health was depressing to Sadie. She loved that gentle, old lady so much.

"Oh, I think she is still sort of recuperating from that trip to Chicago. She is so glad she went, don't get me wrong. All she talks about is the excitement of that adventure." He continued, "But I think it took a lot out of her and will take a while to get her strength back and into the swing of things. Not to worry." He began to amble back to the front door.

"That reminds me of something I have been meaning to talk to you about," said Sadie.

"Shoot! Let's hear it, girl," replied the Colonel with a smile.

"A buzzer."

"A what?"

"We need a buzzer from your house to mine. Just in case anything ever happens and you are unable to come all the way out here to get me and contact me. You could ring the buzzer as an alarm and I would hear it and come running." Sadie looked at the Colonel for approval of her idea.

"Hmmm," pondered the old man. "You know, I think that is a fine idea. I'll look into it tomorrow. That might just be the ticket to keep us from worrying so much. Good idea Sadie," he said. "What in the world did we ever do without you? I'm so glad you came to us."

"I'm so glad you found me on the park bench that day. Where would I be right now if you hadn't come there and sat down beside me and spoken to me?" Sadie shook her head in wonder.

"Must have been the plan of God; that's all I can say," responded the Colonel.

"I totally agree with you," answered Sadie. She walked him outside and patted him on the back. "You and Victoria have a nice evening. Come anytime you want to visit. My house is your house." She thought a minute and added, "I mean that literally."

They both laughed.

Sadie watched the Colonel until he was safely inside with the door shut. She went back into her little warm, glowing refuge and began to ponder the call that Peter had made. *So he is trying hard to settle in there. He is doing the best he can to obtain forgiveness from his two daughters and is trying desperately to establish a rapport with them. Good for him,* thought Sadie . . . . *honorable and noble,* she tried to convince herself. *But oh, I miss him so much.* She stomped her foot a little and shook her head. *Get over it Sadie. Water under the bridge. Move on girl.* Living alone like she did, Sadie found herself talking to herself inside her head. She would reproach herself and advise herself. *I'm my own best counselor,* she decided.

Sadie was still singing in church and playing the piano. A few weeks after she arrived home from Chicago, she sang at the First Baptist church and the people were moved by her song. She sang, 'Safe Thus Far'. The choir backed her up and were even swaying as she sang. Mike Speck's songs could really touch people. Some people were crying and others just smiling really big. But it was obvious that there were still some in the church that did not approve of her taking part in the services. Sadie had to accept the fact that some people in the church were still resentful that she was there. Pastor Harper had talked with her about the coldness of some of the women in the church.

"Now Sadie," he had said, "you can't expect everyone to accept you and love you like all the rest of us do. Don't worry about it. Some of those ladies still hold your ex-husband in high regard. Just the thought of having you in their midst is troubling. They think, 'How can a preacher's wife leave such a holy and devoted man?' and 'Why is she in our church. I wish she'd go somewhere else.'" The pastor laughed a little and smiled at Sadie.

But she was not smiling. "I hate that I've upset the balance and harmony here, Craig. You know I can find another place to worship if it will be better for the whole congregation."

"Don't ever let me hear you say that again," ordered Pastor Harper. "You have been such a blessing to the church with your piano playing and the singing. The choir has grown by leaps and bounds and I love the gospel type music you've introduced to us. We love the Brooklyn Tabernacle music and Christ Church songs. It has been a wonderful addition to our services and the Spirit rises up. You are indeed welcome here Miss Sadie."

"When you call me that, I feel like an old nanny from the south during the Civil War days," she laughed. "But I like it nevertheless."

Sadie also headed up a young singles class on Sunday morning. Her group had grown to about 30 people. They came for her teaching and to talk to her privately afterwards to get her counsel.

The young people wanted to have a get-together at her cottage and so one Sunday she announced that they would be having a BBQ on the grounds of the mansion. She had okayed it with the Shaw's first. The class was so excited and plans were made quickly. The following Saturday they all showed up with friends to boot. Sadie had provided the meat and they had brought all the dishes to go with it. Some brought macaroni and cheese and some brought potato salad, and green salad and deviled eggs, baked beans, buns, cold drinks and iced tea. There was a variety of chips and dips and desserts. A couple of the young men had hauled over three big tables from the church on which to set the food and plates and cups. Everyone brought their own folding chairs.

Sadie made sure that Cherie was invited. She was attending another church, but Sadie wanted her to meet and be with some of these great young people. Cherie had let herself be so wrapped up in raising Joy; and although that was great for her, it was also hampering her social skills. So Cherie was invited to help with the party. She showed up that night delightfully beautiful. She wore a pale yellow cotton dress with full skirt that swirled around when she moved. The bodice was scooped but not low cut. The sleeves were short and loose like a ruffle. She had on white sandals and her toes were painted bright red. *Wow, she looks gorgeous,* thought Sadie. *I'll have to keep an eye out for her.* Little Joy was there too, running around and being picked up by people

They put a huge aluminum tub filled with ice on one table. The drinks were buried in there to get cold. Sadie had brined the meat for 2 days in vinegar and salt and pepper water with spices thrown in for good measure. There were ribs and Boston Butts and quartered chickens. She kept all the meat sitting in the brine in big five gallon buckets. She placed the buckets in the old frig on the back porch and it worked perfectly. She had turned them once a day and just covered them with a cloth. The meat turned out flavorful all the way through and so very, very tender. She slow smoked it on a big smoker that one of the young men had hauled over. Slow cooking from morning till evening made for the most tender, falling-off-the-bone meat. It was succulent. Sadie had used her chef son's famous Andy's Butt Rub on the meat to add that perfect flavoring. It was a little spicy and yet so very flavorful. Everyone loved it.

Some of the people brought guitars and after the eating was done, they sat around on the mansion's wide front veranda and sang and played. Victoria and the Colonel came out and sat on the porch listening. It was a perfect evening. Sadie fixed plates of food for the Shaw's. Victoria insisted that if anyone wanted to use the bathroom to go right in the front door and welcome. Sadie's one little bathroom was certainly not enough. The Pastor and his wife showed up too and the fellowship was sweet.

A young man by the name of Todd Morris was there. He looked a bit out of place and shy. He had on a clean, old cotton shirt and sun-bleached levis and cowboy boots. His hair was messed up some from his baseball cap which he held in his hands respectfully. Sadie liked him right away. He made himself useful carrying things back into the house after the meal was done. Sadie noticed that he and Cherie were laughing together and that he was picking up Joy and carrying her around.

"Well, well, what have we here," said Sadie under her breath.

About that time they heard thunder and within minutes the sky opened up like a giant shower. The young people were screaming and laughing and running for the cover of the veranda.

"Somebody grab the ice cream makers and the dessert," a smart young man shouted.

The Colonel came to Sadie and said very solemnly. "Now listen to me Sadie. I know you won't want to do this cause you will feel like you are imposing on our generosity. But by golly, we welcome a little noise and excitement once in a while. Bring this group of young people inside and let them go up to the big family room at the top of the stairs. They can continue their songfest and talking and you can serve their ice cream up there." The Colonel looked formidable as he stood tall and erect. "Now, I don't want to hear a word from you, Sadie. Just do it!" With that he stomped off and helped Victoria to her feet and inside they went. They left the front door open.

Sadie was stunned at such an invitation. Finally she clapped her hands to get the attention of everyone and said, "Listen up everyone. The Colonel and Mrs. Shaw are enjoying your company so much tonight that they have invited you inside to continue the party. Everyone go up the stairs and settle yourselves in the room at the top of the stairs. There is plenty of room for all. Scott you and Paul and some of the other guys carry more chairs up there from the parlor. I'll show you where they are." With that she pushed on into the house and everyone, in awe, followed her.

They had the grandest time eating ice cream and cake and coffee. They talked and sang and Sadie played the piano for them to sing even more songs. Afterwards several stayed to clean up and replace the chairs downstairs. When they left everything was in order.

Sadie was about to head out the door and lock it when the phone rang. She knew that Colonel Shaw and Victoria were probably sound asleep by now, so she quickly picked up the receiver and said, "Hello?"

"What the heck is going on there, lady?"

She recognized the belligerent voice of Stephen Shaw. At least he'd changed 'woman' to 'lady'. She took a deep breath and said slowly. "How did you find out? Have you got a spy in the neighborhood now?"

"Don't be flippant with me, woman."

Ahhh, there it was again. Sadie smiled to herself. *He hasn't changed that much, has he?*

"I've been very nice for the past months and I didn't even show how upset I was when you gallivanted to Chicago with my folks a while back. But this is just going too far. A noisy, raucous party right in my folks' home? You've got to be kidding."

"No, I'm not kidding. We had a BBQ here and we had a ball. My young single adult Sunday School Class came over for a party. Your parents were right in the thick of it by their own choice, and it was they who insisted we go inside during the thunderstorm to continue the party. I was ready to talk them out of it, but your father is so dear and generous, he adamantly told me to hold my tongue. He is my boss you know. So I had to obey him."

"Well, I wish I were your boss, I'll tell you that. There would be no more shinanigans going on if I were in charge."

"And no more fun, as well, I imagine." Sadie was curt and getting angrier every moment. "And by the way, I'm very glad you are not in charge. You got that part right!"

"You are so cheeky, Sadie. The house is probably a wreck. The person that called me said there was so much singing and laughter coming from inside the house that the neighborhood was bothered. This has got to stop . . . . and right now." He huffed and puffed on the phone and suddenly Sadie saw the humor in it.

She laughed and nearly snorted, "Well, one thing is for sure. You would never be my boss Stephen!" Sadie began. She giggled some and it seemed to inflame him even further. "You know Stephen, I feel sorry for you."

"What? What? How dare you feel sorry for me. I have everything and need nothing."

"Oh you need a lot, I dare say. First of all, you have forgotten how to have fun. I have never seen you demonstrate the joy of letting go and just letting life happen. It must be a terrible burden to always have to be in charge. Were you ever a normal child who just played in the mud and ran and ran for no other reason but to run freely? Wake up Stephen. Life is passing you by. Get on board and enjoy some of it before it is too late." She could hear him spitting on the phone in a high-pressured rage. She had to stop.

Sadie said, "Good bye, I'm tired and need to go to bed. I'll talk to you tomorrow if you want to come by and check out the house, and talk to your folks about this alleged fiasco. Sleep tight and don't let the bed bugs bite. Oh sorry, I forgot. I'm sure you have never had bed bugs to worry about."

She hung up then slowly and gently so he would realize that she was not hanging up on him. *I don't know how much more of Stephen I can take,* she pondered. *He is the most unhappy soul. I wonder if there is any hope for him or if he will always be lonely and end up a bitter man.*

Chapter 47

Summer's Vengeance

Summer came with a vengeance. Sadie woke one morning and the air was oppressive. She felt like she could not get enough oxygen in her lungs. The humidity was rising fast. It felt like steam was radiating from the ground. *Oh dear*, thought Sadie, *here we go; my most 'unfavorite' time of the year.*

As much as Sadie disliked the heat of summer, Cherie and Joy were delighted with it. When they came over later that day, Cherie was beaming. "Oh, Sadie, it is finally here. I love summer: picnics and flowers and warm air, finally, and swimming. I love going barefooted and wearing filmy, light dresses."

"Hurrrumph!" remarked Sadie, dramatically. "I wish that summer would go by in about one week and we would move forward into fall. I'll miss sitting by my fireplace, and I have no air conditioner at my cottage. I don't know how I'm going to stand it," she was ashamed of herself for complaining. "I may have to just install one to make it through the season."

"I'll change your mind, you old lady," teased Cherie. "Come with us to the river. I know of a place where you can lie on the grassy slope and dive off a rock into crystal clear green water. It is so cool you will shiver till you get used to it. Then this summer sun will feel so welcome. Can you go?"

"Old lady is it? I'll show you. I do love to swim and in cold water too. What will Joy do as we swim? Isn't the water just too cold for her?"

"Oh, I'll hold her and dip in her tiny feet and splash her some to get her cool. I have a little light portable playpen and I'll put a big umbrella over it. She will love watching us," said Cherie hopefully.

"That's gonna be a lot of stuff to carry to the river. Is it a long hike?" asked Sadie. "You mentioned a picnic and that will take some carrying too and towels and a blanket to sit on."

"I never pegged you for a worry wart, Sadie," laughed Cherie. "We'll get it all down there."

"Now I'm not only an old lady, I'm a worry wart too? And what's up with 'down there'? Is this going to be a long climb back up after we swim. I hate hills."

Cherie laughed and said, "Yes, it does go down some from the road a bit, but we'll take it easy coming back up." Cherie looked up at Sadie cautiously and said more quietly, "Todd can carry most of the stuff,"

"Well, well, well," smirked Sadie. "Todd, is it? When did this happen? I saw the two of you getting cozy during the BBQ we had, but I didn't know it had progressed from there? What's up with that?" Sadie picked up Joy and swung her around till she giggled.

"Oh Sadie, he is so nice. And he loves being with us too. Joy loves him to come and see us. He started out coming to the café every day and we would talk when I got the chance. Then once or twice a week he began showing up right as I got off work and he walked me over to pick up Joy from the baby sitter and then on to our little apartment." Cherie had a dreamy quality to her eyes. "It is so wonderful to have a man as a friend, Sadie. He's so helpful and we just talk and talk."

"And is that all he wants, Cherie; just talk and friendship?" Sadie asked hesitantly.

Cherie pursed her lips and looked up at Sadie gratefully. "Thank you Sadie, for caring that much to ask that. Yes, right now, it seems to be all he wants. We are holding hands now after the baby goes to sleep and is tucked in. We sit on the back stoop and look at the sky and talk and hold hands." She sighed and looked dreamily up at the sky. "He hasn't even tried to kiss me as yet. But oh, when he touches my hand it just fills me with thrills."

"He sounds refreshingly shy, and I like that," said Sadie. "To find a man who is a little unsure of himself is a blessing in this case. It gives you both time to get acquainted before anything further takes place. You both will figure it out, and when you do, it will be more precious than if he had dived right in there with kisses and such." Sadie hugged Cherie with Joy right in between them. Joy squealed in protest. "I'm so glad for you, Cherie. I like Todd very much. I think he will make you a very nice boyfriend."

"And . . . I promise to take it slow and easy. I already had my heart broken once and I aim to protect it this time."

Sadie looked at her seriously, "Just remember that you and Joy are a treasure and it will take a very special man to be worthy of you both. Think highly of yourself in this regard, and don't be so eager and grateful for attention that you succumb to the temptation to cling to him and possess him. Let the Lord lead you, dear girl. I love you so much and want only the best possible future for you."

"Gosh, Sadie, I didn't say I was going to marry him, did I?" Cherie laughed and pulled away. "One slow step at a time, okay?"

Sadie looked at her and smiled. "You are not a half-way girl, Cherie. You don't play around with people's minds and emotions. I'm just saying to be careful with your own. Guard your heart child."

"I will, I promise. And thanks for caring so much." Cherie took Joy and turned to go. "How about Saturday around 10:00? Can we take your pickup to the river?"

"I don't see why not. I'll make the picnic and bring the blanket." Sadie offered. "Oh dear, whatever am I going to do for a bathing suit? I must go find one. Aaarrrgh! How I hate to shop for a bathing suit. I will have to look in a mirror."

"Don't be a silly goose, Sadie. You are beautiful and you will look great in a bathing suit." Cherie turned to go.

Oh that sweet child has no idea what she is talking about, thought Sadie. *Fifty three years old! A little pudgy from all the good food I cook and imbibe. I'm not exactly somebody that anyone would like to see in a bathing suit. But it will be just us and on a private beach, so I should be okay. I sure do love to swim.* "I'll just wear knee high pants and a big t-shirt," she decided.

That week, Sadie had to go shopping for a bathing suit. She drove all the way into Asheville to shop in the big mall there. She was a wreck by the time she had tried on 10 different suits. *Oh, I just have to stop eating so much,* she complained to herself. *This is getting ridiculous. I used to be a thin rail. Now look at me. Bulges everywhere. Yikes!*

She finally decided on a black one with a built in girdle and yellow trim. It looked fairly well on her. She also bought a gauzy white jacket that was cool and covered up her suit when she was walking. *I'll just wear this over the suit and cast it off at the last minute when I walk in the water,* she decided.

While she was in town, she bought sandals and a couple of cottony summer dresses with scoop necks. The colors were soft and pastel and she felt young in them. *I still have to cut back on my eating. I don't smoke or drink, but I do love to eat. Overeating is just as terrible a sin, and just as dangerous as smoking and drinking,* she tried to convince herself; maybe shame would be a good motivator of discipline. She decided that she would get a hold of her cravings and slim up a bit. *Fat chance!* She admitted.

Sadie woke early on Saturday morning and went into the big kitchen to prepare a feast of a picnic. She made little salmon roll-up sandwiches and wrapped them individually in plastic wrap. A little cooler for easy carrying was set up with ice packs in the bottom. Those rollups went into a heavy duty freezer bag and right onto the cold packs. Then came chicken salad made with crisp celery and mayonnaise and halved red grapes. She added a few toasted pecans just for good measure. Then she washed and patted dry the Rainer cherries all golden and sweet. In another carry on bag she brought Kettle baked potato chips and a loaf of fresh cut bread. The onion dip went into the little cooler. She took some candy bars and settled them in a heavy plastic bag also onto the cooled food. Some cookies and a few slices of sweet watermelon rounded out the feast. Cokes and bottles of water were put in another hand held cooler. She grabbed one of the old quilts from her stack at the cottage and she was ready.

Of a sudden she began to worry about how they were all four going to ride in her pickup. But no sooner had she begun to contemplate this problem, when up drove a lovely silver gold Ranger pickup with double cab seating. Her first thought was, *oh no, company. There goes our picnic and swim.* But lo and behold, it was Todd Morris and he had already picked up little Joy and Cherie. Joy was snug and safe in a car seat in the back seat. There had been some planning going on here.

"I thought it would be good to have a little more room," he offered. "My uncle has this truck and offered to let me use it. My vehicle is a regular three-seated pickup like yours and I was glad we didn't have to bring both of them to the river."

"Me too," chimed in Cherie. "Half the fun will be riding there and back together and talking." She smiled so warmly at Todd that he got shy and had to turn away a bit.

Everything was loaded in the nice roomy truck and Sadie insisted on sitting in the back with Joy. The AC in the van was so invitingly cool. Sadie sat back and relaxed for once, trusting her safety to the driver in the front seat. It felt so good to just look outside at the scenery going by and she closed her eyes a while to just surrender into the freedom she felt. Joy wanted to hold hands. She was trying to talk some and Sadie tried hard to understand a word here and there.

"Aydy," she spouted. She pointed at Sadie and said again, "Aydy."

"Don't you recognize your own name, Sadie?" laughed Cherie.

The drive was beautiful and the foliage lushly green. They finally came to a little turn off country lane and off they bumped and jiggled down the one lane, dirt road. There were ruts in the road and Todd tried hard to miss them. Joy was laughing and throwing up her hands every time they jolted over a rut. After a couple of miles they slowed again and turned onto an even narrower dirt path. The golden truck had its sides brushed and scratched by the imposing bushes on the side.

"Oh dear, I hope your uncle will forgive the scratches we are putting on his nice car," worried Sadie.

"Not to worry, I'll buff them out when I get back. This vehicle was made just for this purpose, to go where no one else dares to go."

Just as he said that they came to a clearing and Sadie could see the water shining and sparkling in the distance. Todd turned to park the car and to her amazement, Sadie noticed at least seven cars and trucks parked in the same clearing.

"Where no one dares to go, you say?" laughed Sadie. "This is a veritable crowd of people." *There goes the privacy I was counting on,* thought Sadie.

It was a hot and dusty walk to the water's edge. But it was not a long one and only barely down hill. "Where is the big hill we were suppose to go down," asked Sadie of Cherie.

"Oh, this is not the place that I told you about. We'll go there another time. This spot is easier to get to, and the river's edge here has been covered with white sand for the children. Todd knew about it and thought it would be better all around." Cherie explained.

There were little groups of people setting up for the day. Todd quickly spotted a tree with shade under it and set up the playpen under there. He laid out the quilt nearby partly in the shade and partly in the sun. *He thinks of everything, that man does,* pondered Sadie. *I like his style!*

Todd went back for the rest of the food and bags. Sadie in all her excitement had forgotten to carry a thing except her own bag and towel. Just like a queen she had marched down that path and made herself at home. She dug into her bag to find the white netted cover up. Then she stripped off her shirt. Underneath was the new black and yellow bathing suit. She looked around quickly and saw that no one was paying the slightest attention to her and so she hurriedly slipped off her jeans and put on the cover up. "I'm going to see how the water feels," she told Cherie.

"Go right ahead. I have to feed Joy first and then I'll join you. Have fun today, okay?" Cherie smiled at her warmly.

I thought I was that child's mentor and now she is acting like she is mine. Well maybe I need one once in a while. Stepping out of her tennis shoes, Sadie hurried across the hot sand and cooled her feet in the water that was lapping over a flat rock. *Oh pure bliss,* she thought. *This is going to be heaven for me.* The water was very cold at first touch, but there were children and adults playing and swimming in it, so Sadie knew it was not dangerously cold. So she rapidly peeled off her white cover up and threw it on a bush and dove in. Her body drew into itself in one quick shock. "Yikes!" she said out loud and everyone looked at her and laughed. "This water is freezing."

"Feels good doesn't it," offered a chubby lady nearby.

"Indeed it does. Indeed it does," repeated Sadie.

It took only a few moments for Sadie's body to adjust to the coolness. Soon she was swimming across the river and feeling the gentle current pulling her down stream. She swam against the current and pulled herself up on a rock to enjoy the sunshine. How long had it been since she had last swum? She could not even remember when that might have been. Probably in that sickeningly warm pool water with her grandson, Treat, that time they shared a motel room on one of the vacations they had taken together. Sadie hated swimming in what felt like bath water. Yuk!! She watched the frolicking children dunking one another and having races. Oh, the joy of it. She was so very glad that she had come.

When Cherie was finished feeding Joy she carried her to the water's edge and stood knee deep in the water. She lowered little Joy so that her tippy toes were in the water and Joy drew up her legs quickly and gasped. They all laughed. Cherie set her baby's feet on the white sand and Joy grimaced at the feel of sand between her toes. "She'll get used to it pretty soon and then she'll love it," Cherie said. And she was right. Just a little while later, Joy was stepping gingerly on the shore and running toward the water to dare the coolness to kiss her toes. Cherie splashed her a little and her squeals filled the canyon.

Todd was a good swimmer. He cut through the water like a fish and dove off the high rocks. *He must know these waters pretty well, and he must know what lies underneath or he wouldn't be diving like that,* Sadie thought.

Sadie held Joy in front of her on a nice flat rock while Todd and Cherie went off swimming together. *My, but that Cherie is a knockout in a swimming suit. I hope Todd can behave himself and keep that shy streak going,* she wished. The sunshine felt so good on her cold skin and she closed her eyes and let it soak in. Joy was resting in her lap and Sadie could see that her eyes were drooping. Soon that baby was asleep. How peaceful it was. Even the other swimmers and families were no bother at all.

Soon Cherie and Todd were coming back toward shore. She saw them come together dog paddling with their legs. Todd reached over to wipe a strand of hair out of her eyes and he gently placed a kiss on her forehead. Cherie smiled warmly at him and then splashed him playfully in the face. Then it was a cat and mouse chase.

Some little fishes had ventured up around Sadie's legs and were nibbling on her ankles. She giggled and Joy woke up. The little tyke was enamored of those fish. She reached out to touch them as they scurried away. Her tinkling laugh filled Sadie with joy. *I hope that Becky has some more grandchildren for me to enjoy. And, please Lord can you nudge my two boys to have the desire to settle down. I hope they can eventually find good wives and have some children also. What a joy the little ones are,* she thought to herself.

The picnic lunch was so good. Todd was beside himself eating it with relish.

"I told you she'd make a tasty feast," bragged Cherie.

"Yeah, but I didn't expect this. Man, this is good. I'm afraid I'm stuffing myself. Have you ladies had enough? I don't want to make a pig of myself," he queried.

"Eat all the rest if you like, I'm sure done with it," assured Sadie.

"Me too. Go right ahead and finish it off. We won't have so much to carry back home." Cherie seemed so pleased at his enjoyment of the lunch. After that, they cleared everything off of the quilt and they laid Joy in her playpen to take a nice nap. She lay on her tummy with her little open mouth drooling and her hands and legs splayed out in surrender. Sadie offered to watch her and rest some herself. The shade had moved so that the whole quilt was covered now. A gentle breeze was blowing. Sadie recognized the familiar scents of the water and weedy growth nearby. The smells of hot dogs roasting on fire rings was just so tantalizing. Even though she was no longer hungry, her salivary glands were appreciating the smells. Sadie piled up the towels to make a pillow and lay back to stare at the blue sky. She didn't realize it happened, but she was soon asleep. What peace she felt.

The trip home was quiet and peaceful. No one felt the need to speak. Happiness exuded from all of them. They dropped Sadie off at her cottage and Todd unloaded the coolers and the quilt. Hugs all around and they were gone. Sadie whispered a prayer out loud for Cherie. "Please, dear Father, guard and guide my dear Cherie to the path you want her to take. It seems so perfect and clear to me right now, but I've been wrong before. Open doors and close them in obvious ways, please. Protect the fragile heart of Cherie and may she and Joy always have this special closeness, no matter what happens."

The next day dawned bright and warm. Summer was well on its way. Could she take the southern heat and humidity? If she did break down and buy a little AC unit, she would have to sacrifice her quiet atmosphere for a noisy coolness.

Sadie dressed for church. She put on a black sheath with a black jacket. The collar of the jacket was lined with silver. She liked just a touch of the bright glittery stuff. She accessorized her ears with shiny silver earrings. A touch of makeup and mascara and she was satisfied that she looked understatedly elegant. Oh, she hated pulling up the panty hose and wearing the tummy pressing foundation garments. She always looked forward to coming home and stripping off all that paraphernalia, letting her body just relax and be normal.

She made some toast from some of her homemade sour dough bread. She spread some ripe avocado on a piece and salt and peppered it. It was marvelous with the good coffee she had brewed. She finished up her coffee just wandering down one of the park paths. Already there were people venturing onto the paths and children playing around the fountains. *What a becoming scene this is,* she pondered.

That morning during church Sadie sang a solo with the choir backing her up. She sang "Somebody's Praying Me Through", and once again the people loved it. *Two Sundays in a row of singing solo. Now that is just about enough,* she thought. She could see the congregation nodding and closing their eyes as she sang. They were remembering their own times that were tough. She knew they were recalling the incidents when other people were praying for them and brought them through the hard moments. She too, was so thankful for her daughter who had prayed her through some rough spots.

After that serious, honest talk with Pastor Harper, Sadie decided to settle in and make a concerted effort to be openly friendly with some of the people in the choir and the church. Sadie knew that there would always be those few who resented her presence in their church and who felt that she needed to be ostracized so as to punish her for her sins. That hurt, she had to admit, but she tried to focus on the majority of the people who had gotten to know her and who had begun to trust who she really was.

She knew from past experience that settling in a new place meant that she had to be patient and let the chips fall where they might. After a while, a friend would always develop out of the acquaintances she made there. It just took time. She knew that it was never good to rush it. The young singles in her Sunday School class adored her. They always hung around after class to just chat and share with her their own problems and concerns.

And she had met some very nice people at Reverend Brown's church as well. She liked to go there at night. The meetings got pretty lively and the Spirit soared there. The people would be so caught up in worship and praising the Lord that they would raise their hands and pray out loud and some would step into the aisles and dance before the Lord. Even a few would speak in tongues when the Spirit moved them. The people would all shush up when that happened and listen respectfully. Then the pastor would solemnly translate the message to the people. It was so meaningful and Sadie was filled with joy just being around that church and the sweet Spirit of the Lord.

Gladys Fortenbrau came to work one Monday in July. She was quiet and sullen. Sadie finally approached her casually, "Heh, Gladys. You feeling okay?" she started. "Why the hang-dog look?"

Gladys burst into tears. "Oh Miss Sadie, I don't know what to do. I don't want to leave. I love it here."

"What are you talking about . . . leaving?" Sadie sat her down on the settee by the staircase. Gladys had developed a pride in her work and the place was kept spotless and dust free. All the surfaces of the old, heavy furniture were shining and smelling of lemon oil. "What's going on, girl?" Sadie took her hand.

Gladys laid her head on Sadie's shoulder and wept into her already damp handkerchief. Sadie quickly pulled out a fresh, dry one from her apron pocket and handed it to Gladys. The crusty housekeeper blew a good, long snort into the handkerchief and then inspected the contents. Then she went on. "My husband wants to take a job in another city. He says he has a chance to earn more money. We don't need no more money! It makes me sick to even think of leaving my home. I just can't go," she wailed. "My old mother is still here roundabouts, and I have some friends at the church where we go. I'm too old to start over again. Can't he see that?"

Sadie patted her on the shoulder and hugged her tightly. "Now Gladys, you are ten years younger than I am. You are young yet. Look at me. I was 53 when I moved here and I started all over. Of course it was scary and worrisome when I was going through it. But look at me now. I love it here and I love my job and my home, and I'm making so many good acquaintances here." Sadie was careful not to say friends, because she was pretty selective to whom she gave that title.

"But Miss Sadie," Gladys started in again, "I've lived in these parts all my life. I know these hills by heart. How can I pack up and leave them for some strange land?" She cried some more.

"Well now," pondered Sadie, "First of all, where is it your husband wants to go? And what job is he trading his old job for? Those questions might be the key to a solution."

"Right now he works at the gravel pit running a scooper and filling trucks. He's been doing that there job for 23 years now." Gladys stopped to blow her nose again. "He says he has a job offer for a crane operator at a railroad yard. Says it pays more money and it is something he's always wanted to do. They are going to train him to work that giant crane."

"Oh Gladys, that sounds wonderful for him. To move up to a more interesting job sounds just right for him. If he gets this chance he may be so much happier and then you will have a happier time too. Where is this job going to be?"

"It is over yonder near Asheville," Gladys replied sadly.

"Asheville? Why that is just a hop skip and a jump from here, Gladys! You will be close enough to come back and visit your friends and these hills. And that wonderful city is right there with the Appalachian Trail running through it. You will be so close to the most beautiful mountains in the world." Sadie wrapped her arms around Gladys. "Oh Gladys, I am so happy for you. You have a whole new set of adventures ahead of you. Later when you look back on what you now think of as despair, you will see how silly it was. You will be happy there; I just feel it. I'll even come see you when you get settled and we can drive around and explore all your options."

"You really think so?" queried Gladys with a little hope shining in her eyes. "It just scares me to death to think of pulling up stakes and movin' somewhere's else."

"Nonsense woman! You are strong and young. If you want, you can get a job there in the city. You'll have lots of choices. If you want to clean houses again, I'm sure you will find a fine mansion to work in. Or you could work somewhere else like Walmart or in the Mall. You'll have lots of options." Sadie stopped and crouched down in front of Gladys and held both her hands. "Listen to me Mrs. Fortenbrau, you are a good woman and you can do this. It is a good choice all around, for you and your husband. Now buck up girl, and stand by your man. Make this work!"

Gladys tried a tentative smile and reached out to hug Sadie tightly. Sadie almost fell over, but she managed to barely keep her balance. She promised she would help her pack up her stuff. She assured the housekeeper that she would surely miss her and her fine work. "And" she added, "I'll miss your company. I like you so much."

This brought a new wave of tears from Gladys, but happy ones. "I'll do it Miss Sadie. I'll go home and tell my Joe that we can move. I'll tell him that I want him to be happy so I can be happy too."

Gladys told Sadie she would work two more weeks, while her husband arranged the sale of their old house and tried to find a place for them in Asheville. She would need at least that long to pack up and say her goodbyes to all the hill folk that she knew and to her church.

Sadie's mind was racing to think about finding someone else for this house keeping position. She would want someone who was planning to be around for a good while: someone young, sturdy and capable. She went back to the kitchen to make Navy beans and ham bone for dinner. She would make a black skillet full of bacon-jalpeno cornbread to go with it. Her mind was racing to consider all the things she must do to fill this position.

Please, dear Lord, help me to make this transition to a new housekeeper. Lead me to someone who will get along with the Shaw's and who will take pride in her work and love this place as her own. I know I bring to you all my problems, but you asked me to. Cast all your cares and lay down your burdens and all that. So I am doing it. Help me Lord, help me.

A sort of peace came over her and she rested in the surety that God would help her in this matter. She began to whistle and continued with her cooking. She would have to tell the Shaw's very soon about Gladys' departure. Maybe they had some good ideas of whom to ask to fill the position. After all they had lived here for all their lives and knew lots of people.

"Well, I'll be," remarked the Colonel, "I just can't even imagine this house without old Mrs. Fortenbrau here roaming the halls and rooms. She has always been sort of standoffish and grouchy, but she's been faithful and lately, since you came here, she has done a bang-up job around here. I'll be sad to see her go."

"Whatever will we do for a new housekeeper, Everett?" asked Victoria. Her face was creased with worry. She too, didn't like change.

"We'll get along fine until we find just the right person," assured Sadie. "I've already turned it over to the Lord and he will help us find someone." Sadie served the Shaw's their lunch of three types of melon and chicken salad with crackers and cheese. She served them tomato juice with V-8 juice mixed in and Worcestershire sauce and poured it over ice. They loved it.

"So don't you fret about it, Victoria," Sadie added. "Things will work out just fine." Sadie added. "I was thinking that maybe the two of you know someone who might fit the bill. You've lived here a very long time and you just might know someone to approach about this position."

"We'll have to think about it, dear," answered Victoria.

"Give me a day or two to ponder on it too," said Colonel Shaw.

And so it was that the answer to their dilemma came to all three of them just a couple days later. Sadie was used to welcoming Cherie's baby, Joy, into her kitchen to play on the floor while she worked. Cherie had to continue her job at the little café in town. Her regular babysitter got another job and was not available anymore. She desperately needed someone to watch over her daughter during those hours when she worked as a waitress. Cherie had been putting out her feelers for someone to watch the toddler and was getting anxious for an answer to her dilemma.

Sadie, can you hear me? You do it. You take care of her on those days when she needs watching. The urging of the Spirit of the Lord was not always a welcome thing. At first Sadie sort of balked at the idea and even panicked a bit thinking about giving over part of her time to this child. Hadn't she done her part raising her own kids? Wasn't it her time to just relax and focus on herself? The answers were yes and yes. But the Spirit said, *Trust me on this, Sadie, you need to do this for Cherie, yes, but for yourself also.*

And so she had suggested to Cherie that she just drop off the sweet child in the mornings and she would see that she was taken care of until she got off work. Cherie protested right away, saying, "I will not take advantage of our friendship like that. You are entirely too busy. You don't need an active child racing around getting into things. I'll find someone. I'm sure I can find someone to help me."

But Sadie lovingly took her by the shoulders and smiled sweetly at her. "Stop just a minute there, Cherie. This suggestion came from the Holy Spirit himself. I can do naught but obey." Sadie feigned a knightly position. "Besides that, I love Joy, and I'm sure I will get adjusted to a child in my midst once again. I did a good job of it with three children in times past, and I'm sure I can do it again. Let's just try it and see what happens."

Cherie had started to cry; from relief and from gratitude that someone so close and dear to her would be willing to share their time for her sake.

"There, there, Cherie, no need for that. We are all family here. You need help and I can give it. Just go with it and no crying."

With that command, Cherie wiped her eyes and sighed a deep satisfied sigh of relief. She didn't make that much money at the Rose Vine Café but it was just adequate to keep her and Joy fed and sheltered and clothed if she was very careful. "I'll pay you just like I used to pay the old woman above the store who watched her for me until she passed away." Cherie looked at Sadie hopefully. "I hope it will be enough."

Sadie looked at her and started to say, "No way. There will be no paying for this service. It is my gift to you." But something stopped her from saying that.

She thought a minute and said, "That will be just fine, Cherie. I'll put it in a little fund for my 'mad money'." Sadie knew in her heart that this little fund would be a savings account for Cherie and Joy in case they had an emergency and needed money right away. This would be her way of helping Cherie to save without realizing it. The thought pleased her.

So here it was on a Wednesday morning at 6:45, and Cherie was dropping off Joy. The sweet child had her little worn out teddy bear, brown and raggedy. She ran to hug Miss Sadie and clung to her legs for a minute.

Cherie handed over her bag of stuff. "Well, I'm off. I'll be back to get her about 2:00 as usual. Just call me if there is any problem and I will take a break and rush over here to take care of it. You have no idea how wonderful it is for me to feel so sure of the good care Joy is getting here. I feel like a great burden has been lifted."

"Don't worry about it. Joy and I are becoming the best friends, aren't we Joy?" Sadie announced as she ruffled the child's hair. "We are making cookies today and Joy will be my helper, won't you Joy?"

Joy jumped in delight and toddled over to the table and tried to climb on a chair to get higher. "Stay down from there Joy," chided Cherie. "You know you are not allowed to climb on things like that." She gently pulled the child back to the floor and shook her finger in the child's face. Joy just giggled and ran off to pick up some toys in the corner that Sadie kept there for her.

After Cherie had left for work, Sadie put some pots and pans on the floor with a wooden spoon and a silver spoon too for banging and making the most noise. She then finished up the breakfast she was preparing. On two trays she set up two breakfasts for the Shaw's. Victoria was getting very fond of soft boiled eggs. Sadie always boiled the water and then gently lowered an egg with a spoon into the bubbling water. She set the timer for 5 minutes and 20 seconds exactly. It assured a perfectly done egg. Whites all set and the yolk hot and still a bit runny. She added some crisply fried bacon to the plates (just two short slices a piece) and some avocado to spread on the toast and some sweet small chunks of orange melon. Victoria got breakfast tea and Mr. Shaw still had his fresh brewed coffee.

She was carrying the trays to the Shaw's personal quarters with Joy in tow coming on wobbly feet behind her. The old couple greeted her warmly and sighed with joy at the smell of the fine breakfast that was in store for them. They lit up with joy to see that baby come toddling in.

"Hello Joy," cried Victoria. "Come here and give grams a hug." She referred to herself as 'grams' because she knew that she was indeed a grandma and that 'Mrs. Shaw' was just too formal and harder to say. Joy ran to her eagerly and crawled up onto her lap.

"This child is just so grand. I love having her around in this house," she proclaimed.

"What about me, Joy? I need my hug too." Mr. Shaw pretended to frown and cross his arms across his chest. Joy scooted off Victoria's lap and rushed to him laying her little head on his knees and hugging his legs.

"Pau pau!" she said.

His eyes lit up with delight. "Oh, that child is like a breath of fresh air," he exclaimed.

Sadie was pleased that they loved having Joy around so much. It really was such a sweet thing to have a baby in their midst adding a light touch to the seriousness of life. It seemed that Victoria complained less of her aches and pains. It seemed that the Colonel's countenance was softer and less stressed.

Of course there were times that Sadie got frustrated at always having to keep a keen eye out for Joy in order to keep her safe and keep her out of the stuff she was not suppose to be near. But every day her presence there was getting easier and easier. She learned to respond to Sadie's warning looks or raised finger. She began to know her boundaries and she learned to be careful of certain things that Miss Sadie told her were hot or sharp. At 11:00 each day she would lie down to take her nap. She learned to do this as routine and didn't fuss about it. Sadie used this time at her cottage to clean it up and do her correspondence and read and plan menus etc. It was a nice quiet time for her that she looked forward to daily.

Sadie and Joy would walk out among the newly bricked paths of the park to check on the progress of the gardens that were being formed up. They always ran into people who were sauntering along enjoying the grounds. Some were resting on the benches in the sunshine. Another had thrown an old blanket on the grass and was reading a good book in the peaceful shade of the big trees. Some would feed the squirrels and pigeons and doves. A big gathering of those birds had begun to grow once they realized there was another park in town where free peanuts and bread bits were being cast out for them. The birdsongs were sometimes deafening in their shrill calls to warn of their territories. It was glorious.

The Colonel had been true to his word and had rigged up not just a buzzer from the mansion to the cottage, but a bonifide phone system. A sweet, soft bell would ring and it would be the Colonel or Mrs. Shaw calling Sadie to talk a minute. They usually called to mention something they had on their minds and didn't want to forget about. But the main reason for the house to house phones was in case of an emergency. That way Sadie could be reached quickly. They felt better knowing if she needed to come and help them, Sadie would be there in a jiffy. Sadie still had no regular phone at her cottage and was so grateful for that.

And so it was that on this particular day, the little phone tinkled during Joy's nap time. She was tucked away in the little cot in Sadie's room. She was softly snoring and Sadie could hear her through the open door as she sat in the living room reading her daily devotionals. Sadie got up quickly to answer it. She didn't want to disturb the child's sleep.

"Yes?" she answered. "Is everything alright?"

"Right as rain, I'd say," exclaimed Colonel Shaw excitedly.

"Okay . . . . good to hear," said Sadie carefully, waiting for the other shoe to drop.

"We think we've found the answer to replacing Mrs. Fortenbrau. When is she going to leave us?"

"She gave us three weeks notice and so that leaves about a week and a half left before we have to fill her position. Whom did you find?" Sadie asked pointedly and with happy expectancy.

"We think it would be great to have Cherie take that position."

Sadie was dumbfounded and the wheels of her mind began to go faster and faster. *Cherie doing the housecleaning and washing of the clothes and ironing. Made sense. She could be trained to do it well. She was young and eager to please. The pay would be better than at the Café where most of her earnings were dependent on the customer's generous tips.* "Well, I'll be. Why didn't I think of that? It sounds like a great idea to ponder," replied Sadie.

"Ponder, nothing! We've talked it over and we can think of no one else we'd rather have. She's a good girl. She gets along famously with you and is not afraid of your authority over her. And here's the clincher . . . . we are willing to allow her to stay in that back bedroom behind the kitchen area with Joy. That way she won't have to pay rent, she can watch her own child and free you up." The Colonel took a deep breath and added, "And . . . . we can see Joy all the time. We will be a family here again." He stopped and waited for her reply.

"Well, well. That sounds almost too ideal. I'm trying to figure out where the flaw in this plan is, and I can't think of one thing that wouldn't work." Sadie was smiling to herself at the prospect of it all. "Now all that is left to do is approach Cherie with the idea. I have little doubt that she would object to the job." Sadie laughed out loud with delight.

"I knew this would make you happy, Sadie. Victoria is the one who thought of it. She is so smart." Sadie could see in her mind's eye that the Colonel was looking at his wife with pride and with love in his eyes.

"She is indeed, Colonel," replied Sadie. "When Cherie arrives at 2:00 I shall bring her over and you can present her with your proposal. One thing, however," Sadie ventured to add. "Will there be health insurance for her and Joy? I know she will desperately need that."

Sadie thought the Colonel would have to pause and confer with Victoria on that added offer. But he answered directly. "Oh, that goes without saying and we shall include life insurance also. You are so correct, she will have to have those things as part of her package."

Cherie and Joy moved in the last week while Gladys was still there working. Gladys and Sadie had that week to train Cherie in how to do her house-keeping duties. There was always plenty of general cleaning work to do to maintain a lovely, clean smelling home. Gladys was pleased with how quickly Cherie learned to do her duties. When it was time for Gladys to move with her husband to Asheville area, she felt assured that she was leaving the mansion in good hands.

The Shaw's with the help of Sadie had a going away luncheon for Gladys and her husband Joe. The Shaw's showed their appreciation for all of Gladys' faithful work over the years. They presented her with a lovely Tiffany lamp, a new winter coat, and a gift certificate from Sears for $200. There were tears all around. Joe sat there embarrassed by all of the emotions being displayed.

"I sure do appreciate all of this. Me and Joe will sure be needing this money to get started up in our new place of living. You all have been so good to me. Ya made me feel like I was family."

"We consider you part of our family," said the Colonel. "You are welcome to come back and see us anytime you like. Thank you for all the fine service you gave to us over the years. We would have been lost without you."

Victoria added, "We love you Gladys and we wish the very best for you and Joe. I don't know if you write or not, but I have some notecards here and envelopes that are already stamped and addressed to us, so you can write a note once in awhile and let us know how you are doing. Would you do that for me?"

A new burst of tears came from Gladys' eyes and she hugged Victoria warmly. She reached down and picked up Joy and hugged and kissed her too. She turned to Sadie, "I guess you know, I didn't much like you when you first come here."

Sadie turned her head a little to the side and smiled wryly. "Yeah, I got that impression for sure."

"Well, truth was, I hated you some. You were so bossy and seemed to be trying to take over and push me out. But then I seen that you was just trying to have us do the best job ever. I could tell you were trying to help me to be proud of the work I was doin'"

Sadie turned to hug Gladys and kissed her on her worn cheek. Gladys was not that old, but she had worked so hard all of her life that she appeared to be older than she was. Joe had to turn away to look out of the window; he was so embarrassed by this show of affection. "Gladys, I'm going to miss you so much. You've become a real friend to me. I like your sharp tongue and how you speak your mind. Underneath, you're just a big softy."

Gladys bowed her head and snorted a little. More tears came and she had to reach for another couple of Kleenex. Sadie reached into the cupboard and pulled out a wrapped present that she'd hidden there. Gladys' face lit up, her mouth opened and her eyes grew wide.

"Is that for me? I ain't never had no present wrapped this fancy. I jist want to look at it, hold it and never open it."

Sadie laughed. "Well, you can do that if you like; it's your present. Why don't you just take it with you and open it when you're ready. It is a gift that I know you can use for a long time. You deserve it. And here's something else you can use on the trip." She reached into the pantry and pulled out a big heavy basket lined with a red checkered cloth and chuck full of good food: sandwiches, chips, cookies, apples, candy bars and drinks.

The Shaw's and Cherie gasped at what a clever and appropriate gift it was. Gladys cried again. More hugs went all around. Finally Gladys took her leave with the beautiful gift under one arm and the picnic basket hanging from the other arm.

They all walked them to the truck. Joe was visibly relieved that they were finally getting on their way. "Oh, I nearly forgot. I have something for all of you too. Gladys reached into the front seat and pulled out three lovely hand-stitched pillows that she had made: one for each of them. Victoria oohed and awed over them making Gladys feel proud and appreciated. Joy grabbed the one for her and Cherie. It had hearts all over it and flowers. Sadie was so pleased to have this memento of Gladys. They made the old housekeeper promise to come visit the old mansion whenever she came back to see her relatives near town. Joe was patient but they could tell he was not that comfortable with all the fancy doings that he'd had to endure. He was anxious to get on the road. They all waved and waved until the truck and U-Haul trailer was out of sight.

As they turned to slowly walk back to the mansion, Victoria asked, "What it is you bought her, Sadie?"

"Well, I bought her a real leather handbag. It is an expensive one that will last her many, many years. I saw what she used for a purse. It was an old raggedy canvas one. She carries everything in it like her life depends on it. This way she can carry lots of stuff, but do it in style." Sadie chuckled.

The next day they finished up the Cherie's move to the mansion. She a had a few items that needed to be moved from her little upstairs apartment across from the café. Sadie took the little blue truck and with Cherie's help loaded up the truck with Cherie's the meager amount of things that she owned. It took all of three hours to get it all done.

The café was very sorry to lose their beautiful, young waitress. Just her presence there had brought in a lot of young customers, especially male customers. They even offered her a substantial raise. But it was not enough to change Cherie's mind. She left her little apartment above the storefront completely spic and span. It was a good indication of what kind of work she would do at the mansion. Sadie was pleased to see her work ethic displayed in this way.

Mother and daughter took over that roomy bedroom on the bottom floor right behind the kitchen area. Joy had her own little bed. Soon it felt right at home and natural to have them living there. A television. was brought down from one of the upstairs bedrooms so that Cherie and Joy could watch it. Sadie worked with Cherie to add colorful curtains and pillows and rugs to the room to make it very cozy and personal. Of course, Sadie made their meals along with the Shaw's, but Cherie had use of the kitchen whenever she wanted to cook something herself. A part of a tall cupboard was emptied out to hold any personal food items she wanted to keep for her and Joy. Sadie was delighted to see that Cherie did not leave any dishes in the sink and always cleaned up her messes after cooking. Joy just blossomed in knowing she was surrounded by loving people who accepted her and enjoyed having her around.

Cherie took to her new job with spunk and enthusiasm. The house was big and there was always dusting and mopping and polishing that needed doing. She had to unobtrusively clean the quarters of the Shaw's each day during the few hours that they were out walking or going someplace. Some days when Victoria was not feeling all that well, Cherie would still go in to straighten up and clean things up for them; but always in a quiet, non-disturbing way. The Shaw's were very pleased with how well she handled her house cleaning assignments. Cherie seemed to take great pride in keeping the place sparkling and smelling great with orange scented polish and fresh flowers in the entry way. Sadie thought how this humble young woman would have made some rich man a fine wife, who appreciated fine things and knew how to care for them.

Life settled down to a routine where everyone knew his or her place in the everyday duties. Sadie still had her privacy and could choose what time she spent with the rest of the family. The Shaw's chose to eat in the kitchen for dinner each night with Cherie and Joy and Sadie. It was a joyful time sitting around the table, and it felt like a real family gathering in the evening to talk about what had gone during the day. Opinions were expressed, jokes made, news recapped and gossip covered. When dinner was over, Cherie would most times insist on helping Sadie with the dishes. They had time to joke around and even sing together. Cherie had a surprisingly lovely voice. She would sing the melody and Sadie would harmonize. Even little Joy tried to get in on the act by bellowing out with her sweet high voice.

Chapter 48

Sadie Gets More Freedom

Sadie made one of her calls to her daughter. After catching up on the family news, Becky informed her mother that the big news around the area was that her daddy was planning to get married to one of the women in the church.

Sadie was stunned. She was resentful and relieved at the same time. *How could that be,* she thought. *I should be so happy that I am now totally free from him.* But the truth was that she knew it would take her a few days to process that news and accept it.

Becky said that it was going to be the biggest event of the year. The church ladies were going crazy with plans. It would be the wedding to beat out all weddings. The President of the Convention was coming to oversee the vows. The choir was singing. The orchestra was playing. The big party afterwards would be at the exclusive country club on the mountain by the city. Becky warned her mother that she might even read about it in the papers.

"Probably not," said Sadie. "First of all, I don't get a paper and secondly, they are not that important in the world of news, dear." Sadie could hear the resentment in her voice and it shamed her. "What is her name, may I ask?"

"Her name is Monica. She's a decorator. He met her at a Christmas party for the singles. She's 44 and has never been married although she came close to doing so one time. She doesn't want children. I found that out from her beautician. Dad seems enamored of her and gives her so much attention. Mom, I have to tell you that she is stunning. Thin and classy with perfect hair and skin. She looks like a grown up Barbie doll. She must think she's found her Ken."

Sadie just shook her head and groaned quietly.

"Mom, I hope you don't mind hearing all the details. Stan and I think it is ridiculous and that Dad is making a fool of himself. He's like an eager young stallion, chomping at the bit. I think even some of the older folk in the church do not approve of the elaborate way he is remarrying." Becky paused. "Mom . . . . Mom, are you still there?"

"Yes dear, I'm still here," Sadie said softly. She knew her daughter and she knew that Becky wasn't saying any of this to hurt her mother. She was just upset and wanted to talk it over with her best friend, which happened to be her mother.

"He is selling the big house because she refuses to live in it after you had lived there so long. They are having another house built in the low mountains nearby. It won't be as big as the old one, but it will be more expensive and have more property. Everything has to be just so, and she is doing the decorating."

"I wish I could say that I am happy for your dad to have finally found the love of his life," said Sadie quietly, "but I am not. I guess I want him to be lonely and miss me. I want him to fret about the mistakes he made in his life with us. I want him to be sorry and repent."

"Would you take him back if he did?"

"Not on your life, dear child, not on your life." All of a sudden Sadie was beginning to feel better. Somehow she knew in her heart that this new, young wife, would wreak havoc in Tony's life. She would reveal herself to be demanding and pouty and not easily satisfied. He would tire quickly of having to pay so much attention to her and thus take away his time to spend with the love of his life . . . . his congregation and himself. They ended their conversation on a good note and Sadie hung up to think about all of this.

During one of her later calls to Becky, Sadie was laughing at something Joy had done that day. She was bragging at what a good housekeeper Cherie was and how she had certainly been an answer to prayer. She was happily relating all the advantages of the new arrangement with Cherie and Joy living in the big house. She suddenly noticed that there was silence on the phone.

"Becky? Are you still there?" She questioned.

"Yeah Mom, I'm still here," came the dejected voice of her daughter.

"What's wrong dear? Are you alright? Did something happen at home?"

There was another long pause and then Becky came out with what was bothering her. "Mom, I don't want to be childish or petty, but there you are being a Grandmother to Joy and treating Cherie like your daughter, and here we sit hundreds of miles away being deprived of your presence. Why can't you be near us and live here and have a job? We miss you," cried Becky.

"Oh dear me," said Sadie softly. "I never even thought about how this would impact you and seem to you. I'm so sorry. I guess I am glad that they are here because I do miss you and Trent so much, and I wish you were here with me." Sadie stopped to consider her next words. "But honey, no one can take the place of you. I wish I could live there near you. But I've got too much history there and the chords of discontent and resentment would hamper my life too much there. I'd be afraid of running into someone from the church. And with as many members as your Dad's church has, you know that would happen all the time. It would stir up gossip and cause problems for your dad and his new wife. I don't want that. So the better choice is for me to stay away from there."

Another pause and a stifled sob, "I know Mom. When I think of it in those terms I agree with you. But when I hear about you having a nice family time each night with Cherie and Joy I can't help but burn up inside with jealousy. I wish it weren't so, but I resent them taking our place in your life." Now Becky was crying full out. "I want my Mama!" She had to laugh at herself even through her tears. She knew that sounded so childish and silly.

"Rebekah, my precious and only daughter, listen to me. No one could ever take your place in my heart. I'm so sorry I had to leave. It is unfair to you and to me both. I wish I knew the answer to this dilemma, but I do not." Sadie was wiping her eyes and blowing her nose. How she wanted to climb into the phone and speed across the line to be with her daughter. *Beam me out there, Scotty,* is what she was thinking

"I think it is time I came out for another good, long visit. With Cherie here now, I think I can safely leave again like that. The Shaw's will surely understand that and will be all for it. When would you like me to be there?"

Becky sniffled and cleared her throat. "How about fifteen minutes from now?" She quickly added, "Now I feel terrible to push you to this, Mom. Of course we'd just leap for joy to see you, but you don't have to do this. I think I should have kept my big mouth shut!"

"No, don't say that, you silly girl! This is going to be just what I need. I just needed a nudge and reminder of how much I miss you all. Think about it and let me know when would be a good time for me to come, okay?"

"How about today?" Becky laughed. "You just make it suit your own schedule and we will clear our agenda to suit you. Oh, I can't believe I'll see you soon. I'm so thrilled."

"I certainly don't want to be there anywhere near the time your dad gets remarried, so it will have to be way before or far after. When is the big date?"

"Oh, you don't have to worry about that. They postponed it for the second time. Monica says she needs more time to get the house completed before she will get married. She evidently doesn't want to spend one night in your house, Mom."

It was easy to arrange to take a break from the Colonel and Victoria. Cherie was there to fill in the slack for a couple of weeks. Sadie felt confident that she could slip away without any bother to their routine. Cherie knew it all, and could keep up with everything.

How good it was to be back with her daughter and grandson. Even her son-in-law, Stan, seemed happy to see her. Their bond from the mountain camping was holding its own. He was sort of hesitant with his hugs and expressions of affection, but Sadie knew that was just his way, and she was not offended by the coolness he portrayed. He was at work most of the days anyway, so that left her to experience lots of grand time with Rebecca. *What a joy it is to have a daughter,* she thought. *Sons are a total blessing too, but daughters present a closeness that cannot be duplicated.*

They would get up leisurely in the morning, staying in pajamas or nightgowns for nice long time, wandering through the house with steaming cups of coffee in hand. They loved to sit in the sunroom and gaze out at the garden in the back. Trent was going to preschool three days a week and that gave them even more time to just talk and share their stories.

Sadie told many tales about the Colonel and his wife. She expounded on Cherie and Joy and what a pure joy it was to have them nearby now. She watched with scrutiny to see if Becky revealed any jealousy in this matter. But she could not detect even a particle of the green curse. Sadie related stories about the Immanuel Baptist Church and the dinners on the grounds. "What grand cooks all those well-endowed women are. They compete to see whose covered dish, cake or pie gets eaten the quickest. You should see how the people dress when they go to church. Honey, you never saw so many bright jewel colors. They look like an Easter parade every Sunday. I feel shabby next to all of them. And the children . . . dressed in crisp cotton dresses and bows. The mothers must devote hours of time to braid their soft black hair, so shiny with oil and braided like princesses. I love seeing them. I've even taken some really good pictures of the children and youth and adults and presented an album to them."

"Oh Mom, you always know just the right special thing to do for people."

Sadie responded with a tiny shake of her head and a screwing up of her nose. "My dear daughter, when I think of how little I do as far as good works go, I am so humbled and sort of ashamed. I see so many people who devote way more time and energy to the work of the church." Sadie looked out the window and paused, "I owe so much to the Lord, Becky, for how he rescued me and showed his tangible love for me." Sadie lowered her head in contemplation. "I can't even seem to find the time to read the Bible. A true disciple is supposed to hunger after the Word. I do, however, pray on and off during the day while I am walking or working. I feel very comfortable with prayer, and I totally believe in it."

"Maybe you should try going to a Bible study once a week. Making a habit of just getting ready and going is a sign of devotion. And you get the benefit of some good Bible teaching at the same time," Becky offered. "I go to one here that is so inspiring. It is a Beth Moore study and combines videos with teaching. I love it."

"Becky, I am so thrilled that you are doing this. You seem so much more settled in your faith and strong in your convictions. How glad I am," Sadie announced.

"Don't be so quick to brag on me, Mom. You heard how I acted on the phone. I was like a child demanding my own way and whining about being jealous. How infantile was that?"

"Rebecca May Myers. If we can't have a moment now and again where we revert to our childish ways, then we must be robots. You were just being real and honest. God loves honesty," Sadie advised.

Becky stood up and gathered their cups and saucers. "All I can say is that I am so thrilled to have you here all to myself for a few days. This is the biggest treat, Mom. I wish we could make it last forever."

"We will just store up some great memories these few days and conjure them up when we are once again apart." Sadie squinted her eyes and looked at Becky sideways. "Why don't we make a special memory today? A really special one."

Becky perked up and said, "What do you have in mind?"

"Is Millie's Corner still running?" Sadie inquired with her hands dramatically clasped in front of her.

"Why yes, I believe it is," replied Becky hunkering down in like manner. "Shall we?"

"I'm right behind you." Becky laughed in excited anticipation. "I don't know why a fancy place like that would have such a simple, common name like Millie's Corner. As expensive as that place is you'd think it would have a complicated French name or something."

"Sometimes the most delectable gifts come in the simplest packages. But I know what you mean. It could have been named . . . 'Mon Cheri's Casaba'."

"Mom, you definitely have unique flair for naming things. You should open your own little eatery. You'd make a mint with your cooking and with the way you make people feel welcome."

"Just what a needed . . . a loyal fan. Thanks, Becky. Tell you what. If I go into business like that, you will be my partner. How's that?"

"Mom, I know you are just fooling around, but I'm gonna hold you to that. One of these days you'll be ready to launch out and take the risk." Becky hugged her mother and remembered to ask, "By the way, did Dad's settlement money come to you yet?"

"I have it tucked away in the bank just drawing interest. It is a poor way to invest that goodly sum of money. But some day very soon I will discover what to trust it in. I'm not a risk taker, as you just pointed out."

"Not a risk taker? Mom, are you nuts? Look at the risks you took leaving here and setting up life somewhere else. If that isn't risk, then I'm a monkey's aunt."

Sadie thought about what her daughter had said, and she had to agree that she did have a little bit of risk-taking in her blood. She began to strip out of her robe and pajamas and shouted, "Last one out of the shower is a rotten egg!"

Millie's Place was set on a residential side street very close to town. Years ago the owner purchased the house and big lot next door. She had that old house carted away. She then arranged for 3/4ths of the land to be paved for parking. On the other piece of land she built the most delectable and inviting little restaurant ever. As time went by, she had added a room here and there. It was strange to see this little restaurant in the middle of a neighborhood of houses. Someone must have pulled a lot of strings and gathered lots of signatures and permits to create this snug little corner. The place looked small, but that was deceiving. There was a second story and the lower structure wandered here and there with added rooms jutting out in all directions. It was painted a drab olive green with little, shining, squared windows trimmed in burnt orange. Each window had a white wooden window box full of Creeping Jenny and tiny purple asylum interspersed with colorful flowers. Bird houses, hand painted and delightful to look at, hung from the eaves. Bird feeders were situated in the midst of the bird houses and a colorful array of birds flew in and out, contentedly eating there. Yellow blossoming Jasmine was growing profusely along the front porch. Big rockers with cushions beckoned visitors onto the wide front porch. Huge pots of bright red geraniums decorated the entrance. The place reminded Sadie of a magic house in a fairy tale that lured the unsuspecting heroine in through its doors. The place was irresistible.

They walked inside and their olfactory senses were rewarded with scents of fresh brewed coffee and delectable lunch items. Crepes Florentine with white Béchamel sauce, puff pastry chicken with mushrooms and tiny diced tomatoes. The place was filled with color. Stained glass lamps graced each table. Each one was a different work of art. The soft glow of their light created a kind and satisfying light that caressed the faces of those gathered there. Since their decision to come had been so spontaneous they had no reservation, but the hostess recognized Sadie and welcomed her with a hug.

"Oh, Mrs. Golden, you're back. I've missed seeing you so much. I loved you being our Sunday School teacher. No one can fill your place."

"It is so nice to see you too, Marissa. I see you are still working here. You'll be running the place pretty soon. I'm just visiting my daughter, Becky. I'm sorry we didn't call, but the idea to come here just popped up in our heads and we decided to take a chance."

"No problem. Let me see what I can do for you. Normally we have no room left, but I think I know of a little table we can give you. Follow me."

They wound their way through a couple of rooms and way in the back was a little corner table overlooking the back garden. "This is perfect," remarked Sadie thankfully. "We have a great view of Millie's garden. Does she still use her own produce to make her dinners?"

"Yes indeed she does. Everything here has to be as fresh as possible or she won't even serve it. She's a stickler for that. I'll send you a waiter. Enjoy your meal." Marissa retreated with a cute wave of her hand.

Lunch was scrumptious. They took their time and savored the sweet potato jalapeno soup, followed by the walnut-raisin, greens salad with Millie's secret raspberry vinegar dressing. Sadie ordered the fresh trout with lemon beur blanc and roasted pine nuts. She also enjoyed tiny, roasted vegetables. Becky got the veal scaloppini with fresh green peas and homemade pasta.

When lunch was eaten, Sadie challenged her daughter, "What do you say? Can we do it? We can't pass up the chance to have some of her unbelievable dessert!"

Becky sighed and smiled at her mother. "Tell you what. I am stuffed, but let's just share one dessert, okay?" bargained Becky.

"Your mother didn't raise 'no fool'," teased Sadie.

They ordered some crème Brule with fresh strawberries and cream on the side. They splurged and ordered two cups of the most delicious fresh-brewed coffee ever. "I love that they serve this so very hot. I cannot abide luke-warm coffee," remarked Sadie.

Just then Sadie noticed a couple walk into the room. The man was handsome as ever and kept his arm on the arm of his new fiancé, guiding her gently through the maze of tables. Sadie gave an involuntary gasp and clasped her hand on her mouth, elbow on the table.

"What is it Mother? What did you see?" Becky turned to look at what had captured her mother's full attention. "Oh, dear God, no!" Becky turned back and remarked. "Oh mom, I'm so sorry. Who would have thought that this would be the day that Dad would bring her here for lunch? Oh Mom, what are we going to do?"

Sadie closed her eyes for a moment and prayed silently, *Lord, you know what I'm going through right now. Be with me, please. Help me to act the way that would be an honor you, Lord. I don't want to embarrass Becky nor cause attention to be drawn to myself. Help me Lord.* She opened her eyes and smiled at Becky. "Not to worry my sweet daughter. Your mother is a lady if nothing else. Everything will be fine."

The waiter brought them their check and Sadie set the money along with a generous tip in the black, leather folder and pushed it toward him. Marissa, the young hostess, came rushing to their table and began profusely, but quietly apologizing. "Mrs. Golden, I am so sorry about this. There is a party of eight coming and I didn't realize your hus . . . Reverend Golden was going to be part of that group. I had no choice but to bring him in here. I hope this won't be awkward for you." She was nearly in tears. Her devotion to Sadie was plain for all to see.

Sadie took her hand and held it in both of hers. "This will be no problem darling girl. Don't fret about it. Life goes on and we must all just be courteous and kind to one another. That's all we can do."

With that she got up from the table folded her white cloth napkin neatly and lay it on the table. She pushed in her chair and waited for Becky to do the same. Their path out of the room led right past the table where her ex-husband was seated with his beautiful new woman. The woman glanced up and then purposefully busied herself looking into the menu. She refused to acknowledge Sadie's presence. But Sadie reached out her hand to Tony and said, "I see that you still like to frequent this delightful place."

He rose from his seat in stunned shock. He took her hand and gave her a slight embrace, then embraced his daughter tightly. "Hi Becky! I had no idea your mother was in town. You didn't tell me she was coming." Then he turned to Sadie and said, "So good to see you. You look very well."

"Thank you, I am very well. I'm just here catching up with Becky and Treat. I'll not be here long." She assured him.

"I'd like to introduce my . . . uh . . . . new . . . . lady friend."

"No introductions are necessary," Sadie returned swiftly. "We used to be know each other very well, as I recall. How are you, Monica? You are looking as lovely as ever."

Before she turned to face Sadie, Tony's fiancé glared at him hatefully. Sadie knew that Tony would get a double blast from her wrath when they got home. But she turned to Sadie with a sudden beatific smile plastered her face and she inclined her head at an angle and looked up kindly.

"It is good to see you again, Sadie." Monica cooed.

Sadie could no longer hold her tongue and said rather pointedly and sweetly, "Well, I'm sure that is not really true, but thank you anyway. We will take our leave. Sorry to have caused a scene. Have a good life, now." With that Sadie turned and walked regally away.

Becky just shrugged at her dad and followed her mother out of the room. It was obvious that people were staring at them as they exited. Millie, the owner, appeared at the door as they were leaving. "Oh, dear Sadie, I just got in and found out you were here. I'm so glad you stopped in while you are here. I've missed you so. I'm sorry about this uncomfortable timing. I hope you won't hold it against me."

"Millie, it is delightful to see you again. I'm so glad your business is still going so well. I miss this little refuge. I wouldn't have missed having lunch here for anything. I am not in the least upset with anyone here for this unforeseen circumstance. That's life. That's all it is." Sadie hugged Millie and planted a kiss on her cheek. "I wish I had more time to catch up with you, but Becky and I are in a hurry to leave right now."

"I don't blame you a bit. God speed. Won't you drop me a line and let me know what is going on with you? Here is my card and address. I mean it. I'd love to hear from you," Millie said sincerely.

Sadie's eyes suddenly filled with tears as she realized just how many friends she had left behind here in this city. "I promise you with all my heart I will write you and fill you in on what I'm up to now. You can count on it." Sadie turned and smiled and waved as they exited the restaurant.

"Oh Mom, why did that happen? Who would have thought that in this huge city we would run into Dad? I'm so sorry. So very sorry."

"Nonsense, dear. Don't fret about it one bit. Maybe this is good that it happened. Now I can truly picture him with her and it is totally settled in my mind. I am happy for them and truly wish them the best." Sadie stopped and could not resist adding, "I just wonder how long it will be before she begins to feel the coldness of his treatment."

Becky looked at her mother sadly, and tears filled her eyes.

"And . . ." added Sadie, "I wonder how long it will be till she makes his life a living hell."

Becky gasped.

"Oh, Becky, I'm so sorry to have said that. I'm a terrible mother. Why can't I just control my quick tongue? That must have sounded terrible. Forgive me?"

"No need for forgiveness, Mom. You can say anything you like. I'm surprised you haven't burned my ears with more details of the marriage. It just makes me so sad to think of all the years you hung on just for our sakes. My brothers are upset about it too. We all love you and want you to be happy again. You hid it so well for so many years." Becky reached over to put her hand on her mother' shoulder. "From now on you must tell me everything on your mind. Let's be honest with each other."

"I'm all for honesty, Becky, and I want that from you too. But as far as unloading my regrets and frustrating memories on you . . . . no, that won't be happening. My life is too good now, and from this moment on, I must go ahead with my new life and not ponder on or hold to that former life." Sadie laughed as she thought about the shock on Anthony's face and the white tint that rose up on his new woman's face. "That poor woman. She will probably not want to eat there ever again."

They both laughed then. The day was still warm and promising. They went to pick up Treat a little early. There was nothing like a fresh, young child's face to whisk away depression or sad thoughts.

It felt so good to Sadie to have confronted Anthony (albeit surprisingly) and not been shaken up or thrown into the doldrums. Mostly, all she felt was relieved and even more free if that was possible. She was glad for Tony to have a new woman in his life. It wasn't that she wanted him to suffer and be unhappy. Now she truly could let it all go. She had to admit that there were some good memories being married to him in the early years, when the children were very small and Tony was not yet a big time 'hot shot' in the ministry. Those struggling small churches were heartwarming and close-knit. Sadie still had wonderful memories of the folk at those places. She still sent Christmas cards to some of them. This past Christmas she had not bothered to send cards, but next year she surely would. Good friends took a little effort and time, but it was well worth it to keep in touch.

The two weeks went by so quickly. Sadie talked to her sons who were so upset that they were both on tight schedules and neither of them could find someone to fill in for them. They desperately wanted to come and be together with the family again. They all agreed that next Christmas they would all clear their schedules and come to North Carolina for an all out shindig of a celebration. Already they were putting in their special requests for favorite foods that their mother had made for years. Sadie was making a few plans of her own.

Sadie was sad to leave her daughter and grandson, but it had to be done. The thing that surprised her the most was the joy she felt arriving home to the big colonial mansion in Rose Creek. The air smelled terrific and fresh. The evening summer air was beginning to let up on the heat and felt like velvet. What looked especially fantastic to her was her little cottage with the warm light streaming out of the windows. She wished it had been cold enough for a fireplace fire. She loved the smell of that wood smoke and the welcoming warmth of a crackling fire.

Wheezer was there to greet her. She scooped up the big old cat and hugged and hugged him. That dear cat began purring almost immediately. Then hopped down and turning his back on her, started cleaning his fur. It was as if he was communicating to her that her absence for so long had not set well with him, and that it better not happen again. There was a delicious aroma coming from the oven. Sadie took a red oven mitt and peeked inside. There was a golden baked chicken and dressing in the oven. It smelled and felt like Thanksgiving. She was so delighted to be home again. *Home! Yes . . . . home!*

There was a knock on the door and then all of a sudden Joy came bursting in with her little hand on the knob. The door banged hard against the wall. Joy stood there with her hands on her hips and a severe set look on her face. Sadie held out her arms.

"Joy, we don't just run into someone's house like this. We have to be invited in. Come back here you monkey!" Cherie said. "I'm sorry Sadie. She was just so excited to see you."

Joy finally decided she was not mad at Sadie anymore for being gone so long. She ran to her and was scooped up in Sadie's arms and twirled around and around. Cherie came walking in to join in the hug. Sadie had Joy all wrapped up in an embrace already, and Cherie joined in with them all clinging together and laughing.

"Group hug!" stated Sadie. "I'm so glad to see you two. I've missed you like you are my own kids." She sat down on the couch with Joy on in her lap. "Who fixed this supper for me? Let me take two guesses. Was it Cherie? Was it Joy?"

"It was me and Mom," Joy chimed in. Joy was now two and a half and her talking was progressing so rapidly. Sadie had never heard of such a young child picking up the language so quickly.

"Well, why don't we all sit down here and have some together," offered Sadie.

"We were hoping you would ask us," countered Cherie with a big grin. "But I'll bet that first you want to go and check on the Colonel and his wife, don't you?" Cherie moved to the cupboard and started getting plates down. "Tell you what. I will set the table and get everything ready and you go talk to them. They are so anxious to see you. They've had a bit of excitement around here."

"Don't tell me. Let me take a wild guess. Big boy has been around again. What's his problem this time?" Sadie questioned with a frustrated sigh.

"If you are talking about their son, you are right. How did you know?" asked Cherie.

"Oh . . . just 'been there, done that' several times. It seems that every chance he gets to see them without me, he makes his presence known. So tell me what he did. Tell me."

"Now Sadie," explained Cherie. "I don't think he purposely came over here to create dissension, but somehow one thing led to another and he lost his cool."

"What in the world is wrong this time?" Sadie asked with irritation in her voice.

"I think I will let you talk to them about it. I wasn't there, so I can't really tell it fully."

"I'll be right back. Joy, you help your mama, hear?"

"Yes, Miss Sadie, I will," piped in little Joy.

"Oh my, if it isn't Miss Manners. I like it, I like it." Sadie kissed Joy on the head. She took two shiny pink bags from her satchel and placed the smaller one on the mantle of the fireplace and took the larger one with her walking toward the door. She was glad that she had remembered to buy gifts for everyone. "I have presents for you both. I'll give them to you when I get back, okay? Don't peek!"

Joy danced in place and clapped her hands. "I wuv pesents!" She ran to hug Sadie's knees.

Sadie knocked softly on the Shaw's door and she heard the Colonel quickly say, "Come in, come in. We've been waiting for you."

She walked in to discover the room rearranged in a delightful new way. Everything was spotless and neat with fresh flowers on a couple tables. Pride in Cherie flowed through her. *What a treasure that girl is,* she thought.

"Hello there you two," began Sadie. "I'm back and glad to be here."

The Colonel helped Victoria out of her pillow laden rocking chair. They both came over for a warm hug. "It just feels right to have you here, Sadie. We've missed you so much."

Victoria had tears of joy in her eyes. "Why did you have to stay so long?" She wiped her eyes with a lace handkerchief. "I sound selfish, but there was something missing with you gone." Victoria retreated to the love seat and carefully sat back down.

"You dear people," said Sadie. "I certainly feel needed and loved. How's everything here. Did anything exciting happen while I was gone?"

The Colonel looked at her sideways and squinted. "Cherie's been talking to you I see."

"Well, she mentioned that Stephen came by and got upset. What's the matter this time?"

The Colonel took a deep breath and let it out in a rush. "Oh, same ole, same ole, I guess. He wants to be apprised of any new decisions we make. He still thinks we are inept due to being old. Why can't he see that my mind is working just fine?"

"He wants to be in charge of our lives, that's what's the matter," added Victoria. "He says we are ruining everything, and he blames you for leading us to consider all these new ideas."

"All what ideas? For goodness sake, tell me what is wrong this time. I get so tired of his attitude and griping." She looked at them and suddenly realized she had said something critical of their son. "I'm sorry for that. It's just that things are going along so well, and he has to step in, again, and make waves."

"That's okay, Sadie, you can speak your mind. Here's the thing that's wrong. Stephen needs to have people to boss. He has no family around to rule, and his job allows for little management, so we are his only outlet."

"Well, he needs to get a big dog to train then. You two don't deserve to be his way of letting off steam and placating himself into thinking he is so all-fired important and in charge of everyone." Sadie put her hand over her mouth. "There I go again. I'm so sorry. I think it is best if I refrain from giving my opinion. Just tell me what his complaint is this time."

The Colonel laughed out loud. "That's what we need around here: a champion. You can speak your mind about Stephen any time you like. We agree with you. It is finally time someone pointed out his controlling behavior and stood up to it."

Suddenly Sadie realized what the problem was. "Let me guess. He doesn't want Cherie working in the mansion here with Joy. He thinks the two of us are planning a take over of some sort. Am I right?" Sadie settled herself in a chair, tired already with this new problem.

Victoria rushed in with words of explanation. "Here's what happened."

The Colonel looked at her with a frown. "Well . . . ," she said, "You were taking too long to let her know what's up." She laughed at her forthrightness and continued. "Stephen came by to check up on us and Cherie answered the door. Joy was coming carefully down the stairs holding on to the railing. With his usual flair he didn't even greet Cherie. He just demanded to know who she was and what she was doing in his parents' house."

"Oh dear, here we go again," muttered Sadie. "Did you forget to tell him that we had invited her to work here? But before you answer that, first tell me why did you tell me about Joy coming down the stairs? Did something happen? She didn't stumble and fall down, did she?"

Victoria and the Colonel shook their heads at the same time. Victoria explained, "She didn't fall or anything. She's very careful now since Cherie taught her how to do it. But that incident gave him the reason to warn us of law suits and ineptness and stealing."

"Does he know that they live here too?" Sadie asked hesitantly.

The old couple looked at each other and turned as one and Victoria said, "Yes, we just let it slip out!"

"What was his reaction to this bit of news, dare I ask?"

Colonel Shaw stood tall and put his hands on his hips. "Well, he paced the room and raised his hands and shook his fists," the Colonel theatrically acted it out. "He frowned and shook his head, all the while huffing and puffing and yelling at us for being so misled and naïve. He wanted to understand how we could trust another strange woman to come in here off the streets and work for us, let alone live in the house."

"He threatened to go right then and fire Cherie and tell her she had two days to get out," cried Victoria.

Colonel Shaw stepped toward Sadie and said, "You would have been so proud of me, Sadie. I stood up to him barring the way to the door and told him to settle down!" The Colonel had had enough of the excitement and went over to sit down next to his wife.

"Yes, he really did do that," joined in Victoria proudly patting his knee. "He told Stephen to simmer down and not be so hasty."

Everett continued, "He finally took a seat and let us explain to him the reason Gladys Fortenbrau had to be replaced. I told him about her having to move with her husband, and that hiring Cherie was our idea, not yours. He just snuffed at that like it was ridiculous and he didn't believe it. I told him that our house was so big that we needed someone in it to fill the spaces with life and noise."

Sadie shook her head. "I can just imagine what he said to that."

"You are so right. He began again to tell us that at our age we needed all the peace and quiet we could get. He asked me what references Cherie came with? How many houses had she cleaned before this? Did the child have her vaccinations? It was laughable."

Sadie did laugh. Stephen was such an ill-informed man. His controlling obsession with his parents had grown to new ridiculous heights. "How did you get him to let the matter rest?" Sadie inquired cautiously, hoping that it was true.

"Oh, it isn't fully at rest," responded the Colonel. "Stephen could see that his mother was really upset and ready to cry. So he left and said he'd be back to discuss this further."

"I was pretending. I even shook a little and breathed really fast." Victoria admitted.

"Why you scoundrel!" Her husband replied, surprised. "You even had me fooled. You're good!"

"Oh it is so good to be home," Sadie admitted joyously. "I love you two. I leave for a couple weeks and both of you can't behave yourselves." She laughed, and went to hug them both. She handed them the big pink bag of gifts. "Here's something I picked up for you at my old home town. Just a little something to let you know I was thinking of you and missing you out there." She placed the bag on the coffee table. "And don't you worry about this mess with Stephen. I'll handle it," Sadie said with determination. "That is . . . . if you will permit it, Colonel."

"With our full blessings, dear girl," he replied.

"Ahh . . . . there it is. You called me 'girl' again. I feel young as a colt when I'm around you. You are so good for me." Sadie promised them a cup of hot lemon tea and some sort of snack as soon as she had finished eating the nice dinner that Cherie had prepared for her. "I'll conjure up something, don't worry."

"Don't even think about it, Sadie. We are too full from the wonderful supper Cherie made for us. Yummm! She's gonna make a fine cook one of these days," the Colonel remarked.

When she stepped into the little cottage out back, Cherie and Joy were sitting at the table with worried expressions on their faces.

"Why so gloomy, you two?" asked Sadie.

"I assume they told you about Stephen and his tirade. I don't think he will allow me to stay and work and live here. What are we going to do, Sadie? My job at the café has been filled, and our little room above the bakery is already leased to someone else," Cherie said nervously.

"What you are going to do is stay put right where you are and continue with the excellent job of cleaning that you are already doing. Leave Stephen to me. We've butt heads before and I guess it is about time we stood our ground together once again. I'll call him and invite him to lunch tomorrow, if he has time. If not, I'll swing by his house when I know he will be home from work. This will get settled."

In her heart Sadie was not so sure. But her words came out confident and cocky. She knew that her knees would be hitting the floor by her bed tonight. The Lord had to consulted in this dilemma. She picked up Joy and hugged her. "I am going to give you your gift whenever dinner is done, okay?"

Joy pouted a little and then a big smile came on her face. "Okay, Miss Sadie, okay."

They sat down to a good, simple chicken and dressing dinner. It was delicious. Cherie had fixed biscuits and peas to go along with it. "This is what I gave the Shaw's for dinner too. They ate early," Cherie said.

"You did well, Cherie. The Shaw's loved your dinner and so did I," said Sadie. "If I don't watch out, you'll be a better cook than I am."

"No chance of that, I'm afraid." Cherie chuckled. "I will be glad to learn all I can from you."

After supper, Sadie pulled out the other pink bag off the mantle piece for Cherie and Joy. Inside she had wrapped up a lovely doll with hand made clothes for Joy. The little girl was so tickled with it. She grabbed and hugged her doll and went to sit on the oval rag rug to play with it by herself.

"Joy, didn't you forget something?" chided her mother. "Don't you want to say thank-you to Sadie?"

The little girl obediently left her doll on the floor and ran to Sadie jumping in her arms. "I wike my pesent. Tank-you!"

"You are the best little girl, Joy. And you are so welcome dear child," said Sadie, hugging her back.

It was a good time. A simple memorable time that none of them would forget. Cherie opened her gift. It was a beautiful, black silk and velvety shawl with golden and pale green embroidery and fringe on the ends. She was so pleased and modeled it draped around her shoulders. Sadie had gotten a teal shawl of the same make for Mrs. Shaw. Sadie knew that it would compliment her glowing, grey hair. For Colonel Shaw she had purchased a set of Corinthian Bells to hang outside their window. The soft sounds coming from those wonderful, indestructible bells would sound like angels hovering right outside the walls.

When dishes were cleared up, Sadie bid Cherie and Joy good night. She changed into one of her many white cotton nightgowns and sat in the lamp light and contemplated her life. She bowed her head and recognized the hand of God in her life. Retreating to the bedroom, she knelt by the bed on the soft rug and prayed earnestly to the Lord. *Dearest father, I mean it when I say that I deserve none of these blessings. You have brought me out of trouble and lostness. You rescued me and set my feet on solid ground. You found a way when there was no way. Thank you, dear Lord. Please help me to know your bidding and have the courage to do it, no matter what. I love you so much, Lord. I place my life in your hands to do with as you will. Tomorrow when I face Stephen, I pray that you will give me the words to say. Curb my temper and fill me with love for this hard man. Nothing is impossible for you. I know that if you choose you can soften that stiff-necked man and reach his heart. Be with me Lord.*

Sadie stopped her prayer and looked up. She then lowered her head once more to add to her prayer. *And Lord, be with my friend, Peter, wherever he is. Keep him safe. Give him success in his endeavors to win back the love of his daughters'. Dear caring Father, won't you please make a way for him, too?. And may he some day recognize that the path he has been following actually was orchestrated by your hand. May he learn to trust you as I do. I pray all this is Jesus' name, Amen.*

After that prayer, Sadie felt at peace and ready for bed. It felt so good crawling into that soft, comfy bed. As soon as she tucked herself in, Wheezer came loping to the bed and sprang up on top of it. He settled himself on her shoulder and arm looking at her. That cat seemed so glad that she had come home. She fell asleep with him there, balancing on her side, guarding her.

Chapter 49

Let's Make a Deal Lunch

The next morning dawned bright and warm. Sadie walked the garden paths looking at all the additions and improvements that were made while she had been gone. Oh, the colors and fragrances that lined the walkways. The birds flitted here and there near the fountains to drink and bathe and sing their songs. What a pleasant place this park had become. Sadie saw couples strolling through the paths on their way to town. A mother had her little toddler, and he was taking some of his first steps trying to reach for a squirrel.

We did 'good', thought Sadie. This is a real gift to everyone. What was walled in and held for only a few is now open and enjoyed by all. I love it.

After breakfast with the Shaw's, Joy and Cherie, Sadie cleaned up the kitchen in the big house. Then almost reluctantly, she took a deep breath and wiped off her hands on the apron she wore and walked to the wall phone. Stephen's number was posted near the phone with several other numbers that were used frequently. She punched in his number and held her breath. *Please Lord, be with me,* she pleaded in her mind.

"Yeah!" It was Stephen's belligerent voice.

"Stephen, hello, how are you?" Sadie started her conversation.

"I should have known you'd call. So you are back home again?" he stopped and cleared his voice and amended his statement. "I mean, you came back to run my *parents'* home again, I see."

"Yes indeed. And you were right the first time. It is my home. I love it here."

"Well, we've got a lot to talk about, lady. I think you've gone just a little overboard this time. We are not running a boarding house in that fine home, I'll tell you that!"

"I hear you, Stephen. I would like to talk with you about all of it. Can you meet me for lunch today?" She held her breath waiting for his refusal.

It took a while before he answered. "I . . . . I guess I could fit you in. Say around 11:30? Where will we meet?"

"This is just a suggestion, mind you, but I'd like to fix you a picnic and eat out on the pathways by the house. It is such a pleasant summery day. Not too hot and it would be nice to be outside, don't you think?"

He was silent for a good while and then answered, "Oh, okay. But there'd better not be a bunch of bugs flying all around me. I hate bugs!"

"I will put in my order immediately for all bugs to stay clear, how's that?" Sadie joked.

"Hmmm! Well, I guess we could try it. I'll only have at most, forty five minutes to spare. I hope you are ready for what I have to say." Stephen said with authority in his voice.

"Oh, I'm ready for it, and I know what to expect, considering our past meetings." Sadie sighed. "And I hope you are ready for what I have to say too," she added.

"Oh, boy! Here we go again!" Stephen said softly. Then louder he answered, "Okay I'll be at your cottage at 11:30. Be ready!"

"You can count on me, Mr. Shaw," replied Sadie.

Sadie got into fast gear and began her preparations for the picnic. She walked the paths and chose just the right spot, out of the way near a corner. There was a nice dogwood tree that had months ago lost its blossoms and was greened out. She set up a little card table and covered it with a nice linen table cloth folded in half. She placed china and silverware and crystal glasses on the table. A tiny bud vase with one red rose sat in the middle of the table. She brought out two wooden kitchen chairs and sat them strategically so Stephen could see the lovely park and enjoy the best view.

For lunch she needed to go to the market, so she trotted on down to Clyde's Grocer and procured some Black Forest ham in very thin slices, some fresh tomatoes and bib lettuce and baby Swiss cheese. She found some kettle chips with pepper on top. She would make her own potato salad and a couple of deviled eggs. She got a solid Pink Lady apple and a ripe peach and kiwi. She went to the pastry counter and got a couple of slices of tiramisu and a can of whipped cream topping. She would serve iced tea with lemon on the side. *It should be enough*, she thought. *How could a man lose his temper in the midst of all that loveliness?*

Stephen arrived on the dot at 11:30. Sadie was ready; dressed in a yellow and white cotton sundress with white thin cotton sweater on top. She had white sandals on her feet. Her toenails were bright red. She had to admit that she looked rather pretty, even if she said so herself. They walked to her spot that was set up for the lunch. Sadie carried a big picnic basket which Stephen insisted on taking from her. "Thank you so much, Stephen," she said.

Stephen seemed confused and taken aback by all the preparations that had gone into this picnic. He tried to hide his satisfaction and joy, but Sadie could see it peeking out from behind his set frown.

"I wanted you to enjoy what this property has turned into: a beautiful park for all the township to enjoy. Isn't it wonderful, Stephen?" Sadie asked being sure to include his name to make it more personal. Oh, how she hoped this sugar-coating would make a difference in his response today.

He looked all around, noticing everything, it seemed. Then he said rather reluctantly, "Yes, I have to admit, it turned out better than I'd expected. It was quite a mess there for a long time. But . . . . I guess it turned out okay after all."

"You can't believe how many people come here daily and sit and read or just sit and enjoy the nature and rest. And the children, oh Stephen, the children are the best part of it. They race around and play in the fountains and skip through the trees playing hide and seek. It is so great to see. Your mother sits on the front porch every day and watches the life that has come into this place. I think it has made a big difference in her health too. Have you been able to see the color in her cheeks and the light in her eyes?"

"She looks fine to me. What I want to talk about, though, is this young girl living in my house with her little daughter. Surely you can see how this is not going to fly." Stephen was on a roll now. There was no stopping him. Sadie sat back in her chair and crossed her arms and decided to just sit it out.

"Imagine what it felt like for me to come in the door and see this woman, uh . . . girl, standing there. Coming down the long stairway was a tiny bit of a child perilously descending. It made me think of law suits and a tragedy in the making. We just can't have these people living in the house and even working there. Mother needs to find an older lady to handle that job. One who can go home at night." He finally stopped to get a breath.

Sadie just remained silent and started setting out the food. Stephen seemed shocked that she hadn't jumped right in to argue with him. He was taken aback. He watched her lay out the sandwiches and olives, chips, fruit and salad. It was all so neatly done. He began to notice how detailed the set up was: the flowers, the china, crystal and silver. Sadie could tell he was impressed.

"I wonder if you'd mind if I said a little prayer over the food." She asked politely.

Stephen could not say, no; he didn't want to object. She had gone to a lot of all trouble already to make this nice for him. So he just nodded. Sadie reached out to grab his hand, which he nearly pulled away in shock. But she had secured it gently and began her short prayer.

"Lord in heaven, for this lovely day and this good lunch, we thank you. Help Stephen and me to speak kindly to each other and get some things settled. I thank you for him and his strong concern for his parents. Bless him Lord. Amen."

Sadie didn't look at Stephen as she let go of his hand. He remained silent, just staring at her.

"Well, eat up, man. You've only got 30 more minutes left."

They ate for a while. He remarked how good everything was. The sandwich was piled high with ham, cheese, lettuce and tomato. It was hard to get his mouth around it. Sadie pretended to be hungry and took tiny bites. Inside her stomach was churning as she thought how she could manage to keep this meeting civil without angry words filling the air.

"I understand," she started, "how shocking it must have been to come in and see Cherie and Joy there. I am kicking myself for not telling you about Gladys having to move. She was so sorry to have to leave. We had a party for her." Sadie took a bite and a sip of iced tea and continued. "I think you were out of town on one of you frequent trips, and no one bothered to leave you a message. But that is no excuse. You deserved to know what was going on."

"You're damned right I deserved to know!" he started.

Sadie hurried to explain herself. "Then I took a two week trip back home to see my daughter, and so here we are. You and I, together again ready to mix it up and have words together. I'd just like for this time to have it be not an angry thing, but a pleasant talk." Sadie looked up at him and put down her fork. "What do you say, Stephen? Can we talk about this without yelling at one another?"

Stephen looked around him. People were walking along the paths glancing over at them and their picnic. The people were far away from them, but Sadie could see that Stephen didn't want to make a scene in front of the community. He finally spoke, "Well, I can see why you planned our lunch this way. It would be rather rude for me to disrupt such an idyllic scene by yelling at you. So yes, I guess we will have to be civil to one another. But it doesn't mean I'm not seething inside at how you've come in here and changed the course of things." His voice had risen a little and Sadie opened her eyes wide to remind him where they were.

"I know that to you it appears that I've bullied my way into your parents' home and changed things around. Things have changed, I admit, but only for the better. Your mother is happier and your dad has purpose again with this project going on. They enjoy their home more, and once again they have life in the house. It was truly rather too solemn and lonesome there before I came."

"Oh, now you consider yourself the savior of the world, heh?"

She gave him a look that would wilt lettuce and said, "Please refrain from being blasphemous, if you don't mind. I do not consider myself to be anything near a savior. I looked at your parents and saw their need, and I moved to meet those needs. Light and sunshine, good food, neatness, flowers, music, purpose in life, love and laughter. These are all essential elements of a happy life. For instance, that Christmas family reunion was all for them; to surround them with the joy of being with their huge family. Bringing everyone together under the same roof again was an elixir to them. Can't you see that?"

"I guess it turned out okay," he admitted. "But I feel like I have no more control over what happens here. I'm left completely out of the loop. It is my responsibility to watch after them and make sure they are not taken advantage of."

Sadie reached over and put her hand on his. He took in a quick breath like she had just burned him. "Stephen, I know that is your purpose here. I see it and appreciate your love for your parents in such a tangible way. But once again, the truth is, your parents are still viable and perfectly capable of still making their own decisions. There may come a day when they won't be able to choose correctly, and you must be willing to take charge then. But right now, it is so good for your father and mother to make their own choices without fear of recrimination from you. They love you so much, but they dread what you will do when you come over. More often than not, it is a big row when you show up. It upsets your Mom no end. It takes her days to recuperate from the stress of it all."

Stephen bristled. "Oh, so now it is all **my** fault when mother has a spell?" He turned in his seat to stare out sideways so as not to look at Sadie. "Here I am still stuck in this no count town, trying to watch after them and this is the thanks I get?" He looked back at Sadie with anger in his eyes. "I might as well be living a day's journey away like my other siblings. A lot they care!"

Sadie passed him some fruit and a plate of tiramisu. "Stephen, listen to me. You are the son who stayed behind. You are to be commended for that. I applaud your love for them and your devotion to their well being." She looked into Stephen's eyes and continued, "But the truth is, you've overstepped your boundaries by trying to completely control their lives. That isn't good for them. They don't need to be so fully dependent on you that they lose who they are. They must still be able to make their own decisions and remain as active and important as they were before, for as long as they can. Just think how you'd feel if your own son, Patrick, decided you were not capable of running your own life. What if he stepped in to take charge of you and rule your life? You'd balk and throw a fit and tell him to back off. And you'd be right to do that. You are a very smart and capable man. You find your importance by being in charge. Just think how it makes your dad feel. He used to be so in charge of companies of men and of his family. Now he is treated as though he is already senile." Sadie stopped and then added, "He is far from senile, believe me."

Stephen looked off into the distance. Sadie was silent and let her words sink in. *Please Lord, open his heart to understanding. Help him see clearly how he appears to his parents and what he is really doing to them.*

Finally, Stephen took a deep breath and let it out. "Well, maybe I was a little forceful. But that is just my way. I can't help it. I've always bullied my way through things. Being the eldest son I always felt I needed to be an example and show the others how to do things." He laughed softly. It was one of the first times Sadie had seen him laugh. It just transformed his face. "I can remember my sister, who is 3 years older than I am, stamping her feet and telling me that she was the oldest and she didn't need me to boss her. We used to go round and round. My poor folks were constantly trying to settle our arguments." He laughed again. "I am a big bull, aren't I?" He looked at her for verification of that fact.

"Yes . . . . you are that, for sure. But your heart is in the right place, I can see that."

Sadie added, "So what do we do to make you feel better about this new housekeeper and her daughter staying here? Let me assure you that she is the finest gal and a very hard worker. She puts Gladys to shame if truth be known. And that little Joy is just what her name implies. Your mother is crazy about her and they even keep their door open so she can wander in and out to see them. A child has a way of adding life to a house, and to those two old people she is medicine."

Stephen took the last bite of his tiramisu and drank his tea to the bottom. He wiped his mouth on the white linen napkin and folded it up neatly. "Okay, here's what we'll do," he began. "We'll see how it goes for one month or two. Then if everything is still okay and things are running smoothly, we can agree to make it permanent. How's that?"

"Sounds fair to me," Sadie answered with relief in her voice. "This has been a good lunch, Stephen. You know something?"

"What?" he said gruffly.

"I really enjoyed myself. Truth is, I was dreading this so much. I hate to fight and you and I have had our history of it, for sure."

Stephen was taken aback, and sat there with his mouth open for a few seconds. When he shut it, he spoke again, "You and me both, Sadie. I was dreading it too. Maybe there is hope for us after all," he laughed.

Sadie laughed too, tentatively, wondering what he actually meant by that. She wanted him to realize there was no hope at all for them to be anything but friends as she worked for his parents. She knew how lonely he was, but she also knew that she was not the answer to that loneliness. "You want to come in to see your folks before you leave?" Sadie asked.

"Well," he looked at his watch, "I guess I could pop in and tell them we settled it all . . . for now," he added, with a smirk. "Let me help you clear all this up," he offered as he stood up.

"Don't you mind about it one bit. I am the chief cook and bottle washer around here and I can handle it by myself. You go on now, and I'll see you later. Thanks again."

He looked deeply into her eyes which made her uncomfortable and said, "It was a great time. It did me a lot of good, if I have the grace to admit it. See you later, gator!"

Stephen had actually tried to make a little joke. She was encouraged by that. He took off toward the house, and she began packing up all the food and cloths. *Lord, thanks a lot. You brought me through. You gave me the words. You are the best. Help Stephen to hold onto what he learned today and help him to make some permanent changes. Is that possible, Lord?* Sadie thought about that question and realized she knew the answer. 'With God all things are possible.'

Chapter 50

The Storm of Happiness

Summer droned on and made a final wicked stab of heat. For such a high little town, Sadie could not believe how warm it could get in the middle of the day. Her little cottage had no air conditioning and she got permission from the Colonel to install a little air conditioner in her bedroom window. If she kept the bedroom door open she would cool the living room and kitchen too. It was at least bearable.

She set up a sprinkler on the front lawn and Victoria and the Colonel would sit on the front porch and watch Joy frolic in the coolness of it. Sadie bought a huge dark green umbrella and table to put on the porch to keep the slanting afternoon sunshine from casting its heat on the old couple. They didn't seem to mind the heat as much as Sadie did. There were many times they ate their meals out there. Sadie would light some citrus candles around the porch to keep the mosquitoes away.

Once in a while Todd Morris, the young man who was sweet on Cherie, would come by to see what was going on. He would eat dinner with them. Some evenings Sadie would watch Joy to let Cherie and Todd go to the movies or out to eat. Cherie assured Sadie without here even asking, that Todd was a perfect gentleman.

"I think he is just too shy to try anything but gentle kisses," she offered in explanation. "He's finally talking more and telling me about himself. In truth, he is an interesting fella. But he doesn't think so. He considers himself just ordinary and not special in any way. Did you know that his father is a local rancher and he works for his dad?"

"I like him," said Sadie. "He's steady and kind and he seems to like Joy very much. She's always running to sit on his lap and show him the treasures she finds in this park." Joy had made a collection of stones and sticks and dead

315

butterflies and bugs and shells of bugs. Sadie had given her a small lidded wooden box in which to keep her precious items. Before Joy woke up, Sadie would often spread colorful stones and smooth pieces of red, green and gold glass around the yard, so that Joy could find them. She even bought some iron pyrite stones, and when Joy found the 'fool's gold' she thought she had struck real gold. She would hold up the stones to the light and watch them flash like fire. It just tickled Sadie, no end, to see her so happy.

Then came Labor Day Weekend, that first Monday of September. The celebration in Rose Creek was a colorful one. They invited Stephen over for the get-together and to view the fireworks show being put on downtown. From the front porch, they could see the sparkling colors shoot up into the sky above the trees and rain down. Joy was exuberant in her reaction to the fireworks. The little town square had a band and the sounds of that rowdy music reached their ears also.

Sadie and Todd had been the chefs that night. They BBQ'd hamburgers on the grill. The air was redolent with fine scents of savory beef cooking over an open fire made of hickory and mesquite. Sadie had onions and bell peppers sautéing on the side in a piece of tinfoil. They had all the trimmings with buns and corn on the cob, coleslaw and hot molasses beans and chips. Homemade ice cream was sitting on the porch under a big towel just waiting to be devoured. Sadie played her guitar and sang a few tunes. Joy sat by her and tried to strum as well. It was a peaceful time. People strolling by wandered up to the porch to sit on the steps. Some were talking softly and some were just sitting quietly. It was truly one of those moments that can be imbedded in the mind then later on drawn forth for a good feeling. Sadie needed those special memories quite often.

Sadie was so relieved to have Stephen enjoying the night with them. He sat and talked with everyone and even played catch with Joy for a short time. Sadie was glad to see him smile a bit now and again. Was it really possible for a man so set in his ways to change? She hoped so.

September finally began to cool off some. The little air conditioner was thankfully turned off. It was now going to be lovely Indian Summer. Some of the leaves at the tops of the trees were falling in a golden blessing. Sadie would watch them fall and stand amidst the colorful dropping leaves with her arms spread wide. Joy and Sadie would try to catch the falling leaves before they hit the ground. "This leaf has never been touched by human hands, Joy. Let's be the first one to touch it."

Sadie hadn't heard from Peter in a more than a month. She kept on remembering him in her prayers and hoped that he was having a real turn around in his life. *Please, Lord, give him a second chance with those girls of his. They seem a bit hardened to his attentions and efforts. I pray they soften up some and give him a chance to be a father to them again.*

She missed him so much. She hadn't realized that having him around had meant so much to her life. It just seemed a bit empty without him around. She wondered if she would ever see him again. Surely he would keep in touch once in a while. Pete had been part of her life for nearly the whole year. If she hadn't found that blasted treasure in the attic room, then the TV cameras would never have come and she and Peter's faces would not have been splattered all over the country. He could have still been hidden away here in Rose Creek. But she knew in her heart that these thoughts were just foolishness. *It is always better to open the wound and clean it out and let it heal. Peter needs to face these demons of fear of being apprehended. He needs to make amends.* Sadie knew in her heart that Peter had to clear up the loose ends and regain his name in order to regain his confidence and purpose in life. Self-imposed exile was not the answer here. Even if she never saw him again, she was glad they had gone to Chicago to help him find his way back to society.

She sighed a deep sigh and got back to making a crumb cake. She liked it with lots of chunks of butter and brown sugar and cinnamon. She had soaked the golden raisins in butter rum and the mixture smelled good. Biting into a piece of that coffee cake, and having one of those plump rum raisins burst in the mouth was a treat for the taste buds.

Victoria had been having some weak spells. She would stand and sway a bit, making an effort to not move until the faint, lightheaded feeling subsided. She would stand with her hand on her chest and she would breathe deeply and close her eyes. If Sadie was around when one of these moments happened, she would rush over with a chair and make Victoria sit down till the weak feeling had passed. The doctor said it was a combination of older age and low blood pressure. Getting up suddenly could cause these reactions because the blood would drain down too quickly. The doctor even suggested that Victoria's heart might just be missing a beat or two from time to time. That in itself would cause that weak feeling. Sadie knew it was something they would have to be careful about, because Mrs. Shaw could lose her balance and fall. Broken hips and arms would not be a good thing for someone Victoria's age.

On top of that, Victoria started to lose her appetite. Nothing tasted inviting to her. Sadie experimented with salty, sweet, and vinegary tastes. She used lemon and lime juices and any spice that might spark up Mrs. Shaw's interest in food again. *Maybe her stomach just can't take normal food anymore,* she pondered. *Perhaps I should begin preparing lighter meals for her; recipes that are easier on the digestion.* Sadie pondered that maybe Victoria's sense of smell had been affected in some way. If you can't smell the food, then you have no appetite to eat it she reasoned.

And so she had begun a concerted effort to make meals that were still tasty and inviting but light and easy to digest. She made broth soups that had fresh veggies and little bits of meat in them: like chicken, or fish or shrimp. She added vermouth or white wine to bring out the flavors and add strength. She made light breakfasts too, with oatmeal and blueberries and omelets mostly with just the whites included. Sometimes she would make a soft boiled egg and serve it with avocado and toast points. Sadie was determined to do all she could to help Victoria recover from this funk she was in. She remembered that decrease in appetite could sometimes mean that a body was choosing to shut down slowly. She hoped this was not the case for dear Victoria.

The Colonel was very attentive to his dear wife. He rarely left her side unless she was taking one of her frequent naps. She complained that she was not able to sleep at night, but felt tired during the day. Things were definitely changing in the Shaw family.

One evening at end of September, the air was scented with a sort of sulfur like scent. Sadie knew that a storm must be nearby and that the wind had carried the smell of lightning to them. She gathered up the nice cushions from the front porch and on the outside swing that hung from one of the big trees. She tucked them away in the back porch of the big house.

The Colonel and Mrs. Shaw had retired long ago to their little suite. Dishes were all cleared up and she and Wheezer sat on the wide front porch of the mansion and watched the late stragglers hurrying along to beat the storm home. She waved at many of them, who recognized her from church or around town.

"Evening, Miss Sadie. You'd better be getting under shelter. Feels like a good one is on its way."

"I hope it is, Fred. We need the rain badly. Have a nice evening," Sadie replied.

How Sadie loved storms. She had always taught her children to relish the wild thunder and to count slowly between the visual lightning strike and the sound of the thunder to determine how far away the strike actually was. She taught them to seek shelter, but to never cower from the fierceness of the storm. For her, hearing a raging storm outside, made her feel so safe and cozy and glad to be inside. She knew that in some parts of the United States there were areas that seemed to work like a magnet for the tornado storms. Year after year the fear of such devastating storms would visit those areas. After a storm like that the ground looked like an atomic bomb had wreaked havoc leaving only waste and rubble and splintered wood. She dreamed often of running from a funnel cloud and hiding in the ditch covering her children with her body. But she had yet to actually be in one of those storms. She hoped she never would have the experience.

Right now, it felt refreshing to feel the cool air rushing in to expel the last of the hot, humid September air. She breathed in deeply and closed her eyes. Joy came out to sit with her. They sang together. Soon they could hear the thunder getting louder and louder. "Well, I guess it is time for us to go inside and enjoy the storm from our safe houses." She ushered her into the house to find Cherie, who was finishing up the laundry and ironing.

"There you are, you little booger," Cherie kiddingly admonished her child. "I saw you out there with Miss Sadie and I wondered how long it would be for you two to come running inside."

"Well, I think I'm going to call it a day. I have a new novel I am reading and I think I'll just go mesmerize and enjoy it while the storm lashes the gatehouse. How I love these storms!" Sadie hugged them both and walked out the back door. Wheezer caught up with her and they both ducked into the house just as the first drops of rain pelted down.

Sadie fell asleep with the book in her lap. Her glasses had fallen on the floor and Wheezer was sitting on her chest purring and kneading with her claws. The storm outside was lashing against the windows. The lightning was fierce and constant. This was indeed a big storm. She hoped that not much damage would be done to the town and the churches. *I'd better get a move on and get into my nightgown,* she thought. She checked the clock and it was 11:45. *I'd better get to bed. I have a big day tomorrow. Church and Sunday School. I have to do the offertory too and I have barely practiced enough.*

She slipped into her white nightgown with the long sleeves. Her little air conditioner had kept the cottage plenty cool and so she enjoyed those long sleeves even through the summer. She was brushing out her hair when there was a knock at the door. Perhaps it was just a branch scraping against the wood. No, it was a definite knock. She grabbed a pale grey shawl and wrapped it around her and headed to the door.

Sadie had no fears in this little town, but someone coming at such a late hour did give her heart a little turn of apprehension. So she called through the door, "Who's there, please?"

She waited for what seemed like a minute and then heard a voice that sounded familiar. "It's a face from the past."

She threw open the door and pushed back the screen door. She grabbed the arm of the late-comer and pulled him in. It was Peter Combs dripping with rain and an umbrella in his hand that was comically turned inside out.

"Why don't you use your umbrella?" she laughed.

He dropped the ruined mess and stepped in to hug her. That hug felt so good, so natural. Her nightgown and shawl got soaked quickly but she didn't care. She never wanted to let go of that embrace. It felt so good, so right. *My but I didn't realize how much I really missed this dear man,* she thought.

They kept on hugging and rocking from side to side. Not a word was spoken. None was needed. He kissed the top of her head and she turned her face up to his. Their first kiss was tender and gentle like new friends getting acquainted. The tears from her eyes joined the rivulets of rain running down his face. They just looked at each other like sojourners in a desert finally seeing water to drink. He kissed her cheeks and her eyes and held up her hands and kissed them too.

Peter turned to shut the door and then he ventured to speak first. "I cannot tell you how good it is to see you again. I've missed you so much. I never knew I could ever miss anyone so much. And what a welcome you just gave me!" Peter was astonished at the response he was getting from Sadie.

She looked at him longingly and held his hands to her face and cuddled them. "Oh Peter, you are a sight for sore eyes. I really wondered if I'd ever actually see you again."

They finally pulled apart and she ran for a blanket in which to wrap him up. He removed his jacket and took the towel she handed him and scrubbed his hair partially dry and patted his pants and shirt. "I'm a big mess. I think I'll just sit on the floor till I can change."

"Take off your shirt and wrap up in this quilt. I'll hang up your stuff so it can dry while we talk. You'll sit on that couch, is what you'll do. You are the guest of honor and you will be treated as such."

She ran in to get water boiling on the stove for coffee. The air outside had turned chilly with the cold front moving in. Could fall really be far behind? A delicious thrill went through her at the thought of the end of summer. "Are you hungry? I'm making you some French press coffee and you can have a sandwich or some of my rum raisin crumb cake or cookies. Name it and you shall have it."

He laughed at her. "Well, one thing for sure, you haven't changed one iota. You are still trying to feed everyone. I think it is your mission in life."

"Well, I have to be good for something," she said as she sat beside him on the couch. He put his arm around her and pulled her in under the quilt with him. They sat in silence again, just savoring the closeness and the satisfaction of being together again.

He pulled away and sat up to look at her. "I just couldn't wait a second longer. I had to see you. I tried up there, Sadie, I really did. I had a pretty good job consulting with an investment firm. But the magic and allure of that life was not there anymore. It was not satisfying to me. I felt so empty and useless."

"What about your girls? Did you see them much? Was there any healing in that relationship?" Sadie noted the sad look on his face.

"I tried there too, again and again. Ellie was kind to me and saw me even though her mother frowned on it and discouraged it as much as she could. Emily had minimal enthusiasm in taking the time and effort to connect with me. That youngest one is still stubborn and responding in like manner to the way her mother thinks of me." He held his head in his hands and put his elbows on his knees. "It was like beating my head against a brick wall trying to break through to them. I love them so, but giving them stuff and trying to buy my way back into their good graces just didn't work for me."

"Perhaps given time and them growing up some, a relationship can still be feasible. We will just pray, hope and trust that it will someday happen. Miracles greater than this happen all the time."

"Oh, it is wonderful to hear your upbeat attitude and view of life." He hugged her again and she laid her head on his shoulder. "It is the elixir that I need so much. How do you do it?"

"Do what?" Sadie honestly had no clue what he was asking.

"Always look for the good and expect the best and deal with troubles like they are a mere bump in the road?"

"Hey mister, I'm old, and I've been through a lot. This kind of wisdom doesn't come easily you know." She grinned at him letting him know she was just joking around and they laughed together again. She thought . . . *the 'old' part is so true and soon he will realize it. He might as well face it right now.*

Peter held her shoulders with both arms as he turned toward her. "Look here woman, I don't care if you are 90. You are amazing and I am crazy about you."

So much for the age factor, Sadie thought.

They talked into the night. Sadie retreated to her room to dress in jeans and a t-shirt and socks. Peter kept wrapped up in his quilt until his shirt dried up by the fire that Sadie made. She served up ham sandwiches and coffee and they ate voraciously. The storm blew itself out and they opened the door letting the cool breezes waft into the room. The air smelled so delicious. Having the AC permanently turned off created a quiet that was therapeutic.

"I can't wait for you to see this wonderful park in the sunshine. You will be thrilled at how your plans for the park have been followed nearly to the 't'," Sadie said enthusiastically. "This place is the wonder of the town. People come here every day to play, sit, ponder and read. Some folk spread out their blankets and sleep like babies in the sunshine. Children run on the paths and feed the squirrels, chipmunks and birds. You have left a legacy here for people to enjoy for years to come. I'm so proud of you."

Pete sat silently and she noted that his eyes were filling with tears. She called the cat to her to give Peter time to compose himself. Finally he spoke. "Sadie, you have no idea how much I needed to hear that, and to know you are proud of me. I have done very little in my life to be proud of. What a dork I was hungering after money and thinking it was the key to all success. How I wish I could go back and fix everything." He caught his breath. "But I can't. The damage is done."

"But life is not done, Peter Combs. It goes on and new chances are just around the corner. God may find us on the junk heap, but he won't leave us there. He can still use us and make us into something grand and workable. You just watch and see." Sadie smiled at him and poured him more coffee.

"There you go again with the Pollyanna attitude." He looked at her teasingly and saw the beginning of a frown on her face. "I meant that in a good way, Sadie."

She could see that he was afraid she might have taken offense at that saying, but she did not.

"What about the judge and the sentencing? Are you here legally or must I hide you?"

Now it was his turn to see that she meant no harm with what she said. They laughed a little and then he answered her.

"No, no, I'm legal. It seems impossible but the judge took such a personal interest in my case that he wanted me to check in with him periodically. He saw that things were not working out for me there, and he noted that I had tried my best to fit into life there in Chicago. I told him how I was striking out with my daughters, and how it was breaking my heart to be so near to them and yet so very far." Peter took another gulp of coffee and set the cup down. "So . . . out of the goodness of his heart, an amazing thing right there, he arranged for me to report to a parole officer close by here once a month. That officer will report back to him and my sentence will wear out in time."

Sadie just sat mesmerized by this wonderful news. "He really is such a nice old gentleman, isn't he? I remember him well."

"And he remembers you well too. In fact, it is just as I surmised right after the trial. I think the reason I got such a lenient deal was because of you, Sadie. By the way, he asked me to tell you hello and that you can visit his courtroom any time you like." Peter squinted his eyes and looked sideways at Sadie. "What kind of magic did you work on that old gentleman?"

"Just honesty and respect, that's all. I think he just had a good heart and wanted to help."

"Well, like I told you before, he has the reputation of being the toughest judge in Chicago. Nobody gets away with anything. He punishes to the hilt, but in my case he was different. People in the courts are still amazed by it."

Finally about 1:30 they decided to call it quits for the night. Peter wanted to go and find a place to stay, but he had flown down to Asheville and ridden a bus to Rose Creek. He had no car to go searching for a motel. Sadie insisted he sleep right there. She made a nice soft bed on the couch, and Wheezer settled in on his arm claiming him as his own property. Sadie thought she would never be able to sleep, but surprisingly, she fell into the best, deepest, restful sleep ever. Once she woke up to hear Peter snoring away. She knew then, that he too felt right at home and safe and at ease.

Chapter 51

Coming Full Circle

The morning after the storm there was such a fresh, pungent scent in the air. Sadie woke and rushed out to see if Pete was still sleeping. He was gone. His blankets were folded neatly on the couch. She opened the door to see if she could catch a glimpse of him. Nothing. She was not worried. Never once did she suspect that he'd run off in the night changing his mind about being there. She put on some coffee in the old percolator and soon the cottage smelled mighty fine. She made her bed and fed Wheezer. Just as she was heading to the door to go search the grounds for Peter, she heard a soft rap on the door.

"Sadie, are you up yet?" It was Peter standing at the door with a white, shiny bag from the bakery. "I decided to walk into town and check things out. I had to wait till 6:30 for the bakery doors to open. The smells coming from that place were driving me nuts."

Sadie took the bag from him and set it on the table. She turned to hug him warmly. She never said a word. Her throat was choked up, and she knew it would be hard to talk.

"I got us some sweet rolls and some bacon and egg-filled klaches. Is that baker from the old country?" Peter looked around at the kitchen and saw the coffee steaming up into the air. "Oh, it smells so good in here. I've missed this place. This little cottage may be humble and small, but to me, it is a mansion."

Sadie took down his favorite red, imperfect cup and filled it with coffee. She was finally able to speak. "Yes, the baker's family was from the old country. Czechoslovakia, I think. They make all the old braided breads with poppy seeds and filled with fruit and such." Sadie opened the white bag and said, "My, but you certainly are hungry. There's enough here for a troop of people."

"Well, I was just thinking that maybe you could skip cooking breakfast for the Shaw's this morning and share some of this stuff with them. Then you and I can go walking the grounds."

"Didn't you already go see all the progress?" Sadie was astonished at the prospect of getting to be the one to show him all that had been done on the park since he was gone.

"Are you kidding me? I wouldn't do that, not without you by my side."

Sadie rushed over to hug and kiss him again. It felt so good to finally be free to show him how she cared for him. *I can hug that man anytime I want, now,* she thought.

"I'm so glad you waited, Pete. But I sure didn't expect you to." Sadie's eyes were wide with anticipation. "Will you come with me to surprise the Shaw's? We will have to do this gently so as not to shock Victoria. They will be so glad to see you. It will be the greatest treat for them."

Peter shook his head and bowed it down. "I can't believe they care for me this much. I certainly don't deserve any of it. What great people they are, Sadie. However did I happen upon all of you the way I did?" He put his hands to his eyes and shook his head.

"Now, Peter, you know how it happened. The Lord loves you and is watching out for you. He has great plans for your life and little by little He is bringing that plan to pass. I know you don't understand or even believe in all of this yet. But you will. The Holy Spirit is working on your heart and helping you understand."

Pete looked at her with wonder in his eyes. "Sadie, I don't really get a whole lot of what you say concerning spiritual things, but slowly I am getting some of it. And it doesn't seem so strange to me anymore."

Sadie and Peter carried the coffee and pastries over to the big kitchen. They set everything up and then walked through the dining room to the Shaw's suite. Sadie knocked on the door softly.

"Is it time for breakfast already?" she heard the Colonel ask. Then the door opened and Sadie grabbed his hand and pulled him into the hall. She reached in and shut the door quietly.

The Colonel stood there transfixed. His mouth was open, but he couldn't say a word. Sadie put her forefinger to her lips in the universal 'shushing' gesture. She whispered, "I don't want to shock Victoria too much."

"Shock me how?" said Victoria opening the door and stepping out.

Peter rushed to her and wrapped her in his arms. He lifted her up for a gentle, but firm hug. "Stand back," she said, "let me look at you. Oh my, but you are really a sight for sore eyes!" Victoria looked up beseechingly to the ceiling. "Thank you, Lord. Thank you for answering my prayers."

The Colonel too got in a good hug and patted Peter on the back. "It's about time you got back home, mister!" he said.

Sadie could hardly see through the tears of joy. They retreated to the kitchen and ate leisurely of the pastries that Peter had brought. Sadie went round to get Cherie and Joy. They, too, were happy to see Peter back. Joy rushed to hug him and planted a big kiss on his cheek. He held his hand over the spot and just smiled.

"I'm going on a walk around the grounds with Sadie as soon as we eat. I can't wait to see what's been done and take a tally of what still needs to be done. This is so exciting for me," Pete admitted.

"Take your time looking and figuring, Peter. When you are ready we'll sit down and reconfigure our plans for the future. I hope and trust that you want to be hired on again to oversee all of this and to maintain it when it is completed?"

"You can count on that, Colonel. I've missed this place so much. I never knew what it was like to be homesick before."

Peter and Sadie let Cherie do the dishes and they walked out into the fresh morning. The sunshine was filtering through the trees and spotting the ground around them. They started out from the front of the mansion and took one of the paths that circled around the perimeter of the acreage.

"Oh, this is nearly how I pictured it in my mind," Pete said about one of the fountains and bench areas. They walked on, hand in hand. Peter went slowly and took it all in. He paid careful attention to all the details and marveled at the intricate stone and brick work that had been done. "This is fantastic workmanship. I hope I get to meet these men who came all the way from Mexico to do this job."

"Oh, you will meet them; tomorrow, as a matter of fact. Today is Sunday, which reminds me I must get ready for church. It is too late for me to get out of my responsibilities this day. But I won't be gone for long."

Peter looked at her and paused a moment and then said, "I wonder if I could go with you?" He thought a minute as Sadie just stood there with her mouth pursed open. She couldn't believe her ears. "But I'd have to run to the bus station and pick up my suitcase from the lockers there. I have some nice clothes that might just do for church.

Sadie was careful not to let the excitement overly show in her voice. "Oh that would be great. I'd love for you to come. I will have to be playing piano and singing and teaching my Sunday School class. But all in all it will only take a couple of hours. Did you want to come even though part of the time I will be on stage and teaching?" She was hoping with all her heart that he would.

"Sure, why not. I don't want to waste even one minute of getting to be near you. It's been too long away."

They stood face to face. The love beaming from their eyes was so obvious. Slowly he bent down to kiss her. It started out gentle and slowly increased in strength and ardor. Sadie sighed a satisfied sigh and leaned into him wrapping her arms around him tightly. They stood in this voracious embrace for a long time with the morning sun streaming down upon them. Sadie did not ever want to pull away. An elderly couple came along the path in their direction and Sadie realized what a spectacle they were making of themselves. "Oh, hello there, Mr. and Mrs. Weatherly. Isn't this a wonderful morning?"

To make a smooth transition, Sadie pointed in the opposite direction. "The stone masons are working on that far corner in the south. The path will lead to and around a huge tree there. The brick path will circle the tree. Flowers will be planted all around with benches along the route." Sadie looked up and added, "Did you see how many birds there are at the fountains and at the bird feeders?"

"Wow! Who fills those feeders? That is a job in itself." Peter was playing along trying to turn away the old couple's interest in them.

"Well, we all take turns. Two days it is my turn, and two days it is Cherie's turn. Then the Colonel does a couple of days a week. We get it done. The birds are so used to us that they hover around waiting for us to finish and nearly knock us over getting to the seeds even before we finish filling the feeders."

"Who is footing the bill for all this marvel?" Pete asked incredulously, this time truly interested.

"Well, the city is funding a good part of it. The mayor and city council are so happy with the recent tourist attraction and they crave the media attention paid to this little town. People come from all around to walk here and picnic. They also come here to take their wedding photos and special family photos. It brings a lot of revenue into this town." Sadie stopped to gaze around her. "I guess this little town has more money than I realized, and there are special donors who give monthly to the upkeep of this park. The Colonel is a generous donor. There are many of his rich, old cronies who also have been cajoled into giving monthly. It is a great legacy for these men to leave to this dear little town."

"You know, I can supplement my income here with consulting fees for people who want to know how to invest money. I'm still very good at that, surprisingly."

"That brings to mind something I've been meaning to ask you," Sadie started. She checked her watch and saw that she still had time to do what spontaneously came to her mind. "Why don't we walk through the town and talk about it."

Peter looked closely at Sadie. He kissed her on the tip of her nose and said, "Now Miss Sadie, are you going to ask me to marry you?"

Sadie looked at him with a twinkle in her eye and responded coyly, "Not yet, Peter Combs, not yet!"

He looked a little disappointed, but covered it quickly. "Well, woman, let's hear it. If it is something I can accomplish for you, I will do it."

They walked and walked holding hands. They didn't talk much. There was no need. They passed the café, the bakery, the grocers, the post office, bus depot, library and several of the churches. In about ten minutes they finally came to the little town square where Sadie had started this adventure. She found the exact same bench at which she had pondered her future nearly a year ago. *Can it be only a year ago that I sat here on this bench praying and waiting for your answer, Lord?*

The sunshine felt so good on her skin. The doves were searching around their feet for crumbs. "This is where it all started for me, Pete. My adventure started right here on this little bench." She told him about her prayer and the almost immediate encounter with Colonel Shaw. He just sat there, quietly, amazed at the story.

"It really does seem that your God had a hand in all of this, doesn't it?" Peter took in a deep breath and put his arm around Sadie as they sat there. She laid her head on his shoulder and sighed too.

"Pete, I'm so happy right now, I can hardly stand it. You talked this morning about not being worthy of such goodness happening to you. Well, I feel the same way. I truly don't think I deserve any of this contentment." She looked up at Peter and hugged him. "But oh, I'm so enjoying it."

"What was it you wanted me to do for you? I'm really curious now."

"Well, I received a settlement from my ex-husband and it was a very good one. I must have had a great lawyer back there, or else Tony just wanted to be free of me so he could marry again really quickly."

"Jerk!" retorted Peter. "But I guess I'm glad he is one; otherwise, he might have tried to fight for you."

"He wouldn't have had a chance if he did, Peter. There was no way I'd put myself in that situation again." Sadie sat up straight and put her hands on her knees. "What I want, Peter, is for you to invest that money for me. I want you to do whatever you think will make me more money. I trust you completely. I will turn it all over to you, no questions asked." She looked at him. His eyes were wide with wonder. "No arguments now. And no humble exclamations of being unworthy. We are done with that." Sadie went on. "The reason I need to do this is because I have the feeling that this little paradise will not last much longer. Who knows how long the Colonel and Victoria will live here. They are getting much older and they will need more care as time goes on. Stephen may have to finally guide them to the care they will need not too long in the future. I hope it is a long time from now, but I need to be ready to move on to another project and way of making a living."

"What? Already planning to run off without me?"

"Not on your life, dear man. But I do have something in mind. It involves a wonderful place in the mountains where I've always wanted to live. I will need money and lots of it. That's where you come in. Make me some money, Pete. I promise that I will be frugal and live carefully and within my means for as long as I must. I know I am getting up there in age, but I finally am free and I still want to make my dreams come true."

"You've got it girl! I'll take your money and make it double in no time. I'm looking forward to a long time of adventure with you. And I want to learn to trust in the Lord. I know you will help me."

"It's a deal then. We will be a team and we will face whatever comes with joy and peace. What an adventure it will be. I love you Peter Combs."

"And I love you best, dear Sadie."

They sat in silence together. It was a little bit of heaven right there on earth. *Thank you, dear Lord. Thank you for everything. I'm ready to be what you need from here on out. Use me, Lord. That's why I'm here. I love you, Lord.*

The End